TWELVE MORE TALES OF CHRISTMAS

(AND A FEW OTHER HOLIDAYS)

M. L. BUCHMAN

PRAISE FOR M. L. BUCHMAN

Tom Clancy fans open to a strong female lead will clamor for more.

— *DRONE*, PUBLISHERS WEEKLY

Superb! Miranda is utterly compelling!

— *BOOKLIST*, STARRED REVIEW

Miranda Chase continues to astound and charm.

— BARB M.

Escape Rating: A. Five Stars! OMG just start with *Drone* and be prepared for a fantastic binge-read!

— READING REALITY

The best military thriller I've read in a very long time. Love the female characters.

— *DRONE*, SHELDON MCARTHUR, FOUNDER OF THE MYSTERY BOOKSTORE, LA

A fabulous soaring thriller.

— *TAKE OVER AT MIDNIGHT*, MIDWEST BOOK REVIEW

Meticulously researched, hard-hitting, and suspenseful.

— *PURE HEAT,* PUBLISHERS WEEKLY,
STARRED REVIEW

Expert technical details abound, as do realistic military missions with superb imagery that will have readers feeling as if they are right there in the midst and on the edges of their seats.

— *LIGHT UP THE NIGHT,* RT REVIEWS, 4 1/2
STARS

Buchman has catapulted his way to the top tier of my favorite authors.

— FRESH FICTION

Nonstop action that will keep readers on the edge of their seats.

— *TAKE OVER AT MIDNIGHT,* LIBRARY
JOURNAL

M L. Buchman's ability to keep the reader right in the middle of the action is amazing.

— LONG AND SHORT REVIEWS

The only thing you'll ask yourself is, "When does the next one come out?"

— *WAIT UNTIL MIDNIGHT,* RT REVIEWS, 4
STARS

The first...of (a) stellar, long-running (military) romantic suspense series.

— *THE NIGHT IS MINE,* BOOKLIST, "THE 20
BEST ROMANTIC SUSPENSE NOVELS:
MODERN MASTERPIECES"

I knew the books would be good, but I didn't realize how good.

— NIGHT STALKERS SERIES, KIRKUS
REVIEWS

Buchman mixes adrenalin-spiking battles and brusque military jargon with a sensitive approach.

— PUBLISHERS WEEKLY

13 times "Top Pick of the Month"

— NIGHT OWL REVIEWS

SIGN UP FOR M. L. BUCHMAN'S NEWSLETTER TODAY

and receive:
Release News
Free Short Stories
a Free Book

Get your free book today. Do it now.
free-book.mlbuchman.com

Other works by M. L. Buchman: *(* - also in audio)*

Action-Adventure Thrillers

Kate Stark
Final Taste
Ice Burn
Knife's Edge

Miranda Chase
*Drone**
*Thunderbolt**
*Condor**
*Ghostrider**
*Raider**
*Chinook**
*Havoc**
*White Top**
*Start the Chase**
*Lightning**
*Skibird**
*Nightwatch**
*Osprey**
*Gryphon**
*Wedgetail**
*Air Force One**

Science Fiction / Fantasy

Deities Anonymous
Cookbook from Hell: Reheated
Saviors 101

Contemporary Romance

Eagle Cove
Return to Eagle Cove
Recipe for Eagle Cove
Longing for Eagle Cove
Keepsake for Eagle Cove

Love Abroad
Heart of the Cotswolds: England
Path of Love: Cinque Terre, Italy

Where Dreams
Where Dreams are Born
Where Dreams Reside
*Where Dreams Are of Christmas**
Where Dreams Unfold
Where Dreams Are Written
Where Dreams Continue

Non-Fiction

Strategies for Success
Managing Your Inner Artist/Writer
*Estate Planning for Authors**
Character Voice
*Narrate and Record Your Own Audiobook**
Beyond Prince Charming: One Guy's Guide to Writing Men in Romance

Short Story Series by M. L. Buchman:

Action-Adventure Thrillers

Kate Stark Stories
Miranda Chase Stories

Romantic Suspense

Antarctic Ice Fliers

US Coast Guard

Contemporary Romance

Eagle Cove

Other

Deities Anonymous (fantasy)

Single Titles

The Emily Beale Universe
(military romantic suspense)

The Night Stalkers
MAIN FLIGHT
The Night Is Mine
I Own the Dawn
Wait Until Dark
Take Over at Midnight
Light Up the Night
Bring On the Dusk
By Break of Day
Target of the Heart
Target Lock on Love
Target of Mine
Target of One's Own
NIGHT STALKERS HOLIDAYS
*Daniel's Christmas**
*Frank's Independence Day**
*Peter's Christmas**
Christmas at Steel Beach
*Zachary's Christmas**
*Roy's Independence Day**
*Damien's Christmas**
Christmas at Peleliu Cove

Henderson's Ranch
*Nathan's Big Sky**
*Big Sky, Loyal Heart**
*Big Sky Dog Whisperer**
*Tales of Henderson's Ranch**

Shadow Force: Psi
*At the Slightest Sound**
*At the Quietest Word**
*At the Merest Glance**
*At the Clearest Sensation**

White House Protection Force
*Off the Leash**
*On Your Mark**
*In the Weeds**

Firehawks
Pure Heat
Full Blaze
*Hot Point**
*Flash of Fire**
Wild Fire
SMOKEJUMPERS
*Wildfire at Dawn**
*Wildfire at Larch Creek**
*Wildfire on the Skagit**

Delta Force
*Target Engaged**
*Heart Strike**
*Wild Justice**
*Midnight Trust**

Night Stalkers Reload
*Guard the East Flank**

Emily Beale Universe Short Story Series
The Night Stalkers
The Night Stalkers Stories
The Night Stalkers CSAR
The Night Stalkers Wedding Stories
The Future Night Stalkers

Delta Force
Th Delta Force Shooters
The Delta Force Warriors

Firehawks
The Firehawks Lookouts
The Firehawks Hotshots
The Firebirds

White House Protection Force
Stories

Future Night Stalkers
Stories (Science Fiction)

ABOUT THIS COLLECTION

WHO SAYS THAT CHRISTMAS ONLY COMES ONCE A YEAR? SETTLE in for twelve tales that celebrate the true Holiday spirit.

It's a season of romance, of old endings and new beginnings. Of acknowledging old friends and finding new ones. A time to celebrate life, each other, and good food.

Anytime of year is the right time to relax by the fire (or at the beach) and enjoy Twelve More Tales of Christmas (and a few other holidays).

CONTENTS

FOREWORD

In my previous Christmas collection, *Twelve Tales of Christmas,* I talked of my dicey relationship with Christmas due to a dysfunctional family. That is reflected in a few of the tales as well.

This collection, I'm pleased to note, has left all of that behind. It is a celebration of the season. Particularly note that I say *The Season.* Other late-year holidays have found their way into my writing. New Years, Hanukah, and even Rosh Hashanah thread through these tales.

Three of these stories are tales of Antarctica. They came out of my interest in the continent, which is leading to my February 2026 plans to sail there by tall ship. Three and a half others come out of my tentative exploration of my Jewish heritage, something my parents left by the wayside before I was six and I've been slow to rediscover.

Overall? This collection is a celebration of love, family (both natural and found), and friendship. I hope that you enjoy it as much as I have.

WHERE DREAMS THRIVE

The *Where Dreams* series were my first ever romances. Three college friends, still single, reunited in Seattle after a decade apart. Cassidy, Jo, and Perrin, three women strong and successful in every way except love. Their circle would eventually grow to include two more, a mother figure and a supermodel, as my planned trilogy became five novels. Each of these strong women, of course, finding the man they deserved. Over those five books, they paid homage to a city I fell in love with after moving there after college. A city I had only a few years before fell in love in myself.

I loved these women and their stories too much to wholly abandon them simply because their happy-ever-afters were complete. From time to time, I added a short love story as a reason to revisit their world.

But it would be years before I wrote a Christmas story.

It is only in retrospect that I understood that Perrin was at the heart of the series. She married a single father and became mother—much to her shock—of a nine-year-old boy and a thirteen-year-old girl. I'd often thought to tell their stories someday but it wasn't until I realized that their stories were connected, and had to happen over Christmas, that I found it.

1

———

"Hey, Gnome!" Tammy threw her arms around Jasper's neck.

"Hey, Loops," he nudged her out of the stream of people coming off the escalator into baggage claim, then patted her on the back just the way you'd expect from a nineteen-year-old little brother, hard, with knuckles.

She hung on just to make him crazy, but he knew her games too well; he didn't even huff out a sigh. It made her so glad to see him that she could cry.

"Missed you, Loops." And it totally melted her that he said that. Of course, Jasper was like a people-genius, and would know that. Didn't matter, it worked on her every time.

"Hey, it's only been a couple months."

"Seven, but I'm so not counting."

Seven months since she'd been home? How had that much time slipped by so fast? She tugged at his collar-long ponytail before letting him go. It might have grown a couple inches. What else had she missed?

"You got any bags? Of course you do." He began leading them over to the wrong carousel. He almost never left Seattle whereas she'd been on so many planes these last few years that the world seriously needed to stop spinning.

She grabbed his ear and steered him the other way through the crowd. God, she'd missed being home so much. Even inside the airport it smelled different. JFK always smelled like it was about to sink into Queens, but SeaTac had that year-round evergreen thing happening because of all the conifers out here. And coming up Christmas, it was even more so.

"Many bags," she whispered in his ear because she always did. Even more now that she was finally coming home from design school in New York City—for good. "Presents!"

"Clothes," Jasp sighed.

"Duh! Fashion designer. Where is everyone?"

"They figured you'd have too much crap, so they sent me to fetch you on my own. Lucky me," he groaned it out. Then, unzipping his jacket, he turned to face her and pulled it open. It was the tailored shirt she'd sent him for his birthday. At least it *had* been.

"What did you *do* to it?" Tammy wanted to claw that grin off his face. She'd busted her ass designing that shirt. Used it to get extra credit in Advanced Tailoring Techniques, a 400-level class—before sending it to him. She'd gotten the A for the matching jacket that was going to be his Christmas present, so the shirt had kind of been spiking the ball in the end zone, but still!

It was the same shirt, elegant lines with just a nod-and-wink at hipster, but it was now a wild tie-dye way out on the neon spectrum instead of a chill off-white. It was actually an impressive job of the technique, but dammit, it wasn't her design anymore. And it sure didn't match the jacket any longer.

"I tie-dyed it."

"Not blind. *Why?*"

"Well I have this friend who—"

"*Female* friend."

His grin acknowledged that. Women flocked to Jasper like… honey didn't have it so good.

"She's a scene painter at the opera. Did a summer art camp thing for her niece's school. I was helping her out, but didn't have anything myself to dye."

"Except the shirt off your back."

"I think it came out great."

It had, but she wasn't going to admit it. No question but Jasp saw both sides of her reaction, too. But his grin wasn't going away.

"Summer? When was this camp?"

"July."

"You still seeing her?" She didn't know why she asked.

Roughly in unison they said, "The power of a great shirt." One of Mom's favorite sayings was *Never underestimate the power of a great dress.* Only fitting for one of the nation's leading fashion designers.

That was why he'd worn the summer-weight shirt to drive to the airport in December. Jasper's way of saying thanks, because she sure hadn't received more than a three-word text after his birthday: *It fits. Nice.*

"Or the power of taking it off at her summer camp," Tammy offered her best sneer.

"Not a total dork; I had a t-shirt under it. It was black, so no-go for the dye job." Making excuses wasn't like him either. Whoever art-camp-girl was had really gotten under his skin.

"You sure didn't wear such a nice shirt to a summer camp to impress the kids." It was weird for her to pull back mentally enough to really *see* Jasper as anything but her little brother. But she managed it this time. He'd been active at the opera since he was eleven working lights and sets. Their dad was the Stage Manager, so it had come about naturally for him. Jasp had gone full-time this year.

The demanding physical stage work had molded his body.

She always had his current measurements in her design book, but it hadn't really sunk in how much he'd changed over the years.

Tammy herself had taken after her birth mother and stopped growing at five-seven. Jasper had topped Dad's six feet by an inch. The year after Perrin had become their new mom, who was almost Dad-tall herself, Jasp had hit his first big growth spurt. Tammy had gone from being the mid-height of three to the runt of the litter.

Only Maxine, their Cairn terrier, was shorter than she was, which wasn't really winning much in the height competition. Her little sister took after Perrin and Dad; she was already the tallest girl in third grade, and would be blowing past Tammy all too soon.

Jasper had always been good looking, but when had he gone all handsome? The sweet-boy face all grown up and in need of a shave?

"She have a name?"

"Yeah. Amelia."

"She have a last one?"

"Clayton." But a strange look slipped across Jasper's face. She knew that face. After their birth mother's death-by-drunk-driver, and the four years until Perrin came along to become Mom, she'd raised Jasper pretty much on her own. That's what three-year-older sisters did even if she'd only been nine at the time. Dad had tried to help, but he hadn't been much better off than Jasper, until he'd met Perrin.

But on Jasper?

She *definitely* knew that face.

"You looking to *change* her last name?" It kind of slipped out before she knew it. She tried to twist it into a joke—did a pretty good job of it, she thought.

But his trademark one-shouldered shrug said he *was* thinking about it.

For half a second, she considered getting all serious about it and cornering him. He was pretty good at resisting for a while, but it still would be seriously fun to do because she always won that game. Then she thought about what Mom would do, and simply let out a *whoop!* loud enough to echo off the baggage claim ceiling.

People crowded close around the carousel jumped or cursed in surprise.

She threw her arms around him and hugged him hard.

"What?" Jasper struggled to peel her off until they were practically wrestling upright.

"I get to design a wedding dress!" She crowed it almost as loud as her initial shout.

That finally stopped him. His eyes went wide and a little desperate as the people around them began applauding, thinking Jasper had just proposed to her. She ignored them.

"Look, Tamara, even *I…me…*" he sputtered for a bit, "*myself* don't know anything yet. Okay? You gotta be chill about this."

"I swear," she did the seal and lock-her-lips thing, and a little cross on her forehead like they were burying the dead. It was an unbreakable vow between them. "Though I bet Mom already knows."

"No way."

"We're talking about Perrin Cullen here, Ms. Super Matchmaker. Remember she set up all three of her friends. Mom knows. She better not have started on Amelia's dress already. She's mine!" If she had, Tammy would take it hostage so that she could do it herself.

Too bad a bride didn't need two wedding dresses.

"How would you feel about wearing a dress at your own wedding?"

His eyes went from merely wild to panic. He grabbed her arm hard enough to hurt.

"What?"

"Wed-*ding?*" His voice cracked really impressively for a handsome nineteen-year-old. That *had* to hurt.

It was almost as cute as when his knees went out from under him, and he sat down hard on the baggage claim floor.

Because of his grip on her arm, she collapsed on top of him in a heap.

There was a lot of laughter, and calls to "get a room" among the crowd as she kissed him soundly—on the forehead.

2

———

SHE CHECKED OUT HIS PHOTOS ON THE DRIVE HOME BY THE sisterly expedient of stealing his phone. Tammy didn't even need to grab his hand for a fingerprint unlock. She took a guess, and keyed in her own birthday. When his phone actually did unlock, she had to look out the window and watch the heavy Seattle traffic go by for a few minutes until her eyes cleared.

They were moving even slower than usual through the slush of a rare December snowfall. The snow was thick enough that the big orange shipping cranes of Harbor Island were barely visible, yet warm enough that almost none of it stuck. Typical.

Snow in the second week of December probably meant a green Christmas, because that's just the way Seattle was. The sky was darkening with sunset somewhere behind the low, heavy clouds. The city lights were becoming visible, but they wouldn't sparkle for most of another hour. Color *du jour*? Gray. Also typical.

His screensaver kicked in; it was the wedoption. Perrin and Dad's wedding with the two of them as Best Man and Maid of

Honor—the day Perrin had also legally become their Mom. It took a while longer before her eyes cleared after that one.

She unlocked her own phone and held them both up for Jasp to see.

"Yeah," was all he said when he saw the same photo on both. It was the moment that had changed both of their lives. Not that their lives had sucked at all, but they'd become way better that day.

Tammy pulled up his photo album.

"Hey, wait. How'd you get into my phone?"

"Duh!" was all she offered him as she began poking around. She didn't need to dig very deep; Amelia was suddenly everywhere. The two of them grinning like idiots in a montage of selfie backgrounds. She knew a lot of them: the waterfall up on Snoqualmie Ridge, backstage at the opera, at the Seattle Center's main fountain with crowds and musicians behind them (had to be the Bumbershoot Festival).

It was like a checklist of Jasp's favorite places. There was even one up in their family's favorite picnic spot. When Dad was too busy to get away during an opera production, they'd all show up with a picnic and climb up into a small loft built into the opera house ceiling. It was a strange anomaly, a work platform with a waist-high safety wall and a great view of the stage, six stories in the air. Sit down and it was utterly private. Picnics there was a tradition Mom had started back during their courtship.

Jasper had taken Amelia there, with a family-style picnic for two in the background. That was *major*.

The next one was even *more* major.

"You coughed up the cash to take her to *Angelo's?*"

"Yeah, why?"

Tammy wondered if the seatbelt would stretch forward enough to let her pound her head against the dashboard. Everything began at Angelo's Tuscan Hearth Ristorante. It had just gotten its second Michelin star, along with two of his other restaurants. Angelo had married one of Mom's best friends. Every courtship in the extended circle, including Dad's with Mom, had gone through there. She and Jasp had even been part of that.

This was *beyond* serious.

The sound changed as they rolled into the new highway tunnel under Seattle's waterfront. Tammy had to pop her ears and blink against the sudden brightness of the lights. Even the tunnel walls fit the day's color palette: concrete gray. Homecomings were supposed to be bright and sparkly.

And without such big surprises!

She stared back down at the photos, trying to figure out how she felt about all this. Jasper falling in love? He was three years younger than she was, so how was that even possible?

But in every photo, no matter how she searched, they looked crazy-close and stupid-happy. Either Jasp was super selective about the selfies he took with Amelia or they really were that gone on each other.

"She's beautiful." Darkly exotic, her face had such great lines. Hair almost as thick as Tammy's own chestnut mane, which flowed past Amelia's shoulders in midnight black and brilliant purple from the middle down.

"Yeah, she is. Some Senegalese, some Apache, a bit of French too, she thinks."

" 'Yeah, she is,' says the mush-boy. That's it, done with 'Gnome'."

"Great! Unless I'm going back to being Troll."

"Nope. That was your kid's name. 'Gnome' was for the teen years.' From now on, you're 'Mush-boy'." She never let him forget how staunchly he'd hated mushiness as a kid. He *was* just a male. She could easily forgive him but that didn't mean she had to let him off the hook.

"You know, she's got an older brother who—"

"No way! Tell me you are *not* turning into Mom."

That got his mouth shut.

"Besides, I've been back for like thirty seconds. Just give me a break."

Again, that one-shoulder shrug. Did it mean maybe he would? Or something more dire and she'd have to sit on him?

When he didn't say anything else, she let her attention drift to Amelia's skin tone. It would support almost anything, jewel tones, pastels, strong patterns... It wouldn't wash out like her own Italian coloring sometimes did. Those high cheekbones and that slender figure would let her get away with fashion murder.

Tammy wanted to hate her for it.

She herself was the only one in the family who had her birth mother's olive skin tone. Jasp had taken after Dad. Perrin, who she'd long since thought of as Mom without the slightest pinch, was a gold-blonde with the light skin to match (and a wicked lean figure) that she'd passed on to Cornelia. With the full figure, that Tammy had inherited along with her skin tone, she looked like the lone adoptee of the family.

Knowing nothing about Amelia except that she'd fallen for Jasper, Tammy stared out at the blank of the tunnel wall and tried to imagine what kind of dress she would want. Classic, racy, *avant-garde*? Please not the last. Tammy could do the runway over-the-top of *avant-garde* but preferred "modern" herself. Her first teen clothing line had been all modern before she'd left it behind to go to design school in New York. Auntie Kari had taken the line over. She would try to give it back, but no way. Kari had finally found her design niche, and Tammy so wasn't taking that away.

Besides, she wanted...something else. She wasn't sure what yet. But it was so close that she could almost taste it. Like...

She was snapped out of her reverie by their abrupt emergence from the tunnel. It seemed that during their brief passage underground, the day had finally found a new palette: dark—with sparkly accents. White and yellow building lights now twinkled brightly. Distant traffic lights added red, yellow, and green accents. Christmas decorations shone beyond either side of the highway like a cheery patchwork of rainbow dots.

Then Jasper took the first right turn immediately after the tunnel.

"Wait, where are we going?" He threaded his way back into town. "I've been awake for like three days straight: finals, graduation, packing, flights. I want to go home. See Mom and Dad. Sleep."

"Sorry, Loops. I'm under orders." And he pulled up to the curb and stopped at the head of Western Ave before it descended past Pike Place Market.

"No way." Tammy looked out the window, and couldn't believe what she was seeing.

"Seriously way, Loops. You're on your own from here."

The nerves shot through her. She knew who was there. It was… "This can't be real." Maybe she was so tired that she was hallucinating. But the engine was idling, the car heat was warm across her knees, and this was utterly impossible.

"Get out of my car already. I'll drop your junk at the house. Though I'll be charging you *beaucoup* for unloading it all."

"I lived in New York for four-and-a-half years. I got *stuff*." Multiple internships had added the six months, despite her taking extra courses every quarter.

"Your stuff is my junk. Now go, before I put *your* junk in *my* Dumpster. I gotta meet Dad back at the opera. We've got a production of *Nutcracker* to get on the stage. Go!"

Numb, she gave him back his phone. Only as he was pulling away did she realize she was freezing. The slushy December night had fallen over Seattle and, while way warmer than New York, her t-shirt wasn't going to cut it. She managed to slap his trunk before he got away. He jerked to halt. Yanking open the passenger door, she grabbed her jacket, then slammed it again. Not fast enough, she still heard his taunt, "Bye, Loops."

She'd gotten the nickname the first morning that everyone was home after the wedoption. Tammy had been so ecstatic to have a whole family around the breakfast table for the first time in four years, that she'd poured Fruit Loops into her milk glass instead of the other way around.

Jasp had tagged her and it stuck; at least from him.

She stood perched high atop the north end of the Seattle waterfront. The towering office buildings to the left rose like flame-lit candles. The cozy alleys of Pike Place Market wended their way in between. She could just see the end of Post Alley where Angelo's was tucked away from the main tourist traffic flow.

More sparklies came from the waterfront Ferris wheel and the massive green-and-white ferries that scuttled over the pitch black waters of Elliott Bay, rushing commuters back to Bainbridge and Bremerton.

And directly in front of her?

Cutters Crabhouse.

It might be a Seattle Landmark, but it was also where all of *la Famiglia* legends began. *All* of them. Well, here and Angelo's Restaurant. But this was where all of the *women's* legends began.

Tammy had never quite figured out anything else to call them, using her birth mother's Italian, with an improper but totally capital F, *Famiglia*. So much more than just her nuclear family. "Extended family" didn't begin to describe it.

La Famiglia had started with Mom and her two best friends from college: Cassidy and Jo.

Mom's business partner—the still impossibly gorgeous model Melanie—was so super-close to them that they might all four have been sisters. And Mama Maria had raised Jo and Cassidy's husbands from diapers while she'd been a personal cook for a shipping magnate. Mama Maria totally pampered all four of the younger women.

For years Tammy had known about the Fabulous Five's "Nights at Cutters."

It was like the female mob: the Godmothers. They'd even done that literally. Every child born into the circle had four actual real-life godmothers to depend upon. The fact that she'd been thirteen and Japer ten when Dad and Perrin had married hadn't mattered. They each suddenly had a whole flock of Godmothers who always had their backs.

The five husbands, including Dad, had turned these nights into their own thing. They'd gather at different houses, drink, argue, play cards, go sailing, all sorts of guy stuff. When it was at their house, she and Jasper used to sit on the stairs and listen in. It was amazing how much these macho guys talked about their wives and kids.

That had been her childhood.

The last time she'd been home, she'd still been too young to go into a bar.

But now?

She was twenty-one and the Fabulous Five were waiting inside.

For her.

3
___

Only when she stepped inside did she remember how she was dressed.

The bar at Cutters was perched high on the hill, overlooking a long sweep of the Seattle waterfront and Elliott Bay right across to the Olympic Mountains towering into the sky—or they would be if it weren't for the dark layer of clouds. Not that anything outside the windows really mattered. Cutters was *the* place to see and be seen.

And she was in the clothes that she'd put on *yesterday* after graduation. There'd been parties and dancing right through the night until she'd had to rush back to get her stuff and catch the plane. Plus a long rumpling flight.

She was wearing a dark red t-shirt with the TJPWC logo. Her youth line had been named for Tammy, Jasper, Perrin, and her dad Bill (except with a W for William so that his and Perrin's initials didn't turn into Peanut Butter). The C got tacked on when Cornelia joined the house—still not yet old enough to be told that she'd been named for being conceived on Mom and Dad's honeymoon in Corniglia, Italy. They'd honeymooned there because Cassidy had insisted it was such a wonderful village. The whole family had gone back twice since which had been only a little weird, knowing about Cornelia, but also crazy romantic.

It was one of the five towns of Cinque Terre, the five earths. That was her family, the Five Earths, plus Maxine the Cairn terrier.

But the Fabulous Five were completely something else.

Tammy brushed at her t-shirt. She'd custom-cut this one to her own figure. On the back was a sunshine-yellow smiley face and the words *powerful* and *confident*. The shirt always made her feel that way, and had been pretty successful. She'd even spotted it three separate times in New York and once during her year abroad in Paris and Milan. But it was still just a t-shirt and the words weren't delivering a whole lot of power or confidence at the moment.

At least these were her favorite jeans, large swirls of white and blue denim that curved down from her butt and wound around her legs. She always thought of it like the fingerprints of a giant who was holding her aloft.

And her muck boots. The streets of New York had been slushed out even worse than Seattle, and the boots wouldn't fit in any of her suitcases. The only place to carry them had been on her feet. Her hair wasn't brushed and somewhere along the way, probably wrestling with Jasper, she'd lost her last rubber hair band. No ponytail. No quick French braid. She was a mess.

Maybe—

Mom plowed into her from the side. "Tamara!" she squealed loudly enough to make Tammy's ears ring. And probably everyone else's in the room.

Suddenly none of that mattered. Tammy hugged Perrin as hard as she could.

She was here. This was home.

4

"I still don't understand what you've been doing with your time. You didn't bring home a single boy."

"Mo-om," Perrin was backlit by the city beyond the window, and looked utterly amazing. The round of news, and drinks, had gone by quickly. It felt as if her sleepy brain had finally deplaned as well and she was all the way here.

All five women were dressed scads better than even everyday but, as always, Mom shone. It was a new design Tammy hadn't seen before but couldn't stop looking at. Her dress was a floor-length swirl of the entire rainbow that should look utterly ridiculous but instead wrapped around Perrin's slender frame in a way that made her look both elegant and sexy as hell.

"You know, if Dad hasn't already seen you in that dress, he's just gonna die."

"He almost did." And Mom's grin said exactly what had followed. Tammy definitely didn't want to be thinking about that. Parents. Having sex. Total weirdness.

"I didn't bring home a married boy either. Nor any girls, straight or not. Except this girl." Tammy tried to point at herself, but it felt as if she'd missed. She tried pointing at herself again with equally little success. She should never have drunk a whole Cosmo. A Cosmopolitan was Mom's preferred drink, a near-lethal blend of vodka, Triple Sec, cranberry juice, and lime that tasted like a sweet delight. Tammy's normal limit was about half of a hard cider, preferably pear.

Mom giggled. It was the greatest giggle on the planet, and she'd done it since they'd first met.

"Were there many *délicieux* boys for our Tamara?" Melanie rested her elbow on the table and her chin on her palm. Always conscious of her public image as a supermodel—and now almost a decade as the signature model and CEO of Perrin's Glorious Garb—it was the most unwound Tammy had ever seen her. Her straight fall of perfect blonde hair only reminded Tammy of the ruffled mess of her own chestnut snarl.

"None were as delicious as your accent makes them sound." She shrugged. "There were some good ones, but no keepers."

"She *is* only twenty-one," Jo hadn't even slouched as much as Melanie. She never slouched; always the serene, native-Alaskan, *gorgeously* curved lawyer. Also always the voice of reason in *La Famiglia*. That she was one of the most powerful women in Seattle was beyond cool.

"I'm going to snitch that blouse, Jo. I bet that satin-green would look really good on me."

"No," Mom polished off her Cosmo, signaled for another round. Then she waved a hand at the plates of appetizers and told the waiter, "More," without any other specifics before turning back to her.

The waiter must be used to them because she just smiled and went.

"Jo's wouldn't fit right. You should steal Cassidy's clothes; you're the same shape."

"No way." Tammy could only gawk. Cassidy had always been her own ideal of a woman's figure. Not lean like Mom or

Melanie who were like pre-designed for high-fashion attire. Cassidy Knowles was "everywoman" embodied.

"Thanks a lot, Perrin," Cassidy groaned. "Now I'm going to have to put locks on my closets. Did you have to be so beautiful, Tammy? I find it kind of depressing."

"Me?" Her voice almost cracked as badly as Jasper's had.

Mama Maria, who'd been watching her quietly just smiled and nodded.

Tammy could doubt all the others, but there was no questioning Mama Maria. Though they weren't related, they shared an Italian heritage—Tammy was often mistaken for her biological daughter. Though Mama Maria was technically old enough to be her grandmother, she'd aged too wonderfully for anyone to ever suggest that; not even when Tammy had been a teen.

Tammy knew she was pretty-ish. But for Cassidy to say that was...weird.

She definitely needed a topic change. "Where are all the men tonight? Jasp said Dad was at the opera."

Cassidy pointed out the window. It was fully dark now and she could see that just beyond the piers of Seattle's waterfront spread out below, ranged a whole array of multi-colored lights. They'd shown up without her noticing.

"The Christmas Boat Parade!" Dozens, tonight maybe even a hundred boats of every shape and size, scooted along the shore, each festooned with Christmas lights. Long familiarity let her pick out Russell's boat—her drink-blurred vision now offering her hyper focus instead. His fifty-foot sloop was a real standout for decoration, each year he and Dad had added something new. It was beautiful—artful rather than garish. She waved though they would never see it. So did the members of the Fabulous Five.

Of them all, only Cassidy was a real sailor—being married to Russell, she didn't have much of a choice. Jo had adapted as

Angelo was his first mate whenever he could escape his expanding empire.

For a bit, they caught her up on the news of Angelo's restaurants, Russell's growing success in nature photography, Josh's latest mystery novel, and Hogan's community work.

The arrival of more appetizers cut off that thread. She was slowly getting the hang of how topics flowed and shifted with the Fabulous Five. Especially as the alcoholic haze rose to wrap her in its warm cocoon. She had to sleep really soon if she was actually waxing poetic. Very bad sign.

But first there were pan-seared crab cakes, bison sliders, and ahi tuna tacos to be eaten. Another waiter added a fresh loaf of Cutters rosemary focaccia.

"I'll bloat," her empty Cosmo was replaced with a full one, "if I don't drown first."

"House rules. As long as we're all together, there are no calories here."

Tammy could only look at the lush spread and laugh.

"And," Mom raised her glass in a toast, "no secrets."

Cassidy practically snorted her white wine. Mama Maria laughed. Jo simply sighed as she thumped Cassidy on the back until she recovered. Melanie offered an elegant shrug of complicity—she and Mom really should have been twin sisters, they certainly acted like it, and came pretty close to looking like it.

Mom leaned close. "The real rule is that we never get drunk unless we're all together. But I like this one, too."

Tammy considered.

"Ooo!" Mom announced to the whole table. "Tammy has a secret. Tell us! Tell us! Tell us!"

Even Jo eventually took up the chant until the whole room was staring at them.

"Shush! I can't! I promised." She made the key-locked lips and dead-man-cross-on-her-forehead sign.

Mom laughed. "That's your and Jasper's sign. You mean Amelia."

Tammy grabbed her own head on either side of her face to stop it as soon as she realized she was nodding in agreement. She only noticed because it was making them all a little blurry, and there might be two of Melanie.

"I purposely didn't start her wedding dress. I knew you'd want to do that."

The reactions around the table weren't surprise, but rather about the rightness of Tammy designing the dress.

"But *he* doesn't even know if he wants to marry her."

Mom just flapped a hand at her. "He'll get there. Wait until you see them together."

"I saw pictures..."

"Then you know," Mom's glass was still up for a toast. "To the lovely couple."

Everyone joined in, clinking glasses all around, then drinking.

"And," Mama Maria's soft voice stopped them before their glasses were back down. "To the Smashing Six."

They all turned and toasted—her?

She wasn't just a visitor here tonight? Not just a homecoming? Even buffered by alcohol, the reality of it almost slammed her out of her chair.

Tammy was now part of *la Famiglia*. The first of the next generation, here among the Godmothers. She managed to get out of her chair without falling to the floor and circled the table hugging each of them in turn.

She didn't realize she was crying until Mom brushed aside her tears when Tammy slid back into her own seat.

"That's the last rule, we don't get to cry unless we're all crying." Sure enough, there wasn't a dry eye around the table.

5

———

Tammy was going to sleep the clock round until dinner.

At least that was her plan.

It was sabotaged by her body still being on East Coast time —and Jasper dropping Maxine on her face.

She and Jasper had picked out the little Cairn terrier shortly after it was born. It had been during the first time they'd had an outing as a family, before they *were* a family. They'd gone to the Seattle Dog Show, and it was totally fated to be. Perrin had brought it home after it was weaned, the evening before the wedoption transformed her into Mom, so that they'd all become a family at once.

When the terrier had settled from ecstasy to snuggle in her arms, she looked at Jasper over the oh-so-comfortable quilt she and Mom had made forever ago—a field of the pinks and golds of a Seattle sunrise, when the city's color palette wasn't being gray. He was sitting at the foot of her bed holding her foot. Whenever either of them was having a tough time, that's what the other did. Close, but not icky close.

Since her only problem was whether or not she'd feel a hangover if she sat up, she assumed this was about him.

"Spill it, Mush-boy."

He grimaced, "Got any lunch plans?"

"Lunch? I'd rather be sleeping." She snugged Maxine closer. "Don't bother us. We're napping." She closed her eyes like the dog's.

When Jasper didn't go away, she reopened one eye. He was just sitting there like a lump. Like he was asking something important. There was nothing important about lunch—considering how often she forgot to eat it. Another trait she shared with Mom. When a design had either of them by the throat, food, sleep, all of it went out the window.

But Jasper was...

"Oh. Sorry, sleep deprived. Got it. How soon?"

His glance didn't go toward the clock. Instead it went toward the stairs.

"You shit! Amelia's here? I'm a mess."

"It's just lunch. She's making sandwiches."

"When did you become an idiot about women, Jasp?" Tammy rolled her eyes. "Never mind. The moment you met Amelia is the answer. Let me guess, Mom and Dad are at work and Cornelia's at school so you could corner me. Go! Get out of here!" She kicked him through the sheets and quilt. "I'll be down in a sec, if only to rescue her from you."

"What? No. That's not what I want you to do. I want—"

"You idiot! Don't you think that she *knows* she's here for the sisterly stamp of approval? She's gonna be nervous as hell. Do not let her handle any sharp objects. Like, I dunno, cheese. Go!"

He went.

Tammy looked down at Maxine. "Sorry, pal. We're gonna have to get back to this later. No. No! *No!* Not the sad-puppy eyes. That's unfair. Besides, it's Mush-boy's fault, not mine."

She hurried for the shower because she'd certainly been

too drunk to take one last night. Her hair would have to wait for another time.

As she dressed and bolted for the stairs, the sad-puppy eyes still followed her from the cozy middle of his sunrise-colored quilt nest.

6

—————

"IF YOU WANT TO KILL HIM, I'M GLAD TO HEL..." TAMMY stumbled to a halt halfway into the big kitchen.

Amelia had dressed very carefully for the occasion. Upscale casual. Her makeup was so perfect that it was invisible—Tammy's was still packed somewhere. Her nails had been freshly painted to match her hair: not a single chip in the purple gloss. Tammy's were ragged and bare. Like her feet.

But that wasn't what stopped her—it was the man beside her. Unlike herself and Jasp, there was no doubting these two were brother and sister. The same lustrous coloring, the same face. He was Amelia's beauty and softness transformed. Not into big and macho, but—

And she was staring.

"I hope you don't mind, I brought Andre along for moral support."

"From me?" Tammy looked down at herself and couldn't imagine. "But why?"

"Because," Amelia waved a hand at her own clothes and Tammy finally focused on them.

"Those are mine." She must be really out of it to not have

noticed. "Well, mine and Auntie Kari's line. And…they look really good on you."

"I know. And that's the dress that got me interested in painting." Amelia was pointing at Tammy's chest.

She looked down at her clothes again. For lack of finding anything handy, and clean, she'd plundered the closet and come up with a more recent version of the first dress she'd ever designed. It was purple, and had been hand-painted in broad strokes with words like *strength, passion,* and *joy.* All closet rumpled, but at least it was clean. "No shit?"

"No shit. I was twelve when Mom bought me this supercool top for a school dance. It was one of yours, aquamarine with the long dark-honey lines."

"I always liked how that came out, and, yeah, I bet it looked utterly brilliant on you."

Andre nodded. Apparently it had.

"Then I looked you up online," Amelia continued in a rush, "and I saw that dress. I just had to have it. Mom made me paint the bedroom to pay for it—it really needed it. I kinda got inspired and painted one wall as a stormy sailing mural. Not a Winslow Homer, actually a mess, but I had real fun doing it."

Andre Clayton spoke for the first time. "Think she redid that wall about fifty-seven times." His voice was deep and warm, and she could hear that he'd probably helped her with every one. Maybe just cleaning brushes and mixing paints, but there was pride in his little sister there, loud and clear.

"That does it, Mush-boy," Tammy turned to Jasper who'd been hanging out on the other side of the island doing one of his fade tricks that let him be inconspicuous to everyone— except her.

Amelia was laughing out "Mush-boy?" in the background.

"Does what?" Jasper watched her with caution.

"You fuck this up, I'm gonna kill you."

He sighed. "That's what Mom told me this morning. Same words even."

"She already knew."

"Knew what?" Amelia looked a little wild-eyed.

"That—"

"No!" Jasper shouted but was on the wrong side of the island to move fast enough to stop her.

"—my mush of a baby brother loves you."

She did the old circle game, staying on the side of the granite island directly opposite Jasper as he scrambled after her. Bare feet on the wooden floor gave her good traction.

"Kinda obvious it's—"

She had to dodge around Andre who grinned as he sidestepped to clear the path, then eased back into Jasper's way. She could get to like him.

"—mutual. I love him too, so it's hard to blame you."

Jasper made a lunge directly across the island—he'd gotten a lot taller over the years and had serious reach—but, by flattening herself against the cupboards on the far side of the kitchen, she scooted clear.

"I can't even tease you that you could do better elsewhere."

And she was back where she started, facing Amelia.

Amelia didn't look shocked. Instead she looked ready to cry. "Can I hug you?"

"Hey, what are future sisters-in-law for?"

"Oh, my, God," Jasper's whisper was barely audible as they leaned into each other.

Amelia's hug was everything one could hope for from a new sister-in-law-to-be. But Amelia's brother standing silently behind her and watching them? Him she was less sure about.

7

Tammy caught the Number 28 bus into town, and enjoyed walking the last couple of blocks to Perrin's Glorious Garb. Mom's store had once stood on a dilapidated block of Belltown. Just north of the business core, most of the area had gone to condos and such.

It was in much better shape now, but Mom's block still had older shops, with unique stuff that couldn't be found in a hundred other places. The old Mexican restaurant where they ate lunch sometimes was still there around the corner. A bike shop, a jeweler, and a florist had the nearby storefronts. A used bookstore had opened that she'd definitely have to check out. They had a big section of vinyl and CDs as well. She'd dodged the vinyl craze but even a peek through the windows said that several of her New York friends would just die if they came to visit.

She hadn't seen Dad yet, but his text just said "Dinner" which meant he was super busy. Then he sent a line of heart emojis. Dad using emojis still cracked her up every time; usually he got it goofy-wrong. This time he got it exactly right.

She sent back a goofy face anyway, then followed it up with even more hearts herself.

The boutique storefront was busy, so she only got to wave at Raquel who wore her ever-so-pleasant you're-going-to-walk-out-of-here-so-much-poorer smile. Brilliant red hair floating behind her, she also wore a power dress that Mom must have designed specifically for the store manager's second baby bump. It looked perfect.

The store's motif had been refreshed a couple times, but hadn't been really changed since she'd first walked in here nine years ago.

A 1950s diner of red leather and chrome. The Big Bopper was pitching *Chantilly Lace* softly on the sound system. The booths lacked tables, allowing full view of the seated and awesomely attired mannequins.

Mom's style had evolved. It stood out for Tammy after not having been home to see any new designs for awhile.

There was still the sexy vibe Mom couldn't help but load up on, but it wasn't so slap-you-in-the-face as when Tammy had been young. She'd found a subtleness that was actually a clearer statement of female complexity. Also, menswear had gone from one or two offerings to a quarter of the displays. And there was a spread of gender-neutral attire. Not that it removed anything, rather, it broke the past presumptions. Whoever wore it, no matter their orientation or preference, would look incredibly sharp. A trio of mannequins—male, female, and androgynous—all wore the same outfit, and each looked totally different.

That was Mom's eye. Her clothes made people beautiful, sexy, and capable.

Tammy's own teen styles had been more about confidence and playfulness.

She'd have to study what Mom had done here...later.

The only real change to the room over the years had been

the door opening knocked through into the next building. Perrin's Glorious Garb and TJPWC had bought out the old hardware store together. This side was Mom's, on the other had been her and Kari's.

Through the glass of the swinging door, she could see Taylor Swift rocking it on one of the big TVs. Perrin's clothes were classy and commanded the prices to match. Tammy had targeted the middle ground. Not cheap like she was a box store or anything, but not out of reach either. It was for the teens willing to push their clothing budget a bit, without having to break it.

And Kari had taken it further, crossing over from teen into New Adult without breaking the design aesthetic, as Amelia's outfit had proven.

No longer hers in anything except corporate structure, she didn't cross through to her old store. Instead she pushed through into the back room and caught Mom, Melanie, and Kari conferring at the table.

Mom and Melanie gave her hugs as if she'd been lost for years, rather than just out drinking together last night. Auntie Kari just clamped her arms around Tammy, and kept whispering, "Little Girl. Little Girl." as her tears dampened Tammy's hair. They looked the most alike of any of the extended family and friends. She and Auntie Kari had started close, and grown closer over the kajillions of hours spent bringing Tammy's clothing line to life.

They were both wiping their eyes by the time she shooed the three women back to their meeting.

For all of its success, online store, and warehouses, the fashion designs that had found such popularity all still came from these few women grouped around this table.

Tammy had interned at Wang, Givenchy, and Prada. Those were massive operations where the lead designer critiqued and built from what their staff created in hopes of striking some spark. Siriano stayed down in the trenches as did a few others.

Mom's vision, with edits by Melanie and Kari, was the heart and soul of every design from Perrin's Glorious Garb.

The big cutting table was covered by an expansive green rubber cutting mat marked in one-inch yellow squares. Cubbyholes of folded fabric now lined three walls instead of two. The hole that had been knocked into the back of the neighboring store to make a sewing room, had now taken over the entire shop except for TJPWC's storefront. All of the machines except Perrin's own pair, which took the short fourth wall, had moved next door as well.

But it was still the same room.

This was her home, even more than the house.

She'd created and run her teen line from this room.

Perrin's looks had walked from this room onto the pages of *Fashion Week* and the Paris, Tokyo, and Milan runways as high-end ready-to-wear. She rarely advertised; no need when even *People* did articles analyzing her latest shows. Of course, that Melanie had snagged a record-breaking sixth *Sports Illustrated* cover in one of Mom's swimsuits hadn't hurt business either.

Leaving them to their conferring—it looked all businessy, and while she'd mostly dodged the hangover, she just wasn't up for budgets and marketing plans—she began to browse the fabrics. Hers weren't here, they were next door. But there was something about these...

She fingered the stretchiness of a plum Jersey. Brushed a corner of daffodil satin across her cheek. Not her color, but it would snap on Amelia. However, it wouldn't have that perfect texture that would make Amelia *feel* like a bride. The tangerine crinoline made her smile, and the crackled brown leather reminded her of her attempts to update a classic bomber jacket. So hard to alter such an iconic image without just being derivative.

Tammy considered the mauve velveteen just to incite a reaction from Andre. Or perhaps a chartreuse neoprene for his sister's wedding dress would make him truly crazy.

He'd been impossible to read during lunch. They'd eaten at stools around the island, cozy, not bothering with the big dining table. Andre had only spoken when she'd directly prodded him, and his equanimity was even deeper than Jo's.

Not her kind of guy.

She plunged into conversations like they were an Olympic sport. When she'd tried to tease him, he'd pushed right back— done it well too, good sharp ripostes that challenged her. But each time she'd tried to escalate, he'd just smiled and wagged a finger, pointing at her and Amelia. It was *their* time to get to know each other; he was staying out of it. Not once during the whole lunch had he introduced a topic.

Amelia, on the other hand, was like the sister she'd never really had. Tammy loved Cornelia, but she'd only been four when Tammy had left for college. With Amelia, they were soon talking as if they'd been together their whole lives, but just hadn't met until now.

Jasper had still cardio-breathing-on-the-verge-of-hyperventilation for most of the lunch, trying to catch up with Tammy proposing for him. She'd have to remind him to do it properly; a girl deserved her moment.

Tammy fingered a frost-blue leather. Amelia would look really good in a bomber jacket made of that. Maybe as a Christmas present. She snipped a sample and moved along to an umber...no...a graphite leather for the trim and snipped another sample. Switch the two: graphite body, frost-blue accent. Yes.

"It wants a pop of color," Mom rested her hand on a magenta. Melanie and Kari had drifted off somewhere. Neither would think to interrupt a design-mode moment. She'd have to catch up with Kari some more before she left.

"No, the dark cherry."

Mom hesitated for just a moment, then tugged out a corner of the dark cherry for her.

Another snip. Tammy plucked a bolt of cotton similar to Amelia's skin color, and she laid the three bits of leather on it. She debated, then snipped samples in spruce and cedar. Amelia's eyes had just a hint of green in their brown depths—definitely the spruce. She dropped the bit of cedar in the scraps bag under the bench.

She set the spruce above the other three swatches.

"That doesn't quite work, does it?"

Perrin looked at her for a long moment.

"What?"

She slipped the scissors from Tammy's hand and took a corner off an obsidian leather, replacing the eye-color swatch.

"Wow! That pops. Weird, because this one is definitely Amelia's eye color," Tammy flapped the bit of spruce.

"For her, you want the magenta accent. But hers are not the eyes you're designing for. Spruce eyes get the magenta accent. Obsidian gets the dark cherry."

"But..." She could see the jacket taking shape, but not the person who'd be wearing it.

"Oh, honey." Mom hugged her hard.

"What?" She sounded like a lost parrot offering some nonsense syllable.

"I'm just so glad...you're home." Like she'd changed the thought midstream.

"Me, too."

Mom was sniffling, which started Tammy off as well.

"I don't ever want to leave again."

Mom didn't say a thing, she just stroked her hair like when she was a teen getting over her first heartbreak.

8

You asleep?

Not anymore, Tammy texted back. The clock said it was seven a.m. Didn't her New York friends understand *anything* about time zones? Apparently not.

There was some kind of a conspiracy going on against her getting enough sleep. The whole family had sat up late last night just catching up. Cornelia had fallen asleep leaning against her on one side, while Maxine twitched happily with doggie dreams against her other one. Mom and Dad leaned together on the couch, and Jasp slouched in his favorite chair. How she'd left this for four-plus long years with only occasional visits, she'd never know.

Breakfast. Out front in ten. Dress warmly.

She sent back a, *K* because spelling *okay* was way beyond her capacity at this hour.

Tammy was three-quarters dressed before she came fully awake. One leg in her silk long johns and one out, she froze. That was a mistake; it sent her nose-diving to the carpet.

Seven a.m. Saturday. Nobody in the house would be up at this hour. The Cullens were *not* an early morning crew.

The message was from a number she didn't recognize. For half a moment she wondered if a boy *had* followed her from New York just as the Fabulous Five had suggested. Vernon? David? Then she saw that it was a local number, one not in her contact list.

Well, sitting on the floor in just her long johns wasn't going to answer anything. A peek out the window reminded her that her view was only the backyard. Jasp's and the master bedroom faced the street.

Out of options, she finished dressing and headed downstairs. Someone rousting her at this hour, they sure weren't getting her at her best.

The storm had cleared off yesterday, and the pre-dawn sky was brilliantly clear. In one of Seattle's quirky twists, it was already in the forties at this heathen hour, probably the fifties by midday. She'd roast in all these layers.

She didn't recognize whose car it was, but it was definitely her kind of vehicle. Low and muscley, and a classic. It was an immaculately restored 1960s Shelby Mustang.

Andre climbed out of the driver's side, and circled around to open the passenger door for her.

"What the hell?"

"Breakfast. You. Me. We're going to be related, might as well get to know each other," he continued to hold the door.

"At seven a.m. on a Saturday? Get a grip. I'm not even conscious."

He eyed the sky. "Should have been earlier, but that seemed cruel since you're probably still jet-lagged. Get in."

"Ordering me around is not a way to get me to cooperate." Then just to show him who was in charge, she got in. He closed the door just as she realized she'd gotten it backwards, and should have gone back into the house and crawled into bed still fully clothed to make her point.

He climbed in and buckled up.

She did her own seatbelt, then thumped her head against the headrest. "I'm so not awake yet."

He headed into town, "We'll fix that."

She wasn't going to ask how.

"Jasp really loves you a lot. Scared the crap out Amelia to meet you yesterday."

"Jeez. I'm just me. Not some *Friday the 13th* serial killer."

"Get that. Didn't matter. Why you two so close?"

"You know we had two moms?"

Andre nodded.

"Well, Jasper had three. I was his mom for four years until Perrin joined us."

"Hell of a burden for a kid."

Tammy just shrugged. She'd heard much worse stories among her college friends. "We were always safe and loved."

"It shows. Mom and Dad are like that, too. Always pisses me off when I hear about parents who weren't. You know, like deep inside makes me mad. I hear those stories, and I want to drop something damn heavy on their narcissistic heads." He didn't seem like the type to get mad easily, but she'd bet he was formidable when he did.

She really needed some hot cocoa or something.

"Jasper is great. You done good, Tamara."

"Only my two moms ever call me Tamara. Or Dad when I really make him nuts."

"Like the sound of it."

"Tough. You get me out of bed at this hour, you play by my rules."

"Sure, Tamara."

She sighed. Even Jasper wasn't this much of pain in the ass —not usually.

The Mustang's tires buzzed loudly as he rolled over the steel deck of the University drawbridge. Lake Union stretched off to the right, just starting to shimmer under the dawn light.

The sun wouldn't climb high enough to clear the hills to the east for another hour to light the water directly, but Andre was right. Half an hour from now, watching the sunrise catch the water would be spectacular.

On the right side of the bridge, she saw the white top of Russell's tall mast; his boat was moored close by the east side. He'd mounted a small Christmas tree for the parade, complete with lights and decorations, right at the very top. It was beyond cute. Something she'd have to rib him about, if she was conscious enough to remember this moment later.

Andre then took the familiar right turn. Not a chance was she going to ask where they were going. But when he turned into the first harbor parking lot, she knew something was up.

"No way did you get Russell up at this hour." Cassidy and Russell were even less of morning birds than the Cullens.

"Nope."

"If you think my idea of a good time is going out on Russell's boat, you're wrong in so many ways." He parked, got out, and circled around.

"Not into sailing?" Andre sounded shocked as he opened her door. She could hear the morning honks of the duck family that lived around these docks.

"They're complaining about you bothering them at this early hour, you know."

"They're saying hello because I do this almost every morning. Besides, I bribe them mercilessly with bread crusts." He held up a couple slices of bread to prove his point.

"Fine. And I can open my own door."

"You weren't. How can you not like sailing?"

Against her will, her better judgment, and several other things she'd think of later, Tammy followed him to the dock. Together they tore off pieces of bread and tossed them to the waiting ducks.

"Because I almost killed Jasper the first time I ever went sailing."

Andre started to make a joke of it, then paused and eyed her carefully.

"Yeah, *for real* almost killed him." Still the single worst day of her life. She'd almost lost Jasper, driven away Perrin, and sabotaged her still-secret dreams of designing fashion—all in the same day. She managed to beg off most sailing trips since then by hanging with Mom and Melanie. Neither one was a big fan, though Mom had gotten over that day, mostly, because Jasp loved it so much. "I'm not getting on that boat."

"Then how about this one?"

An elegant sloop bobbed in the far slip. About a third smaller than Russell's fifty-footer. Like his car, she looked low and fast. And while Russell's boat might be a little rough around the edges, much like its owner, this one was immaculate. Beyond that.

"Yours? Next to Russell's?"

"Uh-huh. That's how we all met. Thought I was just hooking Amelia up with a chance to work at the opera's scene shop: Russell to your dad. Didn't know about Jasper until they were already an item."

He coaxed her aboard by promising to tell her Jasper and Amelia stories that she didn't yet know, which was totally unfair. No way could she resist that, and he knew it.

The sloop was thirty feet long and beyond perfect. Every bit of mahogany trim shone. There wasn't so much as a waver in a single line of the bright-varnished wooden hull or the teak decking. "You did a really remarkable job fixing her up."

"Thanks. Actually, I built her from scratch."

Tammy turned to study him. He was busy starting the engine, pulling in lines, and uncovering the sails. Each item was neatly stowed before he moved on to the next. It was the way she liked to design herself. She was an unusually clean designer. Tammy had never understood how the clutterers could see their design and the images in their head when everything around them was messy.

He'd built it? That was a level of craftsmanship she understood. And it was far too rare, even in the advanced courses at design school. So many designers today thought of themselves as "conceptual artists", and assumed someone else would build their garments properly once they'd made it to the top.

She'd learned from Perrin that doing it right—yourself— gave you a real power. She'd learned so much from every single member of the Fabulous Five. If Perrin hadn't been such a great mom that she deserved the sole honor, she'd have called them *all* her mothers.

Melanie as model and business manager for Mom and her. Cassidy's Pacific Northwest wine collective was already surpassing Oregon and preparing to take on Napa. Mama Maria was still Seattle's best pastry chef. Jo managed the sprawling Pike Place Market and was on the board of every major arts organization in the city... And the Fabulous Five's husbands did no less.

She'd grown up surrounded by examples of doing it right.

It was clear that Andre had been raised the same.

"What's her name?" The boat had been moored bow-in, so Tammy hadn't seen the name across the stern. Then she looked at the boat's perfection. "Never mind. She's the *Amelia*."

Andre eyed her. His silences spoke as much as Jasp's did.

"Your love for her just shines out of this boat."

He didn't bother replying. Andre focused on backing out of the slip, then turning for Lake Union. About a mile long, with the sun still just beginning to color the sky, it started as a beautiful sail on the quiet water. The city was still asleep—like any other rational person at seven on a Decembery Saturday morning.

Russell's boat always seemed so crowded and on the verge of chaos—cheery chaos, but chaos nonetheless. Without the whole family crowded aboard, without Jasper here, she could feel her nerves easing off.

Being on a boat with Andre was a very smooth, controlled experience.

He handed off the tiller to her, as if he just assumed she could handle it, then moved forward to raise the sails. In moments, they were ghosting before the gentle breeze. The silence in the cockpit was deep when he cut the engine.

"You see things," he said softly after they'd eased down more than half the lake's length.

"Hello. Clothing designer. What's your excuse?"

"Hello. Boat designer." He pulled a bag out of the small cabin that he must have stashed her before coming to get her. He handed her a thermos mug.

She sniffed it carefully. "Hot chocolate not coffee."

"I asked." No Jasperish one-sided shrug with him. He was at ease with himself in a way she could never hope to be.

They slipped out onto the main body of the lake. Seattle towered to the south, Queen Anne and Capitol Hill to either side, and the green expanse of Gasworks Park commanded the north. At this lazy pace, they were ten minutes or more between tacks despite the lake's small size.

She could feel the nerves slipping off and floating away across the water. Not just boat nerves, but New York nerves, school nerves, and even homecoming nerves. This was really the first moment she'd truly stopped since...she had no idea when.

Watching Andre was a pleasant surprise too. He didn't pressure or push. He just...was letting her have her morning without being all weird about it. In between silences, he did tell some pretty funny stories about Jasper and Amelia—though she didn't trust the one about the three hamsters and the bicycle. That one had almost made her spill her bowl of apple, yogurt, and honey all over the cockpit as she laughed.

He wasn't reticent, but neither did he waste a lot of words, almost sounding abrupt sometimes. But if she asked, he answered. It was almost a relief to not be second-guessing what he was thinking.

"What *are* you thinking?"

He watched her for a long moment. "I'm thinking I'm incredibly lucky."

"Why's that?"

"That for all the good things Jasper said about you, I'm starting to believe he fell short by some stretch."

Guys never flummoxed Tammy. Being raised by the circle of the Fabulous Five, she was hip to every come-on, cheesy line, and game men could play.

But if Andre was playing a game, it was one she'd never seen before.

If he wasn't, well, she hoped the heat in her cheeks was just from the steam off the cocoa.

9

"Mom! Help!"

She must have sounded more desperate than she intended, because Mom dropped everything and raced around the design table.

"I haven't cut myself. It's just a clothing design emergency. I'm *so* stuck."

Mom huffed out a sharp breath, but looked her over anyway. Once she convinced herself they weren't racing to ER anytime soon, she threw her arms around her.

Tammy just held on.

"Hard to know which is worse, isn't it?"

At the moment, Tammy would vote for being stuck. She'd almost rather be racing to ER, because at least then she'd know what was wrong.

As a designer, this *was* the worst. She'd tried every trick she could think of. For two weeks she hadn't been able to get Amelia's jacket to come together. And, until she had that, Amelia's dress was impossible to think about.

Mom pulled out a pair of stools and sat down shoulder-to-shoulder just as they always had when working on a design.

"Show me."

So Tammy did. "Stacks of sketches. Half a jillion swatches of fabric. And a thousand ideas that totally suck!"

"Okay, first, take a breath."

Tammy did. "It isn't helping."

"Well, take another."

And while Tammy did, Mom gathered up all the sketches as if she was going to—

"No!"

But she was too late. Mom tore the first couple in half with a tear that jolted right up Tammy's spine until she thought her head would explode. "Want to do a couple?"

Tammy just shook her head.

That's how they'd met. The madcap Perrin Williams, tearing up months of another designer's work. Dad had nearly stroked out, because they were the only costume renderings he'd had for a new opera.

Oh...and she'd done it because they were terrible.

Then Perrin had showed her what design really meant. The costumes she'd done for that opera had been a total smash as well as turning them into a family.

"Shit! It sucks that I'm now in 'Carlotta Nightmare'-land." She grabbed a bunch and began shredding them until there was nothing left. Not wanting to do a major cleanup, she tossed just a couple pieces in Mom's face. Mom slipped a few down Tammy's back for old-times' sake, where they itched and crinkled until she managed to fish them out. The rest went into the trash.

Then Mom swept aside all of the fabrics except the original four. She snipped the dark graphite-gray and frost-blue into two pieces, and separated them in pairs. Next to one pair, she laid the magenta swatch.

"Make a jacket for Amelia out of just these three."

Tammy wanted to slap her forehead. The answer hadn't

been to add more, it had been to hone down. To edit. The one trick she hadn't tried, one of the very first Mom had taught her. "I can do that. Maybe."

"I know you can," Mom said in that of-course tone of hers. Then she bumped Tammy's shoulder with hers, before she walked away. She came back with a set of measurements on a Post-it, and placed it with the other set of three colors. "Make a complementary jacket with the dark cherry to this fit."

"But those are a guy's measurements. I want to make Amel—"

"Shush," Mom brushed her hair. "Trust me on this one, Tamara. You'll see it eventually. Do Amelia's first."

She already had Amelia's measurements in her design book —she'd taken them at that very first lunch. And she'd seen her often enough since that she really didn't need them, her figure was so clear in Tammy's head.

The two of them had met for a lunch on their own.

Then the four of them had done dinner together.

Even Jasp had gotten up in time to join in for a couple of Andre's chilly morning sails—he must really be in love with Amelia to do that. Only drenching rain seemed to break Andre's habit of rousting her at a ridiculous hour to sail. She'd also had dinner with their parents, and Amelia had dragged her to the waterfront warehouse where a sawdust-drenched Andre had proudly showed her the half-framed hull of his next boat—a custom job that he already had a down payment for.

Amelia might look like her brother, but she had a fun, quirky side that Tammy wanted to capture in the jacket.

Not even bothering to sketch, she began smoothing out the first chest panel. Curved lines, one of Tammy's favorite signatures. Yes. The hardness of graphite versus the softness of the mottled frost-blue like a cleavage, starting at...the lower quarter of the front zipper—but not low enough to be an arrow at her crotch. Then staying narrow. Not as an arcing race to expose breasts, but instead, making Amelia's face the top of a flower. The magenta, a slender seam between the graphite and frost to soften yet strengthen the arc. Repeated as a rose-petal trim around the collar.

Then...

10

The living room was all Christmas tree, hot cocoa, and scones. Stockings along the bookcase, including a small one for Maxine stuffed to the brim with toys and treats because everyone bought something for the terrier.

Tammy had practically bawled on Mom's shoulder this morning when she saw it all. She remembered their first real Christmas together. Perrin had taught her to knit and they'd made stockings for everyone, covered with goofy pictures and each person's name knit right in. Not just some tube, but Mom had taught her how to properly rib the top, turn a heel, and shape the toe.

A decade of decorations were on every surface and dangling from every branch. Her first family had always decorated a small tree, and many of those were on the tree now. But Perrin had turned it into a joyous and bountiful celebration, requiring a much bigger tree to hold even half of the ornaments.

Each wearing personalized stocking hats and their Christmas socks, they'd opened presents together, taking the time to all appreciate each one.

Jasper went nuts over the tailored jacket she'd made him for Christmas. He instantly raced upstairs to fish out the supposed-to-match tie-dye shirt. It still worked, just...differently. Instead of elegant, it was fun. Jasp had always been a serious kid, even before their birth-mom had been killed, though he was sharp enough to be funny, too. Amelia brought out the fun side of him. The crazy tie-dye under the elegant jacket was the new him in a lot of good ways.

She'd had to reach somewhere really deep for that design, and she was so glad that it hadn't been ruined by Jasper having the crazy idea to fall in love and tie-dye the shirt.

Mom spent a lot of time studying the jacket. Both up close and from a step back.

Her silent hug had tipped something inside Tammy. That as skilled a designer as Mom could like it that much was...perfect.

"Okay. Time for your real present." And Mom had fished the very last gift—a tiny box—out from where it had laid unnoticed behind the tree.

Inside was a key. "To what?"

No one would tell her. Her best target for info, Jasp, didn't know. Mom had known that he couldn't keep a secret from her. Dad's smile said he definitely was in on it, but it took days to wheedle her way past his shields.

He just raised his hands, "Not this time, Kiddo. Not even for the promise of your lasagna."

"Well, okay. I guess. I'm so glad to be home that I'll make us a lasagna soon anyway."

"With pumpkin pie, for New Year's Eve."

She hugged him. Dad had always been nuts in all the best ways.

With her key to...somewhere still clutched in her palm, they piled into the car, and drove down to Perrin's Glorious Garb. Mom's bright logo cheerily splashed across the door was the only brightness on the deserted street. There was even a thin slick of frost on the sidewalks.

"What are we doing here? It's Christmas. Besides, I already have a key to the shop."

Once they were all out of the car, Mom pointed to the other side of the street.

The old tattoo parlor had been resurrected several times over the years, but never lasted long.

For the first time in all the years, the glass storefront was clean. Several mannequins stood in the window, wearing only the simplest plain white for decency's sake, not style's.

They all crossed the empty street together. On the door, in simple yet elegant gold letters was a single word: Tamara.

Done up like it was a logo—as if she was Prada or Chanel.

Not TJPWC.

Not the whole family.

Just her.

Just—Tamara.

Numb, she slipped the key into the lock and opened the front door. Inside was a duplicate of the design room at the back of Perrin's Glorious Garb. A ginormous bow bloomed at the center of the sprawling cutting table. Down the side was an array of machines: a gorgeous Sailrite for heavy sewing, a serger, a Techsew for fine leather, and—

"No way!"

Mom slipped a hand around her waist. It was Mom's Singer Featherweight, the machine she'd taught Tammy how to sew on.

"I can't take that."

"Too late, honey. It's already yours. Besides, it's not really mine. In the beginning, it came from Cassidy's mom to me. It's time it moved on to you."

"But—" Tammy didn't even know what she wanted, what she was going to do. Yes, she could do anything here, but....

"For starters?" Mom could always read her moods. "Jasper, come here."

He came to stand in front of them, with a total Jasp frown of confusion. Mom reached out and brushed a hand over the front of his jacket. "Kari will want to commission this jacket for sale through TJPWC. If you age it up a bit, it's a must-have for Perrin's Glorious Garb, too."

Tammy couldn't even get out a "but" this time.

"And those bomber jackets you made. Those absolutely need to be a line. Different shadings, maybe even set them up as one-off custom exclusives without having to get crazy expensive. You know, 'Send us your photo and we'll tone the color selection for you.' Each custom, each signed. That kind of thing. I've always been good at the clothes, but you—oh God, Tamara, you make me feel so lucky that I've gotten to be your Mom—outerwear is so definitely your thing."

The bell on the front door chimed, and didn't stop for a while. The room soon filled with the Fabulous Five—no—the *other* members of the Smashing Six and their families. Everyone was trading hugs, oohing and aahing over the shop.

Russell and Angelo began popping champagne corks, and serving mimosas around the table. The kids got apple cider. Mama Maria had brought a massive box of her delicious cornetti.

It took a while, but Tammy managed to get Melanie and Mama Maria aside.

"For real?"

Melanie brushed a hand down her cheek, then, rather than a pair of air kisses, hugged her tightly. It wasn't something she did often.

"Remember when I picked your drawings out of all the applications to your Mom, not knowing they were yours?"

"The day I got permission to start TJPW. Even before Cornelia became the C."

"This," she pointed at Jasper. He sat on the floor across the room playing with Cornelia and the other kids. The four younger members of the Fabulous Five had given birth all within the same year. "*This* is more than I ever imagined was possible. Beautiful and perfect. *Très bon!*"

For just a moment she wondered if Melanie meant the design of Jasper's jacket or the gathering of family. Or both.

Melanie sighed happily before turning back to her.

Both.

"The other two jackets, Perrin showed them to Mama Maria and me already—you are *magnifique!* I would be proud to walk your jackets down the runway. Paired with the other two stores, it will be very good business as well."

No one knew the business of fashion better than Melanie, not even Jo.

She turned to Mama Maria.

Maria just wrapped her arms around Tammy.

That was all she needed to know.

11

"This is *your* thing, why am I along?"

Jasper was just looking pleased as he drove them to the Clayton's. "We had Christmas Eve dinner with Mom and Dad last night. I told Amelia we'd be glad to have Christmas Day dinner with them."

"It's the *we* part that doesn't make any sense." Jasper had indeed done it right. On one knee, nice ring, right at Angelo's restaurant where Cassidy had met Russell, and Angelo had courted Jo. Part of their own history with Perrin had been there. Melanie's too. It was only right that Jasper had gotten engaged there.

"Figure it out, Loops." From Jasper, who could always see everything about everyone—except himself and Amelia—that should have been a clue.

It wasn't.

When she went to grab Amelia's jacket from the trunk, there were two boxed presents there. "Who?"

"Mom said to make sure I grabbed the box*es*, plural. So I did. Sue me."

"But I only wrapped one. What's—"

Before she could check the labels, they were swept into the house.

It *was* fun. The Claytons were both software engineers, and had no explanation of how they'd had two such creative children. But they didn't enjoy them any the less for that.

Dinner was a blast, just as the prior one had been. She and Amelia ganging up on Jasper. Andre occasionally plowing them aside before the waters got too deep. A couple times, he'd teamed with Jasper to give back as good as he got. Their parents played half referee and half egging them all on.

But there was some undercurrent she couldn't put her finger on. Something going on that Jasper saw but wouldn't reveal. If she could get him aside, Tammy would get it out of him. But not in this crowd of merry bandits.

They gathered around the tree with pumpkin pie and hot chocolate laced with Baileys Irish Cream.

Jasper gave Amelia one of TJPWC's dresses which earned him a very serious kiss—after she stopped laughing. The laughter was explained when he opened his present of one of Perrin's lovely shirts. "I had to twist your Mom's arm to let me even pay wholesale." Tammy doubted if Kari had gotten a penny from Jasper.

Tammy decided two things. First, Amelia had great taste about what looked good on Jasper. And second, that the gift was also a little bit for her. Switching it out for the tie-dyed shirt, it would look great with the jacket Tammy had made.

After giving a big hug to let Amelia know she'd nailed it, Amelia handed her a small box.

"Please tell me this isn't another key. I don't think my heart could stand another surprise like that one today."

Both Amelia and Andre squinted at her.

"I'll explain after you open your present. I swore Jasper to secrecy so that I wouldn't spoil your gift."

"O-kay," Amelia waved at the box. "It's not a key. We didn't know what to get you, but Jasper said that you really like to draw. Not just sketch, but like pen-and-ink drawings. Andre and I went in on these together, but he picked them out. They're his favorite for drawing boat designs."

"I do love drawing." Something she didn't do enough of. From the box Tammy unearthed a trio of truly fine fountain pens in three different nib sizes. "Oh my God! These are so perfect."

Amelia looked very relieved.

Andre looked…satisfied? Like sailing—which he was slowly teaching her to enjoy—it was apparently a required part of their friendship that they had drawing in common.

Once she could force herself to stop admiring them, she picked up the first present and handed it to Amelia. As Amelia started unwrapping it, Tammy picked up the second box and read the label.

She handed it to Andre, but froze before she could let go of it.

"What?"

Tammy knew exactly what was in the box.

And now knew where Perrin had gotten the measurements for her to build to. *Not* one of the shop's models as she'd kind of assumed.

Mom had understood who her mind had been designing for in the very first instant. That's why Mom had hugged her so hard—for instinctively selecting the dark cherry leather over the magenta. At that moment, Mom had seen all the way ahead to this moment.

Tammy managed to release her hands, and just let it go. Everything racing out of her control.

Amelia and Andre pulled out their jackets simultaneously.

Amelia's looked just as great as Tammy had imagined. Everyone was commenting on it, and Amelia was hugging the thick sheepskin lining around herself.

Andre was brushing a hand along the smooth lines. Rather than a sweeping upward curve of the frost-blue that made Amelia look as if she truly was blooming, on Andre's jacket the curves spread out from his collar. They ran down his shoulders, forming arced points over his outer biceps. It made a strong man look invincible without, quite, tipping over into the superhero vibe.

His eyes. She couldn't look away from his eyes.

Some part of her had known, even after that very first lunch when she'd chosen the dark cherry fabric. The accent color made his obsidian-dark eyes shine so brightly as they looked at her. And she didn't mind looking back one bit as the smile grew on his face.

Tammy now also understood the last thing Mom had said to her before she and Jasper had come here, "Never underestimate the power of a great jacket."

———

If you enjoyed this story, visit https://shop.mlbuchman. com/collections/contemporary-romance and start with *Where Dreams Are Born* and prepare yourself for a romantic journey through Seattle's Pike Place Market.

ICE SHELF RESCUE

You'll find three tales of Antarctic Ice Fliers in this collection. When I first began writing about Antarctica, I didn't realize where this would lead me. I've always enjoyed reading about the great explorers of any era but particularly those who ventured onto The Ice, as it is called by those who work there. At the time I never imagined that I'd soon be setting a major novel there, *Skibird* in the Miranda Chase thriller series. Nor did I contemplate that I would be sailing there on a square-rigged tall ship shortly after the release of this collection as research for an entirely new series that launches there.

This particular romance tale of the New Year was born of sitting for an hour with a Twin Otter pilot in the quiet harbor of Vancouver, British Columbia, Canada. He patiently answered my questions about flying his plane and told me stories of various adventures the aircraft had endured. Some of those are here, a few are in a later story.

Ice Shelf Rescue will always hold a place close to my heart as it was the first time I wrote of The Ice and my passion for it.

1

———

"WHOEVER SAID SCIENTISTS WERE SMART, LIED!" AURORA EVANS glared through Myrtle's windscreen at the white landscape that appeared to spread in every direction—including up.

"Oh I don't know about that, my dear." Doc Tenniel was riding copilot for this flight.

Aurora was too used to flying alone and having only Myrtle to speak with. She and the old de Havilland DHC-6 Twin Otter airplane had been together for a long time. They were each other's constant, and typically only, companions. They could haul nineteen passengers or two tons of cargo just about anywhere. Wheels or pontoons in the summer, but mostly skis down here in Antarctica.

"We scientists have led explorations into every corner of the earth, ocean, and sky. We're quite adept at what we do." He sounded almost...miffed! Which fit, being so British.

She managed not to laugh in his face.

Most "beakers"—Antarctic slang for scientists of any breed, shape, or specialty—wouldn't survive ten minutes without the support crew they never seemed to acknowledge.

"Yet here we are," she nodded toward the non-view, "flying

into the vast nothingness on the shortest day of the winter to save a pair of beakers with less sense than God gave a snail."

"A snail is actually a quite sensible creature. First, it eats its own shell to gather calcium and other essential minerals. Then it is able to continuously extrude his or her shell as it grows, and..."

Aurora tuned him out and looked out at all the white.

Someday she'd learn to keep her mouth shut around beakers. Like most men on The Ice, as Antarctica was known to its residents, Doc seemed incredibly pleased to talk to a woman, any woman, even if she wasn't listening.

Scientists might now be thirty percent women on The Ice, but as support personnel they were still few and far between. Gender rarity had its advantages...and someday she'd think of one. In the summer, it was typically easy to find a big enough clump of women to keep the men at bay, but this was her first winter on The Ice and the slim staff count made it much harder to hide.

Nothing but white ahead, behind, or sideways!

She and Myrtle had been rousted an hour before the Antarctic dawn for a rescue mission. It was actually a misnomer, because there wasn't any dawn during the winter solstice, not at the Brit's Rothera Research Station. This far south on the Antarctic Peninsula, there was a lame twilight for about five hours but that was all she wrote.

She was supposed to be flying back up to Palmer Station today. Located two hundred miles north—clear on the other side of the Antarctic Circle—the US station boasted three hours and forty-four minutes of actual daylight on June 21st.

Except now she wasn't going to be there to see it.

Shortest day of the year but she wasn't going to get a day at all. They'd better get this guy rescued fast, she didn't want to miss the Solstice Night party, too. Even with just ten people of

Palmer's summertime forty-five staff wintering over, it was supposed to be a serious amount of fun.

The rescue report stated that a two-man science team was marooned far out on the ice, one critically injured, and nothing else useful. Something going wrong out in the middle of nowhere in midwinter? The only surprising thing was that they weren't *both* dead.

No matter how bad the emergency, rushing things in Antarctica was a fast way to die. Myrtle had the full cold-weather kit, but Aurora had still spent an hour with gas heaters to warm the engines before taking the risk of turning them over. Even a turboprop didn't start well when it was that cold. And replacing an engine was a real strain down here. In winter, it probably couldn't happen at all because the person to fly in the replacement engine...would be herself.

Doc was running down on his evolutionary pathways of personal housing construction methodologies of gastropods.

She offered him a friendly, "Really?"

That seemed to cheer him up and get him rolling again so that she didn't have to interact.

He wasn't only a medico, but also *just so thrilled* by the science of Antarctica that it made her want to dump him from a great height. Scientists could be a major pain, even if carting beakers about was half of her bread and butter. The other half was shuffling around supplies that kept them alive in the first place.

Totally white!

The only thing to see in any direction were Myrtle's nose and wings.

Aurora knew she was safe. Myrtle's instruments insisted they were in straight-and-level flight at five thousand feet up. They were a hundred kilometers south of Slessor Peak, which rose to almost eight thousand feet. The rest of this section of the Antarctandes Range up the middle of the Antarctic Peninsula were under four thousand.

Aside from their altitude, she had to completely trust Myrtle about the flight *attitude*. Though they'd been together long enough for her to trust the old plane's opinion on that.

The instruments don't lie.

It was the very first lesson any pilot learned. She'd been flying long enough to know that actually, on very rare occasions, they did. But it was always for a reason, none of which were relevant at the moment. Myrtle was a trustworthy beast. Aurora leaned forward and patted the console directly below Myrtle's compass.

"Good girl," she whispered too quietly to disturb Doc's ramblings. It didn't matter, Myrtle heard her just fine.

After a decade of bush flying in Alaska, first with Mom, then on her own—after Mom had found a new husband and gone Lower 48—Aurora and Myrtle had landed the golden ticket. For five years (so far), they'd been cruising up and down the Antarctic Peninsula for fun and profit with few problems. Mom's native Alaskan blood had adapted to the heat of Coronado Beach in San Diego overnight. Despite her mixed blood, Aurora still felt like she was dying when the temperature crossed seventy.

Antarctica never came close. A record hot summer day, high on the Peninsula might approach sixty, but it didn't have the temerity to cross over. And South Pole Station had still never cracked ten degrees. Fine with her.

This year she'd finally landed the lucrative over-winter slot. That ended the last of the quibbles; she was now officially an OAE—Old Antarctic Explorer. Some aspirational geeks said multiple summers counted. But she was with the purists, and a winterover—a single word to a Southie—was required to properly claim the title of OAE.

It was the solstice today, so no matter what happened now, she was in.

Of course, it was only June twenty-first and already a scientist was in trouble out on the ice—the first day of the new Antarctic Year in a very real way. If saving his hide made her miss tonight's solstice party at Palmer, she was going to be rather ticked.

Rather ticked? She'd been spending too much time with the Brits like Doc Tenniel. Majorly bummed! That was better. Pissed off? Yeah!

On the bright side, other than the sun beginning its return, search-and-rescue paid double.

But the white!

Ten miles after she'd taken off from Rothera, she'd torqued the plane enough to look behind her. Yes, she'd still been able to see the spread of buildings, so visibility distance wasn't the issue.

Everything *else* was!

It was all entirely white.

That was a major problem.

She was aloft with no sign of the ground, the sky, or a visible horizon between them.

Aurora listened to the roar of Myrtle's twin Pratt & Whitney PT6A engines. Firm and steady. Even if she wasn't feeling so sure, Myrtle didn't seem to have any doubts which was enough for her.

Myrtle's artificial horizon said she was dead on the mark, the blue half of the instrument floating evenly above the little airplane drawn on the glass with the black half below. With no external visual reference, a pilot could easily fall for a "gut feel" or an inner ear imbalance and end up flying completely upside down without realizing it. When there was no external reference, a body looked inside to find one—and it was always wrong.

The situation reminded her all too clearly about the 1979 tourist plane crash on the other side of the continent. Mt. Erebus was a twelve-thousand-foot peak sticking up out of the flat sea, and the DC-10 airline full of sightseers had run into it head-on, without ever spotting it in a sector whiteout. Two hundred and fifty-seven people, and a DC-10 airliner, all dead.

And she was in the same conditions right now.

The long flat plain of white that was the Larsen Ice Shelf afloat on the Southern Ocean didn't look any different from the ice-clad mountains that formed the backbone of Graham Land, the northern half of the Antarctic Peninsula. By mid-summer, enough of the rocky slopes would have melted out to show the peaks as rock and the valleys as ice.

Not so much in June.

The only real marker in the three-sixty of white was a nebulous brighter-half of the Antarctic haze that said the sun had peeked over the horizon for a few hours somewhere vaguely north...ish. Only her altitude extended her view enough for even that fuzzy hint of morning sunshine; it was going to stay twilight down on the ice until the darkness returned in a few hours.

Their position, close along the Antarctic Circle, meant she had less than five hours of twilight to track down and rescue the two stupid beakers in question.

"See anything yet, Doc?" She had heard enough about gastropods for a lifetime, maybe two. It was far too soon to spot a tent at their last reported position, but at least it gave him something to do.

"Uh, no." He shifted more upright in his seat and began studying the endless white below.

Major science wouldn't start arriving on The Ice until October. By Christmas there'd be four thousand folks scattered across the second largest country in the world, except

Antarctica wasn't a country. But for the thousand year-rounders, The Ice was a planet all its own.

Then there were the ones crazy enough to go out and do midwinter research. Winter was a time for hunkering down at your base and playing with your data. Of course, if they did that, there wouldn't be any winter gigs for her and Myrtle.

Flights into the interior were close enough to impossible for six months of the year that only major medical emergencies called for them—the last one four years ago.

But sixteen countries maintained thirty-four bases along the Peninsula and on the South Shetland Islands alone, and half of those were year-rounders. Even the ones not on islands might as well have been. Air travel was the primary connection between them, and with a little cooperation, it was enough to keep her and Myrtle in business through the cold months. She was the nomad of the Peninsula, never long at any base yet always welcome.

If she had a home base, as such, it would be the US base at Palmer Station perched on Anvers Island. Nowhere on the Peninsula was much harsher than central Alaska. Palmer Station was within five miles of being as far south of the equator as Fairbanks was north. Even at the coldest, about minus forty Fahrenheit, fuel was still thirty degrees from freezing.

Doc Tenniel had found a new topic, thankfully a little more relevant. He again began effusing happily in his slightly too urbane English accent, wholly unaware of the freakish nature of the flying that was going on.

"You know, the breakup of a section of the ice shelf in midwinter is wholly unprecedented. Now is normally the time when it's jolly well the safest to explore the ice."

"If you're into freezing your asses off." She knew it was a mistake the moment she said it and was able to recite his predictable reply along with him.

"All in the name of science, Captain. All in the name of science." *Pip. Pip. Cheerio.* Like he was a throwback to Victorian England. Maybe Doc had seen too many Gilbert and Sullivan operettas during med school.

"Yet it's happened," she couldn't resist pointing out. "The Larsen shelf broke in winter."

"Yes, indeed, it is a tad bit puzzling." Maybe his retro-accent was just The Ice. Personality quirks were honed and cherished down here. When they became too irritating, they were cheerfully stomped back into place by other denizens of the base, but they generally thrived.

And even she knew that this midwinter breakup was very strange. The Larsen Ice Shelf was one of the climate change hotspots, shedding thousands of square miles at a time in massive bergs. Originally larger than any New England state except Maine by a factor of three, Larsen had shed an area the size of Connecticut and Rhode Island combined in the span of her own lifetime.

And somewhere out in all that twilit white was a scientific team in trouble.

Sure, she had their GPS coordinates, but the terrain was still a great expanse of nothing but white.

2

———

"Not one of your smoother moves, Chas."

Chas didn't answer. Hadn't answered once since Tommy had rescued him after the collapse. They were now bundled into their survey tent as the wind slammed it harder than the spring rapids on West River through the Green Mountains. He could do with a dose of Vermont green about now.

But he'd been offered a winterover slot by the Old Man of the Ice himself, Dr. Chas Ellsworth. Tommy hadn't expected to ever even *meet* Antarctica's leading glaciologist. To be selected to assist the Brit with a Larsen Ice Shelf winter study was too incredible an opportunity to pass up. Chas knew more about Larsen than everyone else on the planet—combined.

However, midwinter ice sheets weren't supposed to have surprise crevasses. The only miracle was that Chas had survived rather than plunging to his death.

They'd technically been roped up for safety. Luckily, they were strict on the use of the rope even if it was for an entirely different reason. It was easier to help each other through the blown snow drifts atop the ice shelf when they could haul on each other using the rope.

It was as much security blanket as a communications line—until the ice had disappeared beneath Chas' feet.

The Larsen Ice Shelf was divided into seven sections, A through G. Larsen A had shattered in 1995. Larsen B, over ten thousand years old, had fractured in stages over the last twenty years until only a tiny remnant barely twenty kilometers wide remained. Now Larsen C, by far the largest, was breaking up into monstrous bergs. D through G were all tiny by comparison and, for the moment, safely farther south.

Larsen C was still seventeen thousand square miles and a thousand feet thick. It didn't equate that an area twice the size of his home state of Vermont could just—break. Especially not this far back from the edge.

They'd just unmired their "Doo" and their two sleds from yet another swale filled with wind-blown snow. Chas had stepped aside to take a photo of their rig: Ski-Doo snowmobile, the tow-along supplies trailer stacked high with spare fuel cans, and a second equipment trailer for their ice survey gear. All against the backdrop of the most amazing Aurora Australis he'd ever seen. Intertwined green sheets rippling across the sky like a crazy dragon's laundry. Streaks of gold fire flooding the horizon.

With only five hours of twilight, they started and ended their days in the dark. But what a glorious dark it was.

Astride the Doo, Tommy had turned to face his helmet toward Chas just in time to watch him stumble backward and land on his butt. Which would have been laughable, except a second later, he disappeared from view faster than Wiley E. Coyote after running off the edge of a cliff.

Tommy had already stowed his ice axe alongside the Doo's seat. If he hadn't had his hands on the steering grips, he'd have been yanked off the Doo and dragged across the ice.

They'd both be gone.

As it was, he was fairly sure the harness had cracked a couple of his ribs as he'd fought to arrest Chas' fall.

Tommy had secured the line to the Doo and tied himself to second one before belly crawling to the edge. The crevasse wasn't some little gap in the ice with a snow cap that happened to give way when Chas stepped on it.

Chas' fall had unleashed a ripple collapse that had revealed a five- to ten-meter-wide crack that continued out of sight in both directions.

The first time he'd peered over the edge to see if Chas was alive, Tommy had seen the bottomless pit. His headlamp didn't touch the darkness. The thousand-foot thickness of the ice shelf appeared to have broken all the way down. Somewhere in depths below, the ocean would be rushing to fill the lower eight hundred feet of the new crack in the ice.

It had taken forever, working with the Doo, to haul Chas up to just below the ice shelf's surface. Each time Tommy crawled back to the precipitous edge to check on Chas' upward progress, it was the single bravest thing he'd ever done—harder every time. Thank God no one was around to see how badly he was quaking in his boots.

The thirty-knot wind seemed intent on driving him over the edge himself. Then, when he turned, it resisted his efforts to return to the Doo and goose it forward another ten or fifteen feet before crawling back to check on Chas again. The blown ice particles against his Doo helmet had sounded like a monster hailstorm on a tin roof each time he faced the wind. And scrubbing his ribs across the ice as he crawled hurt like a son-of-a-bitch.

Easing Chas once more over the cliff's edge by hand, all the while wondering if the section under *his own* butt was going to let go, made any earlier fears seem mild.

Just as he'd finally dragged Chas' unresponsive form onto the ice beside him, and lay there trying to catch his own breath,

Tommy had realized the worst of it. The Doo had been parked parallel to the vast crevasse when Chas had fallen. How long had they driven close along the weak spot without knowing? Some glaciologists they were. They should *both* be dead.

Another half hour to get the tent up—far away from the crevasse—and wrestle Chas' dead weight into a sleeping bag. Outside, over the sound of thirty knots of wind chill, it had been impossible to tell if he was even alive. In the tent Tommy could see the tiny cloud of mist each time Chas exhaled—all that gave him away. His own fingers were too numb to feel a pulse over their own throbbing.

He'd called in for a rescue, then just lay there on the tent's thin floor, trying to breathe himself—without moving his ribs.

Some ages later, his radio crackled to life, "This is Myrtle and Aurora calling survey team Larsen Nineteen."

It took him a moment to remember that was him...them technically, but now just him.

"This is Nineteen. Come back."

She verified his GPS coordinates. "I'll be on site in twenty. I need a quarter-mile of skiway with no crevasses or hummocks."

"Right." *Shit!*

He should have thought about that when he called for medevac three hours ago. They'd spent two long weeks winding through the mountains of Graham Land and out onto the ice shelf as part of their survey. Every five miles they'd stopped for ice cores and radar sounding through the ice to map ice thickness and the terrain below. A methodical, unhurried process that had suited him down to his boots.

Now he had twenty minutes to clear a place for the plane to land or it would fly back where it had come from.

"On it!"

He scrabbled into his cold-weather gear and plunged back into Nature's freezer.

While he'd been inside, the morning dark had

brightened into a midday mediocre twilight. Just in case, he reached back into the tent, turned on a high-power flashlight, and aimed it up at the ceiling. From the outside, the tent was now an internally lit bright orange beacon.

That would be one end of the skiway.

Hopefully no worse weather would move in quickly. One good katabatic wind blast, dropping visibility to under three meters in a heartbeat, and he'd be a dead man despite the flashlight.

With no one to rope up to, he selected a ski pole and an ice axe.

Planes landed into the wind. So he turned his back on the wind and stabbed the pole into the surface of ice and snow. Solid. Another step, another stab.

With the wind's help pushing him along, he moved quickly enough. Seven hundred steps, his heart nearly stopping with each one, and he made the distance in under ten minutes without disappearing into an ice crack.

Chance, which had been so unkind to Chas, had favored himself. Not so much as a knee-high drift or an ankle-deep hole.

Now he just needed to get back to the tent so that he could run the Doo up and down the runway a few times to make sure it was smooth enough.

Turning into the wind, he was almost bowled over backwards.

Head-on into thirty knots was a hard push. Like an idiot, he hadn't pulled on his full helmet. Instead he just had snow goggles and his parka's hood—which kept acting like a sail to drag his head backwards.

Out of time, he wrapped a scarf over his mouth and broke into a run. Minus forty degrees with minus thirty more from wind chill. Every breath hurt his battered ribs like a rabbit punch. He was gasping equally from the pain, the effort, and the freezing cold.

"Couldn't stay in Vermont, could you, Tommy Dane? Just had to go be a glaciologist in Antarctica, didn't you?" It was old Professor Farnsworth's fault. There hadn't been a permanent glacier in New England since the last Ice Age. Yet Farnsworth had hooked Tommy's imagination freshman year by showing him how to see that the land had been carved by repeated glaciation like an artist slicing into a woodblock for printing. He'd never lost that wonder; not even now when it was trying to carve him from the landscape—permanently.

Tommy's footprints were long since swept away.

Every now and then he raised his face enough to adjust his course towards the lit tent. It was like looking into the nozzle of a snow machine on Stowe Mountain ski area—ten thousand particles of ice blasted into every exposed surface each second. And the wind didn't just bite, it roared and growled too loud to hear himself think. Which was a good thing right now.

He was running with all the speed of a tree slug.

When he reached the Doo, he nearly collapsed over the seat. Would have, if there was time. Three more minutes.

Taking just enough time to grab his helmet, he could only pray that the ice, which was firm enough to carry his one-eighty, could also support six hundred pounds of snowmobile. Then, however many tons of airplane.

The Doo fired up on the first try which was also a rare blessing. He unhitched the sleds in favor of speed and raced back down the stretch he'd just explored. He'd only have time for a few passes to pack the snow before the plane arrived.

Ruining his day or the fifteen-thousand-dollar machine he'd signed out was a minor consideration compared to wrecking seven million dollars worth of airplane that was pretty much Chas' only chance of survival.

Aurora and Myrtle were almost here.

The Girls.

They had a real reputation on The Ice. Even during his first summer all the way over at McMurdo on the other side of Antarctica, he'd heard stories about them. The stories weren't real clear about which was the pilot and which the plane; they were always mentioned like they were single unit. You wanted someone to watch your ass out on the ice? Apparently, she... they...The Girls were the ones you wanted.

There were plenty of remarks about how pretty a sight they were, usually followed up with a description of the plane slipping into an impossible landing or airdropping a critical load of supplies.

By the sound of the stories, the workhorse Twin Otter cargo plane was a classic "Antarctic Ten"—a great beauty coming to save your ass but so homely that you'd never look at it twice back in the real world. Even when you weren't in trouble, being way out from base made any connection a real gift. In Antarctica it was easy to be hundreds of miles from the nearest camp—a very lonely feeling.

He discounted all the guy-stories about the pilot being even more worth looking at. When women were in such scarce supply as they were down here, they all took on an aura of Hollywood beauty.

At the end of his second run down and back, he carved a turn around the tent to set up his third run and aimed once more down his impromptu skiway.

Then, with a hard correction, he almost drove into the tent and right over Chas.

An airplane had appeared out of nowhere. By the time they'd both stopped nose-to-nose, those spinning propellors looked real damn big.

It must have come in behind him as he raced back toward the camp, the Doo's screaming engine trying to drown out the wind's basso howl.

He understood the stories now. The Twin Otter had seen a lot of hard miles. There were deep paint scuffs in her flanks where the spinning propellers had sandpapered the fuselage with bits of ice. The white underbelly was scraped up as well and the red top paint was sun-faded.

And it was about the most damn beautiful sight he'd ever seen. Nothing had ever looked so good as that big steel sky beast come to the rescue.

Before he even shut down the Doo, the propellors were easing to a halt. The instant they did, someone clambered out the right-side door carrying a small case.

"Greetings, my good man. Where's Chas? Had a bit of a fall, did he?"

"About twenty meters."

"Oh dear, and where is he now? Ah, in the tent I see. Well done." And he ducked inside.

Tommy had met Doc Tenniel briefly when he first arrived at Rothera. Chas had dragged him out onto the ice five times in the three months since he'd come over from McMurdo on the other side of the continent. He hardly knew anyone there, but Doc left an unforgettable impression.

When Tommy turned around, he had to look down abruptly. The pilot was most of a head shorter than he was and had stomped up to stand toe-to-toe with him. Encased in a "Big Red" polar parka, snow pants, and boots, there was little to see other than a shadowed face buried deep within the fur-rimmed hood.

"Nice job guiding me in," she shouted over the wind noise.

If that's what she wanted to believe he was doing, he wasn't going to argue. It—

"Well don't just stand there. I can feel my engines getting cold. Let's go. Go! Go! Go!" As if she and her plane truly were one.

He stumbled back under the sheer force of her words and

landed once more on the Doo's seat. Chas rarely spoke a decibel louder than needed, even when telling a joke—the epitome of a soft-spoken Brit, thankfully without Doc's amateur passion for Gilbert and Sullivan that he was always singing along the hallways.

Raw life force vibrated off this woman.

"Don't we have to wait for the Doc?"

"Sure, if you want me to leave your equipment strewn about in the middle of the ice shelf—we're aloft the second Doc has the patient ready. If you aren't aboard, I'll be leaving your ass behind just for good measure. Now move!"

He moved.

She was right. Antarctica, even in high summer, was far too dangerous to traverse alone.

In midwinter?

This survey project was over.

Time to get the hell out.

3

———————

"Great, Myrtle. Another beaker dullard. Just what we needed. 'Oh, I'm just going to sit here on the ice until I freeze to death.' Fine, if he wants to, but I won't do that to my little sister."

"Little sister?" The man scoffed as he came up behind her.

Aurora patted the deck. "She's a total sweetheart. Now get your damned snow machine over here."

"It's the 'little' that I'm having trouble with. She's definitely the big sister."

Aurora eyed him for a moment. A beaker with a sense of humor? Or the knee-jerk flirt of any testosterone-poisoned Antarctic male—which included all of them in her estimation—around any Antarctic female.

She hauled the loading ramp out of Myrtle's cargo bay, hooked it on the deck edge, and rammed the foot down into the snow.

By the tilt of his head, she knew. He didn't have a clue how to do the next maneuver.

"Okay, get your ass up there. Squat just aft of the door; it's going to happen fast. Whatever you do, don't let me fall back out once I'm aboard."

"What are you—" But he stopped when she walked away toward his Doo which he'd been smart enough to leave on idle.

It was a Ski-Doo Skandic SWT with the full twenty-four-inch tread which was sweet. She raced it a hundred feet or so across the snow to check the throttle reactivity until she had a feel for it.

He was inside, hunched in the four-foot-eleven cabin and close enough to the best spot.

The ramp was ten feet long, only inches wider than the spread of the Doo's skis and rested at about thirty degrees. Easing the skis up onto the ramp, she took a deep breath.

The door was less than four feet high and not much wider. The internal cabin was five feet wide.

And the Doo was ten-six long.

This was always a fun load—not—but she wasn't about to trust some beaker to not drive the Doo through the far side of Myrtle's fuselage.

She goosed and nudged until she was fully on the ramp and the nose was almost to the plane.

When he started to reach out, she shook her head.

"Doesn't he get that you weigh over six hundred pounds, boy? Now you be nice to my Myrtle, okay?"

The low thrum of the Rotax 900 engine offered her a soothing answer.

She rose to her feet but remained hunched low with bent knees. If things went sideway, she was set to spring clear. If they didn't, she had to be low to the machine or she'd catch the top of the door opening in the face.

"Ready?" she called out.

Low thrum from the Doo.

Nod from the beaker.

Afraid of what she'd hear, Aurora didn't wait for her own response.

She gave the throttle a short burst of power.

The Rotax roared to life and jolted her forward.

All in flash, she ducked her head to clear the doorway, the skis hit the deck, and she turned them hard toward the front of the cargo bay. The beaker did a fair job of judging the angle to grab the frame and shove hard *without* jamming his fingers into the drive train. The Doo was now parked facing forward on Myrtle's steel deck.

She nudged the throttle in tiny bursts to walk the Doo up close behind the pair of passenger seats she'd left rigged at the head of the cargo bay, then shut it down.

"You're hired. Now take that litter to the Doc," she pointed up, where it was tied to the ceiling. "Then get your sleds aboard."

He hesitated with the typical thousand questions.

No, she didn't know why Doc was still in the tent, but it sure didn't look good for whoever the patient was.

Yes, the nearest hospital was the hour back to Rothera.

And hell *yes, she'd been doing this long enough to know what she was doing* despite *being merely a woman.*

"Go!" She shouted at him—again.

Thankfully, he went.

She strapped down the Doo so that it couldn't shift on her during flight.

By the time she was done, he had the first of the sleds propped on the ramp. She grabbed the tongue and pulled, watching him as he pushed from behind.

"You're making mighty hard work of that." She eased the first one to the rear.

"Busted a couple of ribs, I think." But he didn't stop with lining up the second sled.

"Why'd you go and do that?" *Weird!* A beaker who didn't

just sit on the ice and wait to have his ass rescued because he had a hangnail.

"It was the best way out of a winter survey mission that I could come up with. Tossing Chas into a crevasse seemed like a good idea before I remembered we were roped together."

"Paybacks can be hell."

"Yep. Next time I'll remember to cut the rope first."

They got the second sled in. She felt bad about making him help heft it on top of the other one, but she couldn't shift it herself. The cargo bay was only eighteen feet long and the first ten of it was now filled with Doo and a narrow passageway forward. They still had to stow an occupied litter and leave room for Doc to work beside it.

"Actually," he knelt to help her strap the sleds in place with only a small groan. "Tossing him in was the only way I could think of to meet the most famous girls on the northern ice."

"Most famous girls on the northern ice? Should I ask for what?" That he included Myrtle was in his favor.

"For being unbelievably awesome. And," he waved a hand toward Myrtle's ceiling, "I've already seen the Aurora Australis, which is beyond gorgeous. I figured I should do a little comparing. One Aurora to another." Then he patted the plane as if he thought she herself was the one named Myrtle.

"And now that you've met both of the Auroras?" She kept her smile aimed away from him.

"Are you kidding? The plane that's fetching our busted-up behinds off the Larsen Ice Shelf in the middle of winter, or some pretty lights in the sky? Zero contest. Though those are some seriously pretty lights. Just saying, so that she knows how high the praise is." He patted Myrtle again.

"If you're trying to get on my plane's good side, you're doing a fine job of it." She finished the last strap.

"How about on *your* good side? Because, damn, I've been

riding Doos since I was knee-high to a ski-lift, and I couldn't have done that half as sweet."

"Where you from, Beaker?"

"Vermont." He didn't even hesitate at the nickname.

"Well, that's the problem. You only get to ride a few months of the year. Fairbanks, Alaska we get to ride October to April— on the short years."

That he was flirting was her standard shut-down switch. It wasn't like the stories of harassment or shut-out that were standard in the '70s through the '90s, but the flirt-wave was still pretty unrelenting anywhere she went on The Ice. And typical of most stations, there was only one other woman at Palmer. It helped that she was the Station Chief but there weren't a lot of crowds to fade into, especially with the winter dropping the staff numbers down.

Still, it was nice that he included Myrtle. That earned him a short-term minimum-level flirting license.

4

———

Tommy hardly knew what he was babbling about. He just knew if he stopped before they were airborne, he was done for. His ribs were killing him, but he wasn't coughing up blood, so he'd still go with bruised or cracked over broken.

"Could use a hand here please?" A high-brow British accent addressed him from the cargo bay door.

Doc didn't even lose his affected accent in an Antarctic windstorm over an unconscious patient. Though, to his credit, he'd dragged the litter over by himself.

"How's he doing, Doc?"

"This chap is alive enough to load him aboard a warm plane. We'll get him aloft and then I'll take the time to assess his condition in a touch more detail."

"Fewer words, more action," the pilot called out.

Tommy jumped down to the snow and collapsed the rest of the way to the ice when his side exploded with pain. It was so bad that his vision tunneled briefly.

"Slipped," he managed to mutter while struggling back to his feet.

The three of them loaded the unresponsive Chas aboard and strapped him in.

A snap in the high wind drew his attention back to the tent. No longer weighted down with Chas's body, it was now struggling hard against the ice screws he'd used in lieu of tent pegs. With the flashlight inside, it still glowed bright orange in the heavy dusk.

He headed over to break it down, but Myrtle the pilot shouted after him. What parent in this age named their kid Myrtle?

"Hey! Leaving now!"

"Get Aurora running. No footprint, remember." Even urine was loaded into bright yellow U-barrels and shipped back out.

If she said anything, it was ripped away by the wind. His few minutes aboard and in the plane's wind shadow had made him forget the abuse the weather was handing out.

The frail dusk was already fading, and the wind was whipping even harder than before. The haze that had moved in earlier assuredly blotted out the Aurora Australis; he didn't waste the time or energy to check.

He didn't bother with any niceties as the first engine coughed to life behind him. He slid free and folded the poles in one fist, pulled the ice screws with the other hand, then threw himself bodily on the fabric as it was tossed downwind.

As if he were some filter-feeding krill using setae like fingers to rake food toward its maw, Tommy scrabbled at the nylon with his fists and feet, bunching it under his body. When the bundle of the tent—with Chas' sleeping bag, and the still-lit flashlight that kept trying to blind him through the thin nylon—and he were about the same size, he struggled to his feet.

The propellors kept beating louder and louder until they drowned out the wind's roar sweeping over the Antarctic ice.

The wind kept catching the bundled-up tent he held in

both arms, and continued to drag him back and forth over the ice.

He gave the whirling propellors a wide berth, though once he passed behind the wings, their backdraft nearly blew him beyond the tail. Next stop South Georgia Island thirteen hundred miles downwind.

With the doc's help from above, he managed to shove the tent into the cargo door before it beat him to death.

But there was no way in hell he could lift himself up.

The propellors changed tone and the wind by the cargo door lessened. At least he could stand now without hanging on. Much.

As he clung to the edge of the cargo deck, the pilot came back. She jumped out beside him.

"Come on, we're not done yet."

He was.

But he followed her anyway. She was carrying a two-step-high ladder and two hanks of rope.

At the end of the wing, she climbed the ladder and slipped one rope through a ring loop on the underside.

"Hold this. We're going to take turns trying to rock the plane."

"Why?" He took the doubled-over line. It kept him upright just as well as the edge of the cargo deck.

"Skis froze to the ice and I can't break her loose with just the engines. I'm going to the other wing and—" She tipped her forearm back and forth like a teeter totter. "Don't worry about hurting the wing. She can take a lot more than we can give her."

It was hard to believe that a woman her size could have any effect on such a large object as the DHC-6 Twin Otter. Then he looked at the thirty-foot-long wing, thought about what could be done with a lever arm of that length, and decided that Myrtle was a smart woman. A hundred-pound force with that kind of lever advantage could produce more than a half-ton of lifting force at the frozen skis. His own weight could deliver well over a ton. They had to rotate the plane and its cargo as well, but he wasn't up for that kind of math at the moment.

He bent down far enough to watch her progress under the plane.

Ladder in place.

Her feet disappearing up the ladder.

Two ends of rope dangling down together.

Then her feet appearing suddenly and dangling a foot in air as she jumped off the ladder while hanging onto the rope like a crazed monk in some mythic bell tower.

His rope barely twitched in his hands.

He took a deep breath and threw his weight into the rope in turn.

It hurt, but not as badly as jumping out of the plane.

Nothing.

But as soon as his wingtip tweaked slightly upward showing she'd jumped again; he gave his best counterpull.

They found a rhythm that built naturally.

Still nothing.

Tommy knew he couldn't sustain this much longer.

He lunged up as high as he could and threw his weight against the line.

Something gave.

At first, he thought it was his ribs as his knees hit the ice.

But then he was being hauled upward by the momentum of the rocking wing.

The opposite ski had broken free from the ice.

Despite his not letting go, the counterswing was enough to break free the near-side ski.

The pilot raced around to the open cargo bay doors. She set the ladder by the door and waved for him to hurry.

Right! They needed to get moving before the plane's weight on the skis refroze the ice.

Dragging the rope behind him, he managed to climb the two steps, turn, and sit on the cargo deck. She shoved his feet hard enough to make him tumble back onto Chas, and make the doctor protest with a hearty, "Here now. Have a care."

She tossed the ladder aboard, hopped up as if the cargo deck wasn't nearly shoulder-high on her, then slammed and latched the cargo doors.

In a flash, she was gone forward.

This time, when the engines roared to life, he could feel the plane nosing down slightly as the engines drove ahead on the high wings. Right. The nose ski would still be firmly anchored in the ice.

Then it all broke loose at once and, with one hard jerk, they were on the move. And...up.

In too much pain to do more, he slumped on the deck, so glad to be out of the cold and wind that he could cry and prayed that the pilot was as good as her plane.

5

———————

"Rothera just won't do," Doc Tenniel came forward to fill her in before she'd climbed Myrtle to five thousand feet.

"What do you mean?" Aurora didn't need any more trouble. They'd come so close to being frozen into the ice that she'd been scared literally spitless.

The wind had picked up another ten knots just in the time they'd been loading. If she'd really been frozen in hard, they might not have gotten her aloft again until Antarctica unleashed one of his hundred-mile-an-hour winds. A katabatic blast that would break Myrtle out of the ice and tumble her to pieces.

"This chap," Doc nodded to the rear, "he's rather busted up."

Aurora had to breathe carefully before she could speak. Her first reaction had been that the helpful beaker, whose name she still didn't know, was the one Doc was referring to. She liked him and didn't like the image of him being worse off than she thought he was. But, of course, Doc would be talking about his patient.

"Dr. Chas Emerson has need of major medical, more than I can provide at Rothera Research Station."

"Where do we have to go?"

"Our choices are Amundsen-Scott—"

"There's no *way* I'm flying to the South Pole in midwinter!" With the waystation refueling camps closed for the winter, it would mean loading up several drums of fuel and taking off thousands of pounds overweight. It would be a massive strain on Myrtle. And the midwinter conditions there were so much harsher than the Peninsula that if she made it there, she might not make it back out—ever.

"The other option is Punta Arenas, over in Chile. The hospital there is sufficient if I can keep him alive that long."

She calced the fuel in her head. It was in range because Myrtle had the extended range fuel tanks and Aurora had made sure that they topped up her fuel at Rothera. In range... barely...depending on the weather.

Aurora reached for the radio to get an update. If they were going to fly over the Drake Passage all the way to the Strait of Magellan, she'd need all the help she could get.

"Patch up Beaker Boy and get him up here."

"Patch him up, you say? What's wrong with him?" She could feel Doc Tenniel raising his eyebrows in British puzzlement even if she couldn't turn to see it.

"Busted ribs. Get them taped or whatever it is you do. Make sure any painkillers you give him aren't sleepies. I need a hand to do this. Now go!"

Three or four *skilled* hands would be better, but she'd have to work with what she had.

6

———————

"HOLY HELL! YOU CAN'T EXPECT ME TO HELP YOU WITH THIS, Myrtle." He'd seen cockpits before, at a safe distance. But to actually sit in one of the pilot's seats and...touch things?

"She has low expectations."

"Why do you have low expectations? Not saying it's inaccurate. And do you always talk about yourself in the third person? Just asking."

"Shut up! Sit down! Buckle up!"

At a loss for what else to do, he followed orders and sat in the right-hand seat. Which was easier to do with the heavy tape Doc had laid across his ribs. Then he began trying to figure out the four-point seat belt harness.

"Sorry," she apologized. "This is just a little unnerving at the moment. What's your name? Mine's Aurora, by the way. Myrtle is my plane."

"Oh, I screwed that up some, didn't I? I'm Tommy," then he looked to his left. "Holy hell!"

"What now?" She said it with a sigh.

Myr—*Aurora* wasn't an *Antarctic* Ten. He was sure that he remembered what beautiful women *really* looked like, and they rarely looked this good. She'd shed her Big Red over the back of the seat. A straight fall of jet-black hair reached past her shoulders. Her skin was the brown of fresh earth beneath a shining sun. And a snug turtleneck revealed...more than he should be thinking about right now.

Her second sigh said she knew exactly what he was thinking.

"Well," he did his best to recover, "you're giving me a major concern now."

"Which is?" She was remaining determinedly focused out the windscreen.

"If your plane isn't named Aurora, did I insult her by comparing her to the Aurora Australis?"

She might have smiled, which he'd take as a good sign.

So, he turned back to the dazzling array of dials and gauges that confronted him. There was also a second steering wheel just like the one Aurora was holding.

"Your big sister Myrtle may have looked like heaven slipping down out of the skies, but she's scaring the crap out of me right about now. Glaciologists are interested in extraordinarily little other than ice and the ground it runs over. We're kind of boring that way."

"Okay, so we'll start with icing factors. We're presently flying in air that is minus thirty degrees with a humidity of eighty percent. What does that tell you?"

"Ice formation occurs rapidly. Like the hoary rime that you see on old sailing ships or Chicago lighthouses. You know, that really cool picture of the storm off Lake Michigan coating that whole lighthouse in massive icicles and—"

"And!" she cut him off. "When we get ice on our wings and propellor?"

"Oh." The answer to that didn't require advanced mathematics. Rough and heavy ice, wrapping around wings and disrupting air flow, would decrease lift. Not something he wanted happening to any airplane he was riding in.

"So, Mr. Glaciologist. Care to tell Myrtle and me what we're flying into?" She tapped a small screen that must be a radar. "Along with this?" She peeled a tablet computer he hadn't noticed Velcroed to one of her thighs and handed it over.

He studied the satellite map, managed to orient that image with what he was seeing on the radar screen, and read through the weather data on the tablet. He wasn't used to the format, but you didn't study glaciers, or live in a place like Antarctica, without knowing weather.

"Um, how high can Myrtle fly?"

"Twenty-five thousand feet."

"Get up there. And veer west."

"Veer? I don't have a lot of spare fuel to go veering about the sky. Punta Arenas is a long way off."

He expanded the view to focus on the storm pattern developing over the Southern Ocean.

"If you start out high. The jet stream will carry you east. But there's a storm developing over the Drake Passage. The winds —man, that's so weird, I'm still not used to the fact that Southern storms spin counterclockwise, it just looks wrong. Anyway, once over the Drake Passage between the Antarctic Peninsula and Tierra del Fuego if you drop lower, out of the jet stream, you should be able to ride the curl of developing storm that will sweep you back to the east a bit. Does that work in flying? I don't know, but I think it makes sense."

She looked at him for a long moment. "Who are you?"

"Hi, I'm Tommy." He held out a hand and she shook it, keeping her left hand on the wheel. Strong grip of a woman who worked for a living. "I'm a glaciologist. Think I already mentioned that. It means I'm a bit of a weather nerd."

Her big eyes were almost as dark as her hair and dominated her slender face.

She held his hand for an extra moment, which was genuinely nice. He'd had an early girlfriend teach him the joys of just holding hands.

"Yeah, that works in flying. And thanks. I've never made this crossing in winter, but you just confirmed my flight plan. That storm will be a rough ride, so let's get you up to speed on some of Myrtle's other tricks. Rest your hand lightly on the controls."

Tommy let go of her hand and wrapped it around his steering wheel's right handgrip. He could feel the warmth of Aurora's hand on Myrtle's cold plastic.

When Aurora shifted the wheel, he could feel it move beneath his own hand. It was far more intimate than he'd ever have guessed.

7

———

Aurora had radioed down to Palmer Station as she passed overhead while Doc Tenniel was still bandaging Tommy's ribs.

It was just as well that he hadn't come forward yet. She'd had a tentative solstice night assignation with Palmer's chief carpenter and fix-it-man. He didn't understand planes, at all, but he was always glad to lend a skilled wrench when she'd needed it. An excuse to "hang with The Girls" was definitely part of it, but he hadn't been pushy which she appreciated.

Not that she'd been particularly looking forward to being someone's ice-wife—because what happened on The Ice stayed on The Ice. But the winters were long and cold, and some companionship would be nice.

Of course, he'd been the one to answer her call to Palmer about her missing the solstice.

He joshed her some about jumping ship the first night of being an OAE, but after five years she'd earned the Old Antarctic Explorer fair and square and it was only friendly teasing. He was dealt with quickly and with little regret, at least on her side.

It was Tommy, after his first flying lesson, who made sure she ate. He'd raided the container where she kept a couple weeks of emergency supplies—because you didn't fly over the ice with less. His own supplies were tied down inside the two sleds.

He somehow made energy bars and near-frozen dried fruit into a droll celebration.

A lunch of a mac and cheese MRE—Meal Ready to Eat— was a pleasant surprise. She forgot she'd stocked those.

She hadn't flown with anyone since Mom had quit and gone south leaving her the old cargo plane. It was…nice. Half of it was a second set of eyes on the instruments, and half just moral support.

Especially when the flying turned hard.

Larsen Ice Shelf to Punta Arenas was only a five-hour flight —which would give her a fuel reserve of half an hour, if nothing went wrong. And it was four-and-a-half hours from landfall to landfall.

Once well clear of the shore, their descent below the east-racing jet stream, which moved at fully half the speed of her plane—over a hundred miles an hour—plunged them down into a rugged storm. Doc Tenniel wasn't happy about her battering his patient, but she wasn't happy about the flying battering Myrtle, so they were even. The advantage was that it was fast, saving her the fuel for when she hit the hard headwind over Tierra del Fuego.

Definitely not an autopilot route, this kind of flying was hard work and there was never a single second's break. She just had to gut it out.

After crossing the harsh mountains of Tierra del Fuego, they finally hit the Strait of Magellan and she could cruise low over the glassy water. Her clenched shoulders began to unwind like slipping into a hot bath—another luxury that didn't happen on The Ice. Fresh water was scarce, collecting and melting snow took a lot of energy, both human and heaters, and showers were regulated to under two minutes.

The descent into Punta Arenas was...startling. A town of a hundred thousand—a hundred times the winter population of the entire continent she'd just left—it lay on the north shore of the narrow Strait of Magellan. The buildings were perched along the water like bright orange, blue, and pink birds who'd arrived during migration then forgotten to move on.

Even though it was winter, and everything was coated in a layer of white snow, there were windswept places revealing brown grasses and occasional trees offering flashes of green. But this was the first natural color other than rock, dirt, ice, or ocean since she'd last gone south last October.

She knew that "greenout" was supposed to be as dramatic as a whiteout—people had told her about not being able to look at anything else when first seeing green. But this was the first time she'd experienced it for herself. Even though the flecks of color were so few and far between, they still distracted her so badly she was amazed that she executed the landing at all.

Doc Tenniel had called ahead and had an ambulance waiting. He took Tommy's number and promised to call the moment there was news.

Within three minutes of landing after the brutally taxing flight, there was just...silence.

No engine roar. No creaking of Myrtle's wings as she slammed through pockets of turbulence like the trooper she was. No more staring at the fast-descending fuel gauge every thirty seconds and rerunning the math of remaining flight time versus fuel flow.

Suddenly it was just her and Tommy, standing on the tarmac. She locked up Myrtle, arranged for refueling, and stood out in the warmth of the setting sun.

"Good job," Tommy grinned, then turned to pat Myrtle's nose. "Oh. You, too," he added to Aurora herself as an offhand afterthought that made her laugh just as he'd intended.

It was two degrees above freezing, sixty-five degrees warmer than the Larsen Ice Shelf, and the wind was a mild five to ten knots. They both stood in light jackets as the ground crew in full parkas and heavy gloves hurried to get the refueling done as fast as possible so that they could retreat back to their warm hidey hole.

She waited only long enough to make sure they were loading AN-8 fuel instead of JP-8 fuel. ANtarctic-8 or Ice-8, as it was sometimes called, froze fourteen degrees lower than standard jet propellant fuel.

"What now?" Seven hours of hard flying had taken it out of her, she could barely stand.

"Do you know Punta Arenas?"

"I've never been past the airport. I fly through here each season for fuel, but that's about it. Southbound I'm eager to get on The Ice and northbound I can't wait to get away."

"Yep!" Tommy agreed. "Sounds about right. I got laid-over here for a week once."

"Are there a week's worth of things to do here?"

"You've got to be kidding me!" She was getting very used to Tommy's laugh. "But I learned some things. Are you a nice sit-down meal kind of woman or—"

"Burger and a beer."

"How about freshies?"

"Oh my god! Actual vegetables?"

"First Caesar salad north of The Ice." Tommy signed out one of the rental cars reserved for pilots.

"That does it, I'm yours!" Aurora couldn't quite believe the words that came out of her mouth but, rather to her surprise, she didn't have a lot of interest in taking them back.

Not as they split a monster salad.

Not as they shared his pizza and her burger.

Not as they tumbled into bed together in a local hotel.

And both crashed into sleep harder than a plane landing with no wings.

8

———

"I'VE BEEN ROBBED!" TOMMY GROANED WHEN HE WOKE UP ALONE in the morning.

His ringing phone had rousted him, and no beautiful pilot lay beside him.

"What?" he snapped at the caller. Then he spotted Aurora's gear bag still dumped on a chair and felt a little better.

"Good morning to you, too." Doc Tenniel sounded typically bright and chipper despite—Tommy checked his watch—it being only six a.m. "Do you always begin your days being surly?"

"Yes!" Tommy rubbed at his face, then became aware of the shower running. That put a much brighter spin on the morning. "It's in the top secret *How to Be an American* handbook."

"Ah, as I always suspected. Well, you'll be glad to know that Dr. Emerson made it through the surgery. A few more hours and we might have had some rather critical issues, but we were able to tie off the bleeder in his head before it damaged his brain. His full recovery looks very hopeful. I told him you were still local, and he is anticipating a visit."

"Uh..." A vision strolled out of the bathroom in a robe that was tied at the waist but was revealing enough cleavage and leg to kill a man.

"Mr. Dane?"

"Uh...huh?"

Aurora strolled over, still rubbing her hair in a towel. She leaned over the bed, offering him an amazing view down the front of the robe, then sniffed loudly before pinching her nose. "Far doo longa on da ice."

Then she slipped the phone from his nerveless fingers. "Hi Doc? Yes, I'm sorry. Tommy is just a beaker, so we can't expect much from him. He's looking a little toasty at the moment—perhaps I should bring him by the hospital for testing."

"Toasty" was an Ice epithet for the brain fog and forgetfulness caused by the dark, cold, and high altitude of much of Antarctica.

He'd show her he wasn't toasty.

She sidestepped his attempt to grab her, then pointed imperiously toward the bathroom, before pinching her nose again.

"Really? That's wonderful news," she continued her conversation with Doc.

Tommy didn't wait around to find out what was wonderful. The faster he showered, the sooner...well...yeah. That was his idea of wonderful at the moment.

Competent women were a major turn-on for any rational-thinking man. And being a "beaker" he considered himself to be very rational.

Aurora hadn't only proven herself competent on the ice and in the air. She'd also been one of the best dinner companions he'd ever had. Bright, funny, and took her adventures head-on. Maybe it was the Alaskan bush pilot in her. Maybe it was the joy of the Antarctic that seemed to strike so few but created a community within the community. The bottom of the world had definitely snared her as thoroughly as it had snared him.

And now he was looking forward to a whole new kind of wonderful.

Except by the time he was out of the shower, she was dressed and leaning against the doorframe watching him.

"Why…"

She handed him back his phone as he stood there naked, dripping on the tile floor. He knew they were headed to the hospital.

"Couldn't Chas have the decency to stay out of it for another few hours like any other decent man?"

"No, but they are medevacing him out on the next flight. So visiting him at the hospital is now or never."

"Shit!"

"Too bad you're all wet or I'd jump you right now, Beaker Boy."

He hurried to dry himself, but she was already in boots and parka by the time he was done. All he had with him were heavy field clothes, but he had one set that wasn't too ripe yet.

9

———————

"WHAT IN THE WORLD HAPPENED?"

Tommy pulled up the new satellite radar image he'd grabbed onto his tablet during the drive over. He turned it for Chas to see.

"You personally created a brand-new iceberg with your butt —about the only thing you didn't break." He did his best not to look at the bandages swaddling Chas' head or the casts on his arm and leg. Life was not supposed to be so fragile. "Depending on how the crack runs, it could be bigger than A-68."

Chas opened his eyes wider then narrowed them...then sighed in frustration. "I can't focus on the screen. I won't remember any of this when the drugs wear off. Send me everything you can so that I can review it when I'm not high on whatever this stuff is. Not complaining. I happily can't feel a thing, but I barely remember you arriving five minutes ago."

"I've been here for hours."

Chas barked a laugh. "I could almost believe you. How did I get to Punta Arenas, anyway?"

Tommy offered a very abbreviated version of his rescue. "Doc Tenniel flew in from Rothera and he insisted on getting you to a real hospital immediately. We flew here direct from Larsen."

Chas was nodding at the ceiling. "Was it The Girls?"

Before Tommy could answer, Chas continued.

"Hell of a pair. You should track them down. Serious pair of lookers."

Tommy cleared his throat and glanced over at Aurora leaning against the wall on the opposite side of the bed. She was grinning at him.

Chas' eyes were drifting shut. "Though she's too smart for you."

"Who's too smart for me, Myrtle the plane?"

"Definitely, but the woman half of that team is even smarter."

"Say what? I've got a PhD from Dartmouth and..."

"Nope. She doesn't stoop to doing it with mere ice men." He raised a hand, dragged along an IV line, a blood pressure cuff, an oxygen meter, and finally tapped his temple knowingly. He added something that might have been a wink or might have been a grimace when he noticed all the gear still attached to him.

Aurora shrugged a "Maybe yes."

He liked that she stayed above the ice-wife/ice-husband shuffling that always seemed to be going on down there. It made sharing a bed with her, even while passed out, and a shower, even separately, all the more special.

"You can admire. But don't try to touch. Shove you...right out of that...plane of hers. At altitude." Chas' voice, which had been fading, snapped back and he reopened his eyes. "Hey!"

"Yes, Chas?"

"When did you get here, Tommy?"

"Hours ago, Chas. Never left your side."

Aurora's snort of laughter didn't draw Chas' attention to his other side.

"Good man. Good man." His eyes were closing again. "You're Head of Ice at Rothera now. Take over for me. Needs someone like you. Smart."

"As smart as The Girls?"

"Nope. Not as good looking either. You'll meet them someday, but don't even waste your time dreaming. I'm old enough to be her father, but you're still a young whipper snapper and probably think that means something. She'll knock that out of you soon enough. Watched her do it to enough other young bucks." Chas closed his eyes again. "You take care of my ice. Time I went back...to the...real...world." This time he went fully to sleep, proven by his heart monitor's slower beeps.

Head of Ice? Had Emerson really meant that?

It wouldn't be nearly that straightforward but... He'd wait to see what Emerson said when he was better, and off the drugs.

Still, the idea didn't just melt away. Chief glaciologist at Rothera Research Station was a height that no one climbed because the fixture of Dr. Chas Emerson was always in place.

After the two summers he'd spent at McMurdo and the Pole, Chas had requested him by name to be the only other glaciologist to do a winterover on the Peninsula. There were still a couple at McMurdo and two more at the Pole, but they all fed their data through Chas.

Duh! He slapped his forehead. The data flow that Chas had him handling for the last three months. Chas *had* been grooming him to take over.

Which meant his drugged-out offer was probably serious.

"Full time on The Ice?"

"That's what he said," Aurora spoke for the first time. She wasn't smiling or frowning. She was...looking thoughtful.

"You thinking of being down there full-time for a while?"

She watched him with those big dark eyes as seriously as when he'd interpreted the weather patterns with her.

That's when he figured out what he'd just sort of asked.

Aurora started to smile as the light dawned.

He'd just asked her if she'd be staying somewhere they could be together. They hadn't done more than share a flight, a meal, and a bed—for sleeping. But the question was still real.

During the flight and over dinner, they discovered a shared love of Antarctica. They were both sufficiently renegade to fit in on The Ice.

Maybe they'd start as ice-wife and ice-husband, but Chas had said she was too smart for that.

Well, maybe he could be smart, too. Because it was sure easy to imagine someday finding someone to fill his shoes just as Chas had found him. Then the two of them—three with Myrtle—could fly off on yet another new adventure together.

Maybe he *was* smart enough to do that.

Her smile said that she already was.

He slipped lower in his chair and propped a foot on Chas' hospital bed.

She raised her eyebrows in question.

"You know," he tried his best to sound as if he was discussing the next spot to drill an ice core. "We kind of fell asleep before we had a chance to celebrate the solstice."

"We did."

At her continued smile, he kept his silence and raised his own eyebrows in question.

"Well," she shrugged as if it had no consequence, "that storm in the Drake Passage is going to take another day to blow out. We could celebrate the New Year a day late. If its important to you."

There was the key word. To be with a woman like Aurora, it had to be important, not casual.

Did he want that? Did he *feel* that? After a single day from twilight on the ice to the sunrise now shining in the hospital window? After a life of only "casual," he now knew that "important" felt completely different.

"Not really the solstice anymore," he nodded toward the light sparkling off the melting snow outside.

"Not really," she agreed. "It's more the first day of *The Ice's* new year." She emphasized it just enough to make it clear The Ice was home, at least for now. He liked the sound of that— a lot.

"Instead of celebrating the solstice, we could celebrate the First Night. The First Night of..." But he was smart enough not to say the next thought aloud.

Her nod and smile acknowledged the thought.

There was no need for words.

Their future began today.

———

For *The Complete Antarctic Ice Fliers* romance collection, visit: https://shop.mlbuchman.com/collections/other-stories

CARRYING THE HEART'S LOAD

This was a challenge story. My friend, author-and-editor Blaze Ward, invited me to submit to an anthology. His chosen theme: *An Interpretation of Moles*. It had to include a "mole" in some form or other. Being me, I chose to include *every* interpretation I could think of.

That it turned out to be a Christmas love story in my Delta Force world is just part of the fun of being an author.

1

"Gonna be a cakewalk, Captain Killer Kristine."

"Pretty arrogant for someone who doesn't have a clue, Mankowski." She'd be damned if she'd call him by his first name. And being the only woman in the squad, there was no way she was using Master Sergeant Connie *Girlie* Mankowski's tag. That just wasn't going down.

Command must have it in for her. Actually, command notoriously had it in for all Delta Force operators but she seemed to draw the short end of the stick a hell of a lot—or maybe it was the electrified end.

"Hey," Mankowski protested as he rewrapped his MREs. "I'm not arrogant. I'm awesome." A Delta operator who liked to talk—which so wasn't a thing on The Unit—and of course he ended up on her team.

Worse, he was one of *those* guys. He wore a Santa hat just because their mission schedule said they were hammering it down hard on Christmas Eve.

He started this whole running debate—with himself because she did say a word—about the best option for Christmas Eve dinner. He finally selected Beef Stew from Menu

9, Barbeque Protein Puffs from 12, and Teriyaki Meat Snack Stick from 10. She reached into the supply box and came out with Menu 17 Pork Sausage Patty and Hashbrowns. Not the worst one, so fine with her.

They both sat on the hangar deck of the USS *Peleliu* helicopter carrier doing the standard mission prep. Last she'd heard, this ship had been decommissioned. But here it floated as big as life, a secret traveling base for the Night Stalkers Spec Ops helicopter guys. Too bad the air jocks couldn't do shit to help on this one except dump them five klicks off the Venezuelan coast and wish them luck.

Standard mission prep included pre-dissecting their Meals-Ready-to-Eat. With a little judicious opening and culling, they could cut down the volume-per-meal they'd have to carry in their packs by as much as fifty percent and mass by thirty percent. Wrap the retained meal packets in a strip of hundred-mile-an-hour duct tape and they were good to go. Every kilo less food equaled an additional pair of thirty-round magazines for her HK416 rifle, five seventeen-round mags for her Glock sidearm, or a generous handful of breaching charges.

The mission was only supposed to be ten hours. The last one-night mission took her five days to crawl out of. She'd be picking up a rescuee, so she packed enough food for two people to last three days as a compromise.

But it really had to happen tonight. Christmas was a big deal in Venezuela, apparently an even bigger deal than back in the hell that was Brooklyn. Distraction level of the OPFOR, opposing forces, would be highest tonight. Church services, nativities, a whole lot of eating and drinking, with—hopefully—a minimum amount of attention among the guards.

"I've walked Syria and Afghanistan. This ain't no worse." He'd made Delta—nothing was harder than that—so why did the guy have to keep taking about it? Was Girlie trying to impress her?

She was so immune to that crap. Her big brother had thought she was an ideal playground, until she'd nutted him so hard that he hadn't walked right for a week. That had set the tone of her life. Uncle Juan was still missing a couple teeth, Steve who she'd benched for a whole season of high school football because she'd had to shatter his foot to back him off, three guys she'd left bloody in Brooklyn, and five she'd left dead out in the Congo.

That had been another fine command decision, Puerto Rican dark didn't pass for African black anywhere except in the two-tone colorblindness of America—white and not. Sure as hell hadn't passed her in the Congo. This time at least they were sending her into Venezuela, so her skin would be okay, if not her accent. Of course Mankowski was a Chicago white boy —target right on his fucking face—she was so screwed.

His answer? "Walking beside a hot number like Killer Kristine, nobody's going to be looking at this old boy anyway. I'm safe as can be."

Kristine wondered who was going to kill this guy first, her or the nightmare that was modern-day Venezuela.

It was a bum assignment anyway: walk into a major military base in an exceptionally paranoid country, find idiot scientist, extract him out of whatever shitstorm political hole he'd gotten himself stuck in, and make sure he comes back alive and in one piece. Command had really stressed the alive and intact part of the mission—while being equally careful to not say one word about what condition Girlie Mankowski had to be in upon his return. Or her for that matter. But they were hella concerned about one Dr. Ray Ewing.

You know, he's one of those *kind of scientists,* her mission briefer had said.

Yeah, and you're one of those *kind of briefers who would be clearly happy to eat his own shit and spew it back out again.*

One of *those* scientists? Absentminded, unworldly, or just an arrogant know-it-all pain-in-the-ass? She *so* couldn't wait to find out which.

"Where you from, Killer?"

"Hell."

"No, really."

She stopped slit-packing MREs and looked at him until he stopped opening his and faced her.

"What?"

"Hell. Really."

2

────────

Once she was done with organizing meals, water, and ammo, she started considering how she was supposed to extract a civilian alive. She sure wasn't going to give him a weapon; he'd be as likely to shoot himself or her rather than the bad guys. But she stuffed one in her pack just in case by some miracle of Mother Mary he *did* know which end to hold it by.

She didn't wear issued armor. Between the weight and freedom of movement issues, she typically wore no more than a Dragonskin vest—even if it wasn't official issue. It worked better and weighed a quarter of the fully-plated Improved Outer Tactical Vest with its heavy ceramic plates; it just wasn't politically correct. But then she wasn't either. This time, she'd layer up with both Dragonskin and the heavy armor of the IOTV, then she'd let the eminent Dr. Ewing wear the heavy shit on the return leg.

Over that, she pulled on her MOLLE. The Modular Lightweight Load-carrying Equipment was a fancy way to say a harness vest. Its entire surface was covered with inch-wide horizontal straps spaced an inch apart. Every Delta operator's was unique because it was wholly configurable. The base MOLLE—pronounced Molly not mole—carried eight magazines. Then various holders of the PALS—Pouch Attachment Ladder System—were added on to an individual's preference. The various pouches interlaced through the straps in such a way that you could probably do a helicopter hoist extraction by any of them, though the rig had the ring on the front for that.

A lot of operators put the med kit on the very back of their rucksack—*Not gonna need it anyway.* She kept it front and center so that she didn't have to dump her pack to access it every time she was patching up some asshole who was too injured to reach the kit on their back, or worse, had dumped their pack in order to survive an op gone bad. Flares, breaching charges, timers, hydration bladder, extra mags for her sidearm and ankle piece, satellite radio, backup radio, batteries...the list was endless of what she wanted to carry. And now she had to dump half of it so that she could carry extra food and fifteen kilos of armor for some civilian who'd probably bitch the whole way.

Girlie Mankowski only whined a little about how much of it there was, but took his share after she offered to remove his pelvis with the Benchmade Infidel blade she wore in a wrist sheath if he said another word.

"Just jokin', man," he muttered to himself.

By some mutual agreement, she didn't point out that she was a woman and he didn't mutter *bitch* aloud, even if she could hear it anyway. Oddly, that's how she'd gotten her tag, she'd threatened to kill the next bastard who called her a bitch. It was Day Two of the month-long Delta Force Operator Selection. *Killer Kristine* had sounded from a Green Beret wag...and it had stuck. As had she. The Green Beret hadn't made it to Week Two —not her doing either.

Besides, the name was far too appropriate, even if no one

would ever know. She let it stick because it was God's honest truth.

Cursing herself before she even did it, she tied another MOLLE harness onto her pack along with a dozen empty utility pouches threaded into the straps. Whatever the good Dr. Ray Ewing felt he needed to take out of the country, he could damn well carry it in his own rig.

"Ready, Mankowski?"

"Gotta pee."

"You've got until I reach the helo, then we're leaving you behind."

"Sure, Killer." But then he looked at her face and hurried toward the can.

Yeah, *Bitch* versus *Killer*. Everyone meant it the same way. Thank God that Delta Force favored individual capabilities over team capabilities or she'd be out on her ass. Delta operators worked in solo or pairs and only came together when they had to. SEALs, however, hated breaking into smaller teams even *when* they had to—it tended to make them snivel like sad puppy dogs.

She did take the steps from the Hangar Deck up to the flight deck slowly, so the Black Hawk was just easing off its wheels when Girlie Mankowski dove through the cargo door.

"What's wrong with you, man?" He was seriously ticked, probably about the long, wet dribble down his pantleg where he'd pulled it in before he was quite done.

She knew only too damned well what was wrong with her.

3

———————

"Five klicks back out through that?" Mankowski whined. "That'll definitely be hell."

The sea had been kicking up rough—slapping a heavy Christmas storm against the Venezuelan coast. Their five-meter-long Zodiac boat had made hard work of reaching the coast from where the Night Stalkers had dropped them. In that short time, three-meter waves had become sixes. It had been twice as brutal because the night was so dark they hadn't been able the see the waves that smashed over them. The powers that be had decided that was a good thing, making their boat invisible to radar in the water's surface clutter.

They never considered that also meant there was no way to drive back to the pickup point into that headwind and through those waves with only a fifty-percent charge on the batteries. Especially not if they wanted their pet doctoral eminence live through it. She was too stubborn to die. And Mankowski? No real skin off her back either way.

"We'll find some other transport. Sink it."

Mankowski groaned, but did as she instructed.

With the charges set, Mankowski aimed the tiny boat out of the inner La Guaira harbor. They'd landed near the entry of the long harbor formed by a massive two-kilometer-long breakwater that arced outward and then paralleled the Venezuelan coast, creating a narrow line of protected wharves. The autopilot held the little boat in line out into the darkness, plunging over the waves that had so inundated them on the trip in.

The Zodiac made it three hundred meters out before the charges fired. Even with night-vision goggles it was hard to see the flashes that ruptured all of the bladders and destroyed the motor as well. Already unidentifiable, in seconds it would be at the bottom of the Atlantic.

"Now what?"

Kristine surveyed the long breakwater of heavy granite stone as another wave shattered on its far side and sent spray climbing skyward. She wasn't going to complain about having a bigger boat when they ventured back to sea. Even if it was physically impossible to get any wetter after their night crossing, she could feel her gear becoming heavier by the second with water weight. Especially all of the extra kit for *himself.* No one had bothered to tell lowly Delta operators why he was so damned important.

"Go pick out a Christmas present for yourself."

"What?"

"Find us a boat, Mankowski. This harbor has commercial, ferry, and naval piers. I can see a half-dozen from here. Night Stalkers will be on station in five hours to retrieve us. You have four hours to find one and pick us up right here. But don't grab it until I radio that I've got him and we're coming out." She always did better on her own anyway.

Mankowski didn't look happy, but he didn't argue.

They went their separate ways. Him scouting the two kilometers of wharves to the southeast while, moving quickly over the big stones that lined the public ferry terminal; her making her way west.

Just as planned, she ducked out of the passenger terminal, closed for the night, and slipped through the fence into the yard for the goods shipping terminal. What the satellite photos hadn't really showed was just how few container ships were willing to deliver goods to a country that could no longer pay any of its bills. Some of the largest crude reserves in the world and they were bankrupt. Beyond bankrupt, the people were starving to death before they could die of poor health care, broken sanitation, and all the other disasters here that made Brooklyn, New York look almost habitable.

She'd planned on dodging through the container field... except there were far more open spaces than containers in the yard. That wasn't at all helpful.

While she was surveying her options, one of the country's notorious blackouts conveniently rolled through. Taking the risk that Christmas and the outage would keep the yard unobserved, she sprinted across a long open stretch. The power and lights didn't come back on until she was out of the yard, across the street, and through the electric fence that was supposed to be protecting Naval Base Antonio Picardi. She even had time to resplice the section she'd cut so that no one would know she'd crossed through. It would also make it that much faster when she crossed back out.

Inside the base, she lay under some leaves of a *palma llanera* that the wind was beating into a frenzy loud enough that she couldn't hear herself think. The storm was really kicking some unpredicted ass, which would make for better cover and made her happier that the Zodiac was at the bottom of the Atlantic.

Straight ahead lay an Olympic-sized swimming pool with diving boards, lounge chairs, folded up and now flopped over umbrellas, and a serious-looking bar and food stand, currently well-shuttered. It was almost midnight, so that made sense.

Long red and green ribbons that had once decorated the area, no snapped like mad cobras wherever an anchor point had held.

It was a good thing that the general populace wasn't starving to death or anything. Oh, wait, they were. Just the military wasn't. No wonder the assholes were loyal—they had the only cushy jobs left in the country.

At that moment, a surprisingly cold rain slashed out of the darkness.

Yep! It was a Delta-style Christmas Eve. Total suckitude.

$$4$$

Thankfully, the Bolivarian Navy of Venezuela felt themselves to be sacrosanct. In the midst of the storm, there were very few patrols and none with night-vision gear or much interest in anything other than getting back under cover after hurrying along their prescribed routes.

In an hour she'd worked around a dormitory, mess hall, and training center—probably could have done it in half the time with how lame the patrols were. The sheeting rain didn't let up and they were doing their duty on the hustle with their heads down.

Ultimately, Building Fourteen was right where the spy for the opposition had said it would be; not all of the military loved their corrupt, paranoid president-turned-dictator-turned-total bastard. The mole had given the CIA the tip about where to find Dr. Ewing—in the secure detention facility on the third floor of Fourteen.

Apparently the CIA had gotten tired of waiting for the government to finally collapse under its own weight. In her estimation that wasn't the issue. The real issue was that if the military and the SEBIN secret police finally went down hard, they sure weren't going to leave behind any prisoners to tell the tale. Either way, tonight was Ewing's lucky night.

Kristine waited for the latest patrol to sweep by. Figuring that the most secure position was close behind them, she hurried along in their wake, circling Building Fourteen. As she went, she strategically placed charges she might need to make good their escape.

The moment the patrol ducked inside, she stepped out into the courtyard and gauged the height of the building—three stories, nine to ten meters. Reaching back over her left shoulder, she snagged the lifting loop on her grappling hook and pulled it and a hank of 9mm tactical line free from its PALS pouch. With a practiced flick of her wrist, she spread the three tines out and they clicked into place.

Five fast spins and she had smooth control of the whirling grapple. With a hard upward release, it soared aloft in a high arc. The coil of tactical line slid off her palm in a neat flow. For a moment she thought a gust of wind was going to ruin her throw, but an immediate counter gust dropped it well over the roof's edge. A sharp tug gave her under a meter of slippage and then a hard set that easily took her weight.

She snapped a pair of hand jumars onto the line, walked her feet up onto the wall, and began working the ascenders. They slid upward without resistance, but not downward unless she hit the release. Two minutes later, she lay on the roof pulling up the line. A Delta operator didn't need no flying reindeer. Besides, no way would Santa be wasting any time in this sad excuse for a country—most wouldn't even have the cash to buy coal.

The wind, which had been blocked while she was down among the buildings, whipped hard at her. Much more and they'd be in a full tropical storm. If it climbed to full hurricane wouldn't that be a sackful of seasonal joy?

A quick tour of the roof revealed a maintenance hatch.

Locked from the inside, she snapped together a thermite torch —about the size of a three-D-cell flashlight—put on dark glasses, and cut the hinges off. Five thousand degrees of fun. There were some things she loved about Delta Force, and the cool toys factor was definitely high on the nice list.

She eased down into the middle of Building Fourteen's detention floor. Nightlights illuminated the corridor and a guard sleeping at the far end of it. Make that drunk and asleep because her entry letting in the storm had been far from silent. She woke him up with a strip of duct tape over his mouth, then cuffed him to his heavy chair with zip ties.

"Which cell is Dr. Ewing in?" Kristine whispered in Spanish as she pressed the tip of the torch under his chin. She'd gave him just enough of a peek to know that it was like nothing he'd ever seen before, not that she was planning to melt his head open with it. "Grunt the number of times for his number."

The guy's eyes rolled in panic.

"Now or I'll tape over your nose too and leave you to rot."

Apparently he believed her and grunted out a six.

5

———

Cell Six was third on the left. Through the observation window she couldn't see shit. Flipping down her night-vision goggles, she could see that it was a much larger space than she'd anticipated. A man lay asleep on a corner cot. To the other side was a long workbench with a computer and an array of stuff that looked like a chemist's lab.

She hit the light switch—which was on her side of the door—and shoved her goggles back up.

The guy on the couch rolled over and blinked his eyes hard. The face matched the briefing and she unlocked the door with the keys she'd lifted off the guard.

"Who?" He grunted out in Spanish, then blinked harder as he focused on her.

"Merry Christmas. I'm here to rescue your ass."

"You don't look like the other military. I mean aside from being female."

"I'm not. I don't fit in even among female military." She dropped her pack and peeled off the IOTV body armor. She suddenly felt thirty pounds lighter. "Put this on. We're on the move."

"To where?"

"What do you care?" Then she cursed herself. He probably did. "The US, if we don't screw this up."

"Rockin'! I'll even risk a ride in Santa's sleigh for that." Not quite the staid scientist she'd been expecting. In fact, he sounded New York. And he was somewhere around her age, another detail the briefing docs hadn't included.

As she helped him into the gear, and ignored his embarrassed grunt of surprise—civilians were so fussy—as she reached between his legs to pull through the strap connecting the butt- to the groin-protectors. "You'll need this MOLLE as well." She freed it from her pack and dumped the vest over his head.

"A vest named Molly?" Ewing switched to English.

"M.O.L.L.E. Modular Lightweight Load-carrying Equipment. The pouches are for whatever you want to take from here."

"Well, that would have a silent E, not a Y sound," he continued as he moved about the room and began stuffing various items into his pockets. It looked almost random, but he didn't strike her as a random sort of guy. Still, it was an odd selection: various sealed flasks, some baggies of assorted powders, and a very dog-eared novel. "Haven't finished it yet," as he tore off the first two-thirds before she could see what it was and stuffed the last third in a plastic bag and then into a pouch. Marks for efficiency, cross off absent-minded. "English doesn't have that sound: Y for a final E. If we go back to the Spanish, you would get mol-lay, like the Mexican chocolate sauce with an extra L. Still not Molly."

"Do you want to talk pronunciation all day or can we get your ass out of here?"

He stopped and glanced around the room, looking at last at the chemist's bench. "If I never have to calculate another mole of cocaine or manufacture another mole of scopolamine (which doesn't work as a truth serum no matter what the SEBIN thinks), I'll die a happy man."

"A mole?"

"Not the small one on your right cheek—which looks good on you by the way—nor the brown furry animal, though a mole of cocaine actually weighs about three brown-furry moles, a third of a kilo. I like that as a unit of measure. A mole, not the brown-furry one but the chemical one, is a six followed by twenty-three zeroes' worth of atoms. It's not actually a weight, but rather a quantity. Because it's such a simpler atom, a mole of pure carbon-12 weighs over twenty-five times less than a mole of cocaine or about point-oh-eight of a brown-furry."

"That's a bunch of atoms," she couldn't help saying. No way was she getting into a conversation about brown-furries, their mass or otherwise. And she already knew men thought she was attractive, which was way more trouble than it was worth.

"A mole, the chemical one, is about six hundred times more atoms than there are stars in the known universe. Atoms are seriously small buggers. Why are we still standing here talking about this?"

There was something about the way he talked that kept her listening. Kristine had to physically shake herself to break the mild hypnosis.

Back out in the hall, she wasn't even halfway back to the maintenance hatch when Ewing called out. "What about all of them?" He was looking at the closed cell doors.

"There's no way I can extract them with you. If I release them all, they'd just be recaptured or gunned down."

"If they're in their cells, they don't stand a chance at all. Give me the keys."

"We don't have time for this."

Dr. Ray Ewing drew himself up to his full height—about an inch over her own five-eight—and did his best to stare down at her haughtily. The effect was also ruined by how gaunt he was.

She was a little surprised that he was still upright beneath the weight of the IOTV's armor plates and everything else he'd been through. But there was no doubting his grimly determined eyes. He'd face down the Devil herself to give his fellow prisoners a chance.

Feeling small in a way she didn't appreciate, she tossed him the keys.

He unlocked the first door, then the second.

"We don't have time for this." But he ignored her mutter.

Ewing walked up to the first prisoner to stagger out into the open. "Here are the keys. Unlock every door before you leave. Every single one, *si?*" The man glanced down the hall at the muzzled guard, then nodded fiercely before snatching away the keys and moving to the next door as fast as his feet could carry him.

"They still don't have a chance, but I feel better about it."

Kristine inspected him and liked what she saw. Liked it a lot. "Do you know how to shoot a gun?"

He shook his head no.

"Good!"

That earned her a confused laugh.

She fished out the spare she'd brought for him just in case he did, and after a moment's debate, her ankle piece as well.

"Who here knows how to shoot?" she asked the prisoners gathering in the narrow hallway. Three came forward. She handed over her two weapons with extra magazines and sent the third person to where she'd kicked aside the guard's rifle. Then she pulled out an explosive's digital timer, without the explosive attached, and set it for three minutes. Starting it, she set her own watch to match a three-minute countdown.

"You," she reached out and grabbed the first unarmed man who came to hand. "Do not let anyone leave this floor until this counter hits zero. At that time, the guards below will think there is an attack all along the north and east side. If you wait for that, then rush out of the building to the southwest, you'll stand a chance. *Comprende?*"

"*Si, bonita señorita. Si! Si! Gracias! Cero segundos,*" he held the timer with both hands like it was precious.

"*Feliz Navidad!*" Ewing called out.

It was echoed dozens of times down the hall.

6

———

THIS TIME, EWING CAME WHEN SHE DRAGGED HIM DOWN THE corridor to the maintenance hatch ladder. He gasped in surprise as he crawled out the hatch into the battering rain and wind. *And here comes the whining...*

"I forgot what fresh air tastes like."

"It tastes wet."

His laugh was encouraging, but he didn't look strong enough to control his own descent. She tied the end of her grapple rope to his MOLLE vest's lifting ring and took a bight of rope about her waist before guiding him over the roof's edge.

"Is it too late to choose the sleigh ride? Please don't drop me," he pleaded as he eased over the lip.

"Well," she grunted as she took his weight, "you weigh a lot more than a brown-furry. More like a mole of brown-furries, but I'll try not to."

"No, that would be roughly two to the twentieth tons and that's—" she lowered him out of sight and let the wind snatch the math right out of his mouth.

By the time he was down, she was running short on time. Kristine took a loop in between her feet and hand-over-handed her way down. On the ground, she grabbed Ewing's hand so that she could gauge his capabilities and sprinted away. In another twenty-eight seconds the Venezuelan Navy was going to have something far bigger than a mysterious rope to worry about.

They rushed out past the corner of the mess hall and the dorm. He didn't stumble often, though he tended to slide around on the muddy ground. She could also feel him lagging even after a twenty-second sprint—she'd have to account for that.

Her watch hit zero just as they ducked out of sight beneath the marginal shelter of a yellow ipê tree. She hoped the freed prisoners hadn't jumped the gun. Pulling out her remote detonator, she selected all the charges she'd set to the north and east, then hit their firing transmitters simultaneously.

The whole corner of Building Fourteen seemed to explode.

"Holy shit!" Ewing cried out.

"Quiet, unless you want a patrol coming up our asses."

"You blew up the building with those poor people still in it. What kind of person are you?" He sounded seriously pissed, but at least he was a little quieter about it.

"I'm Killer Kristine. But try looking again." She needed to be in motion, but she wouldn't mind at least one person in this screwed up world thinking well of her.

Every door and most of the windows had been shattered, but she'd only used breaching charges. A flash and hard bang; most of the energy had been directed into destroying the doors themselves.

"Here," she unclipped her night-vision googles and held them out before pointing off to the west. By the fire's light, she could see the stream of prisoners departing the building in the other direction. The patrols and guards stumbled forward to stare into the firelight to the northeast like so many pigeons staring at the light. Many wore Christmas garb, many still clutched a bottle of liquor, which explained their weaving and their general inaction. It was very tempting to unsling her rifle and start picking them off, but that would draw the kind of attention she didn't want.

"They're getting away," Ewing sounded so pleased.

"We'll see." Their chances still weren't great, but at least they were free for now. "About time we were doing some of that ourselves."

7

———

Clear of the Naval base, out through the bypasses she'd set in the electric fence, they were resting between a pair of containers in the shipping yard that blocked the worst of the slashing rain.

"Do you have any food?"

She should have thought of that, and dug out a pair of MREs from her pack. "Pick one."

"What's the difference?"

She shrugged. "Twenty-four so-called menus; these are two of them. Once you get rid of all the extra wrappings, heaters, and candy, they're all pretty much the same."

"Not even a candy cane? What kind of a Santa are you?" He took one and began futilely tugging at one corner.

She snatched her Infidel blade from it wrist sheath. Hitting the release, the anodized four-inch double-edged dagger snapped out of the front of the handle.

Ewing dropped his MRE pouches in surprise. *Civilian.*

"Candy is bad luck. Never eat it on a mission." She slit open his pouches then peeked in. "You've got the Mexican Chicken.

Not a bad menu, though not great cold." She slit her own. "I've got Spaghetti in Beef Sauce if you'd prefer."

"Cold spaghetti versus cold Mexican chicken. You really live the highlife. Why 'Killer Kristine'? I haven't seen you kill a single person yet."

"I was in a good mood."

"Happen much?" He dug into his pouch with a spork and began eating fast. Most civilians weren't fans of MREs, but he ate it like it was some fancy-kind-of-place good.

"That I have to kill people or that I'm in a good mood?"

"We'll start with the former," he'd finished the chicken, fruit pack, cheddar cheese-filled pretzels, and chocolate bar (which didn't count as candy so it was safe). She slit open and handed over her untouched meal and he started in on that.

Reluctant to answer, she stared up and blinked into the spattering rain that found its way between the shipping containers. *Sure! I've killed all sorts. Psychotic ragheads at two paces and hell-bent Congolese warlords at a thousand. I've taken out narco-runners in Honduras and nacro-manufacturers in Colombia.* Civilians didn't react well to hearing about such things and she'd learned to keep them to herself. *So, you're a killer for the Army?* Rather than taking them down, she'd just say, *I'm a soldier for the same government that builds your bridges and keeps your food safe.* It never seemed to work. Safer to keep her mouth shut.

"I'll take that as a yes," Ewing said between bites of his Chocolate Chip Toaster Pastry and Italian Bread Sticks.

She shrugged. "And?" Kristine waited for whatever weird reaction was coming her way. She wasn't real hungry and didn't bother fishing out another menu.

"Not what you'd expect from a beautiful woman. That's all. Of course, first impressions don't lie, I suppose. You looked amazingly good standing there in my door all kitted up for war. I was down here doing research for their oil fields. Then they showed up one day and I became a government slave instead."

"You mean until you got caught as a spy for the CIA?"

He inspected her carefully.

"It's the only thing that fits. I've worked enough CIA special requests to know the feel of them."

"What are you?"

"You asked that before."

"You said Killer Kristine. But that's when I asked what kind of a person you were."

"I'm Delta Force. Pleased ta meetcha."

"Brooklyn! What part?"

She'd worked hard to knock it out of her voice over the years, but it had slipped out in the old pat phrase. "Along the Gowanus."

"Which side?"

"You know the good parts? Nowhere near those."

He actually laughed. "Didn't know the Gowanus had good parts."

Ewing was right, of course. The mile-long canal in the heart of Brooklyn was still one of the most polluted stretches of water in the entire country. It was a Superfund cleanup site, except no one could figure out how to clean up three centuries of toxic sludge without digging up a whole section of Brooklyn and burying it somewhere that no one cared about, like Queens.

"It *doesn't* have any good parts," as Kristine well knew. "But we lived in the part that killed my little sister when she went swimming in it one day."

"Oh God! I'm so sorry." And Ewing simply reached a hand around her shoulder in a sideways hug.

Something cracked inside her like the lightning bolt of the growing storm that briefly revealed a flash of his concerned face.

"I was supposed to take her out for an ice cream; it was so

hot. Ran into some of my friends and forgot to keep an eye on her. She got bored and went swimming. Even dove down for something shiny in the mud. The toxins took her out in under a month."

And never once since had Kristine told anyone about it. Never told a soul how her family had disavowed her. How she did her best to never use her last name unless she had to in order to avoid hurting the family—another reason to not fight back against Killer Kristine. Now, here she sat with a total stranger in a raging storm in Venezuela, spilling her guts.

How the hell had that happened?

But Ewing's arm around her shoulder felt good. Despite all the gear they both wore and all the pain snarled in her gut.

It felt good.

"I grew up on Carroll Street, just a few blocks up from the canal," he whispered barely louder than the wind shrieking by overhead. "Still live there."

He had grown up on the good side, she definitely hadn't. It hurt that he still had the old neighborhood and she didn't.

"That's how I became a chemist. Trying to figure out how to fix that canal."

"Can you?" The flash of hope hurt almost as much as the cold memory. She'd joined the Army the day of her sister's funeral—a funeral at which not a soul had sat with her or spoken to her.

"Not yet, sorry. But I still work on it when I can. That's what I brought from the cell," he patted the pouches on his MOLLE. "Whenever I could find time, I'd work on finding a reagent that might fix some aspect of that mess without killing everyone who lives near it as a byproduct. I'm a lot closer to an answer than when they locked me up. Probably closer than I would be if they hadn't locked me up in the first place. Very few pleasant distractions in a jail cell." His glance at her absolutely revealed his meaning.

That part of it she was used to ignoring, though she could get to like Dr. Ewing. However, she didn't know whether to be sick that there was still nothing that could save others like her sister or feel overwhelming hope that people were still trying. "Are you a good chemist?"

"Good enough that the CIA recruited me and the Venezuelans didn't kill me when they found out." He offered the first real hope she'd felt in a long time.

She yanked out her radio. "Gotta get your ass out of here so you can finish the job."

8

———

Mankowski had answered right away. "I've got a beauty staked out. Just say go and I'll be there in ten."

"Go!" Then she'd gotten Dr. Ray Ewing on the move. She now had another reason to keep him alive, a far more important one than she'd started the night with.

Again, she took his hand to keep exact tabs on him. It felt like more than that, but...somethings were best ignored. Together, they slipped up to the end of the container alley and surveyed the surroundings. Not a soul in sight and, even though the yard lights were back on, the visibility sucked beyond about twenty meters. With the Christmas Eve factor, it should be good enough.

It took them eight of the ten minutes to scoot across the shipping yard and back to the ferry terminal where she'd left Mankowski.

"We're good here." She got Ray tucked out of sight between some big boulders and a support stanchion for the ferry dock overhead that did impressively little to block the slashing storm. "We just— Oh shit!"

"What?"

She slapped her silenced sidearm into his hands. "It's loaded. There's no safety on a Glock. Just aim and pull the trigger. Try not to shoot either of us in the process." Kristine unslung her HK416, powered up the night sights, and zeroed in on the approaching patrol boat.

It should be out in the middle of the channel right now.

Actually, on a foul night like tonight, it should be tied up at the pier.

It definitely shouldn't be gliding straight toward her position at the ferry landing.

The lights in the ferry terminal above them were off for the night, but there was enough splash from the commercial yard that Kristine knew she wouldn't be invisible much longer.

Only person she could see was standing at the helm inside the high, glassed-in bridge aboard the seventy-five foot long patrol boat. The paint job was light blue, with PG-401 painted on either side of the bow. A Gavión-class patrol boat built in the US decades ago, with fore-and-aft swivel-mounted machine guns. Except there was no one manning the guns.

She zeroed in on the helmsman who was...waving.

9

———————

"Can't believe you know how to drive this thing. I'm so totally renaming you, you're now *Boatman* Mankowski."

"Why thanks, Killer Kristine," he grinned as he backed them away from the ferry dock. "Beats the shit out of Girlie. Never could seem to shed that one. Did some time as a yacht crew off Martha's Vineyard. Pilot gave me lessons when we were running the boat empty to fetch the owners somewhere or other."

"Maybe it's time you shed Killer, Kristine," Ray said softly from close beside her, too softly for Boatman to hear.

Boatman nosed them toward the end of the breakwater, almost invisible in the spray now breaking over it.

She could only shake her head. "I'll take rear gun until we're clear. Stay in here where it's dry, Ray. Santa's still dumping bucket loads on this hellhole."

"Ooo," Mankowski spun the wheel like he knew what he was doing as he called over his shoulder. "Never heard the Captain call any man by his first name. Look out, buddy. She's gunning for you."

Kristine considered giving Boatman a nickname far worse

than Girlie. Or just beating the shit out of him. The latter wasn't a good choice as she'd never driven anything bigger than the sunken Zodiac. She could figure it out if she had to but it wouldn't be pretty, especially not in a storm.

The wind tore at her as she stepped out the door and hung onto the rail heading aft.

"This is a mole, too." Ray... No, Ewing...no...Ray—she sighed to herself—followed her out onto the deck.

"What is? No brown-furries. No stars with twenty-one zeroes after the one—you said there was six hundred times less stars than atoms in a mole." She slogged down the three steps to the rear recovery deck, around the launch cradled there, and stepped up to the rear gun. A .50 cal M2 Browning deck gun. Sweet! Nobody had better mess with her tonight.

"Women who know math are very sexy. You realize that?"

"Soldier doesn't equal stupid," she did her best to ignore his comment. Though it might be the first time a man had called her sexy while not talking about her body.

"Mole, noun," he announced in a professorial tone. "A long pier or breakwater of piled rock. Actually, you get two for one, because a mole is also the harbor protected by a mole. Like a mole squared."

"A thirty-six with forty-six zeroes after it. Or do you prefer a three-point-six with forty-seven zeroes?"

"Very sexy," he whispered just a tone above another gust of wind that slashed salt water in their faces. "A mole of moles being discussed in a mole-harbor protected by a mole-breakwater," Ray sounded very pleased. "Spoken by a smart and lovely soldier lady with a mole on her cheek, who a mole-spy tipped off to my whereabouts—and I now have a belly full of mole sauce—and she's still wearing her MOLLE harness which—"

"I think we've beat that joke to death now, even if you can figure out how to work brown-furries into that sentence." She snapped safety lines from the boat to their MOLLEs and braced herself. The first storm waves were slipping around the corner of Ray's mole-breakwater and slamming into the boat. Even a seventy-footer was making hard work of this weather.

The good news was that there didn't appear to be any unwanted attention due to their departure. If anyone on shore did notice their departure, they weren't doing anything about it that she could see. Noone else was dumb enough to be out in this filthy weather.

"You know you aren't responsible for her death," Ray went suddenly serious.

Kristine could only grunt at the stab that had just bypassed all of her lifetime's defenses.

"You didn't kill your sister," he declared as if he knew what the fuck he was talking about.

"*So* did!"

"No," his voice stayed dead calm. "There's a reason that the word 'accident' occurs in the English language. Have you been blaming yourself for that for your whole life?"

The lights of the inner harbor were falling behind them as the patrol boat lifted its bow into the first big wave.

"I killed her as surely as if I held the gun to her head myself."

"Did you? Goddamn it, Kristine!" Ray yanked on the shoulder strap of her MOLLE to spin her to face him. He practically shook her by it though she was definitely the stronger one. "No wonder they call you Killer. You've been killing your own soul with that load for how long?"

"My entire life since." She could taste the tears coming down her cheeks despite the sea salt spray. She hadn't cried since...since that day.

"Get a clue woman. You made yourself a Delta Force captain. And you just saved my life and the lives of how many others pretty much single-handed. Go ahead, tell me how many women could pull that off. Oh wait, let me guess: one? Maybe two? Gotta rename you Kristine the Incredible or something."

The first big surf slammed against them. They each had a hand on the other's MOLLE and the wave's force slammed them together. She kept them anchored with one hand on the gun.

While the wave disappeared behind them and the patrol boat climbed the next big one, they didn't ease back. Instead, she pulled him the last inch closer.

Maybe Dr. Ray Ewing was right and it was time to drop that load astern.

She kissed him hard as the next big wave rolled by beneath them and lifted them up.

Getting a new nickname for Christmas sounded like a seriously good idea. And maybe, just maybe—Ray latched an arm tight around her waist to keep her close—that wasn't the only present changing her life this holiday season.

———

You can plunge into the completed Delta Force military romantic suspense series at: https://shop.mlbuchman.com/collections/delta-force

CHRISTMAS OVER
THE BAR

One of my US Coast Guard romance stories landed in the first Christmas collection. After its release, I found another to write.

It is set in the same small community on coastal Oregon. I lived along that coast for six years and still love it deeply. I wanted to pay homage to those who live and work there and, especially, to those who put themselves at risk to save lives there.

The series would eventually grow to include five stories, but this one celebrates the Christmas season in a typical Oregon Coast fashion.

1

"THIS IS INSANE!" HAILEY FRANKLIN SHOUTED AT THE STORM.

"When you're right, you're right." Vera replied from the passenger seat.

Hailey had met Vera Chu at the Portland, Oregon airport car rental counter. They'd gotten to know each other driving through the torrential December rain as they forged west to meet their new billet. Spending two hours together, squinting ahead into the darkness through the thick rivers that the windshield wipers on high couldn't clear, created a special kind of bond.

Their US Coast Guard cutter was berthed in Astoria, Oregon at the mouth of the Columbia River, which divided Oregon and Washington. And apparently it was crewed by fish who could live underwater.

"Perhaps there's a reason there are no scheduled flights to Astoria. Only a crazy pilot would fly on a night like this."

"You aren't the one driving," Hailey protested, not that she'd given Vera the chance. When she was in any car, she drove. Ever since her brother had tried to drive under a tractor trailer full of lobster pots and sheared the top off the family car—with her in it—she'd insisted. She'd managed to pull him down in time, so it was just instant convertible rather than instant death...but still!

"I expect this is pretty in daylight." Vera had spent the drive announcing views that her phone map revealed but the pitch black storm hid.

All Hailey had seen for the last two hours was slashing rain on the twisty two-lane Highway 30. Half the time blinded by oncoming headlights and half with her own headlights reflecting off the walls of water that the Pacific storm was throwing at them.

By the time they reached town, her arms were sore from fighting the wind as it slapped their tiny Mitsubishi Mirage about like a hockey puck.

They'd determined three things during the drive.

Vera, the tall Chinese girl from Detroit, was the classy one. Not that Hailey cared. She was fine with being the short black chick from the farthest butthole of Maine. Why wouldn't she be?

They were both USCG born and bred, on both sides of the family, and were both carrying on the legacy by having just re-upped for their second five-year tour.

And third, the chances were good they'd be spending this next tour together. They'd both drawn slots on the USCG cutter *Steadfast.*

She figured that was good grounds for being best buds. Vera had reached the same conclusion even if she was, like, so slender and forever-tall. Though watching her fold into the Mirage economy rental had been pretty funny.

"You're aware that our ship is based from here," Vera asked as they arrived at the town limits sign.

"Shit! I thought we were just going for a scenic drive to a total nowhere town for the hell of it." Not even Astoria was as remote as where she'd been born. There wasn't a whole lot of

America that existed east of Jonesport, Maine—the five hundred residents of Cutler and the Quoddy Head Lighthouse were about it. Maw and Paw had spent twenty years riding the buoy tenders along the coast and into the North Atlantic out of the USCG Jonesport Station.

"I'm simply curious regarding this place where we'll be based for a while."

"Won't see much of it. We'll be out on a cutter."

"This isn't the Navy."

Vera had a point. The cutter would mainly work the Washington and Oregon coasts, voyaging farther to sea only for search and rescue.

"Okay, let's see what we've gotten ourselves into." Vera had been navigator, not that there'd been any real questions. Out of the airport they'd had to make a grand total of one turn to pick up Highway 30.

There was a long silence. Long enough that the town lights were coming up.

"Um... As far as I can tell, the town is essentially one street wide and mostly in a two-mile stretch."

"Party town, whoo-hoo!"

"It means that the men are going to be small-minded provincials. Slim opportunities."

"Urban snob," Hailey teased her for her Detroit upbringing.

"Small-minded provincial," Vera teased her right back.

"Hey, just because I know how to haul a lobster pot and you don't, doesn't mean—"

"That's a pretty building."

"Columbia River Maritime Museum," Hailey read as they rolled by. "Could be fun."

"Oh!" they gasped in unison and Hailey immediately eased over to the shoulder of the road, stopping in a deep puddle.

Just past the museum was the dock...*their* dock. A pair of two hundred-and-ten-foot, Reliance-class Coast Guard cutters bobbed there. Also, an old-style emergency lightship—the kind with a major masthead light that could be driven out to sea in case a lighthouse broke and couldn't be serviced immediately. This one was a museum piece.

"At least we know we're in the right place," Hailey had always liked the Reliance boats. They were the first of the post-WWII cutters. Built in the 1960s, they had a sleek, determined look that said they'd been the workhorse of the Coast Guard for half a century and were still up to the task.

"We're not due for a couple hours."

"Food!" They declared in unison.

Yeah, spending the next five years hanging with Vera Chu could be a good thing.

2

———————

"You lost, Sly."

"Suck on it, Ham."

That was four times in a row that Lieutenant Sylvester Beaumont had lost the draw. He knew that his copilot Hammond Marcus was somehow rigging the game, but he couldn't tell how. This time it was their crew chief, Vivian who'd been holding up the chem lights, and still he'd drawn the red one.

Maybe...

He couldn't quite tell whether or not to trust her smile as she restowed the chem lights in their helicopter's emergency gear.

"Don't forget my horseradish this time, Lieutenant Beaumont," Harvey, their rescue swimmer called out.

"Blah. Blah. Blah." Sly had forgotten it once, like three months ago. Maybe it was Harvey's doing that he'd landed dinner-run duty four times running. The guy was quiet, but real sneaky. Yeah, perhaps it was *him* behind Sly's losing streak.

Harvey was sneaky in more than one way.

"Wedding just two weeks away. Got any nerves, Harv?"

"Not a one."

"Damn straight that better be your answer," Vivian paused in the middle of checking over her gear, long enough to pull Harvey down into a kiss. It quickly became clear that she was making it extra steamy just to mess with him.

"I'm outta here."

"About time," Ham grumbled.

Vivian's and Harvey's kiss broke up in laughter.

Totally messing with him.

He climbed into his pickup and headed into Astoria to get their dinner.

He didn't have a clue how Harvey had done it—and so damn fast. A total babe, Vivian had arrived on base last December 23rd. They'd been dating by New Year's Eve and engaged on Valentine's Day. Getting married on Christmas Day.

For himself, he had no real interest in slowing down yet, but he wouldn't mind that kind of lightning bolt striking him either.

And even though the Pacific Northwest wasn't much given to lightning, this Christmas Eve storm looked all set to deliver.

Wrong kind of lightning though.

There had been a pair of locals that he and Ham had been making good progress with—on that long-ago Valentine's Day. What with Harvey and Vivian getting engaged in their standard dive-bar hangout, it had set a definite romantic atmosphere for the evening—at least until Vivian had busted it up.

She'd sat down with the two hot townies and done the worst thing imaginable, told them the truth.

You girls want a good time, go for it. You want the long dream of escape from this town—because Astoria was the epitome of small town that most wanted to escape from—*Sly and Ham aren't your guys. The trick is, you've got to leave town yourself and go find what you're looking for. Take it from a woman who figured that out the hard way.*

And the two girls had. By the end of the month they'd both moved to Portland.

Vivian was a bad influence.

Vivian had made him think, though Sly hadn't mentioned a thing about it to Ham. Think a lot. (A *really* bad influence as that wasn't his normal mode.) And not exactly comfortable thoughts. What did he want long-term? Other than flying his USCG helo. What kind of woman was he actually looking for?

Damned if he knew.

3

———————

"THAT'S A BRIGHT CHRISTMAS TREE," HAILEY BLINKED. THE thing was oncoming like major high beams.

Vera was doing one of her phone things. "Twenty-eight-foot artificial tree with four thousand LEDs in seven colors."

"Could use the thing as a lighthouse—for passing spaceships." Brake lights blanketed the road ahead of her. "What the hell? Who would traffic jam a one-road town on a stormy Saturday night?"

"That would be the Santa Swim."

"Santa Swim?"

"*Bring your Santa hat and float in our Aquatic Center pool for our annual screening of* Home Alone."

"You're kidding, right?" Then she thought about the blueberry costume parade for the Machias, Maine Wild Blueberry Festival. Maybe it wasn't so odd. Small towns did have their own quirks.

"There's also a Tuba Christmas concert tonight."

Hailey weaved her way through the traffic snarl and made it out the other side. "If we didn't have to report aboard, that would almost be worth it."

"There!"

The car rental was on the main drag. And closed.

They hoisted their sea bags (that they should have dropped off at the ship) and dumped the key through the slot.

Just up the street, there were a number of cars parked close together, lit clearly by red and blue neon lights.

They shared a shrug and trotted that way through the downpour.

"Workers Tavern. Known for burgers and prime rib," Vera somehow ran, avoided puddles, and read her phone.

"Sounds spendy."

"It..." *more* phone thing even though the door was like twenty feet away "...isn't."

As soon as they were through the door, Hailey saw why. The bar looked as if it had needed a major renovation—for at least the last fifty years. Someone had done some recent work on it, but not enough to make it look any better than a total dive.

Perfect.

"They appear to all be different currencies," Vera was inspecting an entire wall covered in hundreds of low currency bills that had been stapled there. Hailey could hear her dripping onto the old wood floor.

Hailey was too busy taking in the marine ambience to check out the wall.

Buoy Beer signs—must be a local brew she'd have to try when she wasn't about to be on duty. Oars, ship's wheels, giant stuffed fish, a couple bowling trophies, so many signs it was impossible to make sense of them—though "Play Meat Bingo Every Sunday" definitely stood out. Only one television, and it was off. Definitely her kind of place.

Battered tables to the front and a big U-shaped bar to the back. Good crowd. Not packed, just cozy and friendly. Group of old graybeards at the far end of the bar harmonizing Christmas carols with no apparent melody and few discernable words.

By the amazing grilled-meat smell coming from the corner kitchen, they'd definitely hit pay dirt.

They dumped their gear and slicks in a corner that didn't look too grotty, then took a pair of stools at the bar.

"Beer?" The barman had a generous beard, shaved head, heavy earrings, and an impressive set of arm tattoos. He also stood about six-five and had a good smile.

"I wish. A Coke and a steak. Still mooing."

"Coastie?"

"Why do you ask?"

"No one except a Coastie comes in here asking for a Coke with their steak."

"Two of us." She nodded to Vera who ordered a burger and a pot of tea.

The barman just laughed and headed to the kitchen at the back of the bar.

"Tea, really?"

Vera just shrugged pleasantly.

4

———

SLY WAS SO PSYCHED.

Ham was totally missing out and he'd get to rub it in for the whole upcoming flight.

In a town not known for having a lot of variety—especially because their crew kept coming to this same place to eat and drink—there were two new women at the bar. With their backs to him, he took his time moseying up to the bar.

He spotted the luggage covered in slicks. Mega-bonus: they'd just hit town. Too bad he was flying tonight. Maybe they'd be around for a while.

One was tall and had straight, jet-black hair down to her shoulders.

The other, much shorter, clearly had curves, and super-curly hair cut short.

"Hey, Teddy," he sidled up to the bar. He handed over the order because he forgot to call it in. "And Harvey is whining about the horseradish again. Could you give me a container of mayonnaise instead or something."

"And mess with my man, Harvey? Dream on," Teddy grinned and headed back to the cook.

Then Sly turned. From the front neither bar babe disappointed.

As advertised from behind, the tall one was sleek. One of those Asian types—Chinese, Japanese, whatever. He could never tell.

The short one did indeed have curves, great ones. Lushly dark skin, and a sideways grin that said she totally knew that he was checking them out.

"His name's Teddy?"

"No, but he's built like a giant Teddy bear, so it works on him."

"Less than you'd think." The bartender planted a glass of water on the bar, hard enough to slop some onto Sly's arm—not that it really mattered with how wet it was out there.

Teddy's wink at the women proved he'd done it on purpose. Sly really didn't need the trouble and waited until he'd moved off to pull some pints at the other side of the bar.

"So, you here for the surfing?"

The Asian chick looked at him in wide-eyed mystification.

The curvy black chick almost snorted her Coke with a bright laugh, so he riffed on it.

"It's big here on the Coast. They even have an app that announces when and where the surf's up."

"It's December, dude." Her voice was low and throaty. Nice.

"Wetsuits. Year round. Honest," he raised a three-fingered Boy Scout salute.

"What? You made Tenderfoot? Can't believe they let you in at all."

"I got to Star."

"Oooo, Vera, we're in the presence of greatness. Too bad he flunked out before he made Eagle Scout."

Well, that gave him one of their names, but the wrong one.

"Actually, I had to choose whether I went Eagle or started lessons in—"

"Remedial 'Being a Human Being'?" She was quick.

"Yeah, that." He gave her a nod, conceding the round. — *flying lessons*. At least that's where he would normally work being a USCG helo pilot into the conversation. But he liked her quick response too much to ruin it.

It lit up that killer smile again. "So, you're, like, Mr. Surfing Man?" She held out her arms as if she was balancing and riding the waves.

"In this weather? Shit no. I'm not that crazy."

And her laugh gave him that round.

Teddy delivered the babes' dinners, so closely followed by a bag of his four orders that it was clear Vivian had called it in. Damn, just when he wasn't in a hurry.

Teddy tossed Sly one of those small plastic containers. "Don't be losing that, or you really *will* piss off Harvey and I wash my hands of whatever he does to your sorry ass. Mayo's in the order, that's his horseradish."

"Dude!" He held up a hand for a high-five, which Teddy ignored just long enough to make the bar chick laugh again, before delivering. Damn but she had a great laugh. Sly then tucked the horseradish container in his slicker's pocket.

"You going to be in town a while?"

"Yes, we are," Vera replied calmly before cutting off a bite of her hamburger—with a knife and fork.

"A fair bit," the other one mumbled around a mouthful of prime rib.

And for some reason he didn't understand, he decided to just play it cool. As if Vivian was watching over his shoulder and telling him not to mess this one up.

"Well, gotta go feed the wolf pack before they get too ravenous," he hefted the bag to make his point.

She waved a knife at him in goodbye as if he was totally unimportant.

"You got a name?" Sometimes you just had to ask.

"Yep. You?"

"Uh-huh."

"Good thing to have," then she made a show of sticking another bite of prime rib in her mouth before turning to her friend.

Only after he was out the door did Sly realize that he hadn't played his best card. "Coast Guard helicopter pilot" never failed to wow the ladies. Though maybe *not* with this one. She had a whole lot of different going on.

5

———

"Welcome to the Aviation Detachment aboard the Cutter *Steadfast,*" the captain had greeted them.

Then he scowled down at them dripping on his pristine bridge deck. The storm had abated enough that they were merely drenched rather than needing gills after the hundred yard crossing from taxi to ship. *Drowned rats asking permission to come aboard, sir.*

"I assume you know your duties when a helo is aboard. Chief Mackey will make sure you know what to do, otherwise."

That and a salute was the entire scope of their welcoming ceremony. The captain was definitely old school. *Yeah, just two new overeager petty officers to worry about.* With a total crew of only seventy-seven Hailey thought he would have at least asked their names.

The captain probably appreciated them arriving together as it saved him repeating his lengthy greeting.

After him, Chief Petty Officer Mackey, a taciturn San Diegan probably built rather than born on the Navy base there, had showed them where they'd be bunked together. As they dumped their bags, the chief had given the entire ship's tour—

which had consisted of him asking one question, "Been aboard a Reliance-class boat before?"

When they'd both nodded, the Chief was nearly as brief as the Captain. "Good. You're the new AVDET team. Prior team rotated out this morning, so no handoff, but you know your duties. Stow your gear, get flight squared away, and then get some sleep." He'd know they'd both just crossed the country from Little Creek, Virginia, and Pascagoula, Mississippi. Which meant, on military transports that never connected the way passenger flights did, neither had slept in two days. Still, first priority was readiness. Sleep was a distant twenty-fifth on any action list.

Coast Guard cutters weren't big on sitting still and the two-hundred-and-ten-foot *Steadfast* was no exception. It had started moving out of port an hour after they'd boarded. Command must have said to start the patrol on today's date and the captain had interpreted that as straight-up midnight rather than daybreak. Hard-charger or total jerkwad had yet to be seen.

By the time they hit the flight deck, *Steadfast* wasn't so steady. She was nosing out of the Columbia River and into the Pacific. The last lights of the North and South Jetty were blinking away dead to starboard and port. Mid-channel markers slipped by in red and green. A peek over the side rail revealed nothing but churning waves.

The seas, which had been slapping the cutter side-to-side was now intent on porpoising her up-and-down as well. It took major waves to do that to a Reliance-class ship.

Full slicks, life jacket, and double safety harness, they'd split up at the rear hatch to survey the status of the flight deck.

Hailey uncoiled and recoiled a couple of tie-down lines just to make sure that the lay of the line was clean and wouldn't snarl if she needed them fast. She liked when she spotted Vera doing the same on the other side of the deck.

Together, they inspected the refueling and rearming status —everything at full inventory. Toolkit was good and spare parts were few. Made sense because a boat like the Reliance rarely carried a helo full time. She could cruise for eight thousand miles between resupplies, but probably rarely ran more than a hundred miles off the coast.

In silence, they did an FOD walk—more an FOD stagger, weaving like drunks back and forth across the pitching deck. No foreign object debris.

Because the HH-65 Dolphin's engines sat high atop the fuselage, it was unlikely that they would suck up any damaging debris. But the heavy blast of a helo's rotors could turn the smallest bit of junk, such as a dropped bolt, into a painful missile for the deck crew. Or even worse, roll underfoot at the wrong moment.

But the deck was clean, and they finally met at the stern rail. The thirty-by-sixty-foot deck was their main domain.

They gripped the stern rail as the bow nosed down into yet another deep trough lifting them several stories into the air. The lights of the four-mile-long Astoria-Megler Bridge, arcing high out of Astoria before touching down in mid-river to continue to Washington, was just visible through the storm.

"This is insane!" Vera repeated her call from the drive out. Now it was almost inaudible over the hard pounding of the rain, driven bullet-loud against the back of their slicks.

"When you're right, you're right," Hailey gave the same reply and they both laughed.

But neither of them moved.

For Hailey it was a blend of exhaustion and exhilaration. Maw and Paw had done their twenty years for the Coast Guard, retiring when she left grade school. They'd moved eighty miles south to teach at the prestigious Maine Maritime Academy in the relative metropolis of Castine—population of thirteen hundred plus a thousand students.

And here she was doing *her* dance.

As she watched the lights of their new homeport fading astern, she couldn't help grinning. Cute guy within an hour of arrival. Not too shabby. Funny too. Major, *major* points for not going for her phone number, or push for her name.

Like he thought they were fated to run into each other again.

The fates of her past had proved pretty damn fickle. The only thing that had held true was the Coast Guard. The men sure hadn't. She'd been hit on by married officers, too crass to even pull off their ring first. At least their new captain hadn't done that.

"Why do so many men assume I'm easy?"

"Looking the way you do, you're surprised?" Vera answered even though Hailey hadn't meant to speak her question aloud.

"What? Why?"

"Hailey. You're beautiful. I'm like this total stick figure of a woman."

"A totally elegant one."

Vera shrugged uncertainly enough for it to show through her gear. "I'm not the one he hit on."

"Mr. Surfing-dude Boy Scout? He's a total hound dog, couldn't you tell? That's what I always draw. Guy who falls for *you* will have a weak spot for pure class. I couldn't wear class even if it came in a dress my size. And trust me, it doesn't."

"So, what happens if you run into him again?"

"Not gonna happen. We're headed out on patrol."

Vera's shrug this time indicated something else, but Hailey wasn't sure what.

6

"THURSDAY. THIS HAS GOTTA BE A THURSDAY."

"It's Tuesday. You and I go off rotation on Thursday."

"Oh, that's why I always thought Thursdays sucked. You sure this isn't a Thursday?" Sly would *always* rather be flying—except maybe tonight. The hangar's inside worklights barely made it out the door. Beyond the windshield of his US Coast Guard HH-65 Dolphin helicopter the sideways rain slashed even harder off the Pacific than when he'd done their dinner run. As the engines continued spinning up, he decided that the night looked very, very Thursdayish no matter what Ham said.

Air Station Astoria was defended from the direct onslaught of the Pacific storms which slammed the Oregon Coast by sitting three miles inland. The problem was that the high point in that three miles was all of eight feet above sea level. The airport lifted a full yard higher into the wind at eleven feet. The stunted coastal pines had been kept well back from the west side of the airport, so offered little defense.

"The storms know, they just know." He continued checking the items on the pre-takeoff checklist as Ham called them out from the copilot's seat.

"Know what? N1 at release?"

"Starter released. They know just how to swing into the mouth of the Columbia River so they can hit us with a straight shot."

"You're now manifesting this poor, little, innocent storm with evil intelligence to make up for your weird Gloucester Nor'easter superstitions? You're a real sad dude, Sly. Engine and transmission oil?"

"Check and rising. Just like this damn storm's temper. Innocent, my butt. Why do people have to go out to sea and get in trouble on nights like this? Why can't they just all stay home?" Sly could hear his past sneaking into his own voice. He still remembered the nine days huddled with Mom until they'd found Dad's fishing boat—or what was left of it—washed up on the remote Sober Island along Nova Scotia. "Unlikely-sober" Island as Mom had called it ever since.

Tonight, the inevitable call came in: crab boat in the shit—and sinking.

"Because if they did, we'd be out of a job. Nav lights, caution breaker, fuel boost?"

"On, in, and in," Sly tapped each switch and circuit breaker to confirm it and kept his tone light. "You're right. That would be even worse. Then who would pay us to fly?"

"Well, no one would pay *you*. But I'm such a handsome and charming brother, they'd keep me on just to make the Coast Guard look good."

"The only way you'd ever look good, Ham, is if they slipped a different corpse in your casket after you died." There'd been a debate ever since they'd hit the same air station on the same day two years back: which of them drew in the women, and which repelled them. Their far superior success as a team made it difficult to keep any meaningful score—not that it stopped them from trying.

He'd long since learned that pointing out his last name,

Beaumont, meant "pretty mountain" was a bad idea. *Talk about mountains out of molehills,* Ham had instantly replied. *You know, you do kinda look like a mole.* Yeah, so not worth the effort. And he couldn't do much with Ham's last name of Markson. And he was a damned handsome black dude. He'd have to make sure *not* to introduce him to the sassy girl in the bar if he did manage to run into her again.

They were all the way down to anti-ice system check, which they'd be bound to need in the December storm, before Ham tried again.

"ELT check? We gotta watch the bar."

Sly glanced over. How could Ham know about the total babe? He hadn't been there.

Oh, the Bar (Captial B). The Columbia River Bar.

"Check." As always, he sent up a brief prayer to Mama's God asking that they wouldn't need the Emergency Location Transmitter tonight. It would only be needed if they crashed.

The mouth of the Columbia River Bar was also known as the Graveyard of the Pacific. The worst and most dangerous stretch of shipping water anywhere in the world. Even the Straits of Magellan at the southern tip of Chile were more traversable. They also had a lot less traffic, instead of servicing three of the top fifteen US agricultural ports like the Columbia. Not to mention enough recreational boaters to make a man choke on his soda.

"Yeah, the Bar." On a night like this—with the Columbia dumping two million gallons of water per second into the ocean, and the storm surge, not to mention the high tide ignoring all that to try for Portland way upriver—there was bound to be some major ugliness. Except the call had come in from much farther out to sea.

"Instruments all normal?"

There was a long silence as they both double-checked for any bad instrument readings—from compass to engine temperature to altimeter (which revealed a depressingly low barometric reading for eleven feet above sea level). There weren't any problems because the Dolphin was an awesome search-and-rescue helo.

"All normal," Sly reported per the checklist then called back over the intercom. "You two still with us?"

Harvey the rescue swimmer grunted an affirmative. Guy hadn't even tasted the mayo. He'd taken one look at it, then held out his hand until Sly placed the horseradish container in his palm. He'd now be belted in at the very rear of the cargo cabin.

Vivian's seat placed her facing backward directly behind his own position. She reported by the numbers because she was that kind of squared-away gal.

"Wedding is Christmas Day. Can we trust the two of you to keep your hands off each other back there?"

"Can we trust you two to keep *your* hands off each other?" Vivian shot back.

"Only because it takes two hands to fly," Harvey offered one of his rare comments.

"It's Sly," Ham joined in. "He can't stand that I'm the pretty one."

"Just get us out there," Vivian gave a long-suffering sigh.

"Your wish is my command, oh Queen of the Skies."

He eased up on the collective, rocked the cyclic forward, and climbed up into the darkening sky.

7

———

"How long were we asleep?" Vera groaned.

Hailey checked her watch and sighed, but put on her most cheerful tone. "Almost two hours. What's your problem, Vera?"

"I'm not some android like you is the problem. I need at least two-and-a-half hours to recharge my batteries."

They dressed fast and reported to the bridge as ordered.

Despite the late hour, the captain was on deck. As well as the XO, two helmsmen, a navigator, and a radio operator. Chief Mackey arrived moments later.

The captain waved them over to the chart table.

"Franklin. Chu. Glad to see you're not sickers."

So, the fact that they didn't puke in bad weather had earned them "named" status in the captain's book. Hailey was okay with that. Because if the Reliance had been lively before, now she was positively active. Quartering waves, with the engines now running at full turns based on the vibration through Hailey's boot soles, gave the *Steadfast* a funky, hip-hop beat motion—one that Hailey's Maine heritage had never been able to follow on the dance floor. However, on a boat? No prob.

"We're in pursuit of the *Savannah Jack*. Forty-six-foot

aluminum crabbing boat that's lost its engines and is in imminent peril of sinking. Crew of five. She's over two hundred miles out."

Mackey cursed, "How the hell did they end up that far offshore?"

"Unclear. Drunk, asleep, driving for Alaska in too small a boat? Who knows. We will *not* arrive in time."

That earned him silence.

"There's an HH-65 Dolphin enroute. Our mandate is to get as close as we can to serve as a landing platform."

Hailey didn't have to do the math. Vera's look said she'd reached the same conclusion.

A four-hundred-mile round trip was close to the helicopter's total range. If they had to linger onsite for a rescue, they wouldn't get back to land. Every mile closer the cutter could get to the crabber was that much longer the helo could remain on-station at the sinking.

"We've checked over everything on the flight deck, sir. We're as ready as we can be for a landing in this kind of weather."

"You will not be losing me a helo on your first day. Are we clear on that?"

"Yes, sir," she and Vera snapped it out in unison.

"Then we understand each other. I let you sleep as long as I could. The helo is already at the *Savannah Jack*. They were able to locate her immediately thanks to the crabber having an ELT. We'll be out past fifty miles by the time the helo will be coming back. They're winching aboard the last crewman and the helo's swimmer right now."

"Must be hell out there," Mackey grumbled.

There was a brief silence as they all sent prayers or whatever was needed out to the rescue swimmer down in that turbulent mess.

"They'll be here in under an hour. Recruit whoever you need, get them safely onto my deck."

"Yes sir."

"I'll send you a pair of MEs," Mackey said before waving them aft. Maritime Law Enforcement Specialist meant a sailor who was good at thinking fast on their feet in chaotic environments.

Hailey could get to like Mackey.

8

———

"Well, that was fun," Ham announced.

Even with the two of them and the four-axis autopilot the rescue had been a major battle. Even clear of the land effects, the waves and wind had been in a contrary mood.

Harvey and Vivian had done their usual amazing task. Harvey had dived into the fray, eventually recovering two bodies and three survivors. While they worked frantically to save the latter from hypothermia, it was now up to Sly to get them to the cutter *Steadfast*. Quickly.

But getting there fast wasn't the problem. They had a ferocious tailwind, which was a good thing. If it had been a headwind, as it had on the way out, they would be in even worse trouble than they were. Having his only available refuge being a hard-pitching cutter just five times longer than his helo was not a comfortable thought tonight.

"Cutter *Steadfast*. This is Dolphin 58 inbound," Ham called ahead on the radio.

"Roger, 58. Winds forty, gusting sixty. Waves at thirty, chaotic." *That* was the problem. Landing on the pitching helo deck.

"Roger that. We'll need immediate medical for the three survivors. Crew plus five aboard." A nice way to say they had two in body bags.

"Sounds like this is going to be even *more* fun." Sly couldn't see a thing out in the utterly foul night and was completely dependent on instruments. Storm dark. Moonless storm dark. And they were still fifty miles to the ship.

"Sure thing. And I'm not looking for a swim, so try actually landing on the deck this time."

Back during training, Sly had misread the markers on the airport runway that were supposed to be the outline of a ship's deck. So, he'd landed *beside* the theoretical ship rather than *on* it. Five years, and Ham hadn't let him off the hook on that yet. "It was my first landing, for crying out loud."

"Whine. Whine. Whine," Ham teased as he entered *Steadfast's* latest GPS coordinates into the onboard systems. "Fifteen minutes," he called back to Vivian and Harvey.

"Okay," Vivian's calm response was a good sign for the three survivors. Not that she was ever *not* calm. But if things were still going badly, she'd be too focused to even hear them.

"Man, that's gotta be a rough ride. *Steadfast* is coming toward us at full steam."

Sly eyed the fuel gauges and hoped that she really was. He had reserve fuel, but he'd have to land dead clean if he didn't want to get caught depending on it.

He hoped he could make it back to shore tonight. Maybe swing by the Workers and see if the nameless woman was still there, crooked smile and all. Wicked hot, but...he hadn't really looked at her body once he'd heard her laugh. Weird thing to stick in his head. He hadn't even lorded their meeting over Ham, which was not like him at all.

Whoever she is someday, Sylvester, Mom was the only one to always use his full name, *make sure she's someone who does* not *go to sea.* She'd never really recovered from Dad going down. Of course, Sly couldn't imagine anyone being prouder or bragging more on her son, than when he'd qualified as a helo pilot for the Coast Guard.

Or more afraid.

9

With the perimeter fence around the Flight Deck folded down and Astoria nowhere in sight, Hailey felt a hundred times more exposed.

Her first tour had been out of Virginia Beach, Virginia. She'd ridden out some rough storms—tail ends of hurricanes and such. But Mackey had said that tonight was nothing out of the ordinary. *Just five thousand miles of open Pacific come to piss on us.*

Clearly, this posting was going to have a whole lot of new experiences for her.

Experiences like the guy in the bar?

Vera had only brought him up about six more times—in that quiet way of hers. As if Hailey wasn't thinking of him enough on her own.

She'd lived in enough small towns to see how completely he stood out in the crowd. Hell, he'd stand out in any crowd.

Hailey again checked the deck. Between them, she and Vera had decided to take turns as the lead Landing Director. She'd immediately claimed first right by order of the alphabet.

"Hailey wins out over Vera."

"What about Chu over Franklin?"

"H plus F equals eighth plus sixth letter of the alphabet. V for Vera plus anything is like a kajillion. My win."

Now she stood at the forward end of the open flight deck and wished she'd gone second. Tonight's landing on the pitching deck was going to be a nightmare.

Vera stood off to the side with a pair of unlit batons just as backup. The two MEs were squatting off to either side. They knew the drill, but she and Vera had gone over it with them again anyway. They'd spent half an hour talking through escape routes if something went wrong, firefighting in case whatever it was went *badly* wrong, and every other scenario she could come up with. Besides, it beat the hell out of waiting and wishing she was still asleep.

"This is Dolphin 58. Have you in sight, *Steadfast,*" sounded over the radio headset built into her safety helmet.

"Say again," Hailey couldn't believe it. She knew that voice, but couldn't place from where. She hadn't heard of any of the guys from her last station at Virginia Beach transferring out West. No, it was more recent than that.

Swiveling around, she spotted the helo coming to hover off the port side.

"Belay that. Roger in sight."

Not quite hover, as the ship would be driving ahead at fifteen knots and the wind blowing the other way at forty-plus. He was actually flying at sixty knots and looked as if he'd been bolted into place against the vast blackness. The pilot was so steady that it was the first time she was really aware of how badly the deck was heaving about.

Her body knew what to do with the pitching deck, but her eyes tracking the helo back and forth were less sure.

"Captain, are we dead into the wind?"

For the moment, she was the master of the ship.

"If this wind *has* a dead into, we're there," he called back.

She could feel him up on the bridge, maybe out on a wing in the storm, watching his newest crews' every move.

She glanced behind her to make sure that she was exactly in front of the foot-wide yellow stripe painted up the aftmost bulkhead. It marked the center of the ship and the center of the Flight Deck for the pilot.

A hard gust and her gut told her that the boat had just made a fierce twist from slamming a wave.

Just gotta surf it smooth.

And then she knew exactly where she'd heard the pilot's voice before.

10

———

The laugh over Sly's headset was as brief as it was unique.

"You've got a sick idea of fun, Ham."

But it wasn't Ham's laugh.

Sly had never put down on a deck when a ship was as breezed up as the *Steadfast*. This was gonna be savage.

He briefly wondered if the nameless woman in the bar danced. He sure hoped so. She'd be something to watch.

And she'd have a laugh like...

"Ha!"

"What?"

"Nothing, Ham. Tell you the joke later."

Green baton pointed to the left, the deck crewman—the nameless bar girl, new to town, USCG new to the *Steadfast* (damn but that *was* really funny)—began waving him inboard with the red.

He shuffled over until the yellow stripe was dead ahead. The problem—that the H at the center of the helipad was rockin' and rollin'—was the baton wielder's problem.

For now, he set aside everything except what she was signaling for him to do. It was one of the hardest things for any pilot. He could see the boat pitching, but he'd never be able to anticipate it well enough to land.

This required absolute trust in the person on deck guiding him in.

Sly shoved aside how much he didn't know about the woman, he locked his attention on staying centered on that yellow stripe of the ship's mid-line, and focused on her two batons.

Down...hold!

Hold.

Hold.

Down! Hold!

He found her rhythm easy to follow.

Batons out to her sides and then angled down when he could descend.

Swinging level to hold.

Only twice did she have to signal him to climb, with upraised batons.

"He's good," Ham mumbled somewhere in the background.

She, but Sly kept that to himself.

The trick was to descend until he was just above the highest point the deck ever swung. Then to be there—the exact moment it swung to its peak.

Down! Hold. Down! Hold.

He could feel the tension between them, the perfect synchronicity of their mutual dance the moment before she gave the final signal.

Two batons straight down.

Sly shoved the collective down. If the ship was in the wrong place by so much as five feet he could pitch to the deck, shatter his rotors, maybe even be thrown overboard.

The wheels didn't even slam down onto the deck. She'd gotten him so perfectly positioned that he kissed down on it.

Following her direction, he pushed the rotor full down, creating negative lift, pinning the helo to the deck.

The disadvantage was that negative lift would drag the tips of the whirling main rotor blades dangerously low.

But he saw the deck crew scramble for the tie-downs practically on all fours. Well-rehearsed.

In less than thirty seconds, she crossed the batons in front of her chest, giving him the Cut Engines sign.

Just before she did, she held the batons out front and back, level for just an instant.

"What the hell is that sign?" Ham asked him.

"Surfin', dude. She's surfin'."

11

———

Hailey tried to figure out just what was happening, but couldn't seem to.

Workers Tavern was packed to the gills.

The Christmas Day wedding had been at the community pool. She supposed it made sense for the wedding of a rescue swimmer, but it was still weird to have the wedding party all in the pool and the bride and groom up on the diving board.

Weird in a gloriously small-town-funny way that she totally dug. The bride's high-brow mom hadn't looked terribly amused, but everyone else was having too much fun to care.

Hailey loved that her bikini had gobsmacked Sly Beaumont straight into stuttering silence.

Vera's shy streak wasn't doing much at fending off a whole lot of male attention. She had looked so perfect in her sleek one-piece that all the guys were hovering, including Sly's copilot.

Most of her crew had returned to the cutter. The captain had said that he wanted at least one of his AVDET people on the boat before midnight—which actually felt pretty damn good. He'd complimented them both on a difficult task well done and it felt as if they really were a part of the team already. It boded well for the five years to come.

"This is insane!" Vera had whispered as she begged off before the party shifted from the pool to the tavern.

"When you're right, you're right," Hailey had hugged her tightly g'night before following Sly to Workers for the wedding dinner and dancing. The latest deluge was so cold after the warm pool that laughter had been the only answer.

It *was* insane.

She'd known Vera and Sly for two whole weeks. And it felt as if she'd never had a closer friend or known any man better.

Now she and Sly were boogieing down to a small up-tempo band, with the four graybeards as backup vocals inventing any melodies they didn't already know—which was most of them.

The giant bartender, in an equally giant Santa suit, handed out eggnog and hearty calls of, "Ho! Ho! Ho!"

Hailey missed when she and Sly switched from dancing with the beat to... The transition from rocking out with Sylvester Beaumont to slow-dancing curled up against his chest had passed without notice. It was just so natural.

For a while, she just let herself soak in how good it felt. *He* felt. No man had ever felt this way.

And somehow it didn't surprise. Everything about Sylvester Beaumont felt easy and natural. The teasing in the bar. The perfect synchronicity during the helo's landing—he'd been masterful. Then they'd talked for hours and hours aboard the cutter despite her exhaustion, and more when they were both ashore, with flirtatious emails in between.

The twinkle lights strung from the ceiling fans...twinkled. The graybeard quartet actually found the harmony on *I Saw Mommy Kissing Santa Claus.* The laughter rippled around the bar in a slow wave while the storm raged somewhere outside in a land Hailey didn't care about at the moment.

"You thinking that you're gonna get lucky tonight, sailor?"

Hailey leaned back enough to look up into Sly's brown eyes. "Isn't that *my* line?"

Sly grinned down at her. "You weren't picking it up fast enough."

"You haven't even kissed me yet."

"Lightning," he whispered.

"What? No man has ever been this slow about kissing me before. Definitely not fast as lightning."

"Wasn't talking about that."

"What are you talking about, Surfer Boy?"

"This," and he leaned down to kiss her.

The chill of the frigid Pacific roaring outside the tavern faded away. As right as landing his helo on the pitching deck. One moment fighting the storm...

And now?

Safe on deck.

Maybe it would be her wedding next Christmas. Right here.

———

For the complete collection of USCG romances, get the whole collection at: https://shop.mlbuchman.com/collections/other-stories

THE APPLE TART OF EDEN

Rosh Hashanah is the Jewish New Year. When I was reading up on it, I discovered that it is also the traditional anniversary of the creation of Adam and Eve. When I discovered that apples served with honey were a traditional food of the New Year's feasting, we Jews do like our feasting, this story became inevitable.

It is naturally set in my Deities Anonymous universe. It's a behind-the-scenes view of how our world works. Joshua, the One God has creation privileges in the Software that Runs the Universe. The Devil has update and delete privileges but, as she and Joshua don't get along very often, our world is far more non-sensical than the designers intended.

This is a small peak through the door into that universe.

1

―――――

THE POUNDING IN THE BACK OF THE DELI ECHOED THE POUNDING in Anne's head. Retired gods and goddesses weren't supposed to get colds, but this one had certainly slammed their household. She and Joshua had finally closed up the deli and retreated to their upstairs apartment, because there were limits after all—even if she was the one who always had to set them.

But tomorrow was Rosh Hashanah and a Jewish deli couldn't be closed the day before the Jewish New Year.

She rubbed at her aching forehead, surprised as always not to find her crown there. She hadn't worn the thing in over two millennia, and still she missed it. There were times she wished she'd kept it, but it had been much more satisfying to heave it in Zeus' face when she'd dumped his sorry behind. After all, it wasn't being married to him that had made her the Mother Goddess Hera; that had been by divine right from Mom and Dad. Well, Mom anyway. Dad had been something of a jerk as well. *Why do we always marry in our father's image?* Pointless path that she wasn't going to think about again...until next time.

After booting Zeus and his latest gaggle of sycophantic

nymphs off Mount Olympus, Hera had played around a bit, but ultimately moved in with the One God.

She only regretted doing so whenever he was sick—Joshua could be such a *qvetch* when he was ill. *Oy vey,* did that man know how to complain. But he was a sweetie at heart.

Anne moved the hands of the plastic clock-sign on the front door to announce they were opening again at noon. Six hours would be plenty of time to set everything to rights. Normally she could do it faster, but it was her first day back on her feet and she wasn't feeling any too quick about it.

She'd started going by "Anne"—the French form of Hannah, which was close enough, but not too close to Hera— shortly after they'd opened a nice Jewish deli out in the countryside not far from Paris. They rode out the Crusades right through the Dark Ages and the Age of Exploration there. Louis had built Versailles nearby and he often stopped in for a cuppa and a piece of rugelach. She'd loved France, but the bloody revolution had been too reminiscent of the testosterone-poisoned Spartans for her taste.

Seattle was a nice change. A little rustic at first, but it had very few wars and even fewer guillotines.

Joshua was still down with the cold—indulging his sniffles as if he was a mortal and his life was ending—but Anne had come down to the deli to tend to the things that couldn't wait. Without much hope she told her lingering headache to please go away because she couldn't face taking another pill or one more swallow some sickly sweet syrup—Nyquil was so completely not the nectar of the Gods.

The cool morning glittered beyond the rain-washed windows. The trees of Ravenna Boulevard had soaked up all of the Seattle sunshine they were going to receive for a while, and were now contemplating the long rains of fall. That reminded her, Persephone soon would be returning to her winter home as Queen of the Underworld beside that old letch Pluto. Anne really must remember to go visit her before she went back to Hades for the winter—snowbirding was fine, but Pluto kept the thermostat far too high for Anne's taste.

The pounding against the back room delivery door started again; she'd forgotten about it. There was a desperate need for coffee, so she quickly started a pot as she crossed behind the long glassed-in case that would soon be brimming with potato salad, knishes, carrot cake, and other Jewish delicacies.

"I'm coming. I'm coming," she shouted out and then wished she hadn't when her headache swelled to proportions she'd thought only Zeus could ever produce. Maybe she *should* go back to bed.

Past the pickle barrel, which her nose was still too stuffed up to smell, and through the swinging doors into the back storeroom which swooshed back and forth behind her.

She unbolted the rear delivery door...but there was no one there. No one driving away up or down the narrow alley. The backyards of houses, parked cars, the deli's Dumpster and recycle bins. The alley was empty except for Myrtle Thomas who waved a greeting as she raced the engine on her Toyota Corolla. She might look like everyone's favorite granny, but she drove with all the panache of Apollo racing his chariot across the heavens and far more style.

Inside the deli, the banging continued.

Anne traced it to behind a pile of boxes a few steps along the kitchen's rear wall. She unstacked several cases of sauerkraut, another of #10 cans of beets, and several cases of those little plastic knives for when customers wanted their bagel and cream cheese to go.

Behind all of those she unearthed a small door, half the size of a normal one. It looked to be carved of a single great slab of wood. She ran a quick hand over the rough surface. Applewood? This hadn't been here before. At least not that she could recall.

The beating on the other side continued.

Rather than a knob or a lock, there was simply a handle carved right into the wood.

She pulled on it.

The miniature door swung open and sunlight flooded into the deli's kitchen and storeroom. Sunlight wrapped in the smells of the harvest. Apple and pear, hazelnut and pomegranate swept into the kitchen and danced merrily in the corners. The sun from this door had an entirely different quality than the wet glitter of the Seattle sunshine. It washed away her headache and the last of her chills.

What in Hade—

"About time," a gruff voice snarled from beyond the threshold. A small man sat cross-legged on the dirt, rubbing at his knuckles as if to see whether or not they had been damaged by his prolonged beating on the door. He was perhaps the leanest man she'd ever seen: narrow-faced, arms and legs so thin they were almost vestigial. He was dirty and wore only a ragged loin cloth made of...goodness, scales. It looked quite uncomfortable.

His eyes traveled up and down her body, dwelling overlong at her chest. "Nice," he mumbled to himself. "Old Joshua finally caught himself a cute one."

"Cute? I'm not cute." As the Goddess Hera she'd been known for being one of the three great beauties of Grecian lore. She'd have been known as the *one* great beauty if Aphrodite hadn't blatantly bribed the contest judge Paris with the promise of bedding Helen of Troy. The fact that he'd turned down Hera's gift to be king of all Europe and Asia only proved how ill-chosen he was as a judge. To add insult to injury, it had been her husband Zeus who had chosen the young prat as judge in the first place.

Of course she couldn't say any of that to this wizened stranger.

"Cute," the old man insisted. "Bet you're even cuter out of those clothes. Care to prove me wrong?"

"Care to get kicked?"

"Not really," he grimaced. "I get that quite enough as it is."

"I'm so surprised."

He leered once more, but it didn't carry to his voice, "You showed your breasts enough to marble carvers and painters over the years. Why not me?" Instead he sounded sullen.

"Most of them were just making it up. The only ones who —" Anne breathed in sharply. Her vanity as a young goddess had led her to pose early on for hundreds of statues and paintings of the Goddess Hera. But Anne, wife of Joshua, was a far more discreet woman. There wasn't a single authentic depiction of her more mature years. "Wait! You know who I really am?"

"Aw, get a clue, sweet cheeks. Joshua and I go way back. Where is the lucky wretch who gets to squeeze these apples?" He made grab-and-squeeze motions toward her chest.

Anne was on the verge of slamming the door in his face, but then she caught another whiff of the harvest-scented air through the low frame. Birds sang and cooed there. Even though it shared a wall with the normal-sized delivery entrance, it opened onto a much more vibrant world. One she didn't recognize.

Beyond the narrow path of dust on which the little old man sat, lush growth flourished beneath a bright sun. It wasn't hot on her sandaled toes, but just ever so pleasantly warm. Her feet hadn't been properly warm since she'd departed Greece and left it to those callous Roman louts. Anne knew that she and hers hadn't exactly been models of decorum, but the Roman gods were truly cads.

"He's sick," though she'd roust Joshua soon despite his whining. They had a deli to run and now this little man to deal with.

"Well, if he wants his delivery, he'd better show up soon. They're ripe now."

"What are? I can take the delivery."

"No, lady, you can't."

Then he reached out a thin hand, shot a final leer at her, and pulled the applewood door shut. It slammed into place with a surprising amount of force. She tried to pull it open, she hadn't bent down to see farther through the low door and now regretted the missed opportunity.

It wouldn't budge.

2

———

"I'm dying here."

"You can't die. You're immortal, remember?" Hera pulled the sheets off her husband.

He made a grab for her that proved he was far from death's door but she wasn't having any patience with that at the moment.

"Come," she captured the hand that had been aimed at her behind and used it to leverage him to his feet. "Shower and shave. There's a delivery waiting for you."

"What delivery?" he moped his way into the bathroom after she dodged his next move. She began stripping the bed to emphasize her point. Besides, after days laying abed with their two brutal colds, it was definitely time for clean sheets.

"He wouldn't say," she stuffed the sheets into the hamper. "A skinny and dirty old man."

Joshua stuck his round face back out around the door jamb, his balding pate and ruffle of white hair looked friendly and grandfatherly on him. "How dirty?"

"He made a whole thing about wanting to see my breasts."

Joshua grinned, "Can't blame him, you have great ones;

especially for a woman in her fifth millennium. Want to join me in the shower?"

"Had one already this morning, dear. He was also filthy. Scrawny little man wallowing in the dust. And you have some explaining to do about..." She trailed off. Joshua's face had gone as white as his hair.

"You saw...*him?*"

"Behind the little applewood door."

"But how? No one but me can see him and...well, one other who hasn't spoken to either of us since."

"Goddess. Wife. Hello. I could see every time Zeus cheated on me just as clearly as I can see you have some explaining to do. You weren't the only god to think up the All-Seeing Eye."

"I'll be right out." And he was gone. By the sound of his morning ablutions, he was now in a hurry.

She strolled into the bathroom—tiled-marble white and lit-sunshine yellow—and called over the noise of the shower.

"Who is he?"

"What?"

Anne knew she'd spoken plenty loud enough to be heard.

She flushed the toilet.

He yelped.

Mortal plumbing did have its side benefits.

"He's nobody."

However, there was one problem with mortal plumbing in this situation, you had to wait for the tank to refill.

She could be patient—when it suited her. So she waited.

Then she flushed again.

"Okay, okay!" he cried out in desperation. "Hold on a moment."

Much of his skin was beet red when he came out of the shower and began toweling off. He wasn't the prettiest god with his rounded shape and little Jewish belly, but he was hers and if she hadn't already stripped the sheets, she just might let him take her back to bed.

Having lost the leverage of the flushing toilet, she folded her arms, just below her breasts to emphasize them, and waited him out. He pulled on the blue underwear with white snowflakes that she'd bought him last year, then his typical gray khakis, button-down white shirt, and loafers.

She offered him a morning hug in apology and kissed him on both the cheeks.

Joshua tried to hurry off, but Anne had anticipated that move and leaned against the closed bathroom door.

"Now talk."

"I hate to keep him waiting. He's not very patient."

"A trait he shares with *your WIFE!*" She raised her voice enough that the walls bowed steeply outward. The trees along Ravenna began shedding their leaves a month early for the hard winter to come, and the Earth hiccupped in its orbit. Scientists would have a new couple hundredths of a leap-second to explain with yet more papers published about the previously undiscovered truths of quantum flux.

Joshua fetched a couple of Q-tips to clean his ears.

"Wow!" he complimented her and leaned in to give a kiss.

She accepted the kiss and caught his hand as it traveled from her backside, where it belonged, to the doorknob, where it definitely didn't. A quick twist on his pinkie made her point.

He retreated, nursing his hand.

"It's a long story."

Anne knew about his long stories. She was glad she'd started the coffee; this was definitely going to require a fresh pot.

3

———

Joshua was slipperier than she'd anticipated. While Anne was preparing his coffee in his favorite ceramic mug—a misshapen old thing with the phrase *Simha,* Joy, painted on it that he'd picked up at Jericho—and toasting his bagel, he'd slipped into the back storeroom without her.

She rushed through the swinging doors and caught Joshua and the skinny old man in mid-exchange. They were on their respective sides of the applewood door, both scowling down at a basket overflowing with the most lovely apples that rested exactly half in one world and half in another.

Hera had never been a big fan of apples. Not since her daughter Eris, the Goddess of Discord, had tossed that apple "for the fairest of all" that led to the Judgment of Paris mess in the first place and the whole Trojan War disaster afterward. You didn't need to be the prophetess Cassandra to see that coming. In retrospect she felt rather bad about it.

"Good crop this year," Joshua said in a neutral voice he was rarely able to achieve.

"It was," the little man replied in a clipped tone.

"Thanks."

The man shrugged.

Men. If Hera lived to be a million, which she was going to, she'd never understand men.

"About time you introduced me," Anne moved forward causing both men to jump guiltily. She knew the One God had any number of things to be guilty about, but why was a basket of apples among them?

"Hi, Anne," Joshua looked about for an escape, but apparently couldn't find one. Besides, she was quicker on her feet than he was and he knew it.

The little man kicked at the dust.

Joshua fidgeted uncomfortably.

"Hi, Ahv!" A tiny angel popped into being and fluttered around the basket. "Is it that time of year again already?" Henrietta.

Anne did her best not to sigh too deeply. The tiny sprite always *meant* well.

Her equally tiny halo was mostly lost in her brown curly locks as she flew about and inspected the apples carefully. Finally, after a long running self-dialogue on their fine form and which Pantone color swatch they matched, she settled with a flitter of her wings to sit on the topmost one.

The ninth-choir angel continued to chatter, her one great skill. "These are wonderful, Ahv. Do you remember the crop the year Cleopatra needed all that help? Awful year for apples. I can tell that these are nice and firm," she tapped a tiny bare foot on the next apple below her perch to make her point. "How did you deal with the drainage problems?"

"Drainage problems?" Joshua managed in a strained voice.

Anne had learned long since that keeping her mouth shut around the chatty little angel was the only real hope of finding a way back *out* of the conversation.

"Of course drainage problems. His orchard has taken a horrible amount of work to maintain."

"His orchard has only two trees in it."

"And the garden. Besides they're really important trees. How would you like to be fighting an infestation of beavers? Well, it's not actual beavers, but the Iraqis have dammed and undammed the Tigris and the Euphrates in so many places that…"

Anne sat down on a stack of boxes of non-dairy creamer. From here she could see to either side of the small man too thin to fill the doorframe. Beyond him she could see lush gardens rampant with growth. Blackberry vines interlaced with bush beans which were overrunning a carrot patch. And though nicely weeded, the carrot tops were wilted from overwatering.

Hand-hacked drainage ditches criss-crossed throughout the expansive garden. Two enormous old apple trees framed the background. It was hard to imagine the thin man doing all that on his own.

Henrietta had moved on to fishes and butterflies falling in love and something about only parrots being able to solve the issue.

Anne began feeling sorry for the man in the garden and not merely because of Henrietta's suddenly lecturing on the "fruitfulness" of vegetables.

"Why don't you get some help?" Anne did her best to regain control of the conversation.

"Ask him!" Ahv jabbed a finger at her husband.

Joshua again shifted nervously from one foot to the other. He only did that when he'd done something bad.

"Joshua?"

"I might, well, have put a guard at the gate," he said the last in a great rush.

"Cherubim and a flaming sword!" Ahv hissed out.

"Oh *skatá!*" Anne didn't curse often, but at the moment she was very glad she was sitting down, even if it was on non-dairy creamer.

$$4$$

<hr>

"AHV MEANS 'SNAKE' IN HEBREW," ANNE'S VOICE WAS BARELY A whisper as it slipped out. Her perch on the creamer was not very stable at the moment.

"Yes, it does," Henrietta agreed cheerfully. "Though in Ancient Hebrew the emphasis on the three sounds is actually—"

"That door. Those apples," too shocked to care about the risk of interrupting the angel in mid-flow, Anne talked right over her. "That's the Garden of Eden," she managed to point through the door.

"Well, of course it is, silly," Henrietta had stood up on her apple, placed tiny fists on tiny hips, and glared at Anne. "What do you think we've been talking about all this time?"

"You're the snake," she shifted where she was pointing.

"Genesis Chapter Three at your service," Ahv made a deep bow that actually rippled up the length of his body. "Though I prefer serpent if you don't mind. Show me your breasts and I'll be glad to tell you how they compared to Eve's," he tried to leer but didn't quite pull it off. He looked too sad.

"I thought the universe was created fourteen billion years ago. That's what you always told me," now she aimed her attention at Joshua. "Have you been lying to me all these years?" She didn't have good control of her voice. As she rose to her feet and began stalking toward Joshua the lids blew off several jars of honey and added to the sweet air that flowed through the low door.

"No, my dear. Not at all." Joshua stopped and looked uncertain how to continue.

"The universe," Henrietta chirped in, "*is* fourteen billion years old. There are just other myths…"

"Like your lovely self, my dear," Joshua tried to slip between Henrietta's words.

"…who were such commonly held belief systems that they become a new reality that is then integrated into the Universe."

"How can reality change like that?"

Henrietta shrugged, "Why do you think they use the Software that Runs the Universe? Universe maintenance is way out of our hands now; even the archangels can't deal with that one. And if they can't do it, none of the rest of us stand a chance. You know that originally the Sixth Order of angels, the Powers, were supposed to be the keepers of history? Well, every time history changed, they changed with it and *so* couldn't remember anything from before."

Anne looked down at her, "Then why do you remember?"

Henrietta shrugged until her halo lifted clear of her curls. "I dunno. Being the littlest angel, I seem to get left behind a lot."

Anne's head was back to hurting as she paced from the seeping jars of honey over to the cases of vinegar and pickling spices, and back.

Then she stopped and squinted her eyes at her husband. At a man she had come to love very dearly.

"Which tree are these apples from?"

"Well, my dear Anne, we already have eaten from the Tree of Knowledge. Courtesy of Adam, Eve, and Johnny Appleseed's hard work, those trees now grow all over the Earth."

"These apples are from the Tree of Life," the snake said. "I tried to give an apple from *each* tree to Eve, but the foolish woman couldn't wait to share Knowledge with Adam right away. Then Joshua came in and threw a fit before she could eat of the second tree."

"I was younger then," Joshua struggled in his own defense.

"Threw a fit, banned them from the Garden, *and* left me to crawl in the dirt," Ahv sounded like one very irritated serpent. Well he wasn't the only one.

Anne walked right up to Joshua until they stood nose to nose.

"You banished a *woman* from the Garden of Eden for gaining Knowledge and then wanting to share it?"

Joshua squinted at her in that way he had.

"Oh no," she knew the look.

His eyes shot wide, "I never thought of it that way."

For all of his wonderful powers and kind heart, he wasn't very well connected to the consequences of his actions.

"Joshua," she managed through gritted teeth.

"I'm sorry, Anne. Seriously, I had no idea. No wonder Eve won't talk to me."

"No wonder."

"What do I do?"

Anne looked at Joshua the One God. A sweet man at a loss for how to undo acts done when he was in one of his rare Old Testament moods.

"You could send her some apples," Henrietta suggested quietly.

Anne was shocked. It was so rare for the angel to say something on point that Anne could only be impressed.

"A great idea, Henrietta. A bit belated, but still an excellent notion."

The little angel glowed until the light off her tiny wings filled the room and competed with the sunshine streaming in through the garden door.

"There are plenty there," Anne turned to Joshua. "We can send half to Eve and still have enough for the Rosh Hashanah dinner."

Joshua nodded happily at her suggestion.

Yet Ahv the Serpent stood on the other side of the door to the Garden of Eden, little more than a sad shadow. All these eons and he'd been left to merely grovel. And garden.

"You never ate of the second tree either?"

Ahv shook his head sadly.

"Don't you think it's about time you had a Life?"

He squinted up at her, "What did you have in mind?"

"I was thinking I'd bake these apples for New Year's dinner. It is the anniversary of the creation of Adam and Eve after all."

"Remember it well," the serpent nodded his head as did Joshua.

"We're supposed to eat apples with honey to bring a sweet New Year. And we have plenty of honey that we need to use up," she pointed toward the seeping jars.

Ahv shook his head and looked down at the apples sadly. "I don't dare cross the threshold. I love my Garden. And if I leave, I've always been afraid that the Cherubim and the flaming sword won't let me return."

"I know! I know!" Henrietta waved a hand over her head and began hopping on one foot atop her apple.

"What?" Anne, Joshua the One God, and Ahv the Serpent asked in unison.

"Easy. The Cherubim got bored eons ago. They're out drinking at this brutish Pictish pub that hasn't been cleaned since Hadrian's Wall was overrun. No one's been guarding the Garden gates since forever." She clapped both hands over her mouth and mumbled out a worried, "Oh gosh! You can't tell that I told you!"

"Why not, Henrietta?" Anne asked as gently as she could.

"If you tell the Seraphim, they'll be very upset with the Cherubim for leaving their post and then the Cherubim will get all angry at me and I'm just a lowly Ninth Choir and I'm—" her voice climbed with each stage of her panic until it threatened to convert the last traces of Anne's headache into a migraine.

"We won't tell," Anne interrupted her and criss-crossed her fingers over her heart. "I promise."

"Oh. Okay." Then Henrietta subsided into a blissful silence and began humming to herself as she polished the apple next to her with the hem of her robe.

"For Rosh Hashanah dinner," Anne decided, "I'm going to use these apples from the Tree of Life to make an Apple Tart of Eden. You're all invited."

She looked directly at Ahv the Serpent.

"All of you. We will all break bread together and share a glass of wine," Anne would have to remember to water Henrietta's; otherwise she got the worst hiccups imaginable. "And we'll toast new beginnings, yes?"

Joshua nodded eagerly and smiled toward Ahv.

The dusty old man directed his smile toward her, the first true smile she'd seen cross his face since she'd met him through the door. He managed to mouth a soft, "Thank you."

Apparently uncomfortable with that, he let the smile slide into a different one that she now knew all too well.

Anne saw the question coming and was already shaking her head no before he asked it.

"Does that mean *now* I get to see your breasts?"

———

For more adventures of the Deities who wish to be Anonymous, visit: https://shop.mlbuchman.com/collections/deities-anonymous-other-sf-f

UNDERWATER CHRISTMAS

The White House Protection Force started out as a series about Secret Service dogs. Through three novels and a still growing list of short stories, it has taken many twists and turns. Though few of those is as curious as when I discovered this real-life competition.

I may have shifted the annual International Submarine Race from June to Christmas, but I liked how it reshaped the story in interesting ways.

1

Glaring at Frank Kootoo's back isn't killing him. My scowls never killed so much as a goldfish, but I keep hoping. Not exactly the Christmas spirit, but I'm past caring.

I don't know why I try, even Kryptonite couldn't kill someone like Kootoo. And confronting his ego directly would bring a whole world of pain I've got zero interest in. Especially not here and now.

Still, if he falls over dead in the immediate future I'll do a happy chicken dance. Or maybe a successful-walrus-hunt dance. Aanaa and Aataa are very traditional after all and they'd appreciate the irony. They tried to instill some of that in us grandkids, though maybe dancing on Kootoo's grave wasn't what they had in mind when passing on their traditions.

Of course my last year had been anything but traditional, especially by our hometown's standards. How many Inuit girls in Nome spent the last year designing a human-powered submarine? One. Me. No boys either, if I'm counting.

Most of my work was remote, virtual connections with the three others of our team at the University of Alaska, Fairbanks campus. That's where Frank Kootoo browbeat Carol and Kane into working with him.

And Malee makes four. Lucky me.

We're the only team without their professor, but he's down with a horrid flu, and we're here with only ourselves to count on. Still, we *are* here and the ISR, International Submarine Races, are on—which is great.

It was only the third time I'd met the team in person and Kootoo is proving to have eight more kinds of horrible in person than I ever knew. Like snow, there should be a name for every type of horrible he embodies: officious, know-it-all, smart enough that he might at least know-most, arrogant beyond belief, takes offense at imaginary...

Maybe he's been culturing new kinds just for this occasion. If so, he's an expert. But seeking the perfect eight, or eight hundred, words to describe his horriblitude only makes me think more about him when I'm trying so hard to think less.

To distract myself, I look around at all of the other submarine design teams that are gathered in the parking lot for the pre-competition photo shoot. The shoot is done now and the teams are starting to check each other out. Not our team, of course, because Kootoo has already alienated everyone nearby.

He even managed to tick off Tricky Gal the sniffer dog and her handler Bethany as we and our gear were checked for explosives. The ISR is held on a Navy base in Potomac, Maryland, so of course there's security. Only Kootoo took it personally.

Tricky never growls at anyone, Bethany had spoken in surprise as she sought to calm her German Shepherd.

She'll growl less after I've turned her into fishbait, was Kootoo's piss-off-anyone-you-can response.

Twenty-six universities from all over the world had sent teams here, hoping for a win from the Foundation of Underwater Research and Education. About half of the submarines are one-person craft, though few as tiny as ours, designed with minimal water displacement in mind. The others are big enough for two powerful athletes to be powering the drivetrain. Though MIT's massive, sixteen-foot boat is crazy to look at.

Finesse versus brute force, I still like the choices I made as our hydrodynamics designer. The overall design and the impeller are mine. Carol and Kane were the builders, and Kootoo browbeat the U of A into financing us with the very best materials. He made sure that we received everything we needed from Kevlar for building the hull to custom aluminum castings for the drivetrain to personalized athletic training for me as the backup driver. Even though he's the sophomore to us three seniors, his skills as a project manager are unquestionable.

His skills as a human being are *highly* questionable—evil space alien in a Kootoo suit. I keep waiting for the *Men in Black* to show up and exterminate him, but Will Smith never does, which is too bad; I'd love to meet him.

I smile at my own joke, which Kootoo turns in time to spot and scowl at.

I wait until he turns away again to resume my useless death-ray scowl. He reaches around to brush at one of his shoulder blades. For half a second I wonder if it's working, then I notice that he's brushing his shoulder with his middle finger just for me. If it was anyone else, I'd bet they were smiling and making a joke. Not our resident evil spirit.

It's still the first morning of the five-day event, and Kootoo has already alienated nine of the teams, three judges, and every other person he has come in contact with. He achieved all that before they'd finished checking in the teams. By the end of the competition? I make sure that my sigh is silent.

At first we other three teammates received sympathetic eye rolls from the judges, but even those are happening less and less already. Day One, Morning One, and us, the U of A Nanooks, are not only the smallest crew but also the outcast crew.

"You have the bad draw," a thick Russian voice whispered from close by my ear. His hidden laugh is almost as rich as his accent.

The whisperer is wearing a Grenoble INP Institut d'ingénierie t-shirt. He's not a big man, only a few centimeters over my own height. But he's the only other person of the hundreds here who looks like me or Frank Kootoo. His skin a shade lighter than my dusky Native coloring, but he has the prominent cheekbones, narrow eyes, and long face of my own people.

"The very bad luck of the draw," I reply...after checking that Kootoo is well out of earshot. He's on the other side of the crowded parking area scowling at the University of Washington's entry and will be annoying their team past reason within seconds.

"I fix this. Come." He snags my arm and leads me toward the people-sized door between the closed roll-up garage doors without asking. Massive US Navy-blue letters above the doors declare *David Taylor Model Basin*. A giant wreath below the name marks that Christmas is fast approaching. Many of the teams are shivering, but Maryland is thirty degrees warmer than Nome and forty above Fairbanks this time of year. Not a single Nanook has zipped their parka; it's barely freezing.

My Russian from Grenoble, France guides me with a half smile that dares me to yank my arm free and return to face whatever new disaster Kootoo is creating.

"Fine. So fix it already."

"Oh, him? No. I don't fix him. I fix you."

I plant my feet firmly which pulls my arm free from his grasp. "I don't need fixing." I know he was flirting with me, a lot of boys do that and I'm fine with flirting back. But I like me the way I am. Mother often forgets that I'm twenty, not seven, but she is the only one I let get away with that.

"Sure you do," he gets behind me and shoos me forward like coaxing a seal pup back to its mother. "You need to join my tour group so that you are away from the bad luck draw for long enough to remember where you are."

I look at the building once more. He's right. I made it here, which is *beyond* amazing.

The scientists and operators of the DTMB are indeed putting together tour groups. The submarine teams range from our four-person squad of Nanooks, to massive eighteen-person teams from Cal Tech, MIT, and the University of Vancouver. Mixed groups of thirty at a time are being led inside. It was with only a minor pang of guilt that I leave Carol and Kane to deal with Frank Kootoo.

He's merely awful to them; for me he has a special barb in his soul. Like he'd be happier if a seal harpoon suddenly sprouted from my chest—starting from my back. For at least several tenths of a second I weigh the unknown Russian's smile against having a break from being Kootoo's primary target, then wave for him to lead the way.

Besides, I've spent a year *dreaming* of walking into this building.

I had studied the DTMB as much as possible, but the reality is so much more.

"Built in 1938," our group's tour leader announces, "the David Taylor Model Basin is the largest of its kind in the world. This basin and its predecessor, built in 1896, have been the testing pool for almost every major US hull design in the last hundred and twenty years. We do water testing for ships and submarines—both military and commercial. The bulbous forefoot on world's largest cargo and cruise ships was developed here. Ships, destroyers, aircraft carriers, and even patrol boats were first built as models and tested here. Even many generations of America's Cup sailing boats. However, any rumors that we did underwater testing for Santa's sleigh to deliver Christmas to submarines on patrol will neither be confirmed nor denied."

He earns his laugh, then keeps rattling on about the history I already know as I try to take it all in.

The building is a kilometer long and shaped like a road tunnel—a half-pipe of concrete arcs above us. No windows. "Blocking the sunlight keeps down algae growth in the pool," our guide tells us. Lights are generally low, giving the tunnel-shaped space a shadowed, mysterious feel. Christmas lights do add cheer though.

The pool itself is well lit and it's the whole reason DTMB exists.

Fifteen meters wide and varying from three to seven meters deep. Nine hundred meters long, it holds twenty-five Olympic swimming pools worth of water. The *singular* swimming pool in Nome is only one-quarter of an Olympic pool, and uses salt water rather than fresh. I can only hope that my model testing holds up. Extrapolating from a carved block of wood with some added metal weights, that I dragged around the pool at the end of a handheld fish scale as a dynamometer to test drag, to a computer model, and then to a finished submarine could be a total fiasco. The actual tests of the finished submarine in the University of Alaska, Fairbanks, Patty Pool weren't much more helpful as it was only half-Olympic in size.

The tour guide continued, "Special carriages run above the water—on stainless steel tracks that are arced by five centimeters, that's two inches—along the whole length of the pool. We do this, because the water's surface curves that much in a kilometer to match the curvature of the Earth. We can move a model through the water at a constant depth of immersion, and run at speeds of up to fifty knots, on the surface or submerged. It's all fully instrumented so that we can study hull flow, cavitation, and any other necessary properties. Your submarines will be moving much slower, of course."

Omer II holds the record of traveling the length of the pool at 6.85 knots, 7.9 miles per hour. The École de technologie supérieure (ÉTS) team from Montreal is back this year and I so want to beat them.

Yes, I want the Speed Award.

I'd love the Overall Design Award, but have given that up seeing some of the other subs. Our sub looks cobbled by comparison with several others that look like they were built at a Naval shipyard they're so perfect.

What I *covet* is the Innovation Award; but that is also probably out of my reach.

Before the races have even started, we've already placed last in the Best Team Spirit Award, so I decide not to worry about that one.

The rest of the tour is a blur as I wish for the Christmas present of winning at least the Speed Award. Maybe even taking over the world record in the process.

The guide leads us down a flight of stairs to the big windows at mid-pool so that each passing craft can be observed from the side as well. At the far end is a forty-meter square tank for testing hulls during turns. Through a metal door into an adjacent warehouse there are towering racks of the models that have been built and tested here. They range from a meter long to massive ten-meter ones for detailed testing of the biggest ship designs. We breeze past them in thirty seconds. I wish I could find the designer of each one to spend a day discussing what they learned.

The Russian gave me his name, which I instantly forgot. Or maybe I never heard. No, we must have exchanged names because he's used mine several times.

His running commentary of small jokes doesn't let me forget about him. As we return down one side of the pool, I can see Kootoo in another group going the opposite way on the other side.

There is a large bubble of empty space around him. No surprise there.

He's glaring Ahab-sized harpoons at me. No surprise there either.

"How can one person be so offensive?"

"Years of practice, Malee Ashoona," my Russian friend jokes. "Years of practice." He always says my last name as if it is somehow more important than my first.

That's when I finally think to look at his ID badge: Vlad Qarpik.

I know several Qarpiks. They have visited Nome from across the *Ice Curtain* of the Bering Sea. For most of the last thirty years since the collapse of the Soviet Union, Alaska natives and those of Russia's Chukchi Peninsula can visit relations without expensive and difficult to obtain visas. My grandparents renewed old friendships with several of the Russian families including the Qarpiks.

I *should* like Vlad for my grandparents' sake; a task that I decide won't be difficult at all. When I switch our conversation from English to Inuktitut, his Russian accent is almost undetectable.

2

Our entry is the *Nanook*—Kootoo insisted that our submarine be the *Polar Bear* after the University of Alaska Nanook mascot because he has all the imagination of a beached whale. I wanted *Natsiq* because I had designed our submarine to be smooth and fast like a seal. And it resembles a seal when it is swimming underwater: a sleek, tapered torpedo. I had decided that I could do far worse than copying Sedna, the Mother of the Sea's design.

During the final planning, I found out that Frank couldn't read or speak Inuktitut or any of our native languages. I had Carol and Kane work *Natsiq* into the paint design below *Nanook*. When evil Kootoo had asked, I'd simply said it was the submarine's name using the Inuktitut syllabary. As I was telling the truth, he detected nothing out of place.

After the tours and lunch, the first afternoon of the races is utter mayhem.

Twenty-six submarines get launched into the massive tank as fast as each team can clear their entry down the ramp of the dry dock. Hundreds of students, team advisors, and DTMB safety personnel are all kitted up in full scuba gear as we begin our testing. University of Virginia's submarine instantly sinks to the bottom of the tank. University of Sussex's sub won't sink at all, bobbing about like a cork.

As teams work on each of their individual issues, I'm glad to see that, with only minor adjustments to the ballast tanks, *Natsiq* floats well and holds its two-meter depth.

I wait until Carol and Kane are submerged with the submarine before speaking to Kootoo as nicely as I can. "Don't show off, Frank. We want to keep our abilities as a surprise. And I need to tune the drive. I've never seen it really work before."

He offers a sea walrus grunt before we both bite down on our regulators and ease underwater to float beside *Natsiq*.

Despite being an inlander—Fairbanks campus lies two hundred and fifty miles and a mountain range from the nearest ocean—Frank Kootoo has incredible endurance. Though we're much the same size, I was never able to match his power in the tests. *Natsiq* needs more finesse than power, but telling Kootoo that had not placed me in the cockpit. It is the one role he claimed for himself as our project manager. Now I'm left to worry how much of the glory he will take for himself over the next five days.

Most of the smaller submersibles place the human pilot face down. The design can be slimmer for a prone driver than a sitting one. This also places their feet by the rear propeller shortening the drivetrain and saving weight and complexity. Their faces are in a small bubble-window at the bow. But the position makes it very awkward to pedal.

The larger ones, typically with two pedaler-pilots, sit upright, either side-by-side or in tandem. They make up for the longer-heavier drivetrain with more power.

I had spent hours balancing myself in different positions on sawhorses in our garage back home, measuring how much power I could apply for how long, to a set of bicycle pedals.

Then I repeated the whole exercise in the pool, nearly drowning myself twice.

The recumbent cycling position won hands-down.

In *Natsiq* the driver sits comfortably, back braced against a mesh seat, and is able to see because the entire upper section is clear acrylic. And with my drivetrain, the point at which the power itself gets generated is irrelevant as half of the drive is at the bow and half at the stern. I sacrificed a few kilos of mass in exchange for an entirely new thrust system.

Most of the submarines use some form of a propeller. Fat blades like an outboard motor, thin blades like an airplane propeller, even a *hélice monopale* single-blade which solves numerous complex flow issues. A few use flapping mirage blades that wash back and forth like paired underwater wings. There is nothing here like my circular impellers.

Kootoo hands off his tanks to Kane, bites down on the regulator attached to the on-board air tank and slips into *Natsiq*. He is barely clamped in under the hatch when he takes off. It's a good thing I didn't use a traditional propeller or one of us might have been hurt.

He recklessly sweeps down the pool's length, scattering other teams. Safety inspectors begin to shout, to no effect as Kootoo is underwater and has left the rest of us far behind.

I'm glad that I didn't show him the real trick to gain speed. Even so, he's ruined most of my surprise.

Then, since we haven't had a chance yet to fine tune the systems, I can see him drifting off course and rising.

My shout spits out my regulator mouthpiece, and I have to surface as I choke out my rage. Kootoo surfaces just in time for me to see him ram the University of Sussex's sub broadside— which, after being stuck on the surface, now sinks abruptly.

3

MY GOAL OF HIDING IN MY HOTEL ROOM UNTIL THE END OF THE apocalypse, or at least until after the races and Christmas, is foiled by Vlad before I even leave DTMB.

"No. The hiding is not good. You are not some seal and he is not a polar bear waiting to eat you."

"No, it only feels that way."

"Exactly!"

Vlad is right. If I sit in the room that Carol and I are sharing, I'll stew about Kootoo on the other side of the thin hotel wall.

Instead of spending an afternoon finally testing and tuning our entry, we spend it helping the University of Sussex fix theirs.

All of our submarines are *wet,* filled with water except for the stream of bubbles rising off the on-board scuba gear. They purposely aren't watertight. This is good because the University of Sussex's boat would never be truly tight again after Kootoo rammed it.

Kane, Carol, and I spent the rest of the afternoon helping them refit their sub. They almost rebuffed our offer. But they calmed down when Kane spotted why they were having buoyancy issues—the flight over from the UK had expanded several air pockets in their lightweight honeycomb fiberglass, which hadn't collapsed on landing. A few judicious holes drilled, the honeycomb compressed, and then the holes patched had solved their excessive buoyancy issues. I also showed them a trick to gain ten percent more power by adding two springs to balance out drive lash and we ended up getting along.

While I was doing this, Kootoo had made several runs at me about the flaky buoyancy trim of *Natsiq*. *Why aren't you working on something important, like fixing our submarine instead of theirs, Ashoona?*

Do trolls have nine lives? I mean if my glare finally kills him, will he come back eight more times?

And now that I'm done helping fix Sussex's sub, he's after me again.

"Why aren't you staying to fix ours now that you've wasted all afternoon helping someone else?"

Before I can waste time explaining to evil-Kootoo that Day One is over and they're starting to chase us out of the building, Bethany the dog handler had strolled up with Tricky Gal. Her German Shepherd, having a good memory, has a snarl ready for Kootoo.

He opens his mouth, then shuts it very quickly when a male handler walks up with a massive Russian Bear Dog. The dog's head is even with Kootoo's gut and probably weighs more than he does even under all that fur.

"Get these stupid beasts—" is as far as Kootoo gets before the big dog unleashes a bark that echoes hard off the rounded ceiling and silences the entire length of the pool.

Kootoo stumbles away, plunging backward into the pool several feet below.

Of course *he* hasn't been hurt. But everyone is delayed because he breaks the arm of one of University of Warwick's swimmers who he landed on.

Carol and Kane are nowhere to be seen. Keeping out of target range, I suppose. The moment the day was declared done, they evaporated.

And I, now that the medics are gone…

"Yes," I looked at Vlad. "Get me out of here fast." Because I could guarantee that Kootoo would find some way to make everything my fault if he found me again.

As good as his word, Vlad had me out the door and into a taxi faster than I could catch my breath. Good thing the evening wasn't cold enough to zip my parka because he didn't leave me enough time for that.

"Thai or Irish?"

"Let's see. In Nome I have a choice of seafood, pizza, seafood, a couple of Chinese places, or seafood. Though there are some good food carts for the Iditarod finish line each year, mostly serving seafood or seafood." In fact, the farthest I've ever been from Nome was to Anchorage for scuba training.

"Meaning?"

"Meaning I have no idea from either one."

"That is meaning the Irish stew we get."

The driver nods and we're on our way.

"Ashoona, huh?" He asks when we settle in the restaurant.

The Irish Inn at Glen Echo has dark wood floors and tables. Twinkle lights and wreaths are tasteful in a way never seen in Nome. And even before I look at the menu, the rolled linen napkins on the white tablecloths tells me that this place is crazy way out of my budget. None of the other diners are dressed in student garb after a day of diving in a Navy boat basin.

Vlad doesn't miss my expression and insists that it's his treat. "You can buy us pizza tomorrow."

Like, of course, we're going to be sharing dinner tomorrow. I'm at a loss. But when I order a safe cheeseburger, he shakes his head so sadly that I tell him to order for me. He goes straight to one of the most expensive items, the Guinness Beef Stew, and a Banger Plate for himself. Maybe he'll hit himself on the head with it.

He also orders two of something called black-and-tans. When they come, I don't point out to the waiter that I'm not twenty-one yet. A Christmas baby, I will be in another seven days. And I'd still love some award from the ISR sitting under the tree—other than Most Reviled Team in History.

Besides, I'm intrigued, the light and dark beers float separately in the same glass, brown-black on top and pale below.

"Different specific gravities," Vlad explains.

I tip the glass slightly side-to-side to inspect the stability of the boundary-layer mixing. More stable than cream in coffee, but less than ice on the sea. Perhaps a slush-water boundary state, stable until disturbed.

"Watch as you drink it, too. The volume shift will change their ratios as you drink and it changes all the flavor. It begins heavy dark. Then more light as the layer of Bass Ale arriving from underneath."

My first taste is dark enough to chew. And only now do I realize that rescuing me probably wasn't Vlad's first priority. Was he thinking this is a date? I try to think of why I'm letting him *rescue* me so easily? That too isn't hard. He's like a sight of home in a blizzard. Until yesterday's flights, I had never been out of Alaska.

"Qarpik, huh?" I move the conversation back to where he'd started it. It will let me talk about home. It doesn't take long to figure out that we aren't related, but that my grandparents and his go way back as friends and that we each have relatives who live near the other.

"Okay, I guess that means that we are fated to meet," Vlad announces as the food arrives.

"Sure, you and I grew up under two hundred miles apart. Yet I had to travel four thousand miles across North America…"

"And I must travel twenty thousand kilometers across Russia, Europe, and the Atlantic Ocean. So, yes, of course, it was fates." Vlad nods as if assuring me that it all makes sense.

"Are you sure it wasn't a *Qualupalik* that brought you here?"

Vlad laughed and it is the laugh of home. Not some great roar that might scare off game, but it came from deep inside. "Do you think that if the child-thieving mermaid had captured me, she would let me go so easily?"

"She must have had some reason. Maybe it is your Russian accent that gave her indigestion." Of course we're having the whole meal in Inuktitut, so his accent is of the Bering Sea Inuit, not Russia.

"Or maybe too pretty to keep."

Now it is my turn to laugh. He is. Handsome and funny.

And it is only when he kisses me outside the room that what he really meant sinks in—he meant me maybe being too pretty for *Qualupalik* to keep.

I know I'm pretty enough. I have my mother's curves and grandmother's straight fall of black hair. I'm fine featured for an Inuit. Boys are always attracted to my body.

But his kiss is only partly about that.

Vlad and I had sat for hours past the bread pudding topped with Baileys Irish Cream dessert, talking fluid viscosity, ramifications of how we each calculated the Froude number for our speed-length ratios, even thermal and pressure effects on composite versus acrylic surfaces.

I let the kiss melt me down like spring thaw, knowing we only have five days together. Four, one is already gone.

I'm past caring when I float into my room with Carol.

She and Kane are asleep under a blanket on the couch.

Avoiding evil Kootoo. I always knew they were both smart. I turn off the TV quietly playing *White Christmas*—I hadn't realized they were Bing Crosby musicals kind of mushes—and crawl into bed.

Somehow, the disaster that reigned supreme for so much of the day no longer touches me.

4

───────

The feeling lasts precisely ten minutes after I get up for Day Two.

"No sign of Frank," Kane announces after going to his own room for a quick change and shower.

I know what evil Kootoo has done. He's decided that he knows best and has worked through the night *improving* my poor innocent *Natsiq*. I should have made sure he left when the rest of us did rather than escaping while the medics were carting away the injured Warwick student. I should have talked to the security teams at DTMB to make sure that none of us would be allowed back into the building. Except they had already said that.

We trade grim looks.

Kootoo has done it before, and been wrong in so many ways.

Day Two will be spent undoing whatever he's done. If it's bad, we could well miss the maneuverability trials today, having already missed the shakedown opportunity.

Even Vlad's cheery wave from the bus that picks us up does nothing to brighten the gloom. No snow in Potomac, Maryland.

No White Christmas. And no merriness under the tree next week if we fail.

Vlad tries a hug when we unload at the Basin, but even that doesn't shake loose my own personal cloud.

The feeling is...*Qapalaqijuq*—whiteout.

I'm out on the ice. There is no snow, no sea, and the sky is hazed white, masking the sun. I can see for miles, except there's nothing to see. The disorienting, flat-light whiteout can send the most seasoned hunter walking in endless circles because the ice and the sky are a single color, a single surface. I can see for kilometers, but the light is so unrevealing that without the horizon I can't keep my balance.

Disaster in every direction I look.

Yet *Natsiq* is in her cradle precisely where we left her last night.

Her bow is still crumpled from ramming the University of Sussex's submarine.

All four of our wetsuits and tanks are lined up together. I check, Kootoo's is dry.

Kane and Carol work on the bow while I go through the rest of the systems. Nothing is out of order. Kootoo crashed so quickly that it isn't even worth topping up the on-board air tank.

In fact, inside an hour, *Natsiq* is ready and the only thing still unaccounted for is Frank Kootoo.

"You sure he wasn't in the room?"

Kane shakes his head and whispers. "Guy's a slob, but there wasn't a wrinkle on either bed."

"Maybe he got lucky?"

Carol shuddered. "Ick! Who would want to touch..." she looked around quickly and lowered her voice further "...*that.*"

No one I could imagine.

"He's gotten way worse than when we started."

"I thought that was just me."

Carol shook her head. I wasn't sure how Carol and Kane had survived being on the same campus with him. I was hundreds of miles away for almost the entire project. Like Vlad, I was the team's design engineer—though his team had three.

By lunch, there is still no sign of Kootoo.

I consider calling the police or the hospital, but I don't want them to find him. I want to drive in the International Submarine Race. Doing it without him? Happy walrus-hunt dance.

We're bumped to the back of the queue because we're missing our registered sub driver.

We keep our silence, finally no longer able to meet each other's eyes. We fuss with *Natsiq* while waiting for the other shoe to drop.

But it doesn't.

Finally, we can't wait any longer and I enter the water as the primary driver. I change out the regulator in the sub for my own spare. I slip through the hatch, shedding my scuba tanks into Kane's care.

I exhale my held breath to clear the sub's regulator and then breathe in carefully. Only a few drips of water, my breathing settles quickly even if my heart rate doesn't.

Once I'm seated and belted in, they seal the hatch over my head. We take a moment to scan all directions, but the only person in view is the swimming ISR official ready to signal our start.

I finally look at Carol and Kane through the acrylic. I offer a thumbs-up and they both thump a fist on the hull for luck. They flutter their fins to swim aside and I'm floating free.

The official places three fingers into an open palm, asking about my air.

I hold up three fingers to indicate that I have three thousand psi on my gauge. Did Kootoo even breathe before he crashed? Maybe he really is an evil spirit who doesn't need air at all. Perhaps he is a *Qualupalik* come to steal *our* souls.

The official signals with an OK sign as a question which I return as a statement.

Then he points two index fingers ahead down the tank, one in the lead, telling me to go ahead and he'll follow.

I drive my right foot down.

In a pedal-powered wet sub, interior turbulence can be almost as big a problem as external. As I drive my right foot forward, special ducting circulates the excess water into the underside of my left pedal. This captures much of the right-foot energy. Rather than being a hindrance, I reuse it.

Meanwhile, the top of my left-foot water is driving water up into another duct which circulates the water downward. As my right foot bottoms out, the surge from the top of my left foot is driving against the bottom of my right. I augment this in turn as I drive down the left pedal.

Within three strokes, the pedal motion is very light, each foot doing half the work for the other—thirty-seven percent actually, but still very efficient. I will tire at least thirty-seven percent less than if I were pedaling in a chamber where the water could slosh at will.

In experiments I tried a two-foot drive like a rowing machine, but couldn't smooth out the strokes from push to pull because of the fluid dynamics.

The push-me pull-you system works so smoothly that I'm up to the first marker before I'm ready. I lose time stopping my foot motion, reversing the gear linkage, taking two strokes to slow, stop again and shift to forward, before I can safely make the turn outside the pylon.

I won't make that mistake again.

So much harder than it had looked in simulations, I twist my way down the course. Evil Kootoo had far more practice time than I did, but I quickly reconcile the differences between the calculated handling, that has filled my head these last months, versus reality. My timing smooths out quickly, and I avoid the point-losing mistake of poor depth control. The last gate is mind-bogglingly difficult. I have to pass through a gate going forward, reverse *around* the gate, then pass through it backwards.

I will definitely make some changes to the steering controls before I try that again.

After I emerge, we three slide *Natsiq* back onto her cart, and roll her up the ramp to dry out. Everyone else is waiting on us to finish before the officials can announce the results. The three of us sit in our full dive gear and drip on anyone who comes close.

Four subs missed the final reverse maneuver entirely. They simply blew through the gate and thought they were done. Another fourteen were unable to complete the maneuver. I feel less awful about my initial blunder and the difficulties with my steering setup as they list the final eight from bottom to top.

"Third!" Carol screams in my ear. Kane picks me up in a bear hug and jiggles me up and down several times.

Then they announce second for *ÉTS*. Which means—

Vlad shoots me a big grin as his team erupts in cheers.

Okay, I'll have to hate him for a while, but I return the smile and add a thumbs-up to show that I won't hold it against him for too long.

5

———

Vlad invites us out, our whole team.

His team is going to mob a local pizzeria.

"It *is* your turn to do the buying," he winks.

"No way am I buying pizza for your entire team." Though after placing third I'm very ready to celebrate.

But there still no sign of Kootoo, evil or otherwise.

With our professor still sick in Alaska and Kootoo missing, the team responsibility has fallen to me.

I promise Vlad that we'll join them after I place a few calls. It takes a half hour; no news from any of the hospitals. Out of ideas, I notify the police.

We don't we get our pizza. I figure out all too quickly that we won't be getting much sleep either. The police discover that Kootoo has been lying to us about being twenty, he's actually seventeen—obnoxious kid genius. That makes him a missing minor, which escalates everything.

I've visited the Nome police station plenty of times. I had seriously crushed on one of the patrolman only two years my senior and quickly learned that, being the youngest on the staff, he had a lot of long quiet evenings manning the desk. Other than drunk and disorderlies, not all that much happens in an isolated town of less than four thousand people. We never dared do much in the police station, but we'd sit and talk for hours while he ate my fresh-baked cookies.

We never talked like Vlad and I did last night, but he was so pretty—until he began dating Sue Renner—all blonde and skinny. After that I was done with him, though once I calmed down and got over the other version of being crushed, I never regretted those long cookie evenings.

In all that time, I never saw the inside of an interrogation room. In Potomac, Maryland I sure did. It's a dismal place: a gray table, chairs that squeak every time I shift my weight, which echoes off the concrete walls painted whiteout white.

They were very clear that we weren't being charged or under arrest. They did roust a public defender for us, but she never protested about a single question or answer. Though she took enough notes that I ended up more scared of her than the police.

The police were nice, but they kept us for hours asking details of Frank Kootoo's habits and ways. Where he'd been when we last saw him and where we'd been since. Soon the military police were involved at DTMB. Then I remembered the two dog handlers, and they were hauled out of bed as well.

We didn't detail his horribleness, but it was easy to state and have corroborated—maybe I've watched *CSI* too many times—that he was universally disliked. We then had to do our best to recall each person he had insulted or injured. It was a long list.

The kid from University of Warwick doesn't remember much other than the pain of fracturing his forearm across the sub's hull when Kootoo landed on him. He tries to shrug it off as an accident, which it was, but I can see how angry he is at having to sit on the race sidelines, too drugged to be of much use and definitely not able to swim with a cast. The shrug apparently punched through the painkillers.

I broke my arm in fourth grade gym class when I fell off the uneven parallel bars. I don't tell him that the itching begins when the painkillers wear off.

We plunge into bed just three hours before we have to wake up.

That Kane slides in with Carol didn't surprise me at all. Other than checking that Kootoo hadn't magically resurfaced, none of us want anything to do with his room.

"No sex while I'm sleeping in the same room as you two."

Carol and I took Kane's snore as an answer.

I barely have time to think of Vlad before we both collapse ourselves.

6

DAY THREE. PRESENTATION DAY STARTED OUT OKAY.

Innovation. I want the Innovation Award. Each sub team has been given twenty minutes to present what is special about their craft. I can't scribble notes fast enough.

A year ago I'd been a physics major, dreaming of getting a high school teaching job when I graduated to help finance a Master's degree that I had no idea what I'd do with. Maybe teach at University of Alaska, Fairbanks some day. No... Anchorage. I didn't want to be so far from the sea. Nome was strictly a remote-access campus, so not an option.

Then my professor had started talking about a senior project. *Design something amazing, Malee. You have the mind for it.*

Total news to me. I decided to design a submarine. I understood boats—sixteen-foot aluminum ones with an outboard engine used for hunting walrus each spring. We weren't a whaling family, but their boats were little different except for the harpoon.

I still don't know quite how I found the ISR but once I did I couldn't think of anything even half as cool. My professor found me a team at Fairbanks, and we were, literally, off to the races.

Still, it had simply been my senior project, which I was plenty competitive about because it's the sort of person I am. That all changed when I saw the video invitation to this year's races. When former ISR competitor Megan McArthur greeted us from the International Space Station and said she'd launched herself from the ISR to become a NASA scientist and pilot, I knew I had a dream.

One I hadn't even told Vlad, though it had occupied so much of my thoughts for nine months now.

McArthur said that her success came from pursuing something she loved with all her heart.

And I loved my design, but especially my drivetrain innovation.

We were presenting alphabetically, which put me in the middle of the pack. University comes late in the alphabet but Alaska was the first of the many universities represented at ISR.

The *Natsiq* was going to be the first one after lunch.

"You aren't afraid of your teammate showing up and having of all the glory?" Vlad sat down across the table from me.

Carol and Kane had taken sandwiches and wandered off somewhere.

"Not until you said that, no." Now I was. That would be so evil-Kootoo of him because he'd get twice the attention than if he'd merely tried to grab the glory as I'd expected. Hiding out until we were so worried about him that I was thinking far less of his horriblity and more of his skills as a project manager. We might be a dysfunctional team, but under his control we had built a wonderful craft with the smallest team here.

The Grenoble INP Institut d'ingénierie eleven-person team had presented early this morning. I had three pages of notes from their twenty-minute presentation. Their drive was nothing special, but they were almost sure to win Smooth Operator because of their immaculate coordination, and Team Spirit for their can-do attitude. Everybody liked their team, who were always helping out anyone who was struggling. And they were a hot contender for Overall Design because while they weren't the strongest, they had the fewest weaknesses. They'd really pulled it together as a team at every level.

"Maybe his ghosting will come to haunt you?" Vlad wiggled his fingers like an invading fog. "And maybe I will humble you completely in the speed trials."

"Only if you drag it down the pool with one of the Navy's high-speed testing carriages." The Grenoble two-person craft is actually a very fast boat. They had decided on a twin-hull configuration using dual propellers, one driven by each pedaler. No steering mechanism, instead they worked as a team and varied their pedaling rates to steer. Simplification had provided lightweight drivetrains and no steering meant fewer moving parts. Their long-blade props stuck out past the sub's turbulence so that they were always biting clear water.

And their depth control was incredible in its simplicity. They had a selectable valve for whatever pressure depth they wished to maintain. It controlled the release of air coming from the diving regulators that had accumulated in the cabin. Brilliantly simple.

"You did the depth regulator." I finally connect that fact to the focus of Vlad's interests over our one dinner together.

He bowed over his lunch tray.

"That was...elegant."

Vlad slapped a hand to his chest as if overcome. "The few. The proud."

"The Marines."

"What?" He squinted at me.

"The United States Marines. That's their recruiting slogan. I didn't know they were recruiting Russians who study in France."

Vlad scratched his head. "I'm not a fighter."

"A lover then." And the heat slammed to my face so that it burned. I had *not* just said that. We'd kissed once. That's all. Yet he'd occupied almost as much of my thoughts as *Natsiq* and Kootoo had in the last thirty hours since he'd gone missing.

I was trying to figure some way out of the flirt-hole I had just cut through the ice, without jumping in to become polar bear bait. I wasn't coming up with anything as my cheeks continued to burn.

Vlad's smile was big and growing bigger by the second.

Then something cold pressed up against my neck and I yelped as Vlad laughed.

"Sorry, he does that," a man's voice spoke behind me.

When I twisted in my seat, I was nose-to-nose with the Great Russian Bear Dog. He licked my face.

"You must be washing that before I try kissing you again," Vlad managed through a laugh.

"He never does that," the handler called for the big dog to heel. "He must like you. Don't tell my wife, she'll be jealous." The dog plomped onto his butt and was still at eye-to-eye level.

"At least he's not a polar bear."

"Wrong color," Vlad remarked.

I ignore him. I understand his growing smile now, he'd seen the dog coming.

"Could you come with us?" The handler isn't looking amused, which has the benefit of cutting off Vlad's laugh.

When I follow him and his monstrous dog, I can't help staring at the white *Police* printed in big block letters across the back of his vest. I jump when Vlad takes my hand, but I decide that I appreciate the moral support.

"Is she in trouble?"

"No, sir. Not that I know of."

I hadn't even thought of that.

He leads us down the length of the pool, past the wave

generator, which can create model-sized hurricane force turbulence in the tank when testing surface ships. We take a left around the broad square tank used for testing turn-maneuverability. There is a cluster of people gathered at the far end of the pool.

A *lot* of them have Police vests. The other patrol dog is there as well. As are Carol and Kane.

"What's going on?"

But the answer is heaved onto the side of the pool as I watch. It's the padded slip-cover Carol had made for *Natsiq* to protect it during shipping from Alaska. The color of the Alaskan Sea, it was nearly invisible in a shadowed corner of the presently unused tank. At only five feet deep, the turning tank isn't of much use for submarine testing, so no one had come by here.

On the concrete at the edge of the pool, the shipping cover looks like a beached blue seal.

Carol has turned her face into Kane's shoulder.

Vlad's strong hand is all that's sustaining my knees at the moment, but I can't look away.

They unzip the cover.

I'd know that face anywhere, it's been in enough of my nightmares.

"That's Frank Kootoo." And now I do turn to hide my face in Vlad's shoulder.

He looks so...dead. Dead and still angry about it.

Even though he's gone, I don't want to do a happy-walrus-hunt dance at all.

7

———

The day blurred on me.

"Valentin," the handler patted the Great Russian Bear Dog's head, "triggered on his scent here at the poolside. But it was so tentative that I didn't pick up on it. Sorry, boy. I missed my cue," he apologized to the dog.

A lot more questions, so I miss most of the other presentations. But I insist that I'm okay to do ours. I've had so many questions about our peculiar looking setup that I told everyone to wait for the presentation.

Of course, with all the police's questions, once again we're bumped to the end of the day. Not that I'm complaining. It has taken me all afternoon to get around the lump in my throat.

I won't miss Frank Kootoo for a second. But he's dead so I should. That I don't is messing with my head.

I test my feelings like a sore tooth. I still feel worse about my very distant Uncle Natak who was killed by that polar bear three years ago than I do about Frank Kootoo.

"I initially thought of my drive system from watching a movie called *The Core*." I start the talk in the big auditorium that is standing-room only with all of the teams and military observers. And several police keeping an eye on the crowd, which I try to ignore.

The movie reference earns me a round of unexpected laughter, including Vlad's. He sat in the front row to cheer me on. What is surprising is how much he steadies my nerves. The biggest group I've ever presented to before was my professor and the three members of my team.

The Core is a ridiculous movie scientifically. It's about an experiment that goes wrong and stops the Earth's spinning core. A team of scientists create a boring-machine ship able to drill all the way down through the crust and mantle, where they fire off a whole series of nuclear explosions to restart the core—which saves the world.

But we're all a bunch of science nerds here, so of course we've watched every science fiction movie that's science-based instead of being a monster hunt—and a lot of those if they did a decent job on the ship design and science.

"I noticed that their ship had paired, counterrotating impellers to drive the ship forward. The counterrotation is necessary so that it doesn't simply make the ship spin the other direction. But I was deeply bothered by their close coupling as the flow dynamics of the molten lava would become highly turbulated by the first set of blades, making the second set useless."

Now everyone who has seen the film is nodding their heads or squinting into the distance as they try to remember it. I show a ten-second clip of the launch where the impellers are very clear. More nods.

"It took me three months of modeling to come up with the flow design for *Natsiq*." I put a detailed image of the computed fluid dynamics of our submarine's drive up on the screen.

I try not to cringe that I'm no longer using Kootoo's *Nanook* name. Am I dishonoring the dead, even though it has always been *Natsiq* in my head? I forge on before that knot can wrap around my throat once more like a scarf wound too tightly and become frozen in place.

"Our forward impeller circles the outside of the boat at one-third of the way along the boat's length. I engineered the blade shape, and added an air bubble layer like the USS *Albatross* submarine to create a smooth flow past the forward impeller." I show a video of a smooth sheaf of air bubbles releasing directly behind the first impeller. "By disconnecting the water friction from the hull's surface, I was able to re-smooth the hydrodynamic flow for the aft impeller as well as significantly reduce drag."

There's a moment of silence and then a small round of applause. This has happened in a few of the other team's presentations and it's exciting that *Natsiq's* unique drive is getting that kind of spontaneous reaction.

I get another round of applause after detailing my pedal-enhancing ductwork.

"Steering is achieved primarily by applying a differential spin rate between the two counterrotating impellers to bank the craft, and then powering straight using the dive planes to control correction to the new course. I sacrificed three percent of the impeller's performance by making them symmetrical fore and aft. Because of this, it is equally efficient and fast in both forward or reverse. Though it needs a rearview mirror," I remind myself out loud.

Which earns me an unexpected laugh and an unprecedented third round of applause.

I include several shots of Carol and Kane machining the drive that I had designed.

And then I know what I have to do.

I put up the last image, the shot of the four of us and our professor gathered together around *Natsiq* at the U of A Fairbanks twenty-five-yard Patty Pool.

"Whatever we may each think of him," not my most tactful,

"we could never have achieved this without the project coordination provided by Frank Kootoo. May we have a moment of silence for him."

And I let the last minute of my presentation run out in a grinding silence. It not only precludes any of the summation applause that the other teams received, but also proves incredibly awkward to break.

But in the silence I figured something out—someone in the room is a murderer.

8

———

Frank Kooto's evil is far from over. Not that I'm thinking ill of the dead or anything.

Day Four is the day for the speed tests. The pool is nine hundred meters long, just under a thousand yards. Our submarines mostly run around five to six knots. Six knots means sustaining an all-out sprint for over four-and-a-half full minutes. If I can sustain seven knots, that saves me forty seconds, and sets a world record. The unimaginable eight knots? That would require only three minutes and twenty-five seconds of flat-out exertion. Maybe.

We never had a chance to test *Natsiq's* full speed because we ran out of pool too fast in Alaska. Now we were jumping from a twenty-five yard pool to a thousand. It's the great unknown for most of the teams and no one has been bragging.

I understand why Frank rushed off that first morning he was in the sub; we were all dying to see what it could do. And now I was thinking of him by his first name. ICK! And using the word *dying* in the same sentence. Double ick!

Overnight we learned that there was no family to contact, just an orphanage. And he'd been so unpopular in his freshman year that they'd given him a single dorm room almost immediately.

But being dead didn't stop him from continuing to make all of our lives awful. The police have a murder on their hands, so we're being guarded.

"Guarded or corralled?" Vlad of course finds a way to make everything funny.

Except his question isn't. "No escaping your foul crimes, Vlad." I try to keep it light as well.

"Hey, I have perfect alibi, I was out to dinner with you."

"Maybe they think we did it together." They've definitely been asking both of us a lot of questions. Well, me, and then pulling in Vlad because we're each other's alibi. "Or maybe you did it after kissing me goodnight at my room?"

"You know, at our normal latitude, I could be kissing you for nineteen hours in the same night."

"In December," I answer, though I wouldn't mind trying that. And it was a *great* subject change. "Of course, you could only do it for two-and-a-half hours in mid-summer."

"We could switch to daylight kissing in summer."

I laugh at the tease.

Of course, after the kiss is where our alibis collapse. Vlad had drawn the single room due to an uneven number of team members. And Carol and Kane were fast asleep when I slipped into my own room.

The police now know that Frank died that first night by analyzing the food in his stomach (*Ew!*): that first lunch and how much it was digested (*Double Ew!*). But they can't pin down an exact time.

"I don't think I was helping our case last night." Unable to sleep after the discovery of Kootoo's body and our presentation, I had wandered down the hall to Vlad's room.

My knock was little more than a scrape of knuckles on

wood, but he answered almost immediately. He'd taken one look at my face and pulled me in.

I was so dazed that until that moment I hadn't imagined he would probably assume I wanted sex.

Vlad was smarter than that. We curled up in his bed together, and he let me sleep on his shoulder, which was exactly what I'd needed. I had slipped away to shower before he woke.

Despite having slept together, we were still at one kiss, at least as far as Vlad knew. I had left him with a kiss of thanks while he slept. It was nice to be held when I was one of the likely suspects for someone's murder.

9

———

Speed Trial Day started exactly as the last several had—talking about Frank Kootoo.

The police showed me footage of him from the night he died. I'd brought along Carol and Kane. Vlad had brought himself and I wasn't complaining.

They fast-scrolled through footage of security sweeping the building and all of us trailing out. Ten minutes later by the timer in the corner, Frank had emerged from some hiding place. A security camera had caught him sitting and staring at *Natsiq*—for hours.

Just staring. Like he was thinking incredibly hard about something.

Not working on fixing the damage, which was just as well, he wasn't much of a mechanic. Just thinking.

"He sat there for three hours barely moving. Do you have any idea what he might have been thinking?"

I looked at Carol and Kane, but we all shook our heads.

How little did we know about our fellow team member? We hadn't known he was seventeen, or an orphan. None of it.

"He kept himself to himself," I finally answered for the others.

"We found out that you three were the ones he was closest to, on campus or off."

Vlad handed me some tissues and waved for me to mop my face. I did, but it didn't stop the tears.

"After three hours he stood..."

He gave the camera so foul a grimace that it should have cracked the glass. Then he did something that made no sense. He bent down and picked up *Natsiq's* ocean-blue shipping cover—before walking out of the frame.

"He walked away from the direction of the exit and didn't appear on any camera again. He must have spotted and avoided all the cameras. We also found this on his phone." The policeman put up a short message on the screen.

I could never be as good as you.
Not that I ever tried before this project.
Thanks for believing in me, Malee.

"What?" I couldn't make any sense of the words. "It sounds like a suicide note. But he was murdered."

The officer shook his head. "He gathered forty pounds of diving weights, tucked them in the bag at the edge of the pool. He appears to have zipped himself in, then rolled off the edge and into the water."

"But...why?" Vlad asked. The three of us were past speech.

The officer put up one last image.

It was an autopsy report, with one section highlighted.

Inoperable brain tumor.
Hard-pressed against amygdala,
center for aggression and fear responses.

Vlad held me tightly as he asked the final question, "He knew?"

The policeman nodded. "The same problem made Charles Whitman climb the University of Texas tower in Austin in 1966. He gunned down eighteen and wounded thirty more in an hour-and-a-half shooting spree. Frank Kootoo knew this, we found it prominently marked on his laptop. Apparently Mr. Kootoo didn't want to do that. Apparently especially not to you."

The four of us huddled together long after the policemen were gone.

10

———

"ARE YOU SURE YOU DON'T WANT ME TO DRIVE FOR YOU?"

I'd spent much of Speed Trial Day crying. So much so that they'd finally sedated me. Not enough to take me to the hospital for observation, but not good.

Vlad had taken me to his room, and I'd spent the night clinging to him whenever the drug didn't keep me under.

The last day was Awards Day, but they'd offered our team a single time trial run early this morning.

"No Vlad," I gave him a kiss. "No, the Nanooks started this and for better or worse, we'll finish it."

He'd made sure I'd eaten and done a workout to clear the last of the drugs from my system. My biggest regret was that we'd had two nights together—and I'd been an utter wreck for both of them.

"You're the best." And I ducked under the water before he could reply.

Carol and Kane helped me lock in.

The ISR official began the signals ritual.

I hadn't ever liked Frank Kootoo, but now I at least understood him a bit. He'd fought against his own nature—

driven mostly mad by that brain tumor—until he'd decided that the world was better off without him.

The real surprise was that he also thought the world was better off *because* of me.

Well, I was going to prove that he was right—for him.

The official gave me the Go signal.

And boy did I go.

11

———————

"AND THE TEAM SPIRIT AWARD GOES TO," THE ISR OFFICIAL opened his envelope, "Grenoble INP Institut d'ingénierie. His team unanimously decided that the thousand-dollar scholarship award goes to team captain Vlad Qarpik."

His team tackled him and hoisted him in the air, almost dropping him half a dozen times before they settled. Once he was on solid ground again, his gaze sought me out.

I realized that it wasn't only me he was wonderful to. He'd treated his people so well that I hadn't even known he was captain until this moment. As sorry as I felt for Frank, I wanted a team like Vlad's.

Again I was doing the crazy crying thing. I'd cried more in five days than in as many years. I didn't have to think about why this time. Tomorrow morning we had a flight back to Alaska. Tonight Vlad Qarpik had a redeye flight back to France. Not quite the antipodes of Nome, which lay where the South Atlantic ran into Antarctica, but close enough.

Awards, honorable mentions, and scholarships were announced and the mood was festive. I did my best to shake it off and leave the pain inside.

Would Frank have felt the joy? *Could* he have?

I'd never know, so I'd better figure out how to live with it. Curiously, I felt as if I was living for two of us now. Excelling was no longer enough. Astronaut Megan McArthur had shown me the possible, and now it was up to me and me alone to do it.

Carol and Kane wrapped me in a crushing hug.

"What?"

"Speed. We got speed!"

I'd never heard the final numbers. Seven-point-seven knots. We'd broken the world speed record by over a mile per hour.

I dragged both of them up to the podium with me. I remembered to thank my grandparents, my professor, had to double back to thank my parents, Frank Kootoo (who deserved it evil or not), and finally, "The two best mechanics I've ever met!" And I held up both their hands in mine as they blushed fiercely.

The Innovation Award I accepted on my own, with a different kind of tears running down my face. I really had done something incredible. That is definitely going under my Christmas tree this year.

When Overall Design went to Vlad's team, I couldn't have been happier for him.

12

———

"We live only two hundred miles apart," it felt like a wail on my part. While it was true, his life was no longer in his Chukchi Peninsula village. It was in France.

Good thing I'd gotten Vlad well away from the others as they finished packing his submarine for shipping or I'd be making a major spectacle of myself. Carol and Kane had scrounged a new shipping bag to replace the one Frank had died in.

How long would Frank dog my footsteps? Years? A lifetime?

I better make his memory a friend if he's going to hang on like that. But I wasn't feeling very triumphant at the moment. In another hour Vlad would be gone and, no matter how stupid, it felt like a piece of me would be as lost as poor Frank the moment Vlad was gone.

That piece of me would be out walking circles in the *qapalaqijuq* with Frank, on the white ice under the white sky until we had no direction, no path, no hope.

"We could live closer," Vlad had that smile of his that said the solution was so simple if only I could figure it out. Even the possibility of a solution gave me enough hope to spar with him.

"Where, the Diomede Islands?" The pair of American and Russian islands were four kilometers apart in the middle of the Bering Sea.

He laughed that rich, quiet laugh of home. "No, you goofball. Didn't you hear, Malee Ashoona?"

"Hear what?"

He rested his hands on both my shoulders to make me focus on him. "Your drive design blew everyone away. Every grad school in the competition would offer you a full-ride ticket."

How had I missed all that? Did that... "Including the Grenoble engineering program?"

"I already asked. How would you like to come live with me in France and design submarines?"

Vlad watches me closely for a long moment but he must see the answer in my eyes, because he leans in and kisses me with that wonderful smile of his.

"One condition," I manage to whisper over the beating of my heart after his powerhouse kiss. "How do you feel about space?"

Vlad leans back to look at the ceiling of the DTMB pool tunnel. But I know that he too is seeing the International Space Station and recalling Megan McArthur's invitation video.

"I am thinking..."

He looks back down at me, but his smile hasn't diminished at all. I know his answer and lay my head on his shoulder. With Vlad's beacon of hope I'll never be lost out in the winter whiteout again.

"First submariners on Mars?" he whispers into my hair.

I don't need to answer, I know he can feel my silent laugh. It's the best Christmas present ever.

———

FOR MORE TALES OF THE WHITE HOUSE PROTECTION FORCE AND their dogs, visit: https://shop.mlbuchman.com/collections/ white-house-protection-force

IN FOR THE LONG HAUL

This is a second *Antarctic Ice Fliers* tale. Curiously, it is the only one in which the airplanes are not front and center. However, the SPoT—South Polar Traverse—supply convoy was so fascinating that once I discovered it, I simply had to give it a love story.

This New Year's romance on The Ice makes me wish that I too could take the long drive from McMurdo Station to the South Pole.

1

———

Michel spotted Clara easily. Even with her back turned and the hood of her Big Red US Antarctic Program parka up, he'd know Clara Poole anywhere—she was just that gloriously herself. The shorter figure by her side would be her best friend Priya.

They were also the only two out on the ice this morning who *weren't* in motion. The South Pole Traverse convoy was leaving McMurdo Station in about five minutes and a lot of last-minute items were being checked over.

They both shoved back their hoods for the warm summer weather—a mere ten below Celsius, about fifteen Fahrenheit. Clara's black hair fluttered about her shoulders. So lovely to play with—it was one of his hundred or so most favorite things about her.

He wasn't quite sure why Priya was here but he suspected that it was important, if only he could figure it out.

They were talking as he came up from behind. Clara's voice was deep and New England curt, "You better stay my best friend even after we leave The Ice. If you don't, I'll die."

Priya laughed. "I didn't think anything could kill a

Gloucesterwoman. Isn't that what you told me the first time we met?"

"I lied. With the wedding coming, I'm rattled down to my boots."

"How is it that you're marrying a man with a girl's name?" Priya began singing the inevitable Beatles' song, *Michelle, my belle.*

"He's Québécois French, he can't help it." Clara crossed her hands over her chest. "I think my heart is going to explode."

"Eww! Don't get any on me." Priya shuffled away across the hard-packed snow.

Clara snagged her by the loose end of her scarf and hauled her back to which Priya made a show of choking and gasping desperately, drawing everyone's attention.

Michel slid his arms around Clara's waist from behind.

Despite the warm day, she shivered even as she leaned back into him. She knew him as easily as he knew her. Their connection was without question. Priya always accused them of being "penguin people," able to find each other without fail in a million-bird colony.

It *definitely* wasn't the cold. Clara and Priya were not alone in easing their heavy winter clothes. All of the winterovers, though none of the summerfolk here for their *life's great adventure* at MacTown, were walking around with their parkas open and hoods thrown back like it was time to hit the water slides at Village Vacances Valcartier back in Québec.

This warm the day after Thanksgiving said they could have whole record-breaking days above freezing by Christmas at McMurdo Station. Priya, being a marine biologist, was already freaking out about shifting food vectors and the potential for massive die-offs when that happened. She compensated with a sharp sense of humor that only reinforced the dire consequences.

For being a *beaker*—an Antarctic scientist—she was actually a lot of fun.

Clara turned inside the curve of his arms, snuggled inside his open parka, and buried her face against his shoulder. He held her tight but addressed Priya.

"How's the maid of honor today?"

"How's the chief lummox?"

"I'm not a lemming," he purposely misunderstood her.

"Sure you are, you're rushing out onto the sea." She waved her hand to indicate the vast sweep the Antarctic continent. "Just warning you. You hurt my friend, I'm going to stuff you down a crevasse."

Clara shivered again, which wasn't like her at all.

He rested his cheek against her temple.

"Hey, Sailor."

"Hey, Jean Pierre."

Since the day they'd met, she'd never called him by the same name twice—ever. She'd also had never used his real name, Michel Charbonneau, or his nickname of Frenchy.

Maybe it really was pre-wedding nerves rather than the cold making her shiver. He glanced at Priya again. Why was she out here instead of already deep in her lab or preparing for a bone-chilling dive? Moral support? Yeah, that fit.

The weather *was* an issue but not a cold one. The sun had first risen three months ago. It had last set a month ago and wouldn't do so again until February.

But the reason Clara was shivering loomed in front of them: a convoy of huge tractors. The SPoT convoy was departing McMurdo in minutes. And he was one of the drivers.

A third of the fuel and supplies for the South Pole Station were flown in from McMurdo by a series of seventy-six flights. The LC-130 Skibirds of the New York Air National Guard 109th Airlift Wing were supposed to start flitting south about now, except they were blocked by a hard cold snap. The plane engines couldn't risk fuel and hydraulics freezing on landing.

But the land-crawling SPoT wouldn't arrive for three weeks, by which time it had to get warmer, so it was time to get a move on now and race the weather south. The tractor convoy delivered the remaining two-thirds of the supplies by dragging them over the ice and snow of the thousand-mile McMurdo-South Pole Highway, more commonly known as the South Pole Traverse—SPoT. As long as they hustled, there was time for three trips a season.

"How *did* I fall in love with a man named like a girl?" Clara sounded a little more like herself. It was also as close as she ever came to using his real name.

"Because you had the good sense to fall for the dashing Québécois hero of Antarctica." He kissed her on the ear.

"Tell me how falling for a Frenchman makes any sense. No, don't." She kept her head on his shoulder. "You'll somehow make it sound wicked sensible, like when you proposed."

"I thought you proposed to me. Either way, I *am* pretty irresistible. I have that on the best authority."

"I should never have mentioned that." She hugged him harder inside his Big Red which had cocooned around them.

"Don't worry, I'll be back in plenty of time for the wedding."

"You'd better." She thumped a fist against his ribs.

He caught her hand before she could get serious about it, because Clara was strong. He pinned it over his heart. "I'm wearing your sweater."

"You'd better. I took a mad risk making that for you." She'd told him there was a knitters' myth—she called it a truth—that when you spent all of the effort to knit a sweater for a boyfriend, that would invariably end the relationship. She'd done it anyway because it was Clara who never quite followed the rules.

That he'd misinterpreted the elaborate colorwork of the

beautiful Fair Isle knit gift as a proposal had earned him one of her electric smiles and a splendid tussle as she peeled him back out of it. Saying *yes* when he'd thought it was a proposal was so obvious that he hadn't hesitated. Something that had made *him* shiver a time or two since. How had it been so ridiculously easy to agree to marry a woman including that death-do-us-part bit?

Right now, she was the one who was all nerves—which actually made him feel a little calmer. They were weird that way and it often made them laugh. Not today.

"Three weeks out, a week layover, and ten days back. We're good for the wedding with a week to spare." He might—not likely but they both knew that—be back for Christmas. But there'd be plenty of time before the planned New Year's Eve wedding. In fact, if he made it back to McMurdo even a day before Christmas, he'd be scheduled south again too soon. To get in the necessary three traverses, the window between them remained very narrow, but he didn't point that out. For the next four months, he'd be spending all but the turn-around week at either end driving back and forth across half the continent.

She kept her face buried against his shoulder.

"Maybe you two should just elope," Priya chimed in.

"Great idea. Let's go." Michel spun Clara free of his arms and grabbed her hand because, at this rate, he'd never be able to let go of her. Her hugs should come with a license. Actually they did, a marriage license. Now he was the one feeling all the nerves.

To mask them, he took one step as if to lead off.

"Wait, where are we eloping to?"

Clara gave him the laugh he wanted.

"The Kiwis?" Priya suggested.

"I don't know. Scott Base is only two kilometers away. Not much of an elopement. You know us Québécois heroes, if we do something, we do it with style. What do you say, my love, do we wait it out or throw ourselves on the goodwill of our New Zealand compatriots?"

Clara sighed. "We wait."

On New Year's Eve, her South Carolina grandparents would be visiting her parents in Gloucester. Her big brother and little sister had agreed to come up from New York and Washington, DC. Michel's parents and brother were driving down from Québec so that the two families could finally meet. And then they were all going to be together to video conference in for the *Big Wedding*.

A wedding on The Ice would also be an excuse for a grand party on their end as well. Any excuse for a party was embraced here but, landing atop New Year's, this one was going to be all out of normal proportion. With McMurdo humming at summerfolk volumes and a wedding to celebrate, mayhem was bound to ensue.

Everything was all arranged. Except Clara would be here doing her job at McMurdo while Michel drove a tractor across sixteen-hundred kilometers of ice to the South Pole and back.

The first tractor engine roared to life.

"That's my cue to kiss the woman I love—"

"—and then leave her standing flatfooted on the snow." Priya jumped in.

"*Mais oui!*" Then he kissed Clara hard and whispered seriously in her ear. "I'll be careful, and safe, and back before you know it, Sailor. I love you more permanently than all the ice in the world," Clara's catchphrase after they'd become engaged. You couldn't be in Antarctica and not firmly believe in global warming.

Rico, the Manager of Traverse Operations, yelled his name and he turned for his tractor.

He glanced back to see Priya slip an arm around Clara's waist. She spoke loudly enough for Michel to easily hear her despite the rumbling tractors, "That man did *not* just whisper a sweet nothing in your ear."

"He absolutely did."

He bent down to check his boot laces at the edge of hearing, because she wasn't hurting his ego at all.

"Damn it! One good man on the planet and you get him. How is that even possible?"

"Well, I have you for a best friend, so I must be doing something right."

"Which means, since you got the man, I must be doing everything wrong. So having *you* as a bestie just makes me a sad sack."

"It does," Michel pushed to his feet and called back.

Priya flicked him the finger and laughed, but Clara just looked sad.

He returned Priya's salute, but he was out of time to do anything about the latter.

2

———————

MICHEL CLIMBED UP INTO HIS CHALLENGER MT865 AND FIRED off the big diesel engine with a throaty roar that shook the very air. The big agricultural tractor, with massive treads like a tank instead of wheels, had been modified for the cold with sealed engine compartments, several engine heaters, and satellite radios which would allow them to communicate from out on the ice.

Rico lurched the lead snowcat into motion. It had a long front boom reaching forward. At its end dangled a ground-penetrating radar for detecting crevasses that had opened since the initial pre-season grooming so that no one drove into one.

There were eight tractors this trip. Six of them dragged massive ten-meter wide, twenty-meter long sleds. On each of these was strapped eight, twelve-thousand-liter fuel bladders for delivery to the South Pole Station. Eighty tons of fuel encapsulated in massive black-rubber beans, each wider than he was tall, ten-meters-long, and filled until they rose a meter high.

Another sled carried several containers' worth of cargo, supplies too big or heavy to be easily flown to the pole.

And the last tractor, Michel's, dragged their living-quarters modules: repair shop, bunkhouse, and the combined kitchen, dining, and living room. Aside from a the turnarounds at either end, for the next four months, it would be just the nine of them: one driver in the lead snowcat and eight in the tractors.

He was late enough to the line, that he was on the move the moment his engine was up to temperature. The line stretched out slowly as they moved down from the station onto the ice. McMurdo perched on Ross Island, the farthest south land accessible by ship—very briefly each year—and they'd be driving across the ice shelf for the first thousand kilometers.

By the time he thought to turn and wave, the big living modules blocked all visibility behind. Yet another reason he was last in line.

He waved anyway, but knew it was lame.

He remembered clearly the first time he'd met Clara, perhaps because it had been her first day at McMurdo just a year ago. She'd walked into the heavy equipment shed and undone her Big Red parka like an old hand, not that it was much warmer inside than outside.

The boss had said they were expecting someone new on the next flight, but that's all he'd said. The FINGY—Fucking New Guy—was a FIN...GAL.

He'd been with the guys, grouped around a fire truck; the fire department was the single biggest team at the US stations of McMurdo and the South Pole. But when stumped, they kicked their gear over to the mechanics and drivers, most of whom served in the fire brigade anyway. The entire cab—seats and all—had been tipped up and forward out of the way, the whole assembly pivoting at the front bumper. Beneath it, the big diesel engine lay exposed on the chassis.

She'd walked into the circle to stare down at the engine with the rest of them as if she'd always been part of their crew. Only because he'd been facing her had he seen the brief hesitation in her step before she did so. Nerves, but nerves of steel as it was the only sign she gave.

Clara always walked with the rolling gait of a captain striding the deck of her ship. Only later did he find out she'd come by it honestly from years of working on her family's fishing boats out of Gloucester, Massachusetts.

"What's it doing?" Clara's idea of a warm greeting.

"It *iz* what she *iz no* doing," Michel had teased her, stressing his French.

"Not working, *eh,* Claude?" She gave the made-up name a heavy French pronunciation.

"Got it in one, Sailor." His tag of Sailor had stuck, which still tickled him no end.

"Symptoms, Henri?" The name *du jour* thing already had the guys laughing with her—*at* him.

"Broken," he continued with determined unhelpfulness. This was too much fun.

She'd laughed in his face. Not nasty, he'd decided, just enjoying herself.

"Won't start," the crew boss had made it clear who was in charge by his tone. "It'll crank, but no fire."

"Meter?" She'd taken the boss' folded arms not as a challenge, but as if he was waiting for her to do her stuff.

Michel had pointed to the nearby tool case. She scanned the shop with a single sweep before turning to fetch a meter. The shop here was pro caliber. There was no sending out the trickier repairs when the next nearest shop was five hours away in Christchurch, New Zealand—by jet. They did it all here and had the equipment to build almost any part they didn't stock.

It had taken her two minutes to ring out the wires—finding the only one that didn't peep when she put the meter's test leads on either end—and find the culprit that had eluded them for the last thirty minutes.

Then she must have noticed their frustrated expressions.

He was feeling some of that himself. She had somehow reached into the massive wire harnesses and found the one fault.

"When there wasn't any fishing, I worked as a mechanic for the Gloucester Fire Department. Took care of their engines." That chilled everyone out, but she'd looked puzzled by the pattern of damage once she found the fractured component.

"Freeze-heat cycle," Michel had explained. "Minus fifty or sixty, then you fire off the engine. The temperature swing will stress crack just about anything."

And in some way that he still didn't understand, his giving her a straight answer when it mattered had started them off on exactly the right foot.

Women were still low density creatures on The Ice, maybe a quarter of the beakers but rarely crossing ten percent in the support teams. Just stepping on the continent upped any woman's hotness by at least a factor of two. That hadn't touched Clara. She couldn't look any other way being who she was—not that she needed the boost. And somehow he'd been the lucky one to snag her attention.

Dammit! He really should have remembered to wave goodbye once he was in the cab.

The SPoT team departure was mostly a non-event at McMurdo. The same crew that had done most of the loading was also doing the driving. Nine people leaving McMurdo's throng, which was almost at its fifteen-hundred-person summer peak, was hardly noteworthy. Small expeditions left almost every day for one summer science camp or another.

And while the SPoT team was driving across the polar ice cap, someone had to keep the home fires from burning. It was Clara's job to stay behind this summer.

He definitely should have waved.

Baptême! He was *un idiot!* He had something far better.

He leaned on the horn, releasing a loud blast. Off to the

sides, he could see people twisting around to look. Not so anonymous today.

When he released the horn, he could hear others in the convoy, blasting theirs. He hit his again.

There was a bright ping from his pager—the only reliable way to send short messages away from base.

He stopped honking to pull it out.

A smiley from Clara. He'd done good.

He hit the horn again.

3

____

When Michel had pictured his life in Antarctica, before arriving, he'd never thought it would be spent as one of the city mice. Most of the McMurdoans never ranged more than walking distance from the largest town on the entire continent. As a fuelie and truck driver, he often drove out onto the ice shelf to build and service the ice runways, but that was still only a matter of a few kilometers from MacTown.

Last year he'd been told he'd be on the next year's SPoT crew if he wanted to stay overwinter. A Challenger MT865 tractor couldn't have dragged him away. He'd turned down a chance for a late summer break in Christchurch, New Zealand. There was always a chance of bad weather closing The Ice early and he wasn't going to risk getting stuck ashore.

He knew he'd made the right choice when Clara had strolled into the machine shop the next day as if she already owned the place.

Her competence was what he'd come to expect from the others who'd made the grade to get to The Ice. Her understated confidence had been captivating. And her Gloucester accent had done him in—the New England-rough just fit her so perfectly.

And now that he finally had his place on the SPoT and his dream of getting out of MacTown was coming true? He was missing Clara. It had taken months into winter lockdown before she'd let him slide into her bed, but in hindsight he could see that she'd slid right under his guard that first day.

He was the last to jostle slowly over the transition from Ross Island onto the McMurdo Ice Shelf. Looking back, his rearview mirror still showed nothing except for the living-quarters module he was dragging along, but he couldn't stop looking. He knew she'd still be there watching him drive out of sight.

That had been the unexpected treat, the truffle-sweet woman inside that hard-candy shell.

They drove out of McMurdo, out onto the ice, and swung wide around Discovery Hut where Scott had started his first expedition to the South Pole. And where he hadn't reached on his second.

"Please don't let that be a portent of what's to come."

Nobody answered, of course. For the entire drive, he'd be alone in a glass box, driving a tractor at eight klicks an hour for ten to twelve hours a day. There would be breaks for meals, refueling, and sleeping, but the main thing to look forward to was utter monotony—or so he'd been told.

"Still with us, Frenchy?" His nickname to everyone except Clara. He realized that this call on the radio hadn't been the first.

"Depends, is today Tuesday?"

"Friday."

"Oh, *non monsieur*. Ne-*ver* on a Friday."

"He's already zoning out in the first five K."

"Buckle down, Frenchy. We've got a long road ahead."

And the banter continued. He did his part to keep it

moving. But it soon faded away, and it was once again him, alone in a glass box, driving over the great expanse of white ice.

His first winter on The Ice, his life had slowed down, just as everyone's did through the long months of darkness and isolation. The Second Winter had spun up like his life was out of control.

Even in the very beginning Clara Poole hadn't just been some pleasant distraction. A woman who understood engines better than he did was to be admired. A woman who knew them *so* much better was a little humbling. He recognized mastery when he saw it. So, he'd made sure that he was always there when she needed an extra hand just so that he could learn.

The payoff of Clara herself...well, he had no reference for that in his life.

He'd grown up chasing slim French girls, so perfectly coy, around the Les Galeries de la Capitale shopping mall. A brash, ballbuster of a Gloucesterwoman wasn't the sort of woman he'd ever so much as noticed before.

Christ, would he have been confident enough to roll into an unknown machine shop and just jump in the way she had? A Québécois might have done it with bravado to take control, she'd done it with blinding skill.

And... *Baptême!*

He yanked back on the speed control and the engine throttle. He'd almost climbed right up the back of the supply sled being dragged by the tractor in front of him. Thankfully, even skidding across the ice, the big loads stopped quickly. But it was a sure bet that the kitchen cupboards he was hauling were going to be a real jumble.

He checked the clock. Six hours, they'd come fifty klicks.

Even *thinking* about that woman wiped out big chunks of time.

He tried looking back, but *again* all he saw were the living-quarter modules. Any hint of McMurdo was long gone. It was just their machines—and the vast white.

To his left was a great expanse of flat nothing and to his right more flat, abutting the white land climbing up until it hit the blue sky. There was no way to tell if it was a two-hundred-foot hummock just a few soccer fields away, or a line of mountains parked along the horizon. Either way, white.

Ahead, the tractors weren't moving.

Only fifty klicks out. That's when he knew why they'd stopped. They were in the McMurdo Shear Zone where the McMurdo and Ross Ice Shelves ground against each other, arguing over which got to go one way or the other around Ross Island while shoving toward the sea. That the convoy had come to a full stop wasn't a particularly bad sign—yet.

The road crew had already been out this way weeks ago, making sure the way through the Shear Zone was clear. But ice was never still. Even at the South Pole, near the center of the continent, the ice cap slipped along at ten meters a year. Out here it was much more lively—a hundred times faster, roughly a kilometer a year.

Up in the lead, Rico in the snowcat would be out prowling around with his radar, checking for any new crevasses that might have formed. Hopefully, any new ones would be small enough to crawl over. If they weren't, the snowplow on the lead tractor might try to fill them in. Rarely, a new one would be big enough that we'd need to scout a route around. It all had to be planned because one thing that a Challenger MT865 treaded tractor towing an eighty-ton sled could *not* do was back up.

Michel toyed with several riffs on, "He's so dumb that he thinks reverse is a gear on a SPoT tractor." But he hadn't come up with a good one by the time the "All clear" was given and they could start edging ahead.

He should have paged Clara while he was waiting, she was really good at things like that. She and Priya often worked out two-person verbal traps for their friends to fall into—he'd certainly been their victim often enough.

Michel reached for his two-way radio, but it wouldn't stretch to McMurdo, now fifty clicks over the horizon. Except for pager pings and spendy satellite calls, they were already well and surely cut off from the world—eight tractors alone on an endless desert of ice.

Cut off from Clara, too.

It was crazy, but the latter was the one that felt far more worrisome.

What had she done to him?

4

———

THE PROBLEM DIDN'T GET ANY BETTER OF THE NEXT TEN DAYS. For a thousand kilometers past the McMurdo Shear Zone he had nothing else to think about.

Crossing the vast flatness of the Ross Ice Shelf offered no distractions—not that it was all that flat, but he knew that way lay ahead ranked far worse. There were only so many hours you could spend envisioning the fuel flow through his tractor's systems. Not being a big fan of audiobooks, it was mostly just watching the world go by. Perhaps it was very Zen, if he knew what that really meant—if anyone did. Most people using the phrase amused rather than impressed him.

It never cracked minus ten outside, but the sun shone twenty-four hours a day. He'd been told to bring shorts and a t-shirt for the drive, which he'd assumed was a prank on the FINGY—despite a year on The Ice, he'd become the fucking new guy all over again when he joined the SPoT convoy. In fact, he was the only new driver on the team this year. One driver had opted out for a warmer clime—as a forest ranger in Montana.

But the shorts hadn't been a joke and he was glad that he'd

276

tucked them out of sight deep in his bag. They were headed to the South Pole, all wearing shorts and t-shirts, sitting in their cabs, and slathered in sunscreen with the door open. Between the engines and the sun, the heat, not the cold, was the problem.

Once he fell into the rhythm of the day, he became more and more aware of how Clara had changed him.

He wondered what she was up to now. Probably servicing all of the pumps on the long fuel lines that stretched across the ice to the McMurdo runways. Tens of thousands of gallons would be transported out to the smaller planes exhausted by their crossing from New Zealand. Hundreds of thousands would be pumped into the Air National Guard planes as they ferried back and forth to the South Pole. During the brief fall-season melt out, an icebreaker-escorted fuel ship would offload five million gallons to restock the McMurdo tank farm.

Other than that, she'd be driving the runway grader and packer trucks, yet another area of expertise for her.

Since when did he spend so much time wondering about a woman?

Since he'd fallen in love with a Yankee.

Being around her was like being addicted to a drug. He was a pretty mellow guy—her figured closer to Zen about his life than anyone who actually claimed to be—but she never settled to rest. And he'd been swept up in it.

Now, he rolled along, fifty meters behind the next nearest sled, one hand on the wheel, the other tapping along to the playlist his little brother kept pumped up for him. There was a certain peace and contentment to the task.

Clara, he imagined, would be worrying about the engine, or listening to an audiobook about the Antarctic explorers, or taking French lessons. Who knew what all the woman did, but she somehow filled every spare moment.

Not that she never relaxed, but she relaxed just as hard as she worked.

Their first movie night together had included fifteen tiny bowls of everything from M&Ms and licorice bits to trail mix, dried apple slices, candied ginger, and other scrounged treats. She'd set up a film fest of *mechanics'* movies. They'd slouched together and nibbled their way through: *The Flight of the Phoenix* (the original not the remake), *Days of Thunder* (for Duvall, not Tom Cruise, she was very clear about that though he'd enjoyed watching Nicole Kidman himself), *Gone in 60 Seconds* (Duvall again but he shouldn't be jealous), and *Apollo 13*. They'd fallen asleep before the old submarine movie *Run Silent Run Deep*.

Out here on the Ross Ice Shelf it felt as if he was taking his first breath since meeting Clara.

The thought made him feel guilty.

He was engaged to Clara Poole. He *loved* Clara Poole. There was no question that he'd ever meet another woman like her, but who was *he* becoming?

5

———

HALFWAY ACROSS THE ICE SHELF, THEY LOST THE LAST SIGHT OF any land. Five hundred klicks behind them, the twelve-thousand-foot volcanic cone of Mt. Erebus had long since faded into the horizon. No land within a hundred klicks in any direction. They were in the middle of an ocean that lay a kilometer beneath the ice.

They made good time over the groomed road, sometimes running as high as a hundred kilometers a day. If they kept that up, they'd make the round trip too fast and he'd be leaving McMurdo for the second SPoT run *before* the wedding. *Baptême,* but The Ice made everything complicated—even a good Québécois religious curse didn't cover the depth of that.

The logistics of everything on Antarctica was just that crazy. By the time they delivered a gallon of fuel to the South Pole and it was actually burned, it's real cost averaged forty dollars US—thirty-nine of that would be transport and storage.

At night, when the sun was a little closer to the horizon than at midday, they stopped the tractors and climbed down from the cabs. It was too dangerous to wander far, they stayed within ten meters of the traverse path. To either side lay the unsurveyed nothingness. Even a tiny crevasse could swallow a man with no one the wiser, no more than a small hole in the snow where he'd disappeared. Whether the crevasse opened a few meters deep—or all the way down to the ocean's surface—the end result would probably be the same.

He really needed to stop finding metaphors of the ice conditions to his mental ones—like wondering just how deep a hole had his heart already fallen down. And should he be attempting to save himself.

In the kitchen, they took turns cooking. One of the hot topics was what the next day's cooks should select. They would then prowl through the ambient temperature—hard frozen—food locker, deciding what to bring inside to thaw during tomorrow's drive.

Another of the hot topics was the upcoming wedding. All guys on the convoy this year, so, of course, the talk kept veering toward the wedding night.

"There won't be one, not until the sun sets." That had sidetracked them from that topic—for almost five minutes.

He couldn't seem to get away from it.

Nine days out on the traverse, Rico waved for him to join in an after-dinner walk. "Come on, Frenchy. We start the climb tomorrow. I want to doublecheck everything."

It was a lame excuse, as they'd already done the daily post-drive full inspections of their rigs. The safety checks weren't optional when the nearest help was now eight hundred klicks away in every direction. Even the next emptiest place on Earth, the center of the Greenland ice cap, was only five hundred kilometers from either coast. By comparison, central Siberia and the steppes of Mongolia were hotbeds of civilization. Here it was only snow, ice, and their pinprick of a convoy.

As soon as they'd stopped for the day, they'd patrolled the treads with an iron breaker bar, knocking loose any snow and ice buildup in the wheels that drove the treads. Left overnight, it could turn steel-hard and damage the running gear. Visual inspections, check the oil, the hydraulic levels, possible ice in the air cleaner...they went through it all every night.

"What are you sitting on, Frenchy?" Rico asked as they began working their way forward along the convoy.

"Other than my ass?"

Rico raised a baseball bat and whacked it against the drive wheel for the tractor's big rubber tread. It offered the right sort of clank in response. Michel's own ear had quickly learned how to accurately read the gear's condition with the tone of that clank. Dull thud, there was hidden ice in there. Any rattle, it was time to check for loose hardware. That clank with just a bit of a ring to it? Sweet.

Rumor said Rico was as old as the ice. One story told how they'd found him frozen in the ice when they built McMurdo. Another that he'd been left behind by the Scott Expedition in 1912 and had built all of McMurdo himself while waiting for the Americans to come back in 1956.

It was also clear that Michel was going to be Rico's next target with that bat, so he did his best to answer the question straight.

"I guess I'm getting more time to think than is good for me." He wasn't exactly *doubting* Clara. He was more doubting her sanity in wanting to marry him. He'd never struck himself as the marrying kind. Shack up with some sexy *artiste*? Sure. He'd always sort of specialized in high-maintenance women. Monogamous? No problem, he'd always been that sort for as long as anything lasted. But marriage? His record longest relationship had been his eight months with Clara. An impressively low-maintenance woman, which only added to his confusion—as if he wasn't doing something right, if only he knew what.

Rico was silent as they poked and prodded their way around the big cargo sled. In fact, he'd didn't speak again until they were checking the ground-penetrating radar on the lead snowcat.

"Frenchy, do yourself a favor."

"If I gotta do one, might as well be for myself, right?"

"Right. Stop thinking so much. My wife said she knew from the first day that we would be married. I was maybe ten, she was nine when we met."

Michel hadn't even heard about Rico being married.

"Married to her was the best twenty years of my life until she died too young." He was silent most of the way back to the living quarters.

"So what's the favor?"

Rico's baseball bat slapped against his butt—not so gently. If his butt rang, he never heard it. "You so dense that you need me to spell it out? Fine. This thing with Clara?"

"Yeah."

"You fuck it up, I'm gonna shove you down a crevasse, an ocean-deep one. Nobody will ever find your body."

Rico stepped inside the living quarter hut and left him standing out in the cold sun.

6

———

Michel supposed that the brutality of the next several days was only appropriate.

The climb from the Ross Ice Shelf through the Transantarctic Mountains—with a few inevitable lame jokes about the T&A mountains—to the polar plateau was a steep one up the rolled front of the Leverett Glacier, one of many that fed the shelf. Depending on how the ice shelf was floating, they started at perhaps a hundred meters above sea level. It would take much of the next week to climb up to the polar plateau over two kilometers above them.

While the tractors were robust enough to haul their loads over rough terrain, the steep climb was too much, so they had to hook up and haul loads in tandem, making two slow trips up the hundred-kilometer glacier. Hooking and unhooking all the sleds and tractors was going to be the most exposed work of the entire trip. That was the first problem.

The second? The air sliding down off the polar plateau was only marginally warmed by the sun, little above minus fifty Celsius, even approaching mid-summer. And the long slope meant that the cold, dense air was blasting downslope at severe-gale speeds which raised a near whiteout of blowing ice and snow. Straight up, the world was blue sky. Looking ahead, it was hard to see the next tractor, never mind the next flag.

Each year, a team ran the route prior to the traverse convoy's passage, staking a flag every five hundred meters for the entire length. Every two to three years, the entire route was resurveyed due to the movement of the ice. GPS was only so useful when some sections of the surveyed-as-safe route moved multiple kilometers in a year and others barely wiggled. It was the flags that marked the safe passage —hopefully.

After the long double-haul up onto the polar plateau, everything else took twice as much effort as well. Even sitting as they drove across eight hundred more kilometers of nothingness was exhausting. The cold was so intense now that it punched hard against the cabin heater's limits. The passage from the tractor cab to their living quarters was "mad cold" as Clara would say.

When Michel decided that he envied the engines—their enclosure modifications ran them as if they were in just minus twenty-degree weather, not minus sixty—he knew he was losing it. It was too cold up here to even crack a window, yet the sun continued to cook them on one side while they froze on the other in their little glass cubes atop the powerful machines.

From the top of the climb southwards, the tractors began having problems. Not mechanical problems; power problems. Hauling thirty tons of fuel with each tractor at sea level made the Challengers seem indomitable. Doing the same thing at three kilometers, up atop the plateau of the polar ice cap, made them gasp and wheeze at every imperfection in the SPoT road.

The *road? Baptême!* The path packed by last year's traverse and then carved up by the constantly blown snow of the long winter was wicked harsh (thanks, Clara). It rarely snowed here, but the drifting never, ever stopped. Driving at speed across the surface, the tractor would abruptly tilt and groan as it struggled over some new drift.

They moved at a brisk walk, very brisk at these temperatures. Without enough air. His body refused to adapt quickly to the high elevation. Even the regulars were pretty subdued those first nights high on the ice cap.

The rest of the passage passed in a blur. A seven-hundred-klick crawl over the plateau.

With a hundred to go, which should have been an easy day's haul, they plunged into hell. Hearing about "Sastrugi National Park" and experiencing it were two very different things.

"Just start the morning by putting all your crap on the floor, it'll end up there anyway. And buckle your damn seatbelt," Rico wasn't the only one to warn him. Unlike the shorts and t-shirt, Michel decided to believe them from the start.

Sastrugi weren't piled-up snow drifts that the plow on the lead tractor could flatten out. It was hard ice that had been deeply wind-carved by the fierce winds plaguing the South Pole. And, in the so-called National Park, the carved ridges were three meters high. Despite the deep seat cushions and springs, Michel knew he'd be black and blue after the first half hour. With full loads, they were beaten and battered for two full days, as they ground over the hard ice dragging their big sleds.

No one slept well the night they spent in the sastrugi, there'd simply been no way to level the living quarters. The constant feeling of falling out of the tilted bunks gave everyone nightmares.

At noon the next day, they emerged from Sastrugi Hell and plunged into the Swamp. With the bright blue beacon of Amundsen-Scott Station looking like a mirage thirty klicks away, it was hard to pay attention to the ice road.

And nowhere could it be more critical. It was a curious region with almost no wind at all. Rather than carved hell, the snow stayed light and fluffy here in broad drifts. Straying from the road, well packed by prior years of passage, was just asking to get high-centered and deeply stuck. Then an elaborate game of unhooking one or two of the other tractors to haul out the stuck tractor and sled, without swamping those tractors in turn, had filled the stories around the dinner table for several nights.

Michel made sure that he stuck right on the tread marks of the machine in front of him the whole way across.

The passage, being the first full traverse of the year, had taken twenty-seven days instead of the more typical twenty-one. They would be spending Christmas out on the ice while headed back to McMurdo. But they were still on schedule for him to be back in time for the wedding—barely.

For four weeks he'd seen and spoken only to the SPoT crew. Other than a few pager-messages with Clara, he'd had no contact with the outside world. Their tiny group had bonded, pulled tight by the shared hardship and isolation.

7

———

Their arrival at South Pole Station was actually a little terrifying.

They were swarmed on their arrival. It was finally warm enough, only minus fifty-three Celsius, for the tractors to drive safely, but a storm up at McMurdo had delayed the planes. The SPoT convoy were the first visitors in over eight months. The forty-one overwinters at Amundsen-Scott Station mobbed them.

For them, the SPoT team were the first new faces of the year and were a welcome relief. Like two old whaling ships meeting for the first time in a multi-year voyage, there was an overwhelming social explosion.

There was also a lot of work.

The cargo sled was unloaded.

The fuel bladders were hooked up to temporary tanks and pumped dry. The team chased the dregs of fuel out of the flaccid rubber bladders with push brooms, salvaging every liter possible from the hard rubber going stiff with the cold. Only three bladders of the forty-eight they'd dragged south were left full, thirty thousand liters to fuel their return trip.

Nothing was thrown out at the Pole, the Antarctic Treaty prohibited it. A lot of the crap went out on the planes, but again, the too big and too awkward were theirs to haul back. A decommissioned building had to be loaded onto the cargo sled along with numerous pallets of recycling, costing them another crucial day.

And through the whole eight-day unload and load operation, it seemed to Michel that he was being pulled a hundred different ways.

Work on the tractors.

Grab a shower. Even limited to two minutes due to fuel costs, it was a *huge* luxury after three weeks of sponge baths. Laundry was another major plus.

Every meal was spent surrounded by the overwinters eager for new stories. That pressure eased a little when the first plane of the season finally made it in—delivering a load of scientists, support staff, and fresh fruit and veggies which he missed so much it was hard to believe it had only been three weeks. At McMurdo, they were five months without freshies each year. How they made it the nine months at the South Pole taught him that his tentative idea to overwinter at the South Pole someday should probably stay tentative.

One of the team mentioned his upcoming Ice Wedding. That made him the center of even more attention. Weddings on The Ice were one of the latest offerings by tour companies. But to have two of *their own* get married on Antarctica was turning out to be a big deal.

The whole week at the South Pole was a dizzying whirlwind that didn't give him time to think.

The only time he felt half himself were the two brief calls he'd managed with Clara. Communications satellite coverage —the only kind there was here—was spotty at the South Pole and there was no bandwidth for video calls. But both times they'd managed to talk and laugh a little. Long enough to get past the *brave front* they each were keeping up for the other.

"Separation makes the heart grow fonder?" she'd asked softly at the end of the second conversation. He'd barely managed to nod before the connection failed. Realizing she couldn't have seen his nod, he paged back, "It does."

Once more in his rig at the end of the convoy, he turned north. From here, every direction was north, though McMurdo drew at him like a compass. Yet it also pushed back against his nerves like the wrong end of a magnet.

He leaned on the horn when a few of the workers who were out to service another Skibird delivery flight waved.

But his heart wasn't in it.

The peace of The Ice wrapped around him long before the station was out of sight. Even when the Number Three tractor wandered into The Swamp and Number Four almost followed it in, he didn't mind—except for the eight hours it took to haul the sleds and tractors back onto the trail.

Mostly it was just him and his tractor.

He was okay with that. This he understood.

His own message still on his pager's screen to Clara's question of whether separation made the heart grow fonder— "It does."—not so much.

8

———————

IT WASN'T SASTRUGI NATIONAL PARK THAT GOT THEM. THAT merely battered them body and soul. Getting seasick at three kilometers above sea level was a little bizarre, but the constant climb and descent over the uneven ice-carved field had him wishing for a stable horizon long before they reached it. Two separate breakdowns happened due to the shaking. It cost them a day he no longer had to spare.

It wasn't the Polar Plateau that got them. They crossed that vast expanse with as few events as they had on the outbound journey—nothing that took over a few hours to fix.

It wasn't even a major crevasse to avoid.

It was "Sonic" Borowski's heart. The big Pole didn't speak much, but he had a laugh that blasted into being like a sonic boom at the strangest moments. You couldn't *not* laugh in response when Sonic launched one.

He was driving the cargo tractor directly ahead of Michel when he abruptly veered aside.

Michel barely resisted the urge to follow him as he had for over thirty days of driving.

Sonic's tractor made it past a hundred meters off the road before it climbed an ice drift—only under one track. The machine tilted in slow motion until it tumbled onto its side. The treads continued spinning as the tractor lay there.

"Man down!" he shouted over the radio. Then he shoved open his cabin door, jumped down to the ice, and cursed. It was minus forty-two and blowing hard. It felt as if he was having a full-body acupuncture by ice crystals. He climbed back into his cab, shrugged into his parka, and grabbed his heavy gloves before jumping down again.

First on the scene, he avoided the spinning treads to reach the cabin door. Through the glass he could see Sonic hanging lax in his seat harness. It was about the scariest thing ever.

He crawled in and killed the engine, stopping the treads, and hopefully before there was any damage to the engine. It was hard not to step on all the detritus that had built up over five weeks in a confined space and now been dumped onto the side window and ceiling. Soda cans, a couple novels, water bottles, a pair of socks and a loner in another color, a whole collection of small boxes—Sonic had a major sweet tooth for Raisinets, which had almost earned him a whole different nickname for how much they looked like rabbit turds.

He still had a pulse, but that was all Michel was qualified to test. That and the man's breath was clear in the cold air. He squatted with Sonic's head supported in his lap until the other guys showed up.

Rico led half the team to haul Sonic to the living quarters. He shouted instructions as he moved off. "Frenchy, get a couple of the guys to right this tractor. Then figure out if it's drivable."

It took them forever in the bitter cold. First they had to get the tractor with the snowplow unhooked from its sled, then cut away the ice dune that had tipped Sonic's tractor. Two more tractors with lines rigged, tipped the beast upright.

Risking the skin on his fingers, he pulled the injectors and cranked the engine with the power off. Only a little oil squirted out the holes—a good sign that not too much had leaked into the cylinders while running inverted.

He slid the injectors back in, and ran the block and sump heaters for twenty minutes before he tried cranking it over. The cloud of white smoke out the stack was so thick that the wind couldn't quite rip it away. But in under a minute, the oil smoke was already tapering off and—he nearly froze his ear to the chassis to check—there was no engine knock that he could detect.

The cab was battered and far from airtight, but it was intact.

They reattached the cargo sled and, using all three tractors, managed to tow it back onto the track.

The outside team conferred quickly. "If Sonic can't drive..." "...we can put his tractor on one of the empty sleds." "Yeah, then we double up some of the empty fuel sleds to free up a tractor for the cargo module."

Michel made a point of high-fiving the whole team for having it down. It would mean moving slower, probably a half day to rejigger the loads and then at *least* an extra day of driving.

He was going to miss his own goddamn wedding. Clara was going to lambast him—because their families would be scattering back to the winds the next day. And family was at the core of who Clara was.

As they hustled over to the living-quarters module, Michel had another thought that almost took his knees out from under him.

It was the first time he'd thought about the crevasses. They were nearing the head of the glacier, where it bent and folded for the two-kilometer drop to form its portion of the Ross Ice Shelf, and he'd been running around on the surface like it was a hockey rink.

Tabarnak! A total city mouse move. It was pure luck that he wasn't dead. Which was a good thing, because if he died before the wedding, Clara would flat out kill him, assuming Priya didn't get to him first.

9

———

"Doc says it was a probably heart attack and we need to get him back to base fast. Didn't say a damn word about how we're supposed to do that." Rico waved at the satellite phone in disgust.

Sonic lay flat on his back on the dining table. It was hard, but Michel forced himself to look at his friend. They were close after five weeks driving on the ice—the whole team was. To see one of their own down was brutal.

But to realize how short time could be was even harder. Just that fast, it could have been him. Maybe not a heart attack, Sonic had a number of issues aside from force-feeding Raisinets, but something else could get him just that fast—like a crevasse.

"Any bright ideas on how to get Sonic to the docs?" Rico asked. "We're still way outside helicopter range to base, even loaded up with extra fuel."

Michel did some quick math in his head. "Two drivers crowd into a cab with no sled load. Figure out how to get Sonic in there too. Then we drive straight through. Bet we could cover the ground in under three days. Even better, at top speed, we could be inside helo range in under twenty-four hours."

"Like the way you think, Frenchy. But we've only got the one ground-penetrating radar. And the tractor would still need to drag a fuel bladder, we don't have any single bladder sleds. We also need to navigate the fall safely, that's a day to do that alone. What else?"

There was a glum silence. Michel wished Clara was here. She'd come up with some brilliant solution that no one else…

"Well," Michel didn't like being the only one talking up ideas. Maybe he could blame this one on Clara.

Rico nodded for him to go ahead.

"I spent last summer and a chunk of this spring making the ice runways at MacTown." Clara, interested in everything mechanical, had asked him about every detail and ended up working part of the spring driving the heavy grooming gear out at Phoenix with him.

"Sonic doesn't have time for us to make a runway."

Michel smiled and pointed out the back door entry to the living quarters. "Don't need to. Have them land an Air National Guard Skibird on the Traverse. We just packed it down with eight tractor loads in two directions. With a little touchup using the plow and another run over the area, that's easily up to spec for those birds. They're tough and we already know the strip is crevasse free."

They were still going to lose a full day by the time all of this was done, but Michel had an idea on that too.

10

After cleaning up the section of the SPoT, they staked a two-kilometer stretch with flags every fifty meters.

One of the LC-130 Skibirds flew from McMurdo and wafted down out of the sky to land smooth as could be on the hard-packed snow.

Sonic was aboard in moments. The plane blew a blinding cloud of snow as it turned and raced back aloft. When the blown snow settled to mere white-out, someone in a Big Red parka emerged from the spindrift. He'd know her anywhere, she walked like a sailor who owned the planet.

Six weeks apart and Clara was impossibly even more familiar. All his nerves and worries were gone in that moment.

He walked up and wrapped her in his arms before Sonic's plane was even out of sight.

"Separation makes the heart grow fonder is utter crap, Sailor."

"Why's that, Antoine?"

He laughed. At her. At himself. At the ridiculous places he'd had to go to discover that he had indeed found the woman he loved.

"Answer the question, Jean Baptiste."

"Separation from you is *utter torture.* I get away from you and all I get is FUD—fear, uncertainty, and doubt. You may be a crazy woman, Sailor, but I seem to go far crazier whenever I'm more than ten steps from you."

She leaned her forehead against his chest for a long moment, "Thank God, Beauregard."

"Why?"

"Because I thought it was just me. That's why I was so nervous when you left. I always made sense to myself until I met you. And now, with you, I make even more sense, but in a whole new way that's so good it's scary. Without you..." and she shuddered once more.

He couldn't see her face, the bitter wind and the needle-sharp ice forced them to keep their furred hoods up, but this was definitely the right woman for him.

"Come on. I need your help fixing up *your* tractor." He thumped a foot on one of the two boxes that the Skibird had dropped on the snow along with Clara. If they drove the SPoT together, they'd never have to be further apart than their machines.

"What about the wedding?"

He thumped a boot on the second box. "I got that covered, too."

11

THEY WERE STILL THREE DAYS OUT FROM MCMURDO WHEN IT WAS time for the wedding. They would still have a grand party once they were back at the station, but their families were only together for this weekend and they absolutely had to take advantage of it.

The Pole and McMurdo kept New Zealand time, mainly because all of their supply flights originated in Christchurch, New Zealand.

So, the SPoT convoy piled out of their beds and onto the ice for a midnight, New Year's Eve wedding on the Ross Ice Shelf. That made for a seven a.m. in Gloucester, Massachusetts, so the families could celebrate over a New Year's Day breakfast.

Priya was at McMurdo on the satellite phone and their families were on another phone. No video conferencing because the satellites just didn't have the bandwidth, but that was okay.

Rico had jumped online long enough to become ordained to perform weddings through the Universal Life Church. And they'd actually bypassed a whole set of problems by not being at

McMurdo. Here, in the middle of the Ross Ice Shelf, they were technically in international waters, so there were far fewer legal hurdles for them to jump over. They'd worry about those later.

The team had unhitched the tractors and pulled them into a semicircle to make what Rico called "a churchy space." It also served to block the worst of the wind.

Down on the Ross Ice Shelf, the temperature stood at a bare five degrees of frost. After weeks up on the plateau, it rated downright comfortable. The driving winds of the Polar Ice Cap had been left behind as well.

They stood in a vast field of white, only the distant peak of Mount Erebus hinted at land. Above them was a cathedral of crystalline blue as if they were getting married inside a perfect jewel box.

After the day's drive, Michel had opened the second box that had arrived with Clara. Priya hadn't missed a single thing on his list, right down to the rings from his night table and two bottles of champagne for afterward.

Standing under the Antarctic midnight sun, he peeled off his parka. He was wearing his tuxedo, complete with a white bow tie (clip-on because he wasn't crazy). It looked ridiculous with his ski pants and snow boots. But it made Clara laugh, he was her kind of ridiculous.

"I knew you'd be late for the wedding. But I didn't know you'd be so dashing, Jean Luc." Then she shed her Big Red parka and he lost his ability to breathe.

She wore the upper half of a wedding dress that wiped out "Sailor" forever.

"You're gorgeous, Clara."

"I'm also turning into a giant goosebump. It's brick out here." The dress was sleeveless, so he slipped his tux jacket over her shoulders and morphed into a giant goosebump himself through the thin dress shirt.

A goosebump, but not one with any nerves or doubts. They were impossible with a woman like Clara standing beside him.

Rico held up the two phones: one linking to the maid of honor (and probably half of McMurdo), and the other to their gathered families.

The SPoT crew stood by their tractors like a whole line of men of honor. They'd actually squabbled over who was escorting Clara and who was standing for him. They finally decided that they were all doing both—but they were really on Clara's side.

He could hear them joking about having chosen a particularly deep crevasse if he screwed this up.

Michel glanced at Rico who just shook his head. Why did everyone seem to have the same idea about him?

For all his preparation, the wedding passed in a blur. He was glad that one of the guys had offered to video it.

One moment they were freezing together...and then he was beginning the New Year kissing his wife.

In the background he heard cheers from the two phones.

"I love you, Michel Charbonneau." Clara whispered for him alone.

"Hey, you just used my real name."

She nodded as she dragged on her parka, keeping his jacket. Her hood nodded. "Guess I don't need to keep you at a distance anymore." Like Rico's, she'd wife, she'd known since that first moment she strode into the McMurdo machine shop.

And, as usual, Clara was exactly right. Keeping her close is what worked for both of them.

Then he was almost bowled from his feet by the sudden blast of all of the tractor horns firing off at once.

"Oh my God. Please tell me we won't have that for every anniversary." Clara had to shout to have any chance of being heard. In the brief gaps he could hear the same sounds coming from both phones, blaring horns.

"Every year!" He shouted back. "The whole world will keep blowing their horns for us on each New Year's Eve."

And he'd be blowing his own horn of triumph as well.

With her permanently in his life, he could finally be his true self. He'd celebrate the Québécois hero of Antarctica who had married the lovely sailor on The Ice as loudly as he could every year.

SKIBIRD (BONUS STORY)

I'm writing a bonus story for each of my novels. Some definitely require reading the novels first as they include: spoilers, inside references, and sometimes whole shifts to the tale's perspective.

This isn't one of those.

Miranda Chase is the premier air-crash investigator for the NTSB—the National Transportation Safety Board. Her challenge, she's autistic. So, while she is a genius about airplanes, planes are all she understands.

At the end of Skibird, Miranda and her girlfriend Andi are sneaking off to their bedroom to have makeup sex after a bad misunderstanding. Everyone else is downstairs preparing the house for a belated Christmas / New Year's celebration. But what happens isn't quite what they planned.

One of my rough draft readers for *Skibird* complained that only my villains get to have sex. In the story that follows, you'll see that there's a problem when my thriller heroes and heroines attempt sex. This scene is wholly unlike the *Miranda Chase* action-adventure technothriller series...but this

Christmas tale is wholly like the characters. Even if the sex scene goes a little sideways, it's something like this:

1

———

At the sharp knock on the bedroom door, Andi mumbled something from where her head lay against Miranda's breast.

"What was that?" Miranda lifted the covers to peer down at the top of Andi's head and to hear her better.

"Tell them to go away."

Even after eighteen months together, Miranda still couldn't believe the sensations that Andi sent rippling through her body. It wasn't merely the sex and the shock waves of release that ensued. The first time they'd tried to make love the sensations of simple touch had overloaded her nerves and she'd had to keep pushing away every few minutes to recover.

She'd been with men before, and had learned to hold her body's reactions at bay for long enough to make them happy. But Andi was her first ever lover who liked to snuggle—to simply curl up together and hold on.

At first it had been a trial to learn to tolerate the physical contact. But, as long as the contact was firm, she rather enjoyed it now. Even for prolonged periods of five minutes or more. She still couldn't tolerate it in sleep. Andi's natural tendency to roll into her as she slept had finally been addressed with a large pillow placed between them at night.

The knock sounded again.

"Wouldn't that be rude, telling them to go away?"

"So be rude." Andi's hair lay heavy enough over Miranda's chest to not tickle—she couldn't tolerate tickling. Instead, it felt like a cascade of dry water on her bare skin. That was inherently illogical and she barely resisted contemplating the necessary molecular structure to create such a thing.

"You know I'm not very good at being rude." Mother had taught her to always be polite. It was written on the front page of her personal notebook under *Rules,* though she rarely had to look at those anymore to remember them.

Andi raised her head, batted at the covers as if they were attacking her, until her face was free, then shouted, "Go away! We're busy here."

The door swung open and Holly strode in.

Andi groaned, dropped her head back onto Miranda's breast, and flipped the covers over her head.

"Being rude didn't work very well, did it?"

Andi responded with a deep sigh that flowed down her sternum, but Miranda tolerated it. She was always cold and Andi was always so warm that the light contact of her breath had its compensations.

Holly stopped at the foot of the bed to look down at them. "You're missing it, you know."

"Not missing a thing here," Andi's voice was muffled by the comforter. "Not even missing you, though I wish we were."

"Jeremy found your box of Christmas decorations and is going wild. Mike is doing one of his holiday cooking things. Roasts and pies and who can tell what. There are Christmas movies on. It's all so...so..."

"What?" Miranda didn't often see Holly so flummoxed. Yes, that was the right emotion. She knew it without checking her reference notebook. Lifting the covers, she peered down at Andi. "I figured out Holly was flummoxed. All on my own."

Andi raised a hand from Miranda's belly and held it up by her shoulder.

Miranda did her best to high five it before dropping the covers back over Andi's head. That left her looking at Holly. "So...what?"

"So...*homey*." Holly mimicked driving a knife into her gut and slashing it back and forth before flopping across the foot of the bed. It was a good thing that she and Andi were both short and the bed so big as they were able to pull their feet clear rather than Holly's landing pinning them uncomfortably.

"Homey?" Miranda wasn't sure if she liked or disliked homey. Neither of her parents had been very good at it. But she and Andi had been slowly changing the house—one thing at a time so as not to upset the overall familiarity. It always took a while, but Miranda had grown to like each one, coral-colored sheets to replace white ones. Extra pillows on the couches for shoving into useful places, like a lap pillow for holding a book. Flowered curtains to replace the plain brown ones she'd grown up with.

Miranda had also learned to enjoy it when the team was all visiting. Was that what Holly meant by homey? She wanted to ask Andi, but she was showing no signs of emerging from under the covers.

"Yeah," Holly lay on her back, staring up at the ceiling.

Experimentally, Miranda pressed her toes up against Holly's thigh through the covers. It felt nice and warm.

"Hey, what's going on here?" Taz stuck her head in through the door that Holly hadn't fully closed.

"Someone please go away!" Andi shouted from under the covers.

Since neither Holly or Taz showed any signs of leaving, Miranda figured that it would have to be her. But the instant she tried to free herself, Andi clamped a hand around her waist, holding her in place.

"Not you. Them!"

"But they aren't leaving."

For the second time, Andi struggled to the surface until she could peer over the covers at the other two women. "Could you close and lock the door."

Taz did.

"I meant with you two on the other side."

"Wow. This is a very comfortable bed." Holly gave no signs of imminent departure.

"Really?" Taz stepped over and lay down on the part of the bed where Andi usually slept.

They always made love on Miranda's side because she found that more familiar and reassuring.

"Hey, this *is* nice."

Andi scooched around and appeared to be trying to force Holly to roll off the end of the bed by pushing her feet against Holly's hip.

Holly simply reached out and grabbed both of her feet with one hand and held them there. "Very comfortable," she declared even as Andi tried to kick free. Holly was far too strong for her.

"But not homey? You specifically said you didn't like homey."

"The men *have* gone crazy," Taz affirmed. "Like ospreys madly building nests for their mates."

"Are they planning on mating with you?"

All three of them turned to face her.

"What did I say wron—"

"No!" Holly and Taz shouted in unison.

"But aren't you each—"

"Doing what you and Andi are?" Holly said but it didn't sound like a question so Miranda wasn't sure how to answer.

"*Were* doing!" Andi didn't sound happy.

"Sure," Taz agreed from where she was lying. "The sex is awesome. But mating implies...you know."

Miranda didn't.

"Little Hollys and Tazs," Andi prompted her.

"Well Taz is already little." The petite Latina was only four-eleven after all, three inches shorter than even Andi.

"Babies!" Holly began beating the back of her head on the bed. Miranda was glad it was soft so that she didn't hurt herself. "They're nesting like they want babies."

"Do they?"

That stopped Holly beating her head against the bed. She looked at Taz who shrugged.

"Maybe. I don't think it's conscious. Mike would probably run for the hills if he had the thought out loud. Jeremy..." Taz sighed. "He's like the only normal one here. Came from a good family and all that. He'd probably go crazy—crazy happy not crazy crazy—at the thought of having a family of his own."

"How can he be the only normal one? He's outweighed by a factor of five."

"Statistics aside, he's the normal one, which all of our messed-up families are measured against. That's how he got past my defenses. He kept being nice to me and saw me in ways I never imagined myself. I never saw it coming, the little sneak."

Little? But he was eight inches taller than Taz.

Miranda studied the edge of the sheet draped across her and Andi's chest. This had been manufactured with very careful statistics measuring material consistency and machine tolerance. Statistics were an inherent element of any process—except humans? That didn't make any sense at all.

Taz frowned. "You don't think the fact that we said the word inside the same house he's in...might have set him thinking about that."

"What word?" Miranda had tried to follow but this was far

less clear than a plane wreck. There didn't seem to be a clear debris perimeter to chart and confine the problem. Data collection was difficult because—

"Babies," all three women said in unison.

"Oh, well you just said it out loud again."

"Ahhh!" Now Taz was pounding her head against the covers like Holly had been.

"Don't you want babies?"

"No!" Again in unison. But their faces didn't match their words and Miranda never knew what to do when that happened. They all settled into a deep silence as if they were either thinking very hard...or starting to fall asleep. The latter seemed unlikely as the bed might be big but the four of them would be distinctly crowded.

"Do *you?*" Andi whispered quietly.

Miranda shook her head. "I think one autistic in the family is enough."

"But you're incredible."

Holly rolled up onto her side, decreasing the room for Miranda and Andi's feet further, and propped her head up on her hand. "She's right."

Miranda shook her head. She knew how she felt inside.

"But why?" Andi's voice had the gentle questioning tone that Miranda could never ignore. "What's wrong with being neurodiverse? Your insides are amazing."

"It's not the insides, it's the outsides. I remember how I never fit in. Not at school or summer horse camp. How many college students have to have their therapist move in and follow them to classes, meals, even the library?" Especially the library. They had instructions not to let her in *without* Tante Daniels as an escort to make sure she didn't try correcting any more historic map inaccuracies.

"Not many," Andi admitted.

"I don't mind being me. Most people think that's the

problem. I *like* being me or else I wouldn't know who I am. But it wasn't easy."

"It wasn't easy for any of us either," Taz was tracing a finger over a stitch line in the comforter.

Holly had closed her eyes. So that she didn't have to look at Miranda? No, that didn't fit.

Only Andi didn't look away. "I think who you are is incredible. I love you, Miranda."

The room seemed to go very still. Taz's finger appeared to have become snagged on a single stitch. Holly opened her eyes to look at Andi, but made no other move.

"I know that's an impactful word." Neither of Miranda's parents had used it, but Tante Daniels had. "I long ago decided to treat it with immense caution."

"Why?"

"A part of being autistic, at least my form of it, is a degree of obsession. I became obsessed with planes after my parents died in one. Before that, I was obsessed with boats probably because I grew up on this island, but I dropped them the day my parents died. If I switch my obsession over to you, maybe I won't care about planes anymore. And then what if I switch after that and you're left—" Miranda couldn't finish the sentence because of a tightness in her chest. Rubbing it didn't help.

"Love doesn't work like that, Miranda."

"How do you know?"

"Obsession is about stuff. Love is about feelings."

Miranda tested the idea. "I do...appreciate the immense clarity you bring to everything. You're saying that it's okay to love you without..."

"Getting all obsessed about it. Yes."

Miranda wasn't sure what that would be like. She looked to Holly who held up her free forearm as if fending off an incoming missile. Taz still hadn't moved her finger from that one particular stitch. Miranda memorized its location so she could inspect it later for possible mending.

Andi continued to watch her.

"You know how terrible I am with feelings."

Andi nodded.

"Especially my own."

And smiled, "I might have noticed that."

Miranda thought about how she'd felt during the last long week they'd been trapped aboard the plane wreck on the Antarctic ice cap. Not daring to speak to Andi. At the same time, unable to tolerate the pain of being apart from her. She had folded into herself, but not like an autistic meltdown. It had almost been worse, as if she'd been collapsing into a black hole—rapidly contracting past the point where even light could ever escape.

Was that what love was? Wanting to be with someone that badly?

Maybe it was. In which case...

"I love you, too, Andi. And I'll try not to get all obsessed about it."

Andi's smile lit up as bright as a plane wreck explosion. Then she began crying and buried her face against Miranda's bare shoulder.

"You're getting me wet."

Andi nodded fiercely but didn't stop crying.

"That's our cue, mate." Holly sat up and tugged on Taz's ankle.

Taz was sniffling, but sat up as well.

Together they headed for the door.

Miranda couldn't see anything wrong with the stitch Taz had been fingering.

"We'll be right down." If Mike was cooking and Jeremy decorating, it would only be polite.

Holly stopped at the door. "I think you two should do a little obsessing first. Join us later."

Andi continued clinging to her and crying on her shoulder. Andi's hair spread smoothly across her chest in a cool cascade. Her tears began to trickle off Miranda's shoulder.

So what *would* be the key markers to distinguish wet water from dry water?

———

If you liked Miranda, you'll love the completed series. Available at: https://miranda-chase.com

THE HANUKKAH PRETZEL PROPHECY

This story is Tracey Cooper-Posey's fault. "I'm doing an anthology of Portal Romances. Do you want to kick a story my way?" "What's a portal romance?" She explained a little, I cooked up the story below, not knowing the hero and heroine were supposed to go *through* the portal. Perhaps I should have asked what the title was first: *Love in Other Worlds.* But she's great and took it the way I wrote it.

Being a fantasy, it landed solidly in my *Deities Anonymous* world. Or perhaps not so solidly, it's hard to tell once Henrietta gets involved.

1

—————

FIRST NIGHT – AARON

"You're an idiot, Aaron."

"Love you too, Miriam." I didn't. But being nice to your older sister on the first day of Hanukkah seemed like a good idea.

First Night of the eight days of Hanukkah, all Jews were mandated to celebrate. Actually, celebrate for all eight days, making it one of my favorite holidays. Miracles were handy that way. The Passover Pig Out, uh, Seder dinner, was another one where loads of good food was eaten to celebrate a miracle. In general, outside of the fast for Yom Kippur, The Day of Atonement, Jews were much more focused on feast. Probably because of all that famining we did in the times of the Torah.

Feasting was also good for the family; who'd have thought that Gloucester, Massachusetts—a decidedly Italian and Portuguese town on the North Shore—would rock a Jewish deli and bakery for over a century.

Also, Miriam is dangerous in an evil-older-sister way, making cautious civility a functional strategy.

After I'd teased her about looking so different from the rest of us—saying maybe ten or twenty times too often that she looked like some demented denizen of Hell had pulled a fast one on Mom—she'd filled my pillowcase with whipped cream...liberally mixed with electric-pink dye.

When I'd plunged into bed that night, it had burst forth and splattered all over my room like a goopy shotgun blast. Everything it touched was stained hot pink: my clothes (which might have been all over the floor), my homework, my rug. My posters, the less said about my taste in under-clad female pop singers at that age...maybe it was high time they were ruined.

I've long since gotten my own apartment but Miriam had somehow arranged to have Mom guilt trip me into taking that rug with me. We're Jewish, guilt works. Jewish-mother-guilt is like an undeniable superpower even Superman could only wish for.

I still live with that rug; so sue me.

Over time, the bright pink polka-dots have faded from Madonna "Material Girl" hot-pink to *Barbie* pastel-pink. Since the movie, I'll admit that having cause to daydream about Margot Robbie knocking on the apartment door some day isn't an all-bad thing.

But I knew why Miriam—too tall and too much lush hair to be a proper Schwartzman—was calling me an idiot this time.

For this first night of Hanukkah, we gathered about the same table that we'd grown up around. Mom and Dad, Uncle Max who's at least half as funny as he thinks he is, Aunt Max (short for Maxine), my two girl cousins (who at least *look* like they belong to the family, though I now keep my mouth shut on that point), and Grandma (on Dad's side).

She'd given me a Hanukkah gift on First Night. We aren't really a gift-during-Hanukkah kind of family. Dad may call our Christmas tree a Hanukkah bush, but he's not fooling anybody; he's into it as much as the rest of us.

No, for us Hanukkah is about fried potato latkes, cheese and blueberry blintzes drowned in sour cream, and smoked salmon on fresh-made sourdough bagels. It's about Mom putting Peter, Paul, and Mary's *A Holiday Celebration* album on because it had the "Light One Candle" song about Hanukkah in among all the Christmas carols. Mom isn't retro, it's Grandma's vinyl and she's never embraced CD never mind digital. We don't try to make the music ourselves as we *are* the Family Schwartzman-can't-carry-a-tune-for-crap non-singers and none of us, not even Miriam, look the least like Julie Andrews.

The most serious endeavor for us other than the lighting of the candles and a bit of feasting was playing the Dreidel game for gelt, gold-foil-wrapped chocolate coins. *Ganz, halb, nischt, schict,* the four sides of the spinning top, deciding who gets and who gives gelt. One year I'd spent hours trying to figure out how to load a Dreidel to always land showing *ganz* so that I could take all the gelt during my turn. But Miriam figured it out, switched our Dreidels when I wasn't watching, and cleaned me out. Worse, she shared her winnings with our cousins, but not me.

Anyway, our household? Not big on Hanukkah gifts.

But Grandma had given me a present—and only me. There are a few advantages to being the only male of my generation on either side of the house. First-born male has a certain gravitas in a Jewish household, especially to someone as traditional as Grandma, which I totally bought into because of how much it irritated Miriam.

It was one of Grandad's first recipes from when his grandad had first taken him to Schwartzman and Sons deli—back when Gloucester was more about fish and less about tourism. Except it was a recipe I'd never seen before, despite playing in the flour bins there since before I could walk.

The index card, faded to mud-brown and handled until it was as soft as fine leather, was covered with a child's scrawl. Half the ingredients were blurred past recovery. I could see there were a lot of steps, but the ones I could read made no sense. Of course, neither did the title.

Root Beer Rye Pretzels.

Grandma tapped the old card with a thwack of her knitting needle almost hard enough to scrape away a few more clues. "You make that. Make it good like your Grandpa. It will be very good for you."

My instinctual agreement to one of Grandma's mandates is what had earned me Miriam's, *You're an idiot* assessment once she'd managed to read the title. Which only made me twice as determined to resurrect Grandad's recipe.

It was just past sunset as I watched Mom set the central *shamash* candle on the Menorah and the First Night one to the far right of the nine-place holder.

Baruch atah Adonai, Eloheinu melech ha-olam...

As I echoed the blessing, watching Mom light the *shamash* then lift that to light the first candle, I could somehow see deeper.

Blessed are thou, Lord Our God, Defender of the Universe...

She replaced the *shamash* and headed for the kitchen. That's when things went kinda sideways. I half imagined that I could see something in the candlelight—Dad as a young man, kneading bread. It made me ask him if he'd ever seen Grandpa's recipe or eaten one of his root beer pretzels. He made a *Hell no* face not all that different from Miriam's.

That's when she kneecapped me with her chair as she rose to help Mom serve dinner and I lost sight of whatever I'd imagined seeing.

2

SECOND NIGHT – TIZZY

"No. No. No. And No!"

"You're being silly. Those soda flavors are all lovely." We'd just finished taste testing four different batches of root beer.

Mum the Encourager wasn't helping. Growing up, everything I did was a success, even when it wasn't. Mum Reality versus Real Reality wasn't often easy to reconcile as a kid. I thought I'd grown accustomed to it but on this one she was dead wrong. "You have Uncle Samuel's gift, Tizzy."

"Lizzy!" I don't know why I bothered. I'd been fighting that nickname since I'd been born. Since I was in Mum's womb. Since Moses first parted the Red Sea, followed closely by his wife Tzipora—the source of my nickname. Or at least that's what I decided. It couldn't be from Mum's favorite saying *Don't throw a tizzy, Tizzy.* I'm a redhead, I get upset. *Nyah! Nyah! Nyah!*

Okay. Maybe I should stop complaining, I don't want to be the *Pride and Prejudice* heroine Lizzy Bennet even more than I don't want to be the wife of Moses.

The fact that I was named for Great Aunt Elizabeth, for reasons no one could agree on, didn't enter into the matter. My

321

vote was for our being the only two with flaming red hair. She'd been hot back in the day, I've seen pictures. Me? At least I got the thick red hair.

When GA Elizabeth had died last month, she'd left The Company to her namesake—me. Good thing or bad? The jury remained deadlocked on that one.

B-Dam—short for Beaver Dam of which we have a lot here on the Massachusetts North Shore but read it as Best Damn, please—was one of the last small independent soda pop bottlers in the US. It had folded three years ago when Great Uncle Sam had stroked out while lifting one of the last-ever cases of Birch Beer Tonic into his rattletrap delivery truck. Probably the way he wanted to go.

But *tonic*? It was a word that, like, one in a thousand people in this century still used for soda. Maybe. GU Sam had refused to change with the times. *Not soda, Tizzy, it was tonic in 1907 when my grandpa founded it, and it's tonic now.* When I tried to shorten his moniker to Gus, he'd shut me down on that too. *I was a newborn named for Uncle Sam during the war. Now that I'm your great uncle, that's good enough for me.* Stubborn old man. Three years gone and I still miss him every day.

Now the formulas and the ancient equipment in the front of the old house that had served B-Dam Bottlers for so many decades were mine. I fought the sniffles, again. GA Elizabeth hadn't let go of her throttlehold on his defunct business until the will had pried it from her dead fingers.

"You've always had the itch," Pop noted as he set the Second Night candles into the Menorah. "You got it from me."

"Maybe I got it from Tzipora," who had certainly patched up Moses enough times during *Exodus*. But he knew I was teasing. I'd inherited the need to fix broken things right down the paternal line.

Mum's eternal patience with the two of us escaped as a

small sigh as she and I raised our shawls for the prayer before lighting the candles.

Baruch atah Adonai, Eloheinu melech ha-olam...

GU Sam's formulas were clear and legible. He'd made eight *soda*—because seriously, *tonic?*—flavors. I'd chosen to start with his all-natural root beer. I'd made the batch straight from his old recipe and three minor variations.

None of which were the flavor I remembered.

Thinking back, I'd never seen him use any recipes. I'd unearthed them on an archeological expedition, from which I'd barely survived, into what had laughingly been called his office. After all those decades, every nuance was in his brain, maybe even instinctively in his fingers as he hadn't exactly been all-there at the end—but his flavors had never varied. How he'd shifted the original recipes was gone, putting me most of the way back to square one.

I'd always loved to hang out with GU Sam while he was mixing syrup and I tried to see his motions as Pop lit the *shamash* and then the two candles, Second Night then First Night, as we intoned the prayers together. Tried to remember the taste. To savor each nuance in a lifetime of having it served on our dinner table. The business had slowly shrunk along with GU Sam's stature until our table and old-timer birthday parties became the only place B-Dam tonics were served. It had smelled of...cinnamon?

Mum set out the fried chicken seasoned with a touch of cinnamon, with a platter of fried leek *keftes*. I could feel my pores clogging simply from the smells. Yes, the oil in the original Menorah had lasted eight days when it should have lasted only one, so fried foods were big on the Hanukkah menu. But I was going to bloat and break out after all this.

Fresh vegetables. I'd get some...tomorrow.

I held out my plate for a taste of home.

3

——————

THIRD NIGHT – AARON

During a break at the bakery, I copied out every character I could read of Grandpa's recipe, but it left me little wiser about how to make Grandpa's *Root Beer Rye Pretzels*. Like a baker's version of the Dead Sea Scrolls, too many passages were missing to prove whether or not Jesus had married Mary Magdelene (my vote was yes because, hey, she'd been a babe).

I know how to make a good Jewish rye bread, what bakery boy doesn't—both yeast-risen and sourdough. Which is also yeast, but slower. And pretzels aren't exactly a big stretch from there. But—

"You think too much. I thought I should come by and tell you that," the small voice was high enough to make me wiggle a finger in my ear like a dog assaulted by a dog whistle.

"Like this is news." Then I startled. I'd thought I was alone in my apartment. The family managed to spend about half of the Hanukkah nights together at my folks'. This year, Third Night wasn't one of them, so I was on my own. Mom and Dad had a dinner invite. Grandma was off with her BWK group, pronounced Bwook—Books, Wine, and Knitting (heavy on the wine).

I looked around the place. It wasn't all that big. Bed, couch, coffee table, a good chair for slouching in, TV on the dresser, a small kitchen...I *was* alone. And talking to myself in a high squeaky voice, apparently.

I glared at my own unlit Menorah. Grandma's actually. Mom and Dad had used the same one since they'd gotten married, so when Grandma had moved in, her Menorah came to me. Another bonus point to being the first-born male.

Miriam had some hot date. Guys never hung with her long, but she did better than I did. Miriams's dusky cream skin, that I'd never admit to envying, reeled them in like Gefilte fish into a poaching broth. A process that ground them up and spat them out in little patties that reeked of demoralization and week-old fish.

"If you looked like your sister," the voice again, "you wouldn't be the first-born male of your generation. You'd be the second-born female. I can tell you that isn't much fun. Try being ninth."

"Ninth?" I looked harder by the last of the evening light easing in through the front window. My room was neat enough —I don't leave things lying about since the fateful pink-pillow night. Of course, that meant the Margot Robbie-pink rug stains were on full display, virulent blotches glowing malevolently in the half light. Which, with my luck, meant I was more likely to get a visit from a pink Teletubby.

With the lack of clutter, it didn't take long to spot who was speaking.

Except it was hard to actually see her. She blurred in and out before coming into focus. Or maybe that was my perception as my mind tried to adjust. The foot-tall speaker sat opposite the Menorah, on the top of my TV, lightly kicking her bare heels against the glass with repeated little plonks. She wore a white smock, had a pleasant round face, and a mass of brunette curls. Half buried in the curls lay a skewed golden halo, like Saturn's rings at a weird angle.

"Aren't you going to light them?" She pointed a tiny finger toward my unlit Menorah. "You know, *He* doesn't care if you light them or not but your Mother does. She'll know if you burned the candles in your own Menorah or not."

"He?" The word stuck in my throat worse than a week-old peanut butter cookie.

"Adonai, Elohim, Yahweh, Joshua. You know, the One God?"

"Yes, I know the One God."

"Oh, you too?" The diminutive angel, I couldn't think what else to call her, clapped her hands together in excitement, making a little pitty-pitty-pat sound. "Isn't He the sweetest God? He can make me laugh until I think my wings are going to fall off. You still haven't lit your candles." She waved a tiny hand at the Menorah and the *shamash* burst alight. "There, that should help."

She said the lighting prayer with me, her hands clasped to her tiny chest and her eyes closed. A real believer. I go through all the motions, but faith comes hard. It—

"Well, if it came easier, then what would be the point?"

"Do you read minds?"

"No," she tapped what might have been a miniature smartwatch on her tiny wrist. "But the Software that Runs the Universe logs all your deeds and thoughts. Not that we really need that, those of us who've worked in Afterlife In-processing. Do you know how many humans come through every year? We've seen all the patterns. People love to *kvetch* even more in the afterlife than during their time here on Earth, so we hear it until our halos are drooping." She reached up to readjust hers but it simply ended up skewed at a different angle. "Of course, I suppose that it's no wonder with the Afterlife In-processing queues so far behind. We're only nine choirs of angels—"

"Making you the lowest order. The ninth. I get it now."

Her sigh echoed inside my own chest like an aching void, and I only had the one sister.

To be ninth... "Sorry."

She wiped at a tear. Who knew angels could cry? Or could show up perched atop a guy's television?

"Uh, not to be rude, but who are you, what are you, and why are you here?"

"I'm Henrietta and I thought the angel part was pretty obvious." She plinked a finger against her halo. It set up a tuning-fork vibration that filled the room until the plates and glasses in the cupboard were rattling together. She yelped in dismay and grabbed her halo, holding tight until the last vibration stopped, the glassware finally settled, and my ears were the last thing ringing in the room.

After carefully releasing her halo and no new sounds emanated, she relaxed. "Don't forget when and how," abruptly so bright and cheery it was like she glowed far whiter than justified by the light of four little candles. "They're very important, too. They'd get lonely if you left one of them out."

"Well, the when *is* kind of obvious, as in now." But I couldn't go any further.

It all sort of caught up with me at once.

What would be...Henrietta the angel? I was talking to a ninth-order angel who claimed to know God and be conversant with the Software that Runs the Universe—*that explained a lot*—which would make sense if she was what she said she was. Which made no sense at all.

"Being the smallest angel, of the lowest order of angels, can be very trying. I was telling Michelle just the other day about—"

"Who's Michelle?" I managed to slip into her stream of consciousness. It was a fast-flowing stream, so I was pretty pleased with my success.

"The Devil Incarnate. I was helping her weed her garden,

which she is *most* inconsistent about. Would you believe that she simply throws seeds wherever they land in her garden and lets them grow? It's so a-jumble, the bees hardly know which way to turn next. I drew them little maps and set up signs for them—in bee, of course." She stood up on top of the TV and did a little dance, not quite falling onto my pink-polka-dot rug or tumbling back to get snarled in the tangle of wires behind. "It's like those word-jumble things, I can never do those; they're even more confusing than Michelle's garden. What was I talking about?" She sat back on the narrow top.

I opened my mouth, but as I had no idea, I closed it again. The angel didn't slow down for even that long.

"I'm here *now* because you called out in some pain."

"Pain?" I looked down at myself. I hadn't nicked myself at the bakery in ages. Nothing broken. No—

She pointed a tiny finger toward the index card I'd set by the Menorah and my insufficient attempts to transcribe it.

"Oh."

She fluttered down to stand on the coffee table that was also my dining table and my footrest. Fluttered, as in flapping a pair of white feathered wings as tiny as she was. I don't remember a lot of dreams, so that didn't seem likely. I was male, so no holy angel was about to pull an immaculate conception number on me—I hoped. Besides, that was New Testament, not something the Jews were big believers in.

I had the *who* (kinda), the *what* (though I still wasn't fully bought-in on that), and the *when*. The *how* and *why* still remained elusive.

Walking over to the index card, Henrietta bent forward to study it by the light of the four candles. She picked it up, as big as a poster in her grasp, and twisted and turned it in the light. "Nope."

"Nope, what?"

"No secret script visible only by Third Night candlelight."

"Is there such a thing?"

She put the card back down with a sad sigh. "Well, it worked during Bilbo's quest to the Lonely Mountain. I thought that maybe if it worked for a hobbit, it might work for me." Her voice faded to a whisper. "You know, one of the little people." She placed a hand on top of her own head as if measuring herself, again tears glistened in her eyes.

I blinked...and was alone.

Me, the stupid recipe, and the glowing Menorah that absolutely I hadn't lit because I didn't have any matches or a lighter in the apartment.

I carried the Menorah over to look at the TV. There was a little dust-free stretch on the top, about the width of a cloaked angel's butt, and two little clean spots on the screen that might have been heel marks. Hey, I said I pick up my clothes, I didn't say I was on top of my dusting except before a Mom visit.

Back to the coffee table with the card.

I tried studying it in the Menorah's light. I tried looking through it with the candles behind. All it did was show quite how primitive the writing was. Grandad must have copied it down when he still counted his years in single digits. But what if he hadn't copied it down? What if he'd been as much a bakery boy as I'd become—and invented it himself?

I stared into the light and thought about Root Beer Rye Pretzels. Definitely a kid's recipe.

Pretend you're a kid, Aaron.

What I saw in the flickering light was the back of a girl's head with a long red ponytail. She wore a poodle skirt as bright pink as the original splotches on my rug (and clothes and homework). Sitting at a strange machine, she appeared to be... filling soda bottles.

4

———

FOURTH NIGHT – TIZZY

I skipped Third Night. And Fourth. Not dinner, just the family gatherings. I'd been weak and swung by the Clam Box in Ipswich for fried haddock and double onion rings. I like their fried clams better, but I'm Jewish, it's Hannukah, and shellfish are *treyf*, forbidden by Jewish dietary rules. So I skipped the clams—this time. If they didn't want Jews to eat shellfish, GU Sam shouldn't have put his bottling operation so close to the best fish-and-chips shop in the state. Okay, maybe it wasn't all that close, on the opposite side of Ipswich, but Ipswich isn't all that big a town.

I wasn't used to this being my home yet. The back of the building was a lovely little apartment but without my GU and GA there, it felt too strange. Instead of easing into my new home, I'd slept for the last several weeks in the old second-floor syrup room.

This setup dated back to before pumps ran the world. Despite its awkwardness, the mixing room still resided on the second floor so that once the syrup was ready, it could be piped down to the bottler in the room below by gravity. But that meant carrying lots of extracts and sugar, especially those heavy, heavy bags of sugar, up the ancient narrow stairs that creaked like they were tempted to drop me into the basement out of spite. I guess I was lucky there wasn't a basement.

Toward the end of GU Sam's life, I'd get off the high school bus each day after school at B-Dam Bottlers to carry the sugar upstairs for him. A hundred pounds of sugar to nine gallons of water, made one batch of simple syrup. Add the extract...and that was the magic I was missing.

I began with cataloging the one- and five-gallon carboys of extracts GU Sam had lined up along the back wall. There had to be some reason he'd left those behind. Most had been there as long as I could remember. Some missing only a few batches' worth. Others must have been more promising but still they'd been sidelined with extract remaining in them, there since even before I got dumped on him for babysitting after Kindergarten let out.

No empties to give me a clue as a syrup-making room had to be kept meticulously clean. The layer of dust over everything when I'd inherited the place hadn't been there the day he died. After a purge worthy of Hercules cleaning the Augean Stables, I'd set it to rights again. It would have been easier if I could have diverted the Ipswich River to flush it clean, but not being the half-god child of Zeus, I'd been stuck with more prosaic methods like a vacuum and mop.

Now, I sat on the cot he'd had installed for toddler Tizzy to nap on that would later support his own after-lunch siestas while the syrup was mixing. As I finished the last onion rings, I poked through the few keepsakes I'd gathered from the apartment but that had been kept here during GU Sam's day. Their Passover Seder goblet, simply beveled with a translucent rim of red-purple glass. I'd always loved its elegance and someday it would sit upon my own Seder table.

Their Menorah and an unopened packet of forty-four candles, the number needed for eight nights of Hanukkah. I placed the candles for Fourth Night, halfway through Hannukah. What would I pray for other than God's blessing?

The patience to relaunch B-Dam Sodas.

But I had a double handicap there. I was about as patient as you'd expect from a *Daddy's-girl* Jewish redhead and Pop's genes telling me to just fix the thing, no matter what it took.

I scrounged some matches and lit the *shamash,* then lit the other candles in turn.

Baruch atah Adonai, Eloheinu melech ha-olam...

I almost dropped the *shamash,* when a small face stared back at me through the lit candles.

Like *Alice Through the Looking Glass'* Cheshire cat. Just the little face, almost overwhelmed by the anime-huge brown eyes. Those eyes studied me intently through the flames for a long moment.

"What? Who?" At least that's what it looked like she said. Then a perky and mischievous smile shone through the light.

I may have screamed. I didn't mean to, and I kept it short, but I was the only critter of any genus or species bigger than housefly in the building, at least that I knew about. There hadn't even been field mouse tracks in the old dust before I'd done my girl-version of being Hercules. And I certainly wasn't built like Xena—I had Mum's lack of big curves despite wishing I'd inherited GA Elizabeth's instead—so that didn't fit any better.

When I dared look into the flames again, I saw a man with an Elvis pompadour, dressed in a dark apron spattered with flour. He was pouring a bottle of something into a mixing bowl. I'd know that label anywhere.

I tapped the side of the Menorah like, I dunno, slapping the side of a malfunctioning computer. The candles were all knocked askew. And the image was gone.

But I knew what I'd seen.

A baker pouring a bottle of B-Dam Root Beer Tonic into his dough.

5

———

FIFTH NIGHT – AARON

HANUKKAH CANDLES ARE MEANT TO BURN AT LEAST HALF THE night, and I had stayed up far longer than that hoping for another glimpse of the redhead at the bottling machine. After the first two minutes, she'd left the machine, gathered one of the wooden cases of glass bottles she'd been filling, and disappeared.

Instead of being voyeuristic about someone's back and ponytail, I was left to stare at the machine she'd been running for hour after hour.

With nothing better to do, I'd tried looking it up online. That's how I figured out it was a Dixie bottling machine...an old one, circa 1950. Back when poodle skirts first became a thing. And I'd had to look those up to see what they were called. Googling *redhead in poodle skirt* didn't help at all except to prove that they did have poodles on them and that they were now worn like costumes.

Yet the girl I'd seen, or maybe imagined, hadn't looked out of her time.

Twice I went and checked. The angel-butt clean spot was still there atop my TV. I thought up an excuse to text a buddy just so I could check the time and date stamp on his reply. It was the day I thought it was, indicating I hadn't fallen into some *Star Trek* time warp.

The more I'd stared at the machine, the more detail I'd picked out. Until I noticed the stack of empty cases beside the machine. Staring harder into a Menorah mostly made my eyes dazzled and watery. I'd finally tried taking a picture with my phone.

Yep, the image was definitely there. And by zooming in, I could almost read the print on the cases but none of them were turned quite right, not even after I thought to rotate the image so that the cases were right side up. But...something about them was familiar.

Getting up for baker's hours wasn't worth it. I'd stayed up so late that it was morning. I'd headed into the bakery early and started working on my root beer rye pretzel recipe. Being part of a Jewish deli meant that we stocked several varieties of root beer.

Over the last two days I'd prepped and baked a batch of rye bread dough for each variety.

Which put me behind on the morning's baking, and the deli was chaos straight through lunch as I scrambled to make bagels and bread fast enough to meet demand.

By the time I returned to my rye dough, it had overproved. I baked it anyway to test for flavor but I was so befuddled with lack of sleep that I'd forgotten the caraway seeds and salt. It didn't matter, none of them had the root beer taste I was after.

The second day, after no more angel visits or visions of redheads, and getting a bit of sleep, I tried again. This time I simmered the root beers until reduced by half to concentrate the flavor. I dropped the barley malt and molasses as being too strong a flavor that would be combative with the root beer.

Closer, but not magical.

Fifth Night I once again sat in my own apartment, staring at my Menorah and the recipe card. No foot-tall angel, so maybe that vision had been an overdose of cheese knishes.

Just as I tried to give up staring into the candlelight for the third time, the image returned. This time a man with graying hair and the first hint of a bald spot was operating the machine. Not nearly as scenic as the redhead. My gaze drifted from his bottler to my card.

With the light passing through the card, there was a word that was clear but made no sense. I checked my transcription notes: *Splotch-Dam Root Beer-Smudge*. I'd never seen *Dam* as an ingredient or instruction in any recipe I'd ever made. Yet there it was, staring at me.

It was also staring at me from the Menorah.

Right there.

On the bottles sliding along the track.

Dam.

In fact, *B-Dam Tonic.*

I compared it to the size of the splotch patterns on my card. That would fit. I did a quick search on my phone for the word *tonic,* archaic term for soda. So, that fit too.

Then I put in the full search string.

Permanently Closed.

Three years ago. It had gone out of business after a hundred and fifteen years.

No way this could be happening. There was something special in the Best Dam Root Beer Tonic that I wasn't going to find anywhere else.

I set the card down and looked at the image in the Menorah. An image seventy years out of date. As old as...my grandparents' Menorah.

If I was going to believe in foot-tall angel visitations, I might as well go for broke.

6

SIXTH NIGHT – TIZZY

No matter how many things I tried, none of them felt right. Had GU Sam used sassafras extract, with the FDA-banned safrole removed? Or had he gone to the sarsaparilla root instead? Had he added licorice root, vanilla, nutmeg, acacia...

The more I guessed, the worse it all muddled up in my head.

But I couldn't move on to the ginger beer or the lemon tonic —*soda!*—until I'd solved the root beer. It had been B-Dam's most popular flavor and I was going to find it! Hopefully before I died of old age and frustration.

In addition to causing liver damage and various cancers, safrole had provided much of the root-beer flavor. GU Sam's recipe must have pre-dated that discovery and the banning of it in the 1960s. Which meant he'd had to adapt, but hadn't written down the changes.

I tried to picture him combining his extracts and spices but—

A knock sounded on the door downstairs. The building had

been abandoned for three years, no one except me cared about the place.

"Go away!" I shouted toward the window closed against the December chill. I'd been close to seeing—

It became a pounding.

Any useful image gone, I stormed down the stairs and threw open the door. "What part of Go Away don't you understand?"

The man standing at the door looked at me wide-eyed. "Red hair," he whispered.

"Yeah. So what?"

"Do you have a bright pink poodle skirt?"

Okay, red hair gets a girl some strange pick-up lines, but that was a new one on me. I shook my head.

"Weird," he squinted at me. "Can I show you something?"

Perfect, a total creep on my doorstep. I was halfway to slamming the door in his face, when he reached into a bag and pulled out a Menorah.

The door slammed loudly enough to make me jump in surprise.

I took a deep breath and eased it open to peek out.

"You're still here."

He nodded.

I glanced down toward the Menorah clenched in his fist. Old brass, as old as mine. "Not quite what I was expecting."

After a brief puzzled look, he nodded. "Oh, right. Yeah, I'm not exactly brilliant about thinking through what I say before I say it."

"Are you licensed to be out in Ipswich after dark wielding a Menorah?"

"If this is the building where the Best Damn Root Beer Tonic is made, yes."

"*Was* made." And then I thought about the man with the Elvis hairdo in the Menorah's light. The same strong hands like the man on the doorstep, I like good hands. And, if I ignored the hair—good jaw, nice face—maybe even related? "Are you a...baker by any chance?"

He offered me a lopsided grin.

"This *is* seriously weird."

"You don't know the half of it." He reached into his bag again and pulled out an empty quart bottle printed with the B-Dam name and logo. The flavor would have been printed on the cap.

I glanced once more at the Menorah still clenched in the other of his big hands. Actually, I'd bet that I knew *precisely* half of it. "I'm not giving you back the five-cent deposit."

"Not asking for it."

"I guess I've got something to show you too."

He teased me with raised eyebrows and we both laughed. Mine sounded maybe a little hysterical. His wasn't all that different.

7

———

STILL SIXTH NIGHT – AARON

ENTERING TEMPLE HAD NEVER QUITE FELT LIKE THIS, NOT EVEN on the High Holidays of Yom Kippur and Rosh Hashanah.

Crossing the threshold left a shiver up my spine like I'd just entered somewhere holy. Either that or how I'd arrived here had been so surreal that I was going to be freaked out for the rest of my life.

This morning at the deli, I'd asked Mom and Dad about B-Dam Root Beer Tonic and got a whole load of reminiscences dumped on my head. Stories about dates walking along the Ipswich River, splitting a bottle of B-Dam Orangeade. Then, at Grandma's suggestion, I'd prowled the back of one of the deli's basement storerooms we no longer used and come up with the empty I'd shown at her door.

From the outside it had looked like a house. Halfway up the drive there was a big picture window that I couldn't help peeking in before I'd knocked. The shadowy view, lit solely by a vague wash of light coming from a narrow stairway, had revealed what simply had to be the same machine I'd seen in the Menorah.

Even thinking a sentence like that rated as a serious

indicator alarm for a mental breakdown. Yeah, maybe less with the holy and more with the freaked out.

But the machine stood there in the shadows.

"Does it still work?"

The redhead, who was as fine looking as the machine beside her, patted it like a good puppy dog. "My girl works wonderfully." Then she glanced up at the ceiling and the briefly radiant smile evaporated faster than wine out of a Passover goblet.

"Then why did you go out of business?"

At that she looked sadder than the teary angel Henrietta had in the moments before she'd departed.

"I just inherited it a few weeks ago. Great Uncle Sam operated it. We didn't have a lot of customers by the end. The Ipswich Riverfest. Long-term customers might order a case or two for a birthday party or wedding celebration. By the bottle if you came to the door." She waved a hand vaguely toward the door I'd entered.

Just inherited. "I'm sorry." For more than one thing. I wanted some of whatever they'd put in those bottles.

She wiped her eyes. "Sorry, my mess, not yours. What did you want to show me?"

"Aaron."

That earned me half a smile. "Please tell me you don't have a younger brother named Moses who I'm supposed to marry?"

Aaron was Moses' older brother in *Exodus*. "Why, is your name Tziporah or something? No younger brother, just an older sister named Miriam." Who had been named for Moses and Aaron's older sister.

She groaned in pain. "I'm Tizzy. No, Lizzy. Wait. Maybe call me Elizabeth."

"Tizzy? Seriously? As in Tziporah the wife of Moses?"

"No, yes, well, mostly no. Just...don't call me that." She

covered her eyes and groaned in exasperation. "Everything's a mess, including my name. Run. Now! I highly recommend it."

"I still have something to show you." I turned back to the machine. "Could you sit on the operator's stool for a moment?"

Lizzy, no, I liked her as Elizabeth, all proud and with a dancer's erect posture. Elizabeth watched me carefully as she moved to do so. She sat with her back to the machine, facing me.

I shuffled until the alignment was right then turned to look behind me. An empty shelf ran above the big picture window. "That's where your great uncle kept his Menorah."

"Elijah's Passover Goblet as well. He was very sentimental that way. He—" She jolted to her feet. "Wait! How did you know that?"

I held up my Menorah as if that explained anything. "Redhead in a bright-pink poodle skirt with a long ponytail almost as pretty as yours."

"Great Aunt Elizabeth had red hair and—" she glanced down toward her body then blushed brightly enough that I could see it in the soft light from the stairwell. "*But*...she never wore it long."

"She used to."

"Huh. And the Elvis imitator?"

I knew who she meant; I'd seen Grandma's wedding photo. "Dad's father."

Tizzy-Lizzy-Elizabeth-Tziporah glanced at my hair.

"No, never. Not even as a Halloween costume."

I didn't know what to make of her thoughtful hum.

"Do you have any of the root beer?" Seemed like a safer topic.

And that brought back the über-sad face. She shook her head. "GU Sam died with the recipes in his head. I can almost see it—" Her fine fingers traced pouring motions through the air, then fell lifelessly into her lap. "—but not."

I was too close to give up now. There was the shelf behind me, the machine in front of me. And pipes going up through the ceiling... "What's upstairs?"

"The syrup room. That's where the trouble is. The bottler maybe be older than our parents, maybe our grandparents, but it works fine."

I tipped my head toward the stairs.

"It's not very exciting. Yeah. Sure. Whatever. I'm lost at this point."

The syrup room could have been a surgical laboratory for how clean it shone. Maybe in need of a fresh coat of paint but it sparkled from a fresh scrubbing. What was also strange was how simple and empty it was. The single workbench filled with historic equipment might have been more appropriate in a museum.

"That's from when they were making their own extracts for flavorings. For years GU Sam was using commercial extracts, but mixing and matching." She tapped a neat pile of crinkly old invoices. "I've ordered the extracts he used, but I can't get the mix right. Maybe he added other stuff. I can't remember. I'm missing something, I just don't know what."

"I've got no idea how the Menorah-flame-vision thing works, or what Henrietta did to make it happen..."

"Henrietta?" she asked then continued before I could answer. "Little round face and big brown eyes?"

I nodded.

"I saw her face in the Menorah's light. She looked like she was up to something."

"Like lighting a burning bush in my apartment." Okay, the Lord of the Universe had not commanded me to go free the children of Israel from Pharoah, but it gave me some idea of how Moses must have felt. Up until then he'd escaped Egypt then become a shepherd for his father-in-law and had a couple kids with Tziporah. Renowned as a great beauty, I could only hope for the old man's sake she was as pretty as Elizabeth.

"That must have been fun."

"Not even close." I looked at the rest of the room and I saw that Elizabeth had spoken the truth about not much here. There was a stainless-steel tank two feet wide and four deep with a motor at the bottom. I peeked inside and saw a big stirring paddle. Beside it, stood a series of three smaller tanks.

She touched the big tank. "Simple syrup of nine gallons of water and a hundred pounds of sugar. GU Sam only used saccharine once and didn't like it. Pure cane sugar only." She pointed at the next smaller one but didn't touch it as if it might burn her. "This is where small batches of syrup are flavored with extract to create a particular flavor. Then it goes through those filter tanks and is piped down into the bottling room. There the bottler adds a splash of the syrup, a blast of carbonated water, and a bottle cap. We mix it by hand."

I made the motion I'd seen Elizabeth's forebears make as they took each bottle off the line. They grabbed either end, gave it three fast, end-over-end twists.

"That's it."

I resisted having a panic attack mostly because I didn't want Elizabeth to think I was that lame.

The rest of the room included shelves of labeled extracts, a cot, and a table on which sat a Menorah as old as the one I still clutched as one might a talisman against evil. "What did *you* see?"

Elizabeth shook her head in a swirl of red hair down past her shoulders. She wore a black turtleneck and had jammed her fists into the pockets of an unzipped forest-green fleece vest. She practically vibrated with nerves.

I stepped over to the table and managed to unclench my grasp to set my Menorah beside hers. My fingers throbbed from holding it so hard. "I saw someone, who must be your great aunt, bottle a wooden case worth of some flavor. She was all dressed up with a pink poodle skirt, a yellow sweater, and black-and-white shoes, like for a party, and took it with her."

"Saddle oxfords," Elizabeth mumbled. "That's the shoes."

"Later I saw a balding man making up a lot of bottles."

"I never met Great-Grandpop, but it had to be him if my GA was in her teens."

"What if..." I waved a hand toward the two Menorahs.

"...we light them both?"

"It is sixth night." I dug into my bag and pulled out a box of candles and a lighter that I'd stopped off to purchase on my way here.

Sitting side-by-side on the cot, we each lit a *shamash* then began the prayer.

Baruch atah Adonai, Eloheinu melech ha-olam...

8

SEVENTH NIGHT – TIZZY

"THIS IS CRAZY."

"No argument from this boy." Aaron hovered without quite...hovering.

At this point I figured anything was possible, but his feet remained firmly on the floor.

Putting our two Menorahs together last night was like cutting their age in half. At least that was our best guess.

Through my Sixth Night-candled Menorah, I'd seen his father—without an Elvis pompadour—making pretzels. No sign of B-Dam soda, or tonic, anywhere in the process.

"We stopped making them back when I was a kid because they just weren't selling."

Through Aaron's Menorah, we'd seen GU Sam and GA Elizabeth making batches of syrup. It went by too fast but Aaron held up his phone; he'd been recording it.

The images were blurry, the blinding light of the seven lit candles of Sixth Night washed out half the image, but—

Well, tonight we'd see if it was enough. We'd sat shoulder-to-shoulder on the cot for hours afterward, playing and replaying the video. What was blurred out in one batch, showed clearly in another.

I felt like I was eavesdropping, but I never so wanted anything more than to watch those endless batches of syrup being made. My notes were a mess and got worse with each repeat. But, by the time the candles burned out, we had them in a reasonable order.

I'm not an idiot.

I might have only been interested in the recipe but I couldn't miss Aaron's growing interest in something else.

Finally, I was holding what simply had to be GU Sam's recipe. It had many expected twists and turns, I definitely had to go shopping, but each step felt right in my memory. The excitement of being so close coursed through my body like a shot of syrup through my bottling machine. I turned to look at Aaron while thinking about what might be fun to do with all that energy.

I'd missed when he'd collapsed sideways onto the cot and passed out.

By the time his alarm rousted him—I checked my watch, baker's hours were harsh—I was too deep planning my batch testing to do more than wave.

"I'll bring some by later if this works," I'd called after him as he creaked down the stairs.

"Okay," drifted back up the stairs accompanied by a big yawn.

Next time I looked up, he was gone and the sun was coming in through the window.

I raced downstairs and fired up the bottle washer and the bottling machine to start the first test batch.

9

EIGHTH NIGHT – AARON

Blessed are thou, Lord our God, Defender of the Universe...

The table was jammed. Mom, Dad at the far end. Grandma, Miriam, and two cousins down one side. Elizabeth's mom and dad with my Aunt and Uncle Max on the other. Elizabeth herself squeezed in close beside me at the foot of the table. I wasn't complaining.

Four Menorahs, each with nine candles alight, blazed over the Eighth Night feast. My parents, her parents, and Elizabeth and I had each brought our own Menorahs.

Every place setting included an unopened bottle of B-Dam Root Beer Tonic—as there hadn't been time to make new labels. Each person also had a Root Beer Rye Pretzel waiting on their plate. Maybe not the most brilliant of meal openers, but no one was complaining.

Grandma patted my knee and whispered, "Such a good boy," before kissing me on the cheek.

"We haven't even tasted them yet." I hadn't dared.

Her smile only grew bigger. I didn't need her glance toward

Elizabeth to hope that her prophecy of this recipe being good for me just might come true.

This afternoon, foggy from so little sleep, I had snapped awake when Elizabeth strode into our deli as if she'd never been anywhere else, and thudded down a case of fresh bottled root beer.

Did you taste it?

She'd shaken her head. Nervous energy, that I was coming to see was an Elizabeth trademark, wasn't enough to sustain her after the long mostly sleepless nights. She collapsed on the small couch in the deli's tiny office and passed out. Lacking blankets, I'd spread my jacket over her.

Then I had turned to do my part. I mixed and rose dough. I wanted to take a sip of the soda to test the flavor profile, but it wouldn't be right if I was the first to taste something Elizabeth cared so much about. So, I'd baked it blind, and managed to track down her family to invite them to dinner while she slept.

Now we were packed around the table, everyone staring at the twist of pretzel on their plate. Caraway rye, Kosher salt sprinkled onto the boiled dough while still wet before baking. Yet no one reached for theirs.

"Well, somebody try it!" Elizabeth finally called out, not reaching for hers.

I took up my pretzel and broke off a bite. I inspected the crumb, many tiny airholes just as a relatively dense pretzel should have. When I squeezed it, it sprang right back showing it was cooked through. I sniffed it carefully. Rye, wheat, salt— I'd stuck with leaving out the molasses or barley malt that I'd have put in without the soda—and...root beer. The smell was there. As to the taste...

"Elizabeth?"

"What?"

The moment she opened her mouth, I tucked the bite in,

giving her no choice but to take it. She rolled those lovely blue eyes at me.

But her focus slowly shifted to the flavors going on in her mouth, and a final whispered, "Oh my God."

I took a bite myself and savored the hard hit of the salt, the chewy texture of the rye bread with the slight crunch of caraway, and then the long after-note of the root beer. Schwartzman and Sons were definitely going to be bringing back these pretzels.

"You know what would go really well with this?" I asked her.

She smiled and we both reached for our bottles of root beer.

It was as good as I imagined.

The kiss that followed was even better.

Somewhere in the background of the buzzing in my ears and the applause around the table, I swore I could hear a small high voice cheering herself hoarse.

FOR MORE FUN SHORT FICTION, PLEASE VISIT OUR WEBSITE AT: https://shop.mlbuchman.com/collections/other-stories

SOUTH POLE RESCUE

This third *Antarctic Ice Fliers* romance story is based on true events.

Kenn Borek Air, a specialist in polar flight, amazingly achieved the first-ever mid-winter medical evacuation from the Amundsen-Scott South Pole Station from June 14-24, 2016. Two critical patients were safely evacuated at immense risk to the flight crew. They were deservedly awarded the Michael Collins Trophy, essentially the Nobel Prize of aviation. Prior recipients include: three of the Mars Rover teams, the Hubble telescope team, and the flight crew of US Airways 1549 that managed to land safely in the Hudson River when their plane lost all power on takeoff due to a massive bird strike.

This story would be an impossible fantasy tale—except Kenn Borek Air did it for real when lives were on the line. Many of this story's details are unabashedly lifted from their amazing flight.

1

———

"Fɪɢʜᴛ ᴏʀ ғʟɪɢʜᴛ?"

"With you? Easy. Fight," Jessica Ryan shot back. "You challenged, so I get to choose the weapons. Thumb wrestle." She held out her still greasy hand in the proper shape without bothering to wipe it on her coveralls. She was always trying to find a way around Ted Donovan's unbending demeanor. He was maybe three years older than she was, but he'd been the senior pilot at Bernard's Ice Air since shortly after she'd joined five years ago.

"Nope, flight," he jabbed a finger toward *Natasha*, the Twin Otter airplane Jessica had been servicing. "You'll need to load the skis." Had the always proper Ted just teased her?

"Last I checked, it was summer outside." She made a show of peering out the hangar doors, opened wide to Montana June sunshine. "It is! Isn't that amazing."

"Snow skis, Hotshot. Auxiliary tanks, all she'll hold, and full winter gear. Including an emergency camp stocked for two for at least a week. Load both *Boris* and *Natasha*."

She stared out the hangar door again to see if it was lying. It wasn't. It was definitely summer in Montana, it would be July any minute now.

Two birds, spare fuel, skis, and a full emergency kit must mean... "Really?"

"You always were sharp, Hotshot."

"But it's...June!" That load didn't fit a mission onto the Arctic ice. The summer melt was so bad each year now that teams would probably never again be able to walk or sled over the ice to the North Pole. They didn't need maximum fuel tanks to reach anywhere on the Greenland ice cap.

"Worldwide, we're there!" Ted recited BIA's motto.

"That means Antarctica. In the winter? That's *crazy*. No one does that. How far in? McMurdo?"

He just stood there with his arms crossed, looking all handsome and confident, while he waited for her brain to reach the only other possible conclusion.

"Amundsen-Scott? You're flying to the South Pole in the dead of the Southern winter?"

Still he waited, his killer smile on full display.

"Me?"

"Welcome to the game, Hotshot. We're aloft the moment you have our birds ready."

She wanted to let out a Montanan whoop, even if she was from Seattle. She wanted to hug him, but women didn't randomly hug men like Ted Donovan no matter how pretty he was. For five years she'd been busting her behind, getting every minute of flight time she could, taking every shitty cold-weather assignment she could get, just hoping to come to his attention as a pilot rather than only as a mechanic. Crossing over to pilot was a dream she'd been nurturing for a long, long time.

But saying any of that just wouldn't do.

She managed a totally chill, "Ready in sixty minutes."

The moment his back was turned, she broke into a happy chicken-dance.

"I see that," Ted called out without turning. Blasted man had eyes in the back of his head.

But she did another couple dance steps just to defy him. Ted was flying into the single most impossible airfield on Earth, and he'd just chosen her as his copilot.

Then she turned to look at *Boris*, the second airplane. There was only one reason to take two airplanes to Antarctica in the middle of the southern winter.

Boris would be there...in case *Natasha* crashed and they survived to wait for rescue. A field camp good for a week? That would be enough only if they were very lucky.

2

———

Ted had spotted the reflection of Jessica's deep red hair flouncing about in the hangar's office window as she danced.

Damn but that woman cracked him up.

She wasn't his top mechanic, but that was only because Bob had spent his whole life working on these planes. She wasn't his top pilot either, but through pure dint of effort, she soon would be. And what he needed on this flight was both an engineer and a top copilot.

"You're stealing her from me, aren't you? Best damned mechanic to come through here in ages and you're turning her into a driver." Bob greeted him with a growl as he stepped back into the office. The old man sat before a series of charts rolled out across his battered desk—he was completely old school. The edges were tacked down with components of different airplanes.

Ted recognized the blown-out fuel pump head that had almost killed him over Yellowknife in Canada's Northwest Territories. And the steering wheel that was about all that had remained after Davy had augered in a Basler-converted DC-3 during an Alaska wildfire. Davy had delivered his smokejumpers on target, but then had nowhere to put it down except in the dense trees when an engine had seized and the propellor had cut his plane mostly in two.

"You want to fly copilot to the South Pole with me?"

"You think I'm a fucking idiot? You damn well better take the best," he jabbed a finger out the office window at Jessica, "for a bejeezus bonkers stunt like this," he slapped the charts.

Out the window, Ted could see that Jessica had two interns, their supply master, and *Boris'* two pilots on the hustle loading up gear. She'd said sixty minutes, he'd better be ready in forty-five or she just might leave him behind.

Ted leaned in over Bob's shoulder and looked down at the chart.

It was a crazy map. Antarctica was half again bigger than the US, including Alaska. In all that area were just four thousand people in high summer—a mere thousand now in dead winter. Forty dots on the entire continent and the surrounding islands had a winter population at all, and only nine of those had more than twenty-five souls in residence.

"The only base within seven hundred miles is summer-only. It's vacant right now. The Russians have a dozen poor souls out at Vostok, but that's eight hundred miles to the wrong side of Amundsen-Scott South Pole Station."

"Real helpful, Bob." Ted hauled over a chair.

Bob had been around since old man Bernard had founded this airline specializing in extremely cold or complex flights. No question Bob had a solution because he always did. He was the one who'd sent him out to prep the Twin Otters as soon as they'd received the call from the US Antarctic Program.

Bob always had a solution.

Ted just had to wait him out sometimes.

Bob aimed a finger at the hangar again. "Twin Otter, it's a primitive bird. Which is a good thing—not a lot to go wrong.

Other than the engines and flaps, she's almost all mechanical. No other hydraulics to freeze up on you."

"That's why you didn't select the DC-3's." The Twin Otter was an unlikely bird to fly halfway around the world and stage a daring medevac. Twin turboprop engines with big three-bladed propellors on a high wing, she could carry nineteen passengers or nine thousand pounds of cargo and fuel. This time it would be crew, a single patient, and all the rest fuel. And even that would be marginal. The South Pole was a long way from everywhere.

"Right. Too many systems to keep warm to make the run in a DC-3. You're going to be flying right near the freezing temperature of jet fuel. Even the specialized AN8 fuel turns to glue at minus seventy-five Fahrenheit. Hydraulic oil might as well be a solid by then. That's why the Air National Guard can't fly their LC-130 Hercules Skibirds in. The moment they land, they'd turn into a popsicle and lie there until spring—if they didn't freeze solid on the flight down."

"How high do I have to climb?"

"You can't. You have to stay low. Temperature drops as you climb into higher altitude. If the ground is at minus seventy, any altitude is gonna freeze your ass and you drop like a brick. The ground there is at ninety-three hundred feet above sea level. You keep your ass under eleven. Down at ten thou is better."

"Christ, Bob. You want me to fly into unknown territory at five hundred feet above the ground? And there's no easy way to visually gauge elevation over ice and snow, white on white. No reference point."

"It gets better."

"How is that possible?"

"It's winter," Bob was definitely enjoying something, but Ted couldn't see what.

"Yeah, cold. I get it."

"Not just," Jessica interrupted, bouncing on her toes in the doorway as if she had too much energy to keep it all inside. "It'll be pitch dark the whole way from the Antarctic Circle."

Ted groaned. He hadn't thought that far ahead yet.

Then Jessica grinned at him. "Unless the Aurora Australis is kicking off."

JESSICA FLEW THE FIRST LEG FROM THE COPILOT'S SEAT. THERE wasn't a moment for idle chatter, Ted remained immersed in planning for the entire flight.

A full load of fuel in the standard tanks covered nine hundred miles. The built-in extended-range tanks added another two hundred miles with a total of four hundred and seventy gallons. And the auxiliary bladder tank the interns had rigged in the center of the cargo bay after pulling out most of the seats, would hold another two hundred and fifty gallons. It would let them fly the final leg of one thousand, five hundred, and fifty-two miles to the South Pole with a ten-percent reserve.

That was the last leg. This first leg was easy.

They were aloft in *Natasha* out of Missoula, Montana forty minutes after they received the call. The backup crew flew *Boris* off their right wing under the mid-morning sunshine. Other than a brief rain squall at the Wyoming-Colorado border, the flight to Texas was uneventful.

Most of the flight was spent discussing every step of the logistics over the intercom. Ted let her fly most of it as he was constantly on the radio to *Boris'* pilots or checking some detail by phone with Bob back at Bernard's Ice Air.

They would only be flying the first and last two legs themselves: Missoula to Texas, then southern Chile to the Antarctic Peninsula, and on to the Pole.

After Texas, she, Ted, and *Boris'* crew wouldn't see the planes again until the southern tip of Chile. Meanwhile, multiple crews would hopscotch the small planes south with refueling stops in Costa Rica, Peru, Central Chile, and finally at Punta Arenas, Chile—the kick-off point for Antarctica—with the briefest stops possible. There better not be any other crises, most of BIA's pilots were involved in just the first hours of the rescue—ten full crews of pilots and copilots were needed to move the planes south this fast.

Her and Ted's job was to be fresh and rested by the time *Boris* and *Natasha* were delivered. Even by jet with the best connections, Texas to southern Chile was going to take them twenty hours and three stops from Austin. No such thing as a direct flight where they were going.

"Business class?" Jessica asked as they slid into the luxurious side-by-side seats on the Boeing 737.

"If the flights had First Class, I'd have gotten it, but the hops are too short. We need to get as much sleep as we can."

Sleep? There was no chance of Jessica falling asleep. Her excitement high had slid most of the way back to normal as the grim realities of this flight had been discussed. But even when deadheading like this, the pilot in her just couldn't let go enough to sleep. "It's five in the afternoon," was the best excuse she could come up with.

"Maybe we can sleep in Chile once we get there," Ted's sigh was one of the first indicators that he was human.

"What, Mister Super-pilot can't sleep on airplanes either?"

"Not a wink," he actually winked at her as if to belie his point. "Mom says even as a baby I'd be quiet but wide-eyed for the entire flight, then have a fit when they carried me off the plane."

"Bet you were a handful."

"Nah! Mom said I was a good kid, except when I had to leave an airplane. I would wager that you were though."

"Totally! Thankfully, I got my red hair from Mom. She understood, though she always griped about how paybacks were hell." They'd also been so close that her loss was still a hole in Jessica's heart.

"Sorry," Ted read her face far too easily as the plane backed out of the gate and began taxiing, "I didn't know she was dead. How did it happen?"

"Her new boyfriend got her started on bicycling. She really got into it. Big charity rides, weekend bike camping, cycle commuting, the whole bit. A drunk clipped her when he ran a red light. She never stood a chance." Jessica did her best to shrug it off. Six years hadn't eased the loss. The month of brain-dead coma before she could bring herself to pull the plug was something she wouldn't be sharing anytime soon.

Mom's boyfriend had been a good guy. Even offered to stand with her when they disconnected Mom, but she hadn't trusted what she might say. It had turned out to be a good call —if she'd had a target that day, she'd have beaten herself bloody against it.

"Well, she'd be damn proud of you if she could see you now." Ted actually rested his hand on hers as the engines roared to life and they began the takeoff roll down the runway.

Jessica held on to his strength as the power of the twin turbofans hurtled them down the runway and aloft.

"Mom and I always held hands for this part." Her voice felt like it had cracked out of her chest.

"Was she afraid of flying?"

"No, she loved it. *We* loved it. She always watched the Internet for those last-minute deals where they're trying to fill seats at any price. Every month or so I'd get out of school on a Friday and she'd meet me with our knapsacks already packed. 'Doing your homework in Chicago this weekend.' Or Pittsburgh, Phoenix, Nashville. It didn't matter, she always made it an adventure. Back in time for school Monday, typically straight off a redeye flight. They were the best weekends of my life. I always loved flying."

"Then why a mechanic and not a pilot?"

"Cheaper. I could get a job faster if I got my A&P license. Airframe and powerplant engineers lack the glory, but we get paid well. We never had a lot of money, but Mom sure knew how to enjoy life."

4

TED WONDERED WHEN HE'D LOST THAT, IF HE'D EVER HAD IT.

He *liked* his life—other than the blood-ugly divorce he'd never think about again. But he'd certainly never done a happy dance at being chosen to fly. Thrilled, excited, sometimes afraid? Sure. So joyously happy that he couldn't hold it in as Jessica had demonstrated on the hangar floor? Not even when he'd banged out his first-ever double with bases loaded in Little League.

The joy simply poured from Jessica. He could feel the fire of it as she continued to squeeze his hand while the plane climbed to cruising altitude.

He did his best not to draw her attention to it, but she eventually noticed and let go.

She blushed until her fair skin was almost the color of her hair.

"Now you're going to have to explain that."

"What?" But pressing her fingers to her cheeks said that she knew exactly what he'd meant.

"I've seen you grab onto someone in the hangar when you're happy with them or laughing at some joke they just told." And he'd done his best not to envy them that easy familiarity. That was a gift he'd never had.

"That's normal people. Not you, Mr. Senior Pilot."

"Am I so untouchable?"

"Yes," she gasped it out in a small voice.

He wasn't quite ready to ask what she meant by that.

He was only a few years older than her, so that wasn't it. Bernard Ice Air's first-generation of pilots had run the operation themselves for years. But when one retired from flight, the others had followed quickly. They ran the place now, and he'd simply been the senior-most of the next generation. Not the oldest, but he'd taken to flight much the way Jessica had these last five years since Bob had hired her.

There wasn't a type of aircraft that BIA flew that Ted didn't certify himself in during his first year. He took every flight they'd give him, even the routine drudge flights no one else wanted. Ice and snow survival classes—he never missed a one. He'd sat for endless hours just listening to the senior pilots talk about this landing or that crash. He'd racked up the hours and experience until he'd been their obvious pick for chief pilot. Maybe he had been a little too focused on his career.

Jessica had done much the same since coming on board. He couldn't seem to turn around but there she was listening, learning, absorbing anything anyone said. He'd quietly fed a lot of flights her way and she'd thrived on them. Yet she exuded life while he...merely lived it?

"There's a lot to like about you, Jessica."

"There is? I always thought I was more a pain-in-the-ass type."

He couldn't help laughing. "I've certainly been told that enough times about you."

"You have? Shit! I'm sorry. I never meant—"

Ted rested his hand on hers again to stop her.

She stared down at his hand, so he pulled it back.

"It's usually accompanied by a comment about your tenacity until you learn everything about whatever it is. I have that same need. It's how I got to my, ahem, *lofty* position."

"Hard to imagine the Great Chief Pilot being a PIA."

"Just ask any of the management guys."

She didn't quite look up at him. "There's a lot I like about you too." Then she determinedly turned to stare out the window.

Their first hop was just across the width of Texas and their conversation had been slow enough that they were already descending.

She didn't take his hand for the landing.

But he hoped she would on the next takeoff.

5

———

Jessica was absolutely losing her mind.

Four flights sitting far too close to Ted Donovan was causing strange reactions that she couldn't quite anchor to any part of her body.

It definitely wasn't her mind because she was rapidly losing that. Maybe she was getting too little oxygen. Thinking thoughts about Ted Donovan as anything other than BIA's chief pilot was simply too bizarre for reality.

She considered switching seats with one of the other pilots from *Boris'* flight crew—also making the leap ahead with them —but didn't want to move away from Ted either.

On each flight, he'd subtly offered his hand. She hadn't taken it out of Houston or Bogotá, Colombia. For both of those long flights she'd pretended that she didn't see the gesture.

But since neither of them were inclined to sleep on the pair of five-hour flights, they had talked. For the Houston to Bogotá leg, she'd carefully kept it professional. Ted was soon drawing diagrams to explain the quirks of handling BIA's various aircraft during extreme conditions. She, in turn, found he was equally interested in the esoterica of airframe and powerplant maintenance—"After all, my life depends on what you do there."

But for the Bogotá to Santiago, Chile leg, they were both tired enough to just talk. They'd slowly shifted three time zones eastward as they traveled south, but that didn't stop it being the middle of the night Montana time. No, it made it worse, as her watch kept reporting it was later and later with each time zone. Actually earlier and earlier because they'd left midnight behind somewhere over Ecuador and it was now the next day. That wasn't right either. Earlier and later? Two a.m., three a.m., in...some time zone.

Whenever they were, her defenses around Ted Donovan were shutting down one by one, even though she wasn't running any checklist she could think of.

He asked more questions about her mother, bringing back so many good memories that it was hard not to weep her thanks out on his shoulder. Mom's ending had been bad and Jessica had shut down *all* memories to leave that behind. But the good parts had been *so* good. Even during the rebellious teen years—"my red-headed years, Mom had always called them"—there'd been far more good than bad. Her first real heartbreak hadn't sent her to her best friend, it had sent her to Mom. He gave those memories back to her.

In turn, Ted had told her about a childhood so normal compared to hers that it was hard to credit. Two parents, older brother, kid sports, school, chasing girls, baseball team captain at his small Montana school. A short marriage and a divorce that he dropped after just that many words. He looked as grim as she'd felt about Mom's death, so she didn't ask.

"Besides, I'd always known I was meant to fly. I shoveled a lot of winter sidewalks and even more manure in horse barns to pay for my lessons. I also didn't waste my time with any other outfits," he teased her. "I was hanging out at the BIA hangar before I even had my private ticket."

"Wasting—" she put on her best offended tone for him. "I was a working mechanic at Harbour Air in Seattle by the time I was eighteen and licensed before I was twenty, I'll have you know."

"Which explains exactly why Bob hired you." He was right. There wasn't a better match than Twin Otter planes with water pontoons to Twin Otter planes with snow skis. Salt water to ice cold. Those were just details, big important details, but details. As if her career had been headed straight to BIA before she'd ever heard of them. She'd certainly applied the day she had.

When he offered his hand after the layover and fast airport breakfast of *huevos con jamón,* which sounded much better than the runny eggs and slab of hyper-salty ham they'd been served, she took it without thinking, though they hadn't even left the gate yet.

She fell asleep while they were still taxiing.

6

TED WASN'T SURE QUITE WHERE TO LOOK.

He simply put his arm on the armrest and she'd taken his hand as if it was the most natural thing in the world. His skin wasn't particularly dark, just a good summer tan, but her fingers appeared alabaster in comparison. They were fine, but the grime under ragged short nails showed she used them hard.

He looked at her face just as her eyes slid shut.

The turn onto the active runway caused her to tip her head onto his shoulder.

He wanted to wake her up and tease her about "I never sleep on a plane." Yet he wanted her head to remain on his shoulder forever.

It wasn't until they'd climbed all of the way up to cruising altitude that he dared rest his cheek on her hair. Soft as a breath on his cheek, it was smooth and silky as the wind over a perfectly formed airplane wing.

Jessica Ryan. Asleep on his shoulder.

Just enjoy the moment and don't read anything into it, boy.

But he wanted to, which was a surprise.
It had been a long time since *that* had happened.

7

Punta Arenas was the jumping off point for forty-six of the seventy bases on the Antarctic continent and islands. But that was in the southern summer. In the winter, the southernmost city in the world was a ghost town—a ghost town of a hundred thousand residents, but still incredibly quiet in the off season. Not only were there no Antarctic flights, there were few research vessels and no tourist cruise ships either. The city's heyday as a coaling station for interoceanic commerce had died long ago with the opening of the Panama Canal.

None of that mattered.

They'd beaten the Twin Otter's arrival in Punta Arenas, Chile, by twelve hours.

The three hours of sleep on that final flight hadn't been enough by far, and Jessica hadn't given it another thought when she'd crashed into one of their hotel room's two queen beds for a straight eight.

But it had been a galvanic shock when she'd woken to hear Ted Donovan taking a shower. She'd feigned sleep until he was done and out of the room before hurrying through her own shower.

He'd left a note: *Meet you in restaurant downstairs for breakfast.*

They'd landed at six p.m., slept until two a.m., and met in the restaurant by three. They were the only people there. Thankfully, the hotel had left the coffee on and a pile of day-old muffins. They also had a hot water tap and packets of hot chocolate which was a nice surprise.

Scott-Amundsen was reporting the patient in non-stable critical condition. Should they try to carry a doctor or a med-tech? He or she would weigh as much as thirty gallons of fuel. The fifty-five fewer miles of range could become critical if they struck a bad headwind.

Their best calculations estimated that a thirty-knot headwind would tap all of their reserve, and thirty-one knots would force them to land on the untested ice before they reached the station. That thirty-mile-an-hour winds were their safety limit—and winds of seventy or even a hundred miles per hour were common during the South Pole winter—was...worrisome.

Basically, it was scaring the crap out of her.

Ted, of course, had remained perfectly calm as they'd verified each other's calculations on that crucial point.

It was presently blowing fifteen knots at Rothera Station—the British base they'd be staging from on the Antarctic Peninsula—and twenty-two at the Pole. It didn't get much more favorable than that. Except there were no winter weather stations anywhere in the fifteen hundred miles between the two.

"That's Seattle to Austin, Texas, with no idea of what's going on in between. You could squeeze a whole hurricane in that gap and never know."

"Except it's a sea of ice and hurricanes are tropical." Ted was always so literal.

"The vasty nothingness," Jessica was just glad to be avoiding any discussion of last night. As the last flight had landed, she'd woken on Ted's shoulder like it was the Rock of Gibraltar, so safe and solid. He too slept with his cheek upon her hair. How was that even possible?

"The great unknown," Ted agreed, looking at the blank expanse on the chart. He also wasn't mentioning last night— Thank God. Or was he? Were they the "great unknown" or was she doing her usual overthinking the crap out of everything? Overthinking. Definitely. Hopefully?

"The planes will be here in about three more hours." And if it was *not* "Thank God?" Ted was a wonderfully comfortable man to be around once she got past the senior pilot role that he wore like a knight's armor.

But they worked together.

There was no way talking about sleeping against each other while holding hands was going to be an easy or comfortable conversation. Of course, since when had she listened to common sense?

Ted looked as if he too was about to change the subject to last night when the *Boris* flight crew wandered in as bleary eyed as she felt.

After that, it was pure business.

It wasn't until her second cup of hot chocolate that she noticed the light pressure of his knee against hers.

He moved it away at her flinch of surprise.

Sticking to her habit of pursuing stupid ideas, she tipped her knee back into his.

It was insane. She was a grown woman playing footsie... kneesie...with her company's senior pilot under a hotel lobby table in southern Chile before flying to Antarctica.

Mom wouldn't have loved it. She would have wondered why Jessica was making up such a crazy story.

Except the pressure of Ted's knee against hers was undeniably real.

8

———

THE PLANES ARRIVED AT SIX A.M., THREE HOURS TO DAWN. PUNTA Arenas only enjoyed seven hours of daylight this time of year. Far more than they'd find to the south. Rothera would have twilight only, but the South Pole would be pitch dark twenty-four hours a day.

Ted tried to help, but Jessica was doing such an I'm-a-force-of-nature-so-look-out mechanic's inspection that he decided it was safer to stay out of her way, file his flight plan, and get a last-minute weather update.

The planes had just been flown forty-two hours straight through, by five different pairs of pilots. Jessica was mounting the snow skis around the wheels, stripping out every extra ounce of weight like removing the seat they'd tentatively planned for the med tech they'd decided against (Jessica would use the satellite radio to be talked through needed care, if it wasn't too awful), checking over every element of the plane, and making sure the fuel was loaded with plenty of reserve to reach their first stop at Rothera.

She was somehow everywhere at once. The copilot from the *Boris* team tried to keep up, he really did, but he was a pilot first and second and a mechanic only as a distant third. He never stood a chance.

In under an hour of whirlwind activity, Jessica had both planes ready. Ted was in the pilot's seat and heading aloft almost without being aware of how he'd gotten there. The two pilots sitting in *Boris* looked equally shocked.

The five-hour flight into the descending darkness left little time for talk. There was a hard blow kicking over the Drake Passage, generally rated as the most dangerous water in the world.

"Wave reports over forty feet, Ted. So no water landings today, okay?" Her voice over the headset intercom made it feel as if she was whispering in his ear.

"Yes, ma'am, Jessica, ma'am. It wasn't on my filed flight plan anyway."

She navigated him around the worst of the weather, but they were riding the twilight south. They were aloft out of Punta Arenas well before sunrise and even though they were flying through the morning and landing at high noon in Rothera, they never quite saw the sun. It remained out of sight, casting a dusky twilight—brilliant with reds skittering through the broken clouds.

"Red in the morning," she said softly over the intercom.

"Sailors take warning. Good thing we're flying."

"Good thing." Jessica repeated. She sounded as if she was testing the feeling of those words far more than she was agreeing with anything.

He could still feel the spot on his knee where they'd brushed together under the breakfast table. How ridiculously sappy was that?

"It's a surprisingly mild ten degrees Fahrenheit at Rothera," she announced as if they hadn't both read the same report an hour ago.

"Milder than a Montana winter. Hardly worth worrying about."

She made a thoughtful noise, then rerouted him around another squall line.

As much as he wanted to know what Jessica was thinking, he couldn't bring himself to ask. Because if he did, she'd ask what he was thinking, and he'd be damned if he knew.

Waking to see her sprawled out, asleep on the bed next to his, her long hair completely hiding her face beneath soft waves... Well, it was a hell of a nice sight to wake up to, he'd give it that.

9

___

Rothera was unremarkable in that Jessica was conscious for so little time there. The British base had just twenty-two winter residents down from a hundred and thirty in the summer. In winter it was the sixth largest population below the Antarctic Circle. In the summer it rose to third, behind only McMurdo and the South Pole.

After a white-knuckle-rough five-hour passage that had sapped their strength, they had a mandatory rest layover of eight hours. Once she'd made sure that both planes were fueled to their very limits with AN8 fuel, she crashed into a bed again. Thankfully, she had her own bunkroom, so she didn't need to think about Ted Donovan sleeping just the other side of the wall.

Or she didn't have to think about him much, because exhaustion took over and she was asleep again.

Now it was all about the weather.

Mid-June and below the Antarctic Circle meant the time of day was fairly meaningless. The fast travel had left her so jetlagged that the time was even more meaningless. She'd slept, she was awake, and she was about to embark on a flight as crazy as Lindbergh crossing the Atlantic or Byrd's first-ever flight over the South Pole.

She tried to remind herself that Admiral Byrd had made his flight in a 1929 Ford Trimotor. To reach the heights of the Polar Plateau, Byrd had littered Antarctica with empty gas tanks and dumped their emergency equipment. He'd also done it in the constant November sunlight across eight hundred and fifty miles from McMurdo.

In contrast, they'd be flying in the dead of night for fifteen hundred miles from Rothera to the Pole because there was no practical way to reach McMurdo—it was far beyond where the Twin Otter's fuel could go. Even if they could get to New Zealand in the first place, all the fuel she could load wouldn't get them across the wide Southern Ocean from there to McMurdo Station.

It was eight p.m. at Rothera when they departed in *Natasha*. The winds were favorable, and the South Pole was reporting a temperature of only minus seventy, which was five degrees above where their fuel would freeze. The *Boris* crew saw them off. They'd be ready if she and Ted crashed in *Natasha*. She could only hope it was enough because there was no one else who could come get them before spring. Suddenly that one week of emergency supplies she'd barely resisted winnowing to save weight looked painfully undersized.

All twenty-two of the Brits came out for their departure as well. It was easy to guess why.

"You made friends for life with that maneuver," she teased Ted as they slid down the ice runway and rotated aloft.

"Me? I didn't do anything special." He'd sent the crews who had ferried the planes to southern Chile to clear out the fruit-and-vegetable section at the Punta Arenas market while she'd readied the planes. The planes had plenty of excess capacity for the Drake Passage crossing, so he'd delivered over five hundred pounds of "freshies" *in the dead of winter.* She wouldn't be surprised if he'd received several marriage proposals for that stunt.

"You were married—" It slipped out before she could stop it as they climbed over the spine of the Trans-Antarctic Mountains before turning south over the Larsen Ice Shelf and the Weddell Sea.

"I was." His acid tone told her to drop it, but now it hung between them in the darkness lit only by the LCDs of the instrument panel. There was nothing to see out the window. The crescent moon wouldn't rise until after they'd already reached the Pole. There was just the burning sweep of the stars and their readouts. Not even a pretty Aurora to provide a distraction.

She tried to concentrate on their route. They'd climbed to ten thousand feet. They'd be more efficient up at the aircraft's twenty-five-thousand-foot ceiling of operation, but the air up there would be fifty degrees colder than it was here and their gas would freeze.

They were well out over the Weddell Sea and most of the way to the Ronne Ice Shelf before he answered.

"She was a needy, passive-aggressive, master of manipulation. I never saw it coming. Got me so damn twisted up that I thought it was all my fault when she started cheating. Took the goddamn lawyer almost slapping me up side the head for me to see it. How lame is that?"

"Pretty lame."

He twisted to look at her in surprise.

Maybe she should have taken the more diplomatic route but that wasn't her. "I mean having to have a lawyer do it. No best friend to straighten you out?"

"That's who she was cheating with."

She cringed. "Okay, so...can we just write my question off to foot-in-mouth disease?"

"Or to my being a total idiot?"

"There's a noun that shouldn't ever be allowed in the presence of the great Ted Donovan. I think it's more that you're a genuinely nice guy."

"Yeah, and look what that got me."

Jessica buried herself in recalculating the fuel, something she planned to do every half hour for the entire flight down and back. Though it had only been twenty minutes since her last check.

What had it gotten him? It had made her really hope that Ted's attraction to her was more than just proximity on a long mission. That it might even match her attraction to him which, she knew, had started the day she'd walked into the Bernard Ice Air hangar for the very first time.

He'd been married then. And whatever his wife had done to him, he'd never shown it for an instant at work. One day he was talking about needing to be home for dinner...and the next day he wasn't. That had been the only change. Word of the divorce had swept through the outfit, but always in quiet whispers and never when he was around.

He'd also never shown his attraction to her, until she'd taken his hand on that first takeoff. Or had he taken hers? She flexed her fingers and couldn't even remember.

There's a lot to like about you, Jessica.

But was there enough?

10

———

TTED THANKED THE BRILLIANT STARS THAT THE FLIGHT TO THE
Pole passed without event.

Sections of the Polar Plateau along their route rose over ten thousand feet, but Jessica's calculations gave him permission to climb as high as eleven based on the ambient air temperature —so plowing sight-unseen into the ice was no longer a worry.

She ran the deicing equipment like a woman conducting an orchestra. Never too much or too little. The ice buildup on the wing, tail, and propellor surfaces were monitored by calculating airspeed versus fuel burn rates.

The wing boots were run through inflate-deflate cycles whenever she wasn't happy with the numbers. The leading edges of the wings and rear stabilizer had been replaced with expandable rubber boots. By inflating them, it cracked the built-up ice, which then blew away. But it couldn't be left too long or the boot might not be able to break it up if the ice was building quickly. Do it too often and a thin sheen of flexible ice would built up and then not crack free.

Heating elements had been placed along the propellor

blades to melt any ice. But they couldn't be left on all the time either. There were power drains and re-icing issues there. Between that and the navigation, there was plenty to keep Jessica fully occupied.

Or at least any lesser person.

He expected that Jessica still had plenty of bandwidth because she was Jessica.

"Don't you ever stop being amazing?"

"Me?" She blurted out in surprise. His ex had been all about careful words and controlled emotions. Jessica had about as much delicate artifice as a bulldozer.

"Yes, you."

"I'm not amazing. I'm just me."

"Yeah, and look what that's gotten *you*." She had so much.

"Like what?"

He could only laugh. "You're BIA's only A&P mechanic who is also a fully certified pilot. Not just to FAA standards, to our standards. You've been to so many places that it makes my head spin. I'm Missoula born and bred. Didn't stick my nose outside the Front Range but once or twice a year to visit the grandparents until BIA sent me there. You dance for the pure joy of being happy. That's a gift and half right there."

"Most people laugh at me when I do that."

"I bet a lot more are laughing *with* you than you think. Or wishing they could be like you."

"You don't ever do a happy dance?"

"Haven't yet."

"That's sad, Ted. If you aren't celebrating life, are you actually living it? Mom used to say that all the time and I think it's true."

Ted kept an eye on their drift rate. They had a rear quartering wind trying to shove them sideways. It wasn't too hard, but he had to keep an eye on it. That wind was helping them now, but it would be a headwind on the return flight when they were traveling back with a patient aboard.

And there it was again. He'd enjoyed his life, except for his three years of servitude with his ex, but he'd never celebrated it.

Jessica seemed to celebrate it with every breath. What would it take to do that?

11

———

Jessica was the first to spot the glow on the horizon.

After seven full hours of darkness, it was a shock.

"The moon won't be up for hours."

Ted laughed but didn't explain.

"Did they turn on all of the station lights for us?"

"Good guess, but no."

She kept her mouth shut and waited. Ted Donovan was known as a real straight shooter, but he was teasing her. She was sure of it. Ever since that moment in the hangar he wouldn't let go of, when he'd caught her dancing. He'd never teased anyone at work even a little that she'd ever heard.

The packed snow of Jack F. Paulus Skiway didn't have an instrument landing system. And because the ice was on the move even here in the center of the continent, GPS wasn't all it could be as a reference.

Jessica saw the light bloom out of the darkness. "It's like magic."

"It's more like oil drums," Ted was laughing.

And that's exactly what it was. A line of oil drums had been partly filled with jet fuel and lit off. A dozen drums down the length of the runway's edge.

"But it *is* like magic. A fairy tale city." Each fire drum lit a great circle of the ice, making the white shine and flicker with a happy orange glow. At the far end of the runway, the main building was indeed well lit. It might be four a.m. on Chile and Rothera Station time, but the South Pole Station was most connected to McMurdo and New Zealand—at least for four months of the summer when flights could make this passage with some semblance of safety—so they set their clocks to match. Here it was just eight in the evening.

At the far end of the runway, she had Ted pause but not shut down. Then, just as she'd instructed, three people ran out and shoved big wooden boards against the leading edge of the skis before backing away.

"Let's do it."

"Oh, you are so good." Ted ran the throttles back up, easing them onto the wood before shutting down.

"I am, aren't I?" Now their skis wouldn't freeze to the ice.

They'd made it to the South Pole, in the dead of winter, with a full hour-and-a-quarter fuel reserve. They wouldn't be nearly so lucky going back. That headwind had her worried.

12

"WELL, THAT WAS A BIG HIT."

"I'm a winning sort of guy." He'd held back one patient's-weight of "freshies" from what he'd given to Rothera. Two hundred pounds of oranges, apples, bananas…the winterovers had gone wild.

Now it was just the two of them. He'd brought Jessica out to see the South Pole marker. Not the ceremonial one at the front of the station where a reflective sphere had been placed atop a candy-striped pole. They were at the real marker that showed how far the ice had drifted since the first one was placed.

It was a quiet corner of the world, close by the station building but also very separate. The two-story structure was mounted atop massive pillars to keep it clear of the snow. A few kilometers to the left was the South Pole Telescope. Ten kilometers to the right was an under-ice seismometer station. Straight ahead there was nothing for thousands of miles other than the tiny Russian station at the geo-magnetic South Pole.

"The silence is astonishing."

Ted listened. After all the hours on jets and in the Twin Otter, the silence made his ears ring. The only sounds were the slick sounds when he moved inside his heavy parka and the wind slid ice crystals along the surface.

"It's like I can hear the world breathing."

"Well, it's certainly moving. We're standing on nine thousand feet of ice drifting sideways at ten meters a year." Which was still impossibly strange, though he'd been here several times before.

"Nine kajillion stars sparkling in the heavens." Her hood was tilted back as she stared up at the sky.

And there were, but all he could see was Jessica. Well, the outline of her massive orange parka etched in the darkness. It was minus sixty-seven on the ground, and the wind chill supposedly made it minus ninety-two—it felt colder.

"You know what night this is?"

He didn't.

"June twenty-fourth, the traditional mid-summer's eve. A night of mystery and magic if Shakespeare is to be believed."

"It is a beautiful sight even if it *is* freezing. Your first trip to the South Pole, I had to show you the true pole. Every direction is north from here."

She made a show of running a small circle around the marker, then pumped both arms aloft. "She did it, folks. She ran around the world!"

For once he didn't think. He didn't plan.

He just pulled her in and pushed the front of their hoods together until their faces were in a tiny shared cocoon of warmth. He hesitated when their lips were just a breath apart.

She didn't.

With the thick layers they each wore, their arms were far from clasping around each other, but that did nothing to diminish the kiss. Locking lips with Jessica Ryan was like kissing summer in the middle of winter. Which was such an appropriate metaphor that he smiled.

She smiled back.

And soon they were both laughing.

"You just wanted to kiss a girl at the South Pole."

"I just wanted to kiss *you* wherever I could."

"Let's go inside and try this again. Or else."

"Or else what?" Would he ever keep up with this woman?

"Or else the tips of our noses will freeze together."

13

———

They'd slept.

It *was* the main purpose of the layover at the South Pole. Their plane didn't want to sit for twelve hours and slowly turn into a block of ice. But even with two pilots, fifteen hours of continuous flight over such difficult terrain—Rothera to the Pole and back—was an unacceptable risk. They had to take a break.

They hadn't made love, but they'd certainly snuggled and finally slept spooned together on her bunk, both holding tight.

Oh, Jessica wished she could hold onto this moment forever. She'd always found the bright side of whatever life threw at her, but it was rare for life to throw something so perfect that she doubted its truth.

That niggling set of nerves woke her while Ted slept on. She slithered free.

She wasn't able to watch him for long, having him in her bed was simply too...something. Odd? Peculiar? Fantastic? A possession by space aliens arriving at the South Pole and replacing them with pod people?

Instead, she'd gone outside to meet the South Pole crew.

They'd worked for days out in the brutal cold and wind fashioning that skiway for them out of the drifting snow. Now they had to prepare her plane to takeoff again. That would take two or three hours.

They attached big hot-air blowers to each engine, but kept them on low. If the metal heated too unevenly, it could crack a fan blade and then they'd be stuck for the winter. Being stuck here with Ted Donovan for the next four months wasn't the worst idea she'd ever heard. Being stuck here with Ted and a patient dying in the station's infirmary, that wasn't a possibility. The doc had at least said he was stable enough for transport —barely.

A third heater was eased into the cargo bay, but that had to be run even lower. It would be all too easy to shatter a windshield with a big blast of heat inside and minus seventy outside the thin piece of glass.

A snow-tracked fuel truck drove up beside her plane and pumped it full of AN8 fuel. She checked carefully to make sure that the sluggish liquid was topped up to the limit of every tank: wings, long-range, and the bladder that lumped in the center of the cabin.

That only left—

"We have a problem."

She whirled to see Ted close behind her. "If that's your idea of a morning-after greeting, we need to have a long talk."

Jessica barely had time to gasp in surprise before he had her pinned against the side of the fuselage and was kissing the daylights out of her. Except there was no daylight here. She kissed him back until she saw stars. There were plenty of stars here.

"That'll have to do for now. We have a problem."

Smug. Ted sounded deeply smug. For herself, she was still a bit star-dazzled. "Are you going to tell me, or is this twenty questions?"

"The doc says that the first patient is stable enough that we should be okay."

"I know. I asked too. Wait a sec... *First* patient?"

"Girl is quick," Ted replied. "We have an *optional* second patient to transport. Our call. Macular degeneration, they're going blind. They need to retreat to a lower altitude and get treatment."

"Yes."

"It's not that simple. Fuel, headwinds, nowhere to refuel in fifteen hundred miles."

"Fifteen hundred and fifty-two. But the answer is yes. Now go get them ready while I figure out how we're going to do that."

Even through his parka, she could read his brief amusement. Then he stroked a gloved finger down the side of her hood as if he was brushing her cheek underneath. He'd already made his choice, but he wasn't going to force it if she deemed it was unsafe. Without a further word, he hustled back toward the station building.

She paced once around the plane. The DHC-6 Twin Otter was the pickup truck of airplanes. It even sounded like one when you were slamming the pilots' doors shut—which was the only reliable way to get them to latch. There was a reason there had been a thousand of these built and most were still going strong. The airframe wasn't some sleek little pretty thing. It was tough and robust. She knew every inch of how true that was from the inside and the pilot-side.

She stepped up to the head of the heater crew. "How long did you make the skiway?"

"We took your maximum takeoff run of twelve hundred feet and doubled it. You have twenty-four hundred feet out there."

"How long would it take to make it three thousand?"

"Well, out past the end wasn't too rugged. The worst of the drifting was here, near the station."

"Even a rough pack would do. I'm hoping we're light on the skis by then but we'll need room to abort if there's a problem."

He looked out into the darkness, then up at the eighteen-inch hoses feeding hot air through the engines. "I can have something by the time these are up to temperature. It won't be pretty. No better than *maybe* able to save your lives."

"Good enough for me."

He was on the radio as he headed away toward the big equipment garage.

She stepped over to where the fuelie was rewinding her hose.

"I've got one more for you."

"Not anywhere to squeeze another drop in this bird, sister."

"I need two fuel drums and a hand crank. I'll burn the bladder tank first, then refill it from the drums. That's a hundred and ten gallons."

While the fuelie was rustling up the extra fuel, she called Ted on the radio. "Tell them that they're going to be lying down for the whole trip. Put them on air mattresses, not even stretchers. That will save us sixty pounds."

"Nine whole gallons of fuel. I feel so much better."

"Every ounce counts, Ted. Make sure you go to the bathroom before we takeoff and eat a light breakfast."

"Ha. Ha. Ha."

"Not kidding."

When he reached the plane, he eyed her two fuel drums and the hand pump. Then he looked down the runway to where a pair of snowcats were racing across the snow, one with a snowplow at the front and the other dragging a big roller.

His hood twisted to either side as if he was cricking his neck.

But he didn't say a word and she wanted to hug him for it.

14

———

Ted almost forgot how to fly.

It wasn't that they were overweight by an extra passenger and two drums of fuel. He trusted Jessica's mechanic's knowledge to make sure that was okay. Even knowing that she'd needed a longer runway just in case the snow was too sticky told him just how much math she'd done to make sure this was okay.

It wasn't that they now had two ailing patients to deliver alive across such an endless stretch of unforgiving ice. They were as comfortable as possible and their chances were tied to his own.

So what had changed since the flight down?

Holding Jessica through the night, and having the easiest sleep he'd managed in a long time. There was a rightness to her that he'd never felt before.

What was new, and giving him problems, was that he no longer had Jessica flying beside him. Their journey had transformed her from amazing to precious. If he'd crashed on the route down, it would have been awful. If he did it now, he'd have lost something so important that its loss was impossible to imagine.

He was also more alone on this flight. She was constantly out of her seat, checking on both patients. Jessica also went to the back to crank the pump and transfer the fuel from the drums to the bladder. And when the bladder had been drained, she rolled and squeezed it so tightly that not a cup of fuel could have remained.

That's when he appreciated the sixty pounds she'd saved by ditching the stretchers for air mattresses. There was no clearer signal of just how low their reserve was going to be.

"What's our leeway?" he asked one of the times she was back in the cockpit.

"With this headwind...not much. We landed at the Pole with fifteen percent fuel reserve, about 75 minutes. I'm hoping we still have fifteen minutes left by the time we land at Rothera. If not, we'll have to risk landing on the Larsen Ice Shelf and *Boris* will have to bring us some more fuel. At least we'll be back at sea level and our engines won't freeze."

"Fifteen minutes after seven-and-a-half hours..." He wished he could cut his tongue out. She was probably already stressing herself out to near her limits. If she even had limits. "Uh, sounds good. I can work with that."

As she rose to once more head back and check on the patients, she rested her hand briefly on his shoulder, squeezing it in thanks. Jessica Ryan did have limits. That was good to know, otherwise she might be just a little too terrifying.

15

—————

SHE ACTUALLY CRIED WHEN THE SKIS TOUCHED DOWN AT Rothera. She couldn't help herself. It was just too much, too big. They all were safe.

But what about their moments on the ice? Had that been real? Or would it forever be a mere kiss at the South Pole? A kiss and sleeping in each others' arms. It was real. It had to be.

So why couldn't she trust it?

She kept the tears hidden.

Once the plane was secure and refueled, and the British medic had both patients in their tiny infirmary, she curled up alone in her bed and slept only fitfully.

She was barely conscious for the flight across the Drake Passage back to Punta Arenas. Ted had tried to start conversations, but she simply couldn't focus on anything beyond the weather and navigation.

At the airport, she was suddenly bereft.

One ambulance whisked away the stroke patient to the local hospital. The one losing his sight was hustled onto a flight headed back to the States.

Now it was just the two of them with *Natasha* the Twin Otter.

She'd finished unmounting the skis and tucking them away in the rear cabin, then she'd sat on the lip of the cargo deck unsure what to do with herself.

Ted came up and leaned on the doorjamb. Because the landing gear were tall on this plane, she looked slightly down at him. But he didn't face her. He faced out toward the water where the Straits of Magellan shimmered under the morning sun.

Sun! It was just past dawn in southern Chile. They'd survived the darkness of the Polar night inside the Antarctic Circle. She became aware of its warmth on her face.

It had been night for four days. Now that it was morning and she was completely out of sync with everything, including herself.

"I was thinking," Ted muttered as if to himself. "You've been a lot more places than I have."

"At least while Mom was alive. Though all our trips were in the US."

"Were they? Isn't that interesting."

She couldn't find the energy to ask why.

"You're going to need a swimsuit."

"You're going to need to get your head fixed. The water here is probably a gazillionth of a degree above freezing."

"I was thinking," he continued as if she hadn't spoken. "We have this plane. We have to fly it halfway around the world to get it home."

"A third."

Again he ignored her comment. "I'm thinking there are probably a lot of interesting places between here and Montana. When was the last time you took a vacation?"

The day after she'd passed her A&P license exam. Mom had

showed up with two prepacked knapsacks and a pair of tickets to Boulder, Colorado. A month later she'd been killed.

"That's what I thought," he spoke into her silence. "About the same for me." Then he fell silent.

A lot of places between Chile and Montana? And she needed a swimsuit? Between here and there were plenty of tropical beaches, cities she'd only ever heard of, places she'd never dreamed she'd get to on her own...

Travel for her had always been about "the two." Her and Mom.

But what if it was about her and someone else?

When she looked down at him, Ted was no longer studying the horizon. He was looking up at her.

He wanted to vacation with *her?* No, it was more than that. He wasn't suggesting some fling. He was talking about trying each other on for size. Like finding just the right airplane for the job.

"For real?" It was all she could think to ask.

"For real. What do you think?"

What did she *think?* "I think it sounds absolutely one-hundred-percent glorious!"

Then Ted did the silliest thing, he started doing a little happy dance right there on the pavement beside their plane.

It was like her world had just opened up. The magic night of a mid-summer's eve had turned into a magnificently radiant day.

She hopped down from the cargo door to join him and together they danced a happy chicken-dance beneath the mid-winter sun.

LIGHT THIS CANDLE

Once again, friend-editor-author Blaze Ward caused me to write a story that I've since fallen in love with. He had room in his *Boundary Shock Quarterly #24: Science Fiction Holidays*. Did I want to add something interesting?

I told him I'd think about it. Twenty-four hours later I sent him this story.

Hanukah may occur in September or October, depending on the year, but it is a timeless story of the battle between doubt and faith that accompanies so many holidays.

1

"Light this candle in ten... Nine."

Esther Levine lay sprawled on the steel deck beneath the lowest tier of bunks with only a stolen blanket for padding.

"Eight."

The number of seconds left in her life?

"Seven."

Seven by seven, all the good girls and boys went to heaven? Well, the heavens. Or was it seven magpies for a secret never told?

"Six."

Unless she ended up broken, with bones scattered like pick-up sticks. She was losing it. Deep breath. Focus. Nothing to focus on except the fiber mesh so close above her face she could practically itch her nose against it without raising her head.

"Five. Four, engine ignition."

It was weird being inside something she'd seen so many times from the outside. Instead of watching the first flash of smoke and fire belching from the great bells of the rocket engines, the deck at her back rang as if she lay on a thin sheet of tin being beaten with a sledgehammer. She'd seen the last of humanity rocketing aloft a hundred, two hundred at a time until there was only…

"Three."

"Two."

She'd managed to blend in and stowaway on the final…

"One."

…rocket…

"Liftoff."

…ever!

With no hearing protection, her instincts told her to cover her ears. Her brain said to keep her arms flat at her sides as the heavy acceleration built. With the conflicting instructions, her arms made it most of the way to her shoulders before they were pinned against her chest, too heavy to move.

Nothing to see here except the mattress that sagged but still held, brushing against the backs of her hands.

Five hundred souls in a rocket designed for seventy-five. If they all lived, six thousand would have parted the heavens and survived. A hundredth the number saved when Moses had parted the Red Sea. This last load carried aloft no cargo, no supplies, only people—the last of humanity to escape the hell of Earth. The final lift from *any* space center.

Five hundred and one, but she hoped no one was counting.

Except they hadn't escaped yet.

Only the pilots rated acceleration couches, every cubic meter had been filled with multi-tiered bunk beds fabricated from any bit of scrap metal that could be scrounged from the base. How many would—

Esther heard a scream off to her right.

She couldn't turn her head, but she managed to shift her eyes sufficiently sideways to peer out the thin gauze that hid her location. She'd rigged a strip on the lowest tier of all the bunks in this section so that her hideaway looked normal.

Two of the four tiers of the opposite bunk section had collapsed. The screams had been shock, not pain—from the survivors. Anyone in the pancaked tiers had been crushed too quickly to scream; the nine-g acceleration turned an eighty-kilo human into a seven-hundred kilo jackhammer.

Barukh ata Adonai Eloheinu, melekh ha'olam...

Blessed art thou, Lord our God, King of the Universe...

Esther couldn't remember the rest of the blessing, of any blessing.

Blessing for what?

For the death of the Earth?

For the death of Mother and the assured death of Father left behind?

The heavy acceleration dragged tears from her eyes that dribbled into her ears like cannon shots.

She couldn't tell Father what she had planned. Didn't dare speak it aloud for fear of being monitored. Simply because they were inside the hermetically sealed enclave didn't earn them a ride to space: Father too old, Mother dead on the Outside, and she, a late child, too young. Father had slipped her inside the quarantine before the base was permanently closed to the Outside but with no hope of salvation, only of prolonging survival.

Esther and Father had worked together in Uniform Distribution, issuing two for every space-bound refugee. Last night the count had come out two uniforms over.

Father had opened his mouth to ask how it might have happened as each recipient had to be fully registered. Then he'd glanced down at a small official daypack tucked under their workstation, all anyone would be allowed to take aloft. She scrounged it from the discard pile and sewn a careful patch inside the long tear. Without a word that might alert the security forces—and there were a *lot* of security forces here at the end—he reset the uniform counter.

Then he'd hugged her tight and kissed her on the forehead —all the blessing she needed.

2

LIGHT THIS CANDLE.

Esther assured herself that the flight, despite being the last ever off the face of the Earth, was happening according to plan.

The captain announced the dropping of the First Stage during a brief moment of weightlessness but warned everyone not to move. There was no countdown before they lit the Second Stage engine to lift them to a higher orbit.

There were the groans of the injured and the blood offering of the shattered, dripping onto the deck in a silence wrought of sonic overload from the liftoff and the new roar of the Second Stage. She witnessed each splash of red like the drops of red wine flung on a white plate during the Passover Seder service.

One drop for each of the ten plagues on Egypt, sent by God to punish the Pharaoh for not setting the Jews free from slavery.

A rain of blood. Frogs. Locusts. Only the foulest of all, the tenth plague sent by the Lord of the Universe, had broken the Pharaoh's bitter grasp: the death of the first-born sons of all Egypt—people, cattle, all of them.

Of course, the Torah said that God had hardened Pharaoh's heart at each plague so that he would not relent. That had always seemed like cheating to her, never giving the man a chance to escape his own wickedness.

It had been the first of her many questions about a faith her parents still held so dear.

Father was a first-born son and would soon be dead of the final plague.

With the rocket away, any atmospheric seal on the base would be meaningless. There was no more hardware to send aloft, even this last one had been more salvage than rocket. There was no escape on the surface from the global plague; too virulent to allow a last-minute miracle of salvation. Only a matter of time before The Pale Horseman, as the bug had been dubbed, found a way in, or the base's cache of food ran out. Anything that would last had already been sent aloft.

Rumor said The Pale Horseman had been engineered to wipe all except pureblood Chinese from the face of the Earth. Escaping their lab untested, as lesser plagues before it had, China had actually been the first to die as the fourth horseman of *Revelations* rode forth and spread death.

And I looked, and behold a pale horse: and his name that sat on him was Death, and Hell followed with him.

Was Hell a *fifth* horseman? Yet another question never answered to her satisfaction.

Being Jewish and therefore not counting *Revelations* as Holy Writ, His word offered no more sanctuary than being Chinese. Lamb's blood painted over the lintel did not turn aside the wrath of The Pale Horseman as it had in *Exodus 12.*

The new kick of the Second Stage's engines elicited no more collapses in the tiers of bunks. What was going to shatter already had.

3

———

LIGHT THIS CANDLE.

The words remained stuck in her head.

Esther had waited for those still alive to leave the rocket's cabin. Then she'd wiggled clear of the bottom bunk and slipped on her daypack.

When she'd taken one of her two precious uniforms from the bag before stowing away, she'd found a package. It was small, but heavy, as if densely packed. Little bigger than a large book. On the front Father's unmistakable scrawl simply said, *Open when you arrive.*

In space? Or their final destination? Assuming they ever reached it. *Later* was the only meaningful concept at the moment.

The stench of death here was somehow clean: the iron of blood, uric acid of panicked bladders unleashed. But not The Pale Horseman, which was reported to smell like jasmine.

She took three more breaths, shallow ones through her mouth rather than her nose, to gather her nerves. At worst, when they discovered her, they could shove her out the airlock.

At least it would be quick. The Pale Horseman rode slowly through the bloodstream.

With nerves of wet matzoh, she stepped into the corridor. The lights didn't flicker, they stuttered as if they'd forgotten how to speak.

"You!"

She hadn't even made it two steps past the threshold and she was already caught.

"Take his other arm." The man who'd hailed her had a bloody gash on his forehead. His eyes didn't focus well. The man he was supporting didn't *have* another arm. Nor was any blood pumping from the stump where it had once been.

She eased the man with the head injury against the wall. With his friend's remaining arm still wrapped over his shoulder, he and the corpse slid down to sit on the deck.

Esther looked up and down the steel corridor, hoping to spot help in the flashes of light, but there was no more to be seen than during the War of the Maccabees. That had been a desperate battle, a Jewish rebellion against the Grecian Empire of Seleucus—a fight destined to fail. Yet the Jews had triumphed, though at such a brutal cost.

Here on the ship, blood marks splattered many uniforms. Very few had their packs with them. She considered shedding hers to fit in better.

Fit in. There was a laugh.

She didn't belong here at all. Five years below the age limit, sixteen still lay a month in her future, if she survived. What place did she have amongst these people?

Her namesake had been one of the few great heroines *not* purged from the ancient texts. Esther Levine, the fifteen-year-old stowaway had no place here. No purpose.

Esther had one arm out of her pack when she had an idea.

"You rest here, I'll find you help." She shrugged her pack

firmly back into place. Snapped the front buckle to make sure it stayed on her shoulders.

The man nodded in such a way she couldn't tell if he heard or his body was finally catching up with his injured state.

Her father had been employed at the gate within the base that divided those headed aloft from those to be left behind. He had proven himself both trustworthy and capable of controlling chaos. It was in her to do no less than honor her father.

In minutes she'd gathered a team of people who had managed to keep their packs as she had. It was a marker of clear thinking in a crisis.

Making her own cabin a morgue and the one beside it a *desperate need* center, they set to work.

By the time the rocket had finished coasting up to their final orbit, two long days later, she hadn't slept and eaten only once. Her team worked tirelessly throughout the ship.

Mother's death had aged her, Father's work at the base had offered her wisdom...or so she'd thought. But the naive girl who had stowed away in fearful hope two days before was burned away by the tragedy and the small acts of heroism that happened all around her. The long climb to final orbit stretched endlessly ahead, like a path with no promise of salvation.

She'd struck a match of hope and passed its light forward to all who could carry it. Each who did, came to the aid of those who couldn't spark their own.

4

———

LIGHT THIS CANDLE.

Esther lay down in her Deep Sleep capsule. Safe. She didn't know whether to laugh or cry.

The crews of the interstellar colony ship, who had streamed aboard the moment her ship was docked, had been horrified. *Can't believe this piece of crap survived the launch at all.*

Six weeks ago the colony ship itself had been a year from completion. An effort worthy of the Old Testament had finished and peopled the ship.

And she'd been accepted aboard—not for her work. Not for anything beyond her mere presence. All of the worrying that she'd been too young to meet the requirements no longer mattered.

She was here. No other security or safety checks were required.

And then the sobs came.

The Final Cull of her rocket had been horrific. Yet another cost of battle to free themselves from the final rule of The Pale Horseman.

The Deep Sleep process for interstellar transit required a

person be very healthy for the system to work. A mild concussion or a broken arm could be allowed to heal. Organ damage, traumatic brain injuries, and the like were a death sentence. Nor could they spare the supplies to give any marginal cases a chance to heal. The supplies aboard were meant to buy the surviving crew a window of opportunity—if they ever reached a viable destination. Mars had fallen to The Pale Horseman before its virulence had been understood. The Moon had never supported more than a few small mining stations and could never be a viable home for humankind.

There had been much discussion but, like the Jews trapped by the siege of Masada, the mortally injured had chosen the solution themselves.

Late on the eighth night since docking to the colony ship, Esther had once again been aboard the final rocket that had brought her aloft, tending to those who could never survive Deep Sleep. At the darkest watch, she and the few with her were ushered to the airlock linking to the colony ship. The man who she'd first met in the corridor had been among those to guide her and the others off the ship; one eye focused on her, the other following a will of its own.

Before her weary mind had thought to protest, the marginal survivors had detached the old rocket and drifted clear.

Before she could even scream from inside the colony ship's airlock, they blew their own open to space.

After that, there was nothing to recover.

5

LIGHT THIS CANDLE.

It was so odd that the father of American spaceflight, a good Christian, had spoken the words Esther couldn't shed. Alan Shepard, sitting atop the first-ever Mercury rocket, stalled by one safety check after another, had finally demanded *Let's light this candle.*

Esther could only stare at the wrappings of the gift that Father had secretly tucked into her daypack. She'd decided that by *Open when you arrive,* Father had meant her new home.

By some miracle, she had lived to honor that request.

The centuries of transit had passed in Deep Sleep. The inevitable slow aging meant that she was now over the minimum age limit, though still the youngest by six years in the new colony.

She sat beneath a tree that only partly fit the word but offered shade from the white dwarf sun. A blue giant circled far away. New Earth had no true darkness for half the nights. The seasons weren't driven by axial tilt, but by the light of the blue giant, a tiny yet brilliant beacon burning high in the night.

Cross-legged on the woven mat that people called grass but

had more in common with a lichen, including the rich golden color, she opened Father's package and lay it out before her.

Under the outer wrapping lay Mother's *tallit,* her fringed prayer shawl.

Within its folds, a hand-sized Torah rolled on a pair of spindles, a physical copy in case electronic ones failed. A Haggadah had also been included for conducting a Passover Seder to celebrate the freeing of the Jews from Egypt. A small branch, withered and desiccated with age, that must have come from the launch base's hydroponics. She would add it to her hut built to celebrate the first successful harvest during Sukkot. And while there'd been no room for the family's fragile goblet for Elijah, there was a small vial of festival wine for Purim, to celebrate the Jews' rescue from the evil vizier of Persia. A rescue performed by her namesake Esther when she was still a year younger than Esther herself had been on launch day.

But the largest and heaviest item had been the family Menorah and the forty-four small candles needed to celebrate the Festival of Lights. The simple brass had always run smooth under her fingertips. The soot of the final candles from a time now centuries gone dusted her fingers. Mother had lit those candles on a world lost.

Hannukah.

After the sacking of the Temple in Jerusalem, after the triumph of the Maccabees over the Seleucid Empire, only one day of sacred oil had remained to relight the Temple lamps. The nearest cache lay a four-day ride away and four days back. Yet the lamps had burned for all eight days. A miracle, if one chose to believe in such things.

Yet eight fires *had* brought her to New Earth: first and second stages of the lift rocket, the interstellar acceleration and deceleration burns while she slept, the deorbit and landing burns. Those six had been born of heat and flame.

But first, she had burned all of the bridges behind her,

leaving all she loved in order to stow away aboard the final rocket.

And most importantly the inner fire when she'd proven herself to *herself* in the bowels of the broken ship after the launch. Proven that she had value in this new society despite her youth. That *anything* was possible if one believed hard enough.

And perhaps that was the final answer to all of her questions about faith.

Esther wrapped Mother's *tallit* about her shoulders, then pulled it up over her hair. She felt her parents kneeling beside her.

Placing one candle in the center and one in the rightmost hole of the eight-arm Menorah, Esther used a sparker to light the central candle. Then she lifted it out and lit the first-night candle with it.

Barukh ata Adonai Eloheinu, melekh ha'olam...

Blessed art thou, Lord our God, King of the Universe...

...asher kid'shanu b'mitzvotav...

...who made us holy through Your commandments...

———

FOR MORE SCIENCE FICTION TALES, START WITH *THE LIFT*.

SANTA AND THE PIRATE QUEEN

Sometimes you just have to have fun. This Christmas romance is exactly that. I often dreamed of going deep sea. And though I owned a sailboat and learned to single-hand her—except for one horrid passage through the Chittenden Locks in Ballard, Washington—it would be four more decades before I would venture out onto the ocean, three months *after* the release of this collection.

The Choy Lee belonged to two good friends and Captain Master Howl to another. As to the rest of it, it's surprising how little I had to make up to tell this story.

1

———

THE WIND GUSTED PAST SIXTY KNOTS OUT OF THE WEST-
northwest. Not an issue from any other point of the compass,
but WNW winds slid past the marina's breakwater, took a stroll
down the lane between T and U docks, and hammered into
slip T19.

Her slip.

Anything over forty-seven knots made her boat bob and
weave like a drunk penguin.

"November storms suck!" Janine yelled at the boat. Ship's
Captain Master Howl opened one eye, rolled onto his back and
began to purr, forcing Janine to rub his furry black belly. Not as
if she could do anything else. Her forty-one-foot Cheoy Lee
sailboat, *Tārā,* twisted badly enough that she was far more
likely to type *Gwko~* than *Help!* or *Sthj@* than *ARGH!* as the
laptop slid one way and her fingers went the other.

Giving it up, she slapped the cover closed and tucked it into
the drawer under the chart table. Scooping up Master Howl in
her arms, Janine staggered forward—banging a shoulder
against the starboard door to the head, almost dropping Master
Howl as she crashed her hip against the cooktop in the portside

galley, and finally shuffled fast enough to plummet into the starboard-most seat of C-shaped settee rather than plunging into the closet.

The settee was the oddest feature of the Cheoy Lee's design, but one she'd come to love. Most boats would have two sofa seats with some awkward arrangement to raise a table in the middle of the aisle when guests and meals were happening. Her boat had a circular sofa that could seat eight. The mouth of the C-shape opened to the stern to either side of where the mast punched through on its way to the keel. A fold-up table hung from the back of the mast.

She shuffled around the seat until the two of them were ensconced in the backmost position. This part of the seat could be folded aside to access the forward cabin, which she rarely used except for sail storage. Once seated on the centerline of the boat, the action felt much less violent, now no more than a gentle rocking. Books flopped side-to-side on the shelf with a gentle slap. Spice bottles rattled against each other in the galley. Miscellaneous gear clanked to one side then another in the various storage cubbies. And though she couldn't hear the water sloshing about in the bilge, she could hear the pump engage and shut down as it was alternately submerged and exposed with the rolling of the boat.

All the sounds of home. Then a blast of rain and hail pounded on the deck over her head, drumming like an all-percussion marching band.

"Gonna be a long night, Master Howl."

He answered with an orca-sized yawn as befit his black coat and white chest patch. Though his hair fell more into the shaggy category than the sleek and dangerous one.

He *had* been a howler as a kitten but age had mellowed him. It was now far easier to picture him snoozing in a rope coil, sipping a White Russian (without the vodka or Kahlúa diluting the cream, of course), and occasionally rousing himself to batter his catnip toy crew into submission. It made him the perfect ship's captain. Though he still did occasionally give full voice to his discontent—especially if his dinner was more than three seconds late. He considered her ignoring that while navigating tricky archipelago passages to be grounds for mutiny. She had taught him quickly enough that batting her with his claws out counted as a gross breach of the ship's articles under which she served.

Of course it was better than being saddled with a dog. She'd trust Joshua Slocum on that point. On sailing the first solo circumnavigation of the globe in the 1890s, he'd considered taking on a local to help him pass through the Strait of Magellan. But the man had insisted that no one in their right mind would attempt that passage without a *doog* on board. Per his book *Sailing Alone Around the World,* Slocum *drew the line at dogs.* Janine had cleaved to that advice and never regretted her decision to do so.

Here, at the centerline with a warm cat in her arms, and the boat rocking side-to-side like the perfect cradle for a grown woman, she wanted to fall asleep. She really did. She tried.

Master Howl succeeded easily enough.

But her? Oh no! Tomorrow was *her* day and it wouldn't stop churning up a turbulent wake in her head.

With kind words and the hints of how much fun it would be, the secretary-general of the local yacht club had suckered her into organizing the annual Christmas Sailor's Potluck. A crime for which she'd never forgive him.

The reality had no relation to the purported ease and fun.

The other volunteers' expectations were that they could have everything exactly their way, that it was fully under their control, and that the louder they protested the more likely they would succeed.

However, Janine had been sailing far too long to be fooled. Everyone who had ever skippered a boat, even an eight-foot rubber dinghy, would gladly don a t-shirt declaring *I'm the Captain so, of course, I'm right!* She tried not to wince at the one in her own collection stating *I'm the Captain. Rule #1: The Captain is always right. Rule #2: Any questions? See Rule #1.*

Organizing a potluck should be merely sending out a few fun invites and reminders. A little bit of dish coordination so that not *everyone* brings a package of QFC chocolate chip cookies, and make up a few fun door prizes.

Except Georgina Anne wanted there to be fixed seating and a size limit.

Michael wanted to turn it into a fifty-dollar-a-head fundraiser (that Janine was sure was actually to keep the riff-raff like herself out but that Georgina Anne took personally).

Bethany had organized a decorating committee with her two BFFs, and they'd wanted a committed budget several times the yacht club's annual membership fee.

This wasn't the Seattle Yacht Club costing tens of thousands of dollars with thirty-six-month payment plans (for those in need). Nor was it the Sloop Tavern Yacht Club with a ninety-dollar fee, which also registered your boat for all of their races. She'd chosen one that cost in the hundreds—after having broken up with the head barman at the Sloop, which had definitely cancelled her prior membership there. Danny had been cool about it, but not the patrons.

The Lakefront Yacht Club landed in the casual zone between the two. A little upscale from the guys chugging pints at the start of a race no matter what the hour. It made for a nice change. Except the LYC also gathered all of the wannabes who the Seattle Yacht Club would never allow on their clubhouse verandah much less as members. And the worst of the lot had harangued her hourly on every social media platform known to womankind.

Finally sick of them all, she'd issued the invite to the full membership for the Annual Christmas *Pirate's* Potluck, set a suggested door price of a wrapped present for a homeless kid, and called it done. Once out, no one had the balls to take it back. When Bethany and her BFFs had attempted to vote her out, she'd invoked the *I'm-the-Captain* rule. Finally, the club's secretary-general had backed her up over Bethany's protests with a simple e-mail: *Janine's the organizer.* Three whole words from a man who typically communicated in story-length volumes.

Tomorrow would either be immense fun. Or—

"Worst they can do is keelhaul me, right, Master Howl?"

On a particularly rough buck of the boat, her cat rolled out of her arms to plop into her lap, more like a beanbag than a cat with an actual skeleton somewhere beneath all that fur.

Janine sighed and began beating the back of her head against the partition that separated the settee from the forward stateroom. Not hard enough to knock herself out, though the thought did come to mind.

2

———

Howie Liebermann loved Christmas. Or at least the Christmas season. Mom loved having the annual *Hanukkah bush* in the living room. Dad always turned surly for a week or so after its arrival before caving in. It was hard to blame him. Each year he caught hell from Grandma when she visited, which seemed unfair as Jews didn't go in for the whole Hell thing—more of a Limbo-like retraining center for souls destined to enter the Garden of Eden on high.

Howie and his two sisters could always count on the worst presents under the Menorah. How many wooden dreidels and cheap milk chocolate wrapped in gold foil did three kids need after all? Grandma's Fifth Night gelt always eased the pain a little. The five-dollar *fortune* they'd received as little kids had never crossed twenty even in the lean college years. She paid their tuitions—her and Grandpa's sewing machine business had been very successful—but never more than a twenty on Fifth Night. The best presents always landed *under* the Hanukkah bush—which they had trimmed with twinkle lights and eclectic ornaments. Presents that just happened to be opened on December 25th, though nothing from Grandma, of course.

That wasn't why he loved Christmas.

His passion for the holiday season had sprung into being when he'd escaped Brooklyn under the impetus of a cool job and cruised into Seattle's land of year-round sailing.

And the best part about Christmas here was definitely the great sailing parties and races. The Seattle Yacht Club Championships close before Halloween, typically coincident with the Sloop Tavern's Great Pumpkin Race at the other end of the spectrum. The Turkey Bowl race that the Corinthian Yacht Club on the Friday after Thanksgiving. Again, the Sloop's Dark & Stormy Christmas Light Cruise (and inevitable after-party). All the nights with parades of Christmas boats along different sections of Seattle's vast waterfronts were illumination spectacles.

And every club had an annual Christmas potluck.

Howie had never joined any of the clubs, though he'd enjoyed the round of *Introduction* dinners every club offered as they sought new members. Instead, he'd made a small name for himself on the local race circuits as on-call crew when a boat came up a person short.

He learned that it was a *thing* two years ago while hanging out at Fremont Brewing's Urban Beer Garden after a long day cutting code at Adobe. Their offices commanded the waterfront by the Fremont drawbridge.

At the next table, a couple were fighting about whose turn it was to helm the boat in that night's race. Watching the summertime Tuesday Duck Dodge evening races out on Lake Union in the heart of Seattle was fun. But he'd never given any thought to being aboard, until the guy had stormed off and the woman looked around the bar like a lost soul. Short, cute, and curvy, they'd dated long enough for him to learn the basics of sailing and have a good laugh together. She let him and other volunteers crew every position, except the helm—that was hers alone now that she'd canned the fiancé.

Howie had quickly learned to read the local racing calendars and started making a few educated guesses. The Fremont Brewery or Duke's on Tuesday afternoons led to Duck Dodge slots. The bar at Ray's Boathouse the night before a race out of Shilshole turned out to be a great place to be picked up as last-minute crew. Laurelhurst had too much money to ever consider wanting crew like him, but Anthony's Homeport along the Kirkland waterfront was a consistent winner.

There were now a score of boat skippers with his number on speed dial. Two, even three races a week came his way almost year round. He'd never spent a dollar past his bar tab, one pint and an appetizer limit unless some winning captain was buying for the crew. There'd been no need to join any of the yacht clubs.

Except for missing the Christmas parties.

Despite his initial introduction, sailing women were in a special class all their own—rare. Men dominated the sport. Howie soon learned, however, that grown-daughters-of came out of the woodwork at special moments...like Christmas parties.

But he had to adhere to his policy of minimal expense. He was only about halfway to affording his own boat big enough to live aboard but fast enough to be fun. Or maybe even rigged for the ultimate: going deep sea. Circumnavigating. Hard to imagine but it sounded very cool. Until then? He'd stay focused on hitting those great holiday parties.

He'd built enough connections to enough different boats that he always heard about the various parties. This being the self-proclaimed sailing capital of the US of A, there were a lot of them. Between Halloween and the end of the Christmas boat parades on December 23rd was in many ways the peak of the sailing season—or at least the *social* sailing season.

But finding a date, even on a one-evening basis to attend a party, was tricky because the sailing women were so rare.

Then the great idea came. Who could turn away a gate-crashing Santa, even one with a Brooklyn-Jew accent?

3

———

Janine surveyed the yacht club decorations. Thank God last night's storm had played itself out, which would be a boon for attendance. She so didn't want to be the person who organized a party and no one came. From the crackling fire at one end of the hall to the giant Christmas tree at the other, it was beautiful.

"This is amazing! Great job!" Janine had to give credit where credit was due.

Bethany and her pair of BFFs offered her thankful smiles that didn't reach their steel-like eyes, but they *had* done well. And it had cost the club only fifty dollars.

In keeping with her Pirate's Christmas theme, the Queen Bethany Trio scrounged among the membership for old manila lines, wooden block-and-tackle, battered wooden chests, and the like. The tables, that Janine had insisted be set up in long communal-style rows over Georgina Anne's protests, were scattered with well-worn seafaring paraphernalia. The QBT had also raided various long-grown-children's toy boxes; rubber swords and daggers had been strewn about as well. Bethany had found nautical-chart paper tablecloths to spread

428

along the tables, which had cost the fifty dollars and were sure to be conversation starters with any sailor.

Janine's personal playlist—of mixed sea shanties by the Cornish Fisherman's Friends group and Christmas carols—lent a cheery background.

Georgina Anne and Michael had eschewed festive wear beyond very conservative Christmas sweaters.

But not to be outdone by Janine's chosen theme, the QBT wore matching pirate maiden costumes that included high leather boots, alarmingly short skirts, and seriously low-cut bodices. Bandanas side-knotted as headbands allowed their latest hair styles to be on display while adding to the piratical air.

Courtesy of a brief fling several years ago that had overlapped Halloween, Janine possessed full Elizabeth Swann attire. Keira Knightley had rocked it in *Pirates of the Caribbean,* and their builds were similar enough that Janine had gone all in when putting it together—right down to the sheathed long sword dangling from a well-worn broad leather strap. Unsure why she could never throw it out, especially when space was always such a premium on a sailboat, she now knew. Without a word, simply by standing beside them, it changed the Queen Bethany Trio from sexy pirate maidens to cheap working girls in a pirate bar.

The fact was not lost on the BFFs, though Bethany pretended not to care. Of course, rumor said that Bethany was searching for a new *captain* for her personal boat, having divorced the second (or perhaps third) one two months ago. She appeared fully prepared to leverage all that the costume implied at the least hint of a major checking account.

Oddly, this was something relatively easy to assess in the boating community. Finding out the size and make of a person's sailboat, a natural conversation starter in a yachting club, quickly separated the pretenders and the wannabes from the truly affluent. A C&C 27 earned a scoff at best, though a J24 might command a little respect as it was a racer rather than a wallowing daysailer. Anything over fifty feet commanded attention. Her 41-foot boat floated in the murky middle ground, though it being a Cheoy Lee did earn her more attention than a longer Gulfstar or Cal might.

By the time of the official start of the potluck, the hall was already half full—a good turnout. About half had taken her challenge with costumes ranging from a simple bandana to a few other kits better than the QBT. Too bad she was judging the best costume competition, as so far she would be an easy win.

Her top choice so far was a family who had dressed as space pirates with obviously recycled astronaut Halloween costumes. They weren't incredible but the family absolutely owned it, especially the five-year-old girl brandishing her kid-sized red light saber.

Steaming pots and great platters of food soon had the buffet table groaning under the weight. Three sets of Swedish meatballs, several lasagnas, salads in every variety from Asian noodle to orange-cranberry. Two whole sides of salmon were sufficiently massive that even a concerted attack didn't kill them off until past the first hour. Not a single Jell-O salad—a staple of her Iowan youth—reared its ugly head.

The dessert table was like a light show: blueberry cobbler, a great sheet of golden baklava, the round eyes of orange pumpkin and lemon-yellow meringue pies were interspersed with M&M oatmeal cookies larger than her hand with the fingers spread.

Yet Janine could feel the change like a good skipper reading the winds before they wholly shifted and left your boat stranded on the wrong side of the course.

Second helpings tapered off. The dessert buffet slightly resembled the docks after a fish-cleaning session. An hour in and the event showed the first signs of fading. It was too early to start on the door prizes. The Spring Fling had revealed that this wasn't much of a dancing crowd. She cursed herself for not thinking up any games, probably because she'd always hated them when someone else did.

This evening was on the verge of winding down long before she was ready, considering all the effort and pain she'd put into the event. Desperate enough to approach the Queen Bethany Trio? Sadly, yes.

But when she went looking for them, she could only find the two BFFs.

"She's showing her boat to someone." The BFFs' shared look said that she wouldn't be back anytime soon. The Solaris 40 might be a foot shorter than her Cheoy Lee 41, but the interior was pure luxury. Bethany and her latest target might not resurface for days.

The BFFs were far more tolerable on their own, but neither had any brilliant ideas to keep the party going either.

Maybe she should bow to the inevitable and start the door prizes early. Of course, with her luck, she'd then be accused of cutting short such a lovely evening. It was the no-win scenario with Captain Jack Sparrow nowhere in sight to rescue her. If she—

"Merry Christmas, ye blaggards!" The shout sliced through every conversation and focused all attention on the door.

4

"Heya! Heya! Heya! Can Santa make an entrance or what?"

It earned him a polite round of applause. Kinda middle ground. Not the polite patter from the Medina Yachters nor the round of cheers and a beer thudded on the bar before him at the Sloop Tavern.

He jumped up onto a table, brandishing the sword that he'd spiral wound with red-and-white electrical tape.

"Arrrr! Come on people. Give Pirate Santa a proper arrr. ARRR!"

The response, especially from the kids and their families, improved by several levels. His little sister Stacey had been hyped on Broadway since seeing *The Lion King* at age six. She'd rarely been the lead in any school play, but she *always* nailed the scene-stealing comic relief. Good enough that this year Yale Drama gave her a major scholarship. For this event, he'd channel Stacey.

Howie flourished the hook clamped over his left hand. He'd picked it up at a local costume shop along with the sword, see-through eye patch, and tricorn hat. Though he'd never been *Pirate* Santa before, he couldn't resist the challenge when a buddy had forwarded him a copy of the invitation.

"ARRR!" he roared out again and the kids ate it up.

As he swashbuckled down the table, people yanked empty plates and glasses out of the way.

"So, who here has been a good lad or lassie—and who's been baaaad?"

A small voice popped up on cue. "I've been good," a pint-sized pirate with a raggedy shirt, a bandana, and an eyepatch flipped up.

"Good?" Howie blustered. "*Good?*"

He tucked his sword away and reached down to lift the little boy onto the table.

"I oughter make ya walk the gangplank. Less'n you was a-sayin' you were a good *pirate*." He'd lost the kid, so Howie helped him out. "You been a good *pirate* for Pirate Santa, young lad?"

His sister had taught him that one of the keys was to dress the part. So, he'd done the full Santa fat suit and beard, and layered on the pirate with eyepatch, tricorn hat that he'd spray-painted bright red, and latex-makeup scars on the bits of cheek and forehead that showed. The other key, she'd insisted was to ham it up and never break character. So, he laid on the Brooklyn accent, the one he'd done his best to leave behind along with his youth, as thick as a Katz's pastrami on rye and dove into the pirate role.

"Yes, Pirate Santa."

"Well done, lad!" He unslung the red gift bag he'd been wearing on a wide leather strap. Peeking inside, he found a Matchbox fire engine, the full ladder truck with the pivot in the middle, and handed it over. In moments, the pirate-in-training was once again in his chair, racing his new engine around the plate holding the last few bites of an apple pie.

"Har! Har! Har! Merry Christmas, lad!"

5

———

Janine slid over to stand by Georgina Ann and Michael. Now there was a match made in hell. Maybe she should push them together simply for the sheer spectacle. Of course, what if it worked? The vision dancing in her head of miniature versions of these two ruthlessly organizing the world was enough to stop the thought.

"Okay. Who hired the Pirate Santa from Brooklyn?"

They both shrugged. "We thought you did."

"It *is* rather crass," Georgina Ann continued. "Hadn't you already made a sufficient mockery of the event as it is?"

Michael was nodding his agreement.

"Gods, you two *do* belong together."

"We what?" they said in unison. Then they both looked at her before turning to inspect each other.

Crap! Now she really had unleashed the Christmas Gorgon or Hydra or whatever mythical monster it was that got released at Christmas.

Well, it *was* her event. Which meant whatever happened was up to her.

She moved up to Santa who'd returned to floor level as he dug deep into his bag for a little girl.

"Ah!" he spotted her. "Santa's Pirate Elf just when I needed her. Sit. Sit." He pointed at the floor.

Caught unawares, Janine sat cross-legged on the floor, placing her eye-to-eye with the little girl.

Santa fished out a stethoscope.

"Put these in your ears," he instructed the little girl as he helped her. "And you'll hear something amazing."

He handed the business end to Janine. Without any hint of risqué, the V-neck of her blouse still opened enough for her to place the pickup close above her left breast.

The girl's eyes shot wide.

"You can listen to anyone's heart," the Pirate Santa told her.

"Even Mr. Tom's?" she asked in an overloud voice.

He tickled the side of her ribs with the tip of his plastic hook. "When ye get home, lass, listen right there, just behind Mr. Tom's front leg on either side. And try right here on his throat," the hook touched the side of Janine's throat, "when he starts to purr. Do you purr?"

Janine hadn't expected the last to be addressed to her.

Snagging her wrist with his hook, he moved the stethoscope from above her breast to beside her throat.

She pressed the pickup there and did her best to purr.

The girl giggled in delight. "You don't sound nothing like Mr. Tom." Then the shyness kicked in. She leaned in to whisper to the man in the well-padded red-and-white suit that was at least as high quality as her own pirate outfit. "Thank you, Santa." The girl scurried away, clutching her stethoscope tightly to her chest.

"I hope she has a patient cat," Pirate Santa appeared to be grinning behind the fake white beard.

"Who—" But her attempt to ask who he was, and each

subsequent attempt after that was cut off by the arrival of another child. He soon had a waiting crowd.

Each time, he listened carefully to them, asking questions. Then he'd fish around in his bag. Nothing was wrapped, nor was any of it new. Some showed signs of repair, touched-up paint and so on. But each gift delighted its recipient.

"How—"

She was as unsuccessful with that question as *Who.*

But during the quiet in-between moments, Santa explained. "Pirate Santa hits the thrift stores. Picks over the toy sections—"

"And the doctor ones," she interjected, realizing that the girl now owned a genuine stethoscope, not some imitation that would break before she could listen to her cat's heart.

"Sure. Marine stuff, farmer, chef—though no knives. Whatever comes to hand. Fix it up and give them away. It's a good goof, all in fun, dat fer sure. Pirate Santa and his pirate elf," he offered her a broad wink, "take care of his wee crewmates, dat's all o' the game." Only a lone eye was clearly visible, and one of the fake scars tugged the wink askew.

She'd swear that his Brooklyn accent grew thicker the longer she stayed near him. Janine was about to fade away, though not too far as he remained an unknown, when she caught onto the pattern of the gifts. Boys wanted the little cars and trucks along with the occasional action figures. For the girls, there were a few dolls, but most received a next-level gift like the stethoscope, a small hand telescope, or a children's book of knot-tying with a length of line. One of the older girls received a scientific calculator complete with a printed-off copy of the instruction manual.

That was what kept her closer than merely keeping an eye on him.

6

————

Howie had been following a routine that he'd honed a dozen or more times with great success. Though he'd never had an elf assistant before, especially not one who looked so incredible. At her first attempt to slip away, he placed the next little kid in her lap to keep her in place.

Long and sleek. Thick hair, the chocolatey brown of Santa's reindeer, flowed down over her shoulders and offered a glorious distraction. The low brim of her black tricorn hat shaded her eyes so that he couldn't see their color. And dressed in a costume that looked like it was straight out of the 1700s. She was utterly astonishing. Exactly the woman any pirate king would want by his side to make him the envy of all far and wide.

He set himself up on a chair on one of the tables and had her assisting *Those who sought an audience with Pirate Santa* to step up onto *Pirate Santa's throne*. She had the poise and build of a dancer, but demonstrated a surprising strength when handling even the stoutest boy or girl—a sailing pirate's strength for sure.

From up here, he could also judge the ebb and flow of the

room. He could usually sustain this game for ten or fifteen minutes. It was over half an hour before he finally closed his bag for the last time. Then he stood and bowed to the four corners of the room, honoring the four winds. The applause was almost a roar, his best yet. He could see why his sister was so hyped on it, even if he never wanted to do it out of a Santa—or a Pirate Santa—suit.

Then he reached out a hand toward the lovely elf. Not down, but coaxing her up to stand on the table beside him.

Her blush shot bright, but she stepped on a wobbly chair with perfect surety and joined him aloft.

Then he took her hand, raised their joined grasp high, then swung it down. Only a bit off the cue, she took the indication to bow. The applause continued.

As it died away, he called out, "Santa sees there's still plenty o' fine desserts awaitin'. What kind of a pirate crew are ye to be leaving such vittles laying about?" It earned a laugh and turned the crowd's attention back to the buffet line.

The elf retrieved her hand and jumped lightly down from the table. But she didn't walk away. Instead, she held the chair steady for him. He was far less graceful in his heavy boots, fat suit, and a hook for a left hand.

"Party crasher?" she asked from mere inches away once he stood again on *terra firma*. Her eyes were the color of a darkening sky, but he didn't see any storm brewing there.

"What else would ye expect from a Pirate Santa?"

"Far less than this one has earned tonight." She kissed him on the cheek above his white beard but below the latex scar that was squinting up his exposed eye—a mistake he'd never make again as it was seriously annoying.

By the end of the evening, Howie knew several things.

First, the elfin pirate had almost no skills with people. She was as forthright as her pirate attire suggested. While she didn't offend, she was crap at superficial chit-chat. He recognized it as a trait they absolutely shared.

Second, she was organized enough to lead an entire pirate rabble to victory. The whole evening finished smoothly. Including the family of space pirates winning best group costume and a gift certificate to the Museum of Science.

Third, he remained his usual awkward real-life self despite being the Pirate Santa. He departed well-fed and thanked—without discovering her name or asking for her phone number.

Fourth, he was completely gone on the woman who had set a whole new standard for attractive piratical elves.

7

THE CHRISTMAS SHIP PARADE OF BOATS WAS ALWAYS A TRICKY challenge. Tourists paid top dollar to ride on the Argosy tour boat with fine cocktails, appetizers, and a caroling choir. No self-respecting Seattle boat skipper would be caught dead on such a cruise—or paying that much money for a ninety-minute outing.

However, it was the lead ship on the final night of the parade of boats dressed up in Christmas lights. On evenings throughout December, there were parades along different sections of Seattle's waterfront—something the city boasted a lot of. But December 23rd counted as the big one and she'd hate to miss it.

Janine had sailed every parade this year, and after going to so much trouble dressing up *Tārā,* she'd hate missing the final one. But her normal call-up crew felt that their office Christmas party was more important. She hoped that they told the truth about having to put in an appearance, rather than what she suspected—that they'd have more fun at their office than with her. Personally, she was always happiest alone on her boat.

She could single-hand *Tārā* in all conditions except for the busiest of races. But passing solo through the Ballard Locks was just begging for trouble. She moored at Shilshole Marina on Puget Sound, and tonight's cruise was along the Lake Union waterfront, five miles and one tricky set of locks away.

A few calls up and down the docks to the other liveaboards revealed they were having similar crew problems. Alice and Jake gave her a number to try. *He's a good hand, dead reliable. Decent guy.*

Her excitement about inviting a strange guy onto her boat for a six-hour cruise ranked mighty low. But when, six calls later, Quint gave her the same number, she caved.

A couple quick texts and she had her crew, for better or worse.

At T dock, pinged into her phone.

Janine glared at the text, then ponytailed her hair under her hoodie and pulled on a windbreaker. It was a good night, calm and dead clear, which meant chilly headed for downright cold. Sure enough, by the time she reached the head of the dock to open the security gate, she had to snug down the hoodie and was wishing for a mug of hot chocolate.

Though he was silhouetted by the parking lot lights behind him, the guy on the other side of the wire mesh didn't look dangerous. His height was all she could really tell, a few inches over hers. A cable-knit orange wool hat was tugged down to his eyebrows. A multi-colored scarf around his neck, and the heavy jacket said he knew what he was getting into. He was carrying a satchel.

"What have you got there?"

"My standard kit, though I hope I don't need it tonight: inflatable life vest, slicks, and a change of clothes."

"Okay." She opened the gate.

"There's also a dozen cookies from Dahlia Bakery in Belltown."

"You're hired."

He had a good laugh. Down at Slip T19 he came to a halt. "Is this a Cheoy Lee?"

"The 41." Janine was more than a little charmed. It was unusual enough that not many could pick one out of a crowd. "Her name is *Tārā*." She liked the way he scanned the boat. Not wide-eyed neophyte, but rather pausing only briefly as he cataloged the deck layout, line paths, and tiedowns.

"You don't strike me as the sort to be burning down the South."

Everyone always assumed that her boat was named for Scarlett's plantation in *Gone with the Wind*. Even if they saw the odd spelling, which this guy couldn't without going to the stern and bending down to look.

"Uh, I never got your name."

"Howie."

"Hi, I'm Janine. Thanks for lending a hand tonight."

"Always glad of a chance to cruise in the Christmas parades." He tossed his bag inside the lifelines.

She hopped aboard. "*Tārā* was a female Buddha or a bodhisattva, depending on who you talk to. She's the Mother of Liberation. Success in work and achievements also fall under her purview." She started the engine.

"Cool! Liberation from the hum-drum life. I like it." Howie caught the end of the spring line after she untied it, flipped it off the dock cleat and tossed it aboard forward in a neat coil. Without needing any prompting, he untied the stern line, left a loop over the dock cleat, and handed her the loose end. That would let her keep the boat in place until she was actively backing out of the slip. Finally he undid the bow line and stood ready to walk the boat out.

No questioning his familiarity with proper line work.

In minutes they were sliding through the night waters. He clipped the safety lines securely, then cleared the rubber bumpers that had dangled off the side between the boat and the dock. He continued until he'd dressed all the lines as neatly as she always did.

After snagging his bag, he hesitated at the head of the companionway down into the boat.

She waved him ahead as she navigated her way along the back of the Shilshole breakwater. Manners too. Who was this guy?

8

———————

HOWIE DIDN'T WANT JANINE TO THINK HE WAS SNOOPING; THE woman came across as seriously serious. He'd intended to toss his bag on a bunk and return to the deck immediately, but the interior required a good long look.

She was no simple daysailer—neither the woman nor the boat.

There were obvious signs that not only did Janine live aboard, but that her boat was capable of far more serious adventures than a parade of Christmas lights. The instruments at the chart were top quality gear. Not merely an ICOM two-way, but also a handheld and a satellite radio. The GPS and navigation equipment was sufficiently impressive that he'd want a good long spell with the instruction manual before approaching it.

And the interior. Janine was a very practical woman. There were only hints here and there as to the owner's gender. But she had a fantastic physical library of the great mariners from Bligh to Chichester. There were also travel guides that appeared to include most major countries with a coastline. A slim set of volumes about Arctic and Antarctic exploration were particularly intriguing.

Too long below, though the thoroughly efficient and comfortable interior tempted him to linger, he turned to ascend the ladder to the deck.

Except his way was blocked. Sitting there at the base of the ladder, a large black-and-white cat regarded him suspiciously.

"What's his or her name?" he called up to Janine loudly enough to be heard over the engine rumble as he knelt to let the cat sniff his hand.

"He. Ship's Captain Master Howl. Be sure to salute."

He glanced up the ladder at her. What little of her face he could see between the hoodie and the darkness showed no sign she was joking. So, he knelt as straight as he could, then saluted sharply before reaching out to pet him. The cat had a ready purr.

Howie scooped him up and carried Master Howl up to join his mistress above decks.

"Now you're spoiling him rotten." She showed the first hint of humor since his arrival.

"And you don't? You made him ship's captain."

"Oh no, he did that on his own. I merely bowed to the inevitable. Here, take the wheel." And she simply walked away from him.

In all his sailing, it was the one thing he did the very least— as in never. It was part of how he'd fit into every crew, by never going for the wheel or tiller.

She disappeared below.

The steel wheel radiated cold against his palms, cold enough it almost burned. But he didn't dare let go to fish out his gloves. Instead, he held on for dear life and did his best to stay on track for the opening at the south end of Shilshole and the turn into Salmon Bay and the locks.

Foolishly trusting him, Janine stayed below forever—at

least a minute, perhaps two. Other boats were coming out of darkened docks. Picking their running lights out of their extravagant Christmas finery was tricky.

Then she must have thrown a breaker and the *Tārā's* lights blinked on. Which was a massive understatement. The boat glittered with a galaxy of multi-colored lights. After that, everyone stayed out of his way as if he was Neptune, God of the Sea.

She finally reappeared, only to set down a pair of bowls on the floor of the cockpit. Master Howl thumped down from the seat he'd been lounging on and began eating his dinner.

Then Janine was back out of sight, reappearing only to set out a big thermos, then two mugs, and finally his box of cookies.

When she returned to the deck, she didn't take the wheel. Instead, she sat on one of the side seats and filled the two thermal travel mugs from the thermos.

"Hope hot chocolate's okay. I can't drink coffee past the first cup of the morning or I end up more jittery than Master Howl." As her cat seemed more likely to yawn than jitter, he wasn't terribly worried.

"Hot chocolate born and bred." He accepted the mug and managed the turn into Salmon Bay without crashing her boat into a channel buoy. A minor triumph in his opinion.

He could feel her eyes on him. "What's wrong?"

"I've never taken the helm before."

"Never? Why?"

He shrugged, though that probably didn't show through his heavy parka. "Earned my first ride as crew because of a couple fighting over control of the helm while they were still ashore. Figured my best way to keep sailing was to keep my hands off."

"But the rest of it?" She waved a gloved hand at the rest of the boat.

"A hundred and thirty-seven races from winch grinder to foredeck sail handler."

"Over hard right!" She snapped out.

He didn't see a reason but wasn't going to mess with that tone. He looked right to make sure no one was in the channel beside him and turned the wheel to starboard.

"Spin it! All the way!"

So he did through two full turns until the wheel hit a stop with a solid *thunk!* he could feel through his palms. The boat turned like it was dancing.

"Back the other way!"

He spun back to port, four turns until the wheel thunked against the other stop. The boat spun with equal agility in the other direction.

"Settle straight up the channel," her voice turned utterly patient.

She sat in silence as he tried but overcorrected one way and then the other before he found the center position again *and* had them headed in the right direction.

"That gives you a beginning feel for how she handles, agile without being twitchy."

And that set the tone for the evening.

She handled lines, but never touched the wheel or the engine controls. Instead, she offered clear, precise instructions on boat handling and then explained what he was feeling as he did so.

"Put the engine in neutral and feel how she coasts. Twelve-six beam on a forty-one-foot hull weighing twelve tons fully loaded, she glides longer than you'd expect. Skeg keel, so if you nudge it into reverse, she only walks a little to the left."

He put it into reverse and, as they slowed, the bow did indeed swing to the left, but was easily corrected with a light turn of the wheel.

9

———

Twenty-two feet up through the busiest set of locks in the entire US, she kept a hawk eye on Howie, ready to leap in at the least provocation. But he tended to under- rather than over-control, which was a pleasant change and avoided the most common mistakes.

He learned incredibly quickly. It made sense once she thought about it. She typically set neophyte friends at the helm to get a feel for a boat. It was strange to have someone who was an experienced sailor in every way *except* steering.

Howie's attempts to relinquish control tapered off as he became more and more used to how the boat reacted. In her early days, she'd had to fight for even moments at a boat's helm, until she was so fed up that she'd bought her own. Janine had long ago sworn that she'd never be one of *those* skippers.

And if she were to take Howie at his word, he wasn't one of those control-freak-effing-asshole guys either.

They slid along the Washington Ship Canal in the company of the other eight boats that had been in their same lift through the locks. Others were joining them from the commercial yards to either side of the passage.

As they emerged into Lake Union, Howie lost all control. She didn't take the helm away from him, but did stretch out a foot without disturbing Master Howl in her lap and nudged the throttle back to idle.

"Holy shit!"

She could only smile. There were some experiences he clearly hadn't had. The various boat parades typically included twenty boats. This final-night gathering on Lake Union, in the northern heart of Seattle downtown, was an outright extravaganza.

Argosy Cruises had all three of their big tourist boats out and lit up like birthday cakes. Several boats in the hundred-foot-plus class floated like pylons in the middle of the lake for the other boats to swirl around. Powerboats abounded, from tiny skiffs to luxury yachts.

Sailboats stood out clearly because most had a string of lights that traced from the stern, up the mast's backstay to the peak, then down the forestay to the bow. Others enhanced that with a string of lights down the mast so that it looked as if their sails were up with edges alight.

Not quite sure why, Janine had gone a little crazy this year. She'd run lights up every shroud and sidestay, and wound them around the main boom. More lights outlined the edge where deck met hull and others traced the top of the cabin. She'd done it all with colored LED twinkle lights so the cockpit itself remained shrouded in near darkness, but *Tārā* glittered.

A hundred or more boats littered the water, providing a kaleidoscopic ever-shifting light show. Hers was a standout, drawing applause from those ashore every time they drifted close.

And somehow in that moment, she understood what she'd been doing as if everything suddenly, finally made sense. *Tārā,* the Mistress of Liberation, had been setting her up for a long time without her being aware of it.

Like breaking through a bank of fog, the course she'd been sailing was so clear now that she could see it.

First, her entire library had gone digital, *except* for the tales of the great explorers and circumnavigators.

Then, she'd collected travel guides simply for the fun of imagining what was out there.

Third, *Tārā's* gear and sail-set were utterly ridiculous for kicking around Puget Sound—but perfect for heading off deep sea.

Even her job, she'd shifted to online and lately focused strictly on contract piecework. Log in, get it done, get paid, and move on.

It would have been nice to have someone to voyage with. Some part of her had kept her plans on hold, out of her own sight, but to no avail. In three years of waiting, she hadn't found the right fit once. Someone both serious and funny—the first to put up with her and the latter to lighten her up a little. She'd certainly heard that diagnosis from enough exes to believe it necessary. They had to be smart, independent, adventurous…

Yeah, her cat was, sadly, as close as she'd ever come.

Officially sick of waiting, only one question remained.

When?

Spring. Once the winter storms had abated, she'd head out. March, April at the latest.

And that's why she'd ultra-decorated this Christmas. She, *Tārā,* and Master Howl were saying goodbye to Seattle with far more style and flair than she usually managed in her day-to-day life.

She looked down at Master Howl.

"If we're off to conquer the high seas, I should have worn my pirate outfit."

10

"YOUR *WHAT?*" HOWIE HADN'T MEANT TO SHOUT. HE SUDDENLY had the undivided attention of every sailor within a dozen boat-lengths, as well the party currently rocking out on the nearby Ivar's Restaurant barge.

Janine had gone quiet for the last twenty minutes or so, leaving it up to him to slowly adapt to navigating an unfamiliar boat through such heavy traffic. His nerves had finally pushed him to the far quieter northeast corner of Lake Union near Ivar's.

The Number 12 red marker buoy below the I-5 overpass bridge was a common turning point for summertime Duck Dodge races and he knew it well. He'd been using that to practice various turns as he learned more of how the boat handled under power. It would be very different under sail and he'd love to learn that too.

The parts of his mind that weren't occupied with learning were busy debating the best way to ask Janine if she needed a regular crew. Maybe she'd let him try the helm under sail.

And then she'd spoken—to herself and her cat—but with the engine barely above an idle her voice had carried clearly.

"Your…" he tried to catch his breath. There was no way. She was several inches shorter than the woman who'd been stuck in his mind for the two weeks since he'd played the Pirate Santa. He'd considered breaking his rule and joining the yacht club simply to find her.

"My what?" She looked up at him. There were enough work lights in the nearby boatyard that he had his first really clear look at her face.

"Your…pirate outfit?"

She looked away—exactly as she had when he'd beckoned her to take her bow on the tabletop. "It's silly."

That's when he remembered her stepping so lightly on the chair to climb up on the table beside him. Her leather pirate boots had several inches of stout heel.

He considered not saying anything. *Oh, hi. I crashed your yacht-club party once, acting like a total lunatic. By the way, I think I may love you.*

Not a good start.

I've had this huge fantasy crush on you since…

Please let me bow at your feet, my pirate elf.

Yeah, a fast track course for a cold swim to shore.

And she thought that *she* was the one who'd been silly?

"Tell me," he eased the boat to port to avoid ramming a Christmas canoe that had twinkle lights twisted around the paddles. They even wore black outfits so that only the paddles showed. "I'll bet I can out-foolish you."

She shook her head and kept her silence.

"C'mon," he knew he was pleading, "how am I supposed to talk you into teaching me how to really sail if you won't tell me the embarrassing shit?"

She turned to face him, studying him in that quiet way he couldn't believe he hadn't recognized earlier.

"Okay. This is going to sound beyond stupid."

"I can out-do it. I swear on Master Howl's food bowl." That earned him a brief smile.

"I was recently in charge of a Pirate Christmas party. And there was this guy." Again one of those vast silences that shouted so loudly about who she was.

"I hate him already."

"He crashed the party as, you're not going to believe this, a Pirate Santa. He was loud, ridiculous—"

And curling up to die at the helm of your boat.

"—and probably the most decent guy I've met in years."

11

———

Howie had gone strangely quiet until they'd returned down through the Ballard Locks and had retied the boat at Shilshole. The only thing she could figure out was he must now deem her to be a total idiot. Who ever would get a crush on a Pirate Santa whose face she'd never seen.

His silence had let her dredge up thoughts she hadn't found in the last two weeks since the events of that night.

The way he treated those kids.

With simple gifts, he gave those girls lofty visions of what they could be.

Without her realizing it, he'd sailed into her thoughts as smoothly as *Tārā* slicing through a wave. He'd been too loud and brash for her, and his Brooklyn accent had often grown almost incomprehensibly thick to her Iowan ear. But he'd... well, she'd liked him.

And the idea of finally heading out to cross the seas was so big and fresh that it too had spilled out of her. The fantasy of sailing from one exotic place to another, seeing the world. Making some money when she hit a port and could connect in;

she owned her own floating home, so the costs were low and she could carry on for...years.

And why she'd dumped all of that on Howie still mystified her. He'd been quiet and listened. Somehow he made it okay for her to speak the thoughts she never said to anyone, not even Master Howl. Or herself.

It was only as they were tying off the spring line on the boat and plugging in the shore-power cable that she realized something. He'd convinced her to give him sailing lessons next weekend. And even made a tentative date for New Year's Eve if they went well.

But... "Hey, you never told me how you could *out-foolish* me."

Howie stood in the darkness beside her on the dock. The temperature had dropped enough that their breath issued as white clouds. By that alone, she could see that he'd tipped his head back to stare up at the stars.

They were crystal bright, at least for being so close to the parking lot and the low wash lights that lit the dock's planking. From deep sea? Janine couldn't wait to see them.

"Well, I'm not sure how to say this."

"Try." She'd laid out every ridiculous dream she had and needed someone, anyone, to tell her it wasn't a pile of steaming hooey, even this near stranger.

Howie leaned back against the hull of her boat, which drifted away from the dock, almost enough to plop his butt down into the water before the lines snubbed it to a halt. Once he stood squarely on the dock again, he let out a big cloud of breath, then turned to face her.

"Your dream is beyond beautiful, Janine. I can't find a way of saying how much I want to do it with you without sounding like a total stalker."

And he saw he was right as Janine shifted a step back along the dock.

Howie reached out a hand to stop her, but withdrew it before he touched her. He *so* wanted to touch her.

"Except maybe this…"

"What?" she asked when he didn't continue.

He took hope from how she'd described him and dug deep for his best Brooklyn-Jew-pirate, and spoke softly…

"Arrrr! The lovely Pirate Queen needs a Pirate Santa in her life, don't she?"

———

FOR MORE TALES OF ROMANCE UNDER SAIL, SET COURSE TO *THE Complete Sailing Stories.*

AFTERWORD

Thank you for joining me for *Twelve More Tales of Christmas (and a few other holidays)*. I hope that your holiday seasons are as enjoyable as mine and may they always find you somewhere fun!

———

For the author's Root Beer Rye Pretzel recipe from "The Hanukkah Pretzel Prophecy" story, visit: https://mlbuchman.shopify.com/blogs/nerdguy-cooks/root-beer-rye-pretzels

ABOUT THE AUTHOR

USA Today and Amazon #1 Bestseller M. L. "Matt" Buchman started writing on a flight south from Japan to ride his bicycle across the Australian Outback. Just part of a solo around-the-world trip that ultimately launched his writing career.

From the very beginning, his powerful female heroines insisted on putting character first, *then* a great adventure. He's since written over 75 action-adventure thrillers and military romantic suspense novels. And more than 200 short stories, and a fast-growing pile of read-by-author audiobooks.

PW declares of his Miranda Chase action-adventure thrillers: "Tom Clancy fans open to a strong female lead will clamor for more." About his military romantic thrillers: "Like Robert Ludlum and Nora Roberts had a book baby."

His fans say: "I want more now...of everything!" That his characters are even more insistent than his fans is a hoot.

As a 30-year project manager with a geophysics degree who has designed and built houses, flown and jumped out of planes, and solo-sailed a 50' ketch, he is awed by what is possible. He and his wife presently live on the North Shore of Massachusetts. More at: www.mlbuchman.com.

Other works by M. L. Buchman: *(* - also in audio)*

Action-Adventure Thrillers

Kate Stark
Final Taste
Ice Burn
Knife's Edge

Miranda Chase
*Drone**
*Thunderbolt**
*Condor**
*Ghostrider**
*Raider**
*Chinook**
*Havoc**
*White Top**
*Start the Chase**
*Lightning**
*Skibird**
*Nightwatch**
*Osprey**
*Gryphon**
*Wedgetail**
*Air Force One**

Science Fiction / Fantasy

Deities Anonymous
Cookbook from Hell: Reheated
Saviors 101

Contemporary Romance

Eagle Cove
Return to Eagle Cove
Recipe for Eagle Cove
Longing for Eagle Cove
Keepsake for Eagle Cove

Love Abroad
Heart of the Cotswolds: England
Path of Love: Cinque Terre, Italy

Where Dreams
Where Dreams are Born
Where Dreams Reside
*Where Dreams Are of Christmas**
Where Dreams Unfold
Where Dreams Are Written
Where Dreams Continue

Non-Fiction

Strategies for Success
Managing Your Inner Artist/Writer
*Estate Planning for Authors**
Character Voice
*Narrate and Record Your Own Audiobook**
Beyond Prince Charming: One Guy's Guide to Writing Men in Romance

Short Story Series by M. L. Buchman:

Action-Adventure Thrillers

Kate Stark Stories
Miranda Chase Stories

Romantic Suspense

Antarctic Ice Fliers

US Coast Guard

Contemporary Romance

Eagle Cove

Other

Deities Anonymous (fantasy)

Single Titles

The Emily Beale Universe
(military romantic suspense)

The Night Stalkers
MAIN FLIGHT
The Night Is Mine
I Own the Dawn
Wait Until Dark
Take Over at Midnight
Light Up the Night
Bring On the Dusk
By Break of Day
Target of the Heart
Target Lock on Love
Target of Mine
Target of One's Own
NIGHT STALKERS HOLIDAYS
*Daniel's Christmas**
*Frank's Independence Day**
*Peter's Christmas**
Christmas at Steel Beach
*Zachary's Christmas**
*Roy's Independence Day**
*Damien's Christmas**
Christmas at Peleliu Cove

Henderson's Ranch
*Nathan's Big Sky**
*Big Sky, Loyal Heart**
*Big Sky Dog Whisperer**
*Tales of Henderson's Ranch**

Shadow Force: Psi
*At the Slightest Sound**
*At the Quietest Word**
*At the Merest Glance**
*At the Clearest Sensation**

White House Protection Force
*Off the Leash**
*On Your Mark**
*In the Weeds**

Firehawks
Pure Heat
Full Blaze
*Hot Point**
*Flash of Fire**
Wild Fire
SMOKEJUMPERS
*Wildfire at Dawn**
*Wildfire at Larch Creek**
*Wildfire on the Skagit**

Delta Force
*Target Engaged**
*Heart Strike**
*Wild Justice**
*Midnight Trust**

Night Stalkers Reload
*Guard the East Flank**

Emily Beale Universe Short Story Series

The Night Stalkers
The Night Stalkers Stories
The Night Stalkers CSAR
The Night Stalkers Wedding Stories
The Future Night Stalkers

Delta Force
Th Delta Force Shooters
The Delta Force Warriors

Firehawks
The Firehawks Lookouts
The Firehawks Hotshots
The Firebirds

White House Protection Force
Stories

Future Night Stalkers
Stories (Science Fiction)

SIGN UP FOR M. L. BUCHMAN'S NEWSLETTER TODAY

and receive:
Release News
Free Short Stories
a Free Book

Get your free book today. Do it now.
free-book.mlbuchman.com